Secretary of Defense Scott began to chuckle. Finally he said, "Dr. Nilstrom, we all know your love of science fiction. Now you have come here trying to convince me, the President of the United States, and the rest of the Cabinet that we are literally on the verge of being invaded—from outer space!"

He laughed some more and wiped his eyes with a handkerchief. "I find that pretty hard to believe!"

Nilstrom's eyes were needles and his voice a scalpel as he said, "*Why,* Mr. Scott?"

Nobody spoke or moved. Everyone felt the impact of the simple question.

The idea seemed incredible only because it had never happened before. . . .

INVADER

INVADER

ALBERT FAY HILL AND
DAVID CAMPBELL HILL

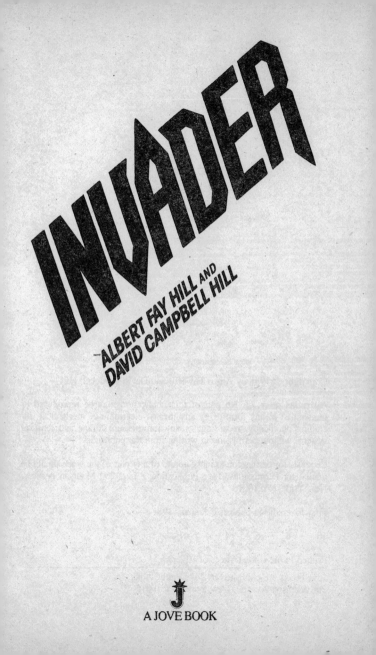

A JOVE BOOK

First Jove edition published January 1981

10 9 8 7 6 5 4 3 2 1

Printed in the United States of America

Jove books are published by Jove Publications, Inc., 200 Madison Avenue, New York, NY 10016

THIS BOOK IS

DEDICATED

TO

THOSE WHO

ONE DAY

WILL HAVE TO FACE THIS THREAT

ACKNOWLEDGMENTS

While it is obviously impossible to thank every person who gave assistance in the preparation of this novel, we do want to express our appreciation to those who made major contributions. Bill Levisay graciously conducted us around and explained the procedures in the Denver Control Tower. Pat and Dick Oburn provided us with information about the Canadian terrain. Ed Safford helped us get certain facts concerning the NORAD control center in Cheyenne Mountain. The Public Relations office of NORAD was also courteously helpful. Dave Stacey provided much invaluable scientific advice and assisted in some of the mathematical calculations. He also made many suggestions about the Large Orbiting Optical Telescope. It was he who first suggested, as one possibility, the "balloon telescope," which we then named for him. Kristin and Cydney Hill made shrewd comments on the characters and structure of the novel. And most of all we owe to Nancy Hill more than we can express for her unrelenting vigilance in detecting, and her remorseless ruthlessness in extracting from the novel, excess verbiage. She was more than an editor; she was a loving partner and we thank her for it.

Part One

Chapter 1

CHRISTIAN NILSTROM was undeniably an exciting man. But he was also exasperatingly difficult. The thrill Linda McCoy had felt when he asked her to dinner had now been replaced with annoyance. He sat across from her in the booth, frowning in concentration—and didn't even notice that she had stopped talking in mid-sentence when she found he wasn't listening.

It was the first time Linda had seen him since the funeral of his wife Kay, two years before, and she had looked forward to this evening with a twitch of hope that he was interested in her romantically. But the brilliant college professor was as remote as ever, his dark eyes seemingly trained on something outside the restaurant window. She shook her head and waited for him to return from his thought-world.

Linda had been attracted to Chris from the moment Kay had introduced her to the intense young Ph.D. student twenty years ago in Berkeley, and she was still fascinated by him. Full of contradictions, he was charming and arrogant, compassionate and contemptuous, endlessly good-natured and strangely irritable. Tenderly patient with a slow student, he could be vicious with a colleague bent on displaying his erudition. Exasperatingly conventional one moment, Nilstrom had people gasping at his revolutionary ideas the next. Before long, people who knew him were divided neatly into two groups: those who hated him for the challenge he presented, and those who were hypnotized by his dynamism and brilliance.

Following Kay's death, there had been a time when Nilstrom seemed becalmed. Now, as she looked at the preoccupied man, Linda knew something had happened; his life was moving again. Certainly he was sadder and had lost some of his optimism, but the burning ambition, the furious drive, the incandescent intellect were still there.

3

Irritated at his lack of attention, Linda studied him now.
The short, dark beard he had recently grown added a rugged
strength to his appearance, making him even more appealing.
But suddenly she realized she would never be close to him.

She sighed and said softly, "How are the kids? So big I
wouldn't know them?"

Nilstrom tried to focus on what she had asked. "Oh, fine,
Linda, fine. Uh, Mike is eight now and big for his age. Susan's
six and as pretty as her mother." His face softened and his eyes
smiled as he spoke.

"I hope you have time to spend with them. I know your
mother and father are fine grandparents, and the kids are lucky
to have them, but they need *you*, too."

He chuckled at her motherliness. "Don't worry. I've been
home most of the time since Kay died."

"You're here *now*, though."

"Well, I couldn't dodge this one." He frowned.

"Top secret?"

He looked out the window at the runway as a huge airliner
landed. "As a matter of fact, Linda, it *is*. Sorry..."

They were at the 94th Aero Squadron, a restaurant located
beside the east-west runway of Denver's Stapleton International
Airport. Built in the style of a French farmhouse used as an
aerodome in the First World War, its walls were covered with
old pictures of aircraft and pilots from the era, and occasionally
the sound of those early airplane motors was piped over the
loudspeaker system.

It was late November, the Wednesday night before Thanksgiving, and an inch of snow lay on the ground. From their
table, Linda and Chris could see airliners landing every four
or five minutes. As the huge planes thundered in, snow swirled
up from the runway in a white cloud. But the sky was clear
and the stars shone brightly.

Linda gave Nilstrom a few minutes, then interrupted his
thoughts again. "That sounds like more UFO work for the Air
Force, Chris. Don't tell me you've found that flying saucers
really do exist?"

"Well, it's no secret that *I* think *something* exists."

"Little green men from Mars?"

He smiled. "We don't know where the devil UFOs come
from. Nobody on earth can produce aircraft capable of doing
what they do, and no other planet in our solar system can
sustain life as we know it. But to get here from any other planet

orbiting any other star, they'd have to travel many light-years."

"You mean it *isn't* mass hysteria or swamp gas or Venus in the evening sky or something like that?"

"Right. The damned things have been seen on radar screens and by hundreds of observers who'd have no reason to make anything up."

"But . . . they *are* harmless, aren't they?"

Outside, a huge Boeing 747 touched down. Nilstrom watched the monster and tried to find an answer that wouldn't break security.

He turned back to Linda. "That was the conclusion of our report three years ago."

"You so carefully put that in the past tense. If you've just been to Colorado Springs, then it's almost certain you've been to NORAD, and that must mean more UFO sightings. Are they hostile now?"

Nilstrom didn't want to get in any deeper, but he didn't want to lie to her, either. He *had* been to NORAD, where he'd met with the recently appointed commander, his friend General Nicholas Beck. And what he had learned had left him stunned and alarmed.

He pointed at the 747 disappearing down the runway. "Amazing things, those. They may be old, but they're the safest planes ever built . . . even safer than the old DC-3s. Did you know they're twice as long as Orville Wright's first flight? And that his plane never got as far off the ground as those things stand on the runway?"

Linda was amused at his attempt to change the subject. "Really, Chris, you're the world's worst at hiding anything. You've just about convinced me something *has* developed with the UFOs."

He grinned and looked mildly guilty. "You know that if I *were* working with the Air Force again I couldn't discuss it."

She hesitated, wondering how he might take what she was about to say, then said it anyway. "You *are* being careful, aren't you? I mean, you know your statement about the UFOs three years ago almost ruined your standing in the scientific community."

He nodded. Linda was right; his career had been in serious jeopardy. He had been frozen by contemptuous looks from his peers, laughed at behind his back, actually denounced by some, and patronized even by his friends. Only the publication of his brilliant paper on pulsars, and the immediate sensation it caused in scholarly circles, saved him from being cast aside in favor of a more conventional man, and assured his appointment as head of the astronomy department at Wisconsin University.

"I've learned my lesson, Linda. I keep very quiet about my unorthodox opinions." He smiled and took her hand. "How about another drink before we order?"

Chapter 2

"CHRIS, THE waitress wants to know what you'd like to eat."

There was an edge of anger in Linda's voice that jerked Nilstrom out of his reverie . Once again he'd allowed himself to drift off. He grinned and shook his head. "I really was wool-gathering, wasn't I? Sorry."

He glanced at the menu, frowned, took his glasses out of his breast pocket, and ordered a steak. This time he was determined to keep his mind from wandering, and he looked Linda in the eye. She was smiling at his obvious dislike of having to use glasses.

"Thanks for suggesting this place, Linda. I like the atmosphere. Pilots in the First World War were the last of the romantic warriors. That was the end of chivalry."

They chatted about mutual friends as they waited for dinner. The restaurant was almost empty and their meal came quickly. As Chris bent to cut his steak, his mind strayed once more and he found himself thinking again about his meeting with Nick Beck.

Years before, in the 1970s, Nilstrom had joined Beck's staff as a reserve officer serving as scientific advisor on a task force appointed to study UFOs. He had been impressed by the similarity in reported sightings from all over the United States, and even the world. Those who insisted they had seen flying-saucer-like craft tended to give essentially the same description. They were people who had nothing to gain, and indeed, risked being branded crackpots. Of course, there were also the usual nuts who rushed in to capitalize on the phenomena, but most reports were made by reliable witnesses.

It was apparent that the UFOs posed no threat to the security of the United States. Most often they appeared in sparsely inhabited areas, or even over forests and farmland. Not once had a UFO harmed persons or property. There were instances of circles of burned grass where they had allegedly landed, and the spots remained radioactive for months, but otherwise no damage was done. Eventually the task force gave up trying to find an answer that would satisfactorily explain the various incidents, and concluded only that, whatever the UFOs were, they were not a threat.

But Beck and Nilstrom were not satisfied. They tried to carry on the investigation even after funds were cut off. Chris urged a further study, which was promptly rejected. Then Beck was swept into the stream of Air Force duty, Kay fell ill, and the two were forced to give up.

During Kay's illness, Nilstrom spent more evenings at home instead of attending university meetings or going to the observatory, and since the evenings were quiet, he turned his own restless mind to the problem he had posed to the Air Force. What he had suggested, and what he now pursued himself, was a contingency study on what the U.S. could do if the unidentified craft proved to be from another planet, and if they became hostile.

He thought about the weapons mankind might use to defend itself against an invasion of extraterrestrial visitors, the weapons the invaders might possess, and the kind of propulsion that would be required for them to travel such great distances. He had even written a report and sent copies to Beck and to the Pentagon. Washington thanked him, but cautioned him not to expect remuneration.

Now, months later, the call had come from Beck. The general informed Nilstrom that UFO sightings had increased within the last several weeks. And now there was a difference: the UFOs were behaving aggressively. They had appeared over defense installations, usually alone, but often in pairs, and once there were three. Visual sightings had been confirmed by radar.

Chris had never seen Beck so grim. Usually the general was overly cheerful, often giving the impression that he wasn't very bright.

"Chris, those bastards are testing our defenses, and you know better than anyone what that means."

"Trouble," Nilstron said.

"Affirmative! And it also means we need you, full time."

Linda watched Nilstrom in silence after finishing her steak. Anger at being so ignored fought with the desire to know what he was thinking about. Finally she gave up and looked around the restaurant. Her eye caught a set of earphones hanging against the wall.

With them she could listen to the conversations between the tower and incoming planes. She knew the talk was boring, but at least it would be better than staring at a man so preoccupied he didn't even know she existed. She put on the earphones. Immediately she heard the controller.

"Continental 445, continue. Number two in traffic behind Frontier 112 turning base, over."

There were moments of silence, and the, "Frontier 112, cleared to land."

"Frontier 112, roger."

"Continental 445, begin final approach."

"Continental 445, roger."

"Continental 445, cleared to land."

"Denver Ground Control, Frontier 112, landed, taxi instructions, over."

The huge Continental plane shot by the window of the restaurant in a cloud of blown snow and blinking lights.

"Denver Ground Control, TWA 678 beginning final approach."

"TWA 678, continue, cleared to land."

A sudden squawk, a sound of terror, a sound Linda would never forget, shrieked through the earphones.

"Denver Tower, West Central 165 Heavy, sixty east, flight level two-five-five. Mayday! We are being attacked by a damn it!—it's a flying saucer! It buzzed us twice, and we have passengers injured when we took evasive action. Oh God . . ."

Linda started at the terrified message, and Chris's dark eyes were immediately alert.

"What is it?"

She didn't hear him. She was listening to the voice of Denver Control.

"West Central 165 Heavy, say again."

Silence.

"West Central 165 Heavy, say again."

"Denver Tower, West Central 165. We are being attacked—repeat, attacked—by an unidentified aircraft. I am diving lower for safety. We have injured passengers. Request help. Over."

"Roger , West Central 165. Will call NORAD for interceptors. Will have ambulances. Describe attacker. Acknowledge."

Linda tore off the headphones. Her voice was shrill. "A West Central plane is being attacked by a flying saucer—or something—"

Nilstrom grabbed the headset and clamped it on in time to hear the pilot say, "...faster than anything I've ever seen—turns on a dime. It's round; like a disk—no, oval, with fire coming out the rear, and the whole thing glows. Son of a bitch is right on my tail—I can't shake him. He's *playing* with us."

"West Central 165, we have you on radar, but we see no other craft. Over."

"Denver Tower, West Central 165. You can't see the bastard because he's hanging right under my tail. No! There he goes, like a bat out of hell. *Now* do you have him?"

"West Central 165, affirmative! He must be doing three thousand knots. Look out! He's turning!"

Nilstrom tore off the headset, pulled out his wallet, threw down two twenties, grabbed Linda's hand. "Come on, I've got to get to that control tower!"

They dashed through the dining room, past the startled hostess. Chris ran down the winding stairs to the landing four at a time, and pushed open the door to the parking lot. Linda struggled into her coat as she followed. He ran to the car, opened the door.

"You drive, you know the way. But burn it!"

Linda gunned the motor of her little blue Plymouth and they shot out to the street, turned at the corner to Montview Boulevard, then roared west through the sparse traffic. When they came to a red light, she hesitated, but Chris put his foot on hers, pushing the accelerator down.

"Move it, Linda! Move it!"

Chapter 3

WHEN THE alarm rang, Captain Thomas Randall couldn't believe it. It was bad enough to be out here in the middle of the Colorado prairie, two thousand miles from his home base and his wife and children. Indeed, when he and the others had first received the order to come to Colorado Springs, they'd thought it was a joke. Interceptors are for the periphery, to ward off an invasion of enemy bombers. But Colorado?

And now, in the middle of the best poker hand he'd had all night, the alarm was ringing. Old Ironass Beck couldn't be satisfied with just having them here. He had to put them through a drill on a cold night!

Captain Richard Beed's thoughts were much different. The alarm had saved him from a drubbing. He chortled to himself as he threw down his cards and bolted for the door of the temporary shack they were using for a ready room. He didn't mind drills that much, anyway. He loved to fly, especially the Eagle.

They ran across the field to where the huge interceptors were hulked on the runway, already screaming their banshee salutation to the stars. The planes were kept warm all the time, which Randall thought a terrible example of over-security. The crew chief moved aside and Randall climbed the ladder and lowered himself into the cockpit as if he were a well-oiled part of the plane. But Beed was big, and it took an extra second for him to get seated.

Randall looked over the instruments with a practiced eye. Everything was in shape, as usual. The Eagle throbbed under him as the polycarbonate canopy slammed down over his head. Then the blocks were pulled away, the engines screamed at a still higher pitch as he advanced the throttle, and the huge plane moved. Behind him, the tornado of his engine blast blew snow for two hundred yards. He made his turn and caught a glimpse of Beed making his.

Immediately, the tower came through. They were cleared for takeoff. Randall smiled inside his oxygen mask. He always wondered what would happen if some little Piper Cub wanted to come in for a landing in front of a scrambling interceptor. His hands moved through the last-second preparations as he swung around for take-off. Then, with Beed's plane beside his, he eased his brakes off, his throttle forward, and he began to roll. The Eagle accelerated so rapidly that Randall was pinned to his seat. The runway lights streamed past in a solid line, and in what seemed an indecently short time, the plane left the ground.

Men rightly called the Eagle the smartest plane ever built. Packed into its sleek body were millions of microcircuits that saw and analyzed things in a way no man could. Its radar was capable of tracking nine different targets at once; its sensors could guide it through clouds, rain, and radar jamming. Unerringly it sought the target, its eyes keener than man's, its brain swifter. Terrain-avoidance radar allowed it to fly low and fast, reacting more quickly than any pilot could to avoid hitting trees and hills.

Once an Eagle found her target, it was doomed. Her missile, the Falcon AIM-47A, was itself a marvel of the electronic age. It could home on its target a hundred miles away at Mach 6, guided first by the pilot, then terminally by its own pulse-Doppler radar.

Now, climbing at forty-five degrees, Randall was already nearing supersonic speed. Ahead, he could see the lights of Denver mirroring the millions of stars above. He loved it, the whole mission, now that he was in the air. Then too, a training mission wasn't any big deal, and this flight couldn't be anything more than that. It probably wasn't even an investigation of an airliner running off course. And as for a real threat? A bomber penetrating the rings of defense around the United States and appearing suddenly over Denver? He smiled.

The radio crackled in his ear. "Foxtrot Leader, this is Foxhole. Intercept vector is one-niner, altitude one-five. This intercept is Hotel Alpha Seven. Repeat, Hotel Alpha Seven. Proceed on minimum-intercept time. Acknowledge."

Randall turned cold inside his heated flight suit. Hotel Alpha Seven was code for "intercept and destroy." It was no drill. On his radar, Randall could see two blips—one large, one small, side by side—at the location given by Foxhole.

The airspeed indicator had passed Mach 1, but the two fighters continued to increase their speed. Minimum-intercept time meant maximum speed. The indicator swung further, approaching Mach 2.

The radio crackled again. "Foxtrot Leader, this is Foxhole. Acknowledge intercept vector and mission code."

Randall shook himself and said, "Roger. Intercept vector

one-niner and mission is Hotel Alpha Seven."

The planes reached, then exceeded Mach 2. The chill night air around them was pierced, ravished, thrown aside, and it shrieked in horrified protest. At these speeds, the air was rock-hard, an overpowering force that had torn earlier planes apart. But the Eagle was designed for it. There was nothing for the outraged air to grasp on the sleek plane. She slipped away from her own shock wave, riding it as a surfer rides a wave of the ocean.

Randall and Beed banked southeast of Denver and fixed on their coordinates for the target. Any second now would come the recall notice; this couldn't possibly be for real. Already there'd be hell to pay for the damage they'd done. At this speed, at this altitude, the F-15s trailed a cone of furious air, sweeping behind them like the wake of a motorboat. When the wake broke over the city of Denver, it would do so as an earsplitting boom that would wake children, and disrupt parties, and set dogs to howling. The switchboard at Cheyenne Mountain would be jammed with calls of protest.

A different voice came on the radio. "Foxtrot Leader, this is Foxhole One."

Randall jerked in his seat. The commander of NORAD himself, General Beck.

"Foxtrot, this is confirmation Hotel Alpha Seven. Commercial heavy, fifty east, is under attack by hostile UFO. Destroy the bogie, but be careful not to destroy the heavy too."

"Roger. Willco."

The jets hurtled eastward, mere metallic tips on ramrods of fire pushing them at speeds now approaching Mach 3. Randall's stomach hurt and he felt an intense desire to urinate. It was always that way just before he went into combat. But combat over Colorado?

Chapter 4

FROM SYRACUSE STREET, Linda careered around the corner. The airport was directly ahead. Chris shouted in her ear as she wove in and out of the heavier traffic on Thirty-second Avenue, "Stay on the lower level. Let me out and you park. I'll meet you later in the lobby."

The little car fishtailed on the packed snow as she passed two Yellow Cabs, but she kept going, and skidded to a halt at the south end of the lower level. Nilstrom jumped out.

He almost fell on an icy spot as he ran to the swinging doors. Inside, he turned right to the corridor at the back of the baggage room, saw the tower through the window, and took the door to the outside. At the foot of the tower he found the door locked, but saw another and yanked it open. He was in a hallway, separated from the elevator by another door. It too was locked. He swore, then saw the telephone. He jerked it off the cradle and dialed the tower.

The answering voice was breathless. "Yes?"

"This is Colonel Nilstrom of Air Force Intelligence. I want to talk to that West Central pilot—the one who's being attacked."

"Well, I'll have to ask the night supervisor. I'm not supposed to let anyone in without—"

"Fuck your night supervisor. Open this door!"

The door buzzed immediately and loudly, and Nilstrom pulled it open, slamming the phone back on its cradle with his other hand. The elevator was at ground level, and he got in, and pushed the button for the twelfth floor. The car rose slowly, and Nilstrom snarled at its leisurely pace. When the doors opened he lunged out, expecting to be in the control room, but he found himself in a small entryway. Two locked doors were marked No Admittance. He tried a third, found a circular stairway, and sprinted up to the next level, through a fire door, and up again, this time directly into the control room of the tower.

Five men were there. One came to meet him—a young man nattily dressed in a dark blue blazer with a shirt and tie. His face was unusually lined for one so young.

"Colonel? Bill Straws, night supervisor." He offered his hand.

"How's that plane? Where is he?" Nilstrom shoved his credentials under Straw's nose and moved quickly across the room to the long-range radar.

Three men in sports shirts leaned over the screen. A fourth stood behind them, watching over their shoulders. He turned as he heard Chris. "Our pilot is only fifty miles away now, and down to fifteen thousand feet, but look at that other bastard!"

The voice of the frantic pilot came over the radio. "Denver

Tower, help! He's coming at me again. *Where's that inter-cepter?* Oh shit!"

On the green radar screen, Chris clearly saw the brighter green blip labeled WC 165. It was turning sharply. But right behind it was another blip, hurtling at the hapless airliner with astonishing speed, only to veer off at almost a right angle at the last second.

"My God! What kind of plane can fly like that—and what kind of pilot can take such a maneuver without blacking out?" Straws almost whispered the words.

The smaller, indistinct blip circled and seemed to disappear inside the larger one. The pilot spoke again.

"The son of a bitch is right beside me, I can almost touch him. Denver Tower, where the hell's that interceptor?"

"West Central 165, keep your course. You are only forty miles away now."

Chris grabbed the microphone from the controller's hand and spoke into it. "West Central 165, are there any identifying marks on the aircraft?"

"Denver Tower, I can't see any. It's just a big oval disk. There's a dome, but it's glowing so much I can't see anything inside."

"West Central 165, can that glowing be from overheated metal? At that speed he must have thermal problems."

"Denver Tower, I don't know. He's still there, just watching me! God, it's eerie! Hey! Something's different . . . God!"

Instinctively Nilstrom and the others lifted their eyes from the screen to the night sky in the east. Suddenly, out over the prairie, a brilliant orange light flared and hung in the air. On the screen, the bright blip was gone, but the smaller one re-mained, standing almost still.

"That son of a bitch shot him down. Killed all those people!"

"Who *is* that? Look at him, just sitting there, watching. Bastard!"

The three controllers stared at the radar screen. But it was Chris who saw the interceptors closing fast. He turned to Straws. "Can you put me on their frequency?"

"Sure. Here you go." He leaned over the console, pushed a button.

"Interceptor flight, this is Colonel Nilstrom, Air Force In-telligence. Unknown hostile just shot down the 747. Go get the bastard! But be careful! He's armed and capable of great speed and maneuverability. Acknowledge."

"Roger, Colonel."

The men in the control tower watched the screen as the interceptors approached the almost stationary dot.

"Go get him!" Straws said. "Zap the son of a bitch!"

Chapter 5

RANDALL'S EYES were on his radar screen as the blip got larger, nearer. A red light showed that the missiles were locked on target, but he didn't fire until he was at point-blank range. Now! The Falcons roared away, arrowing toward the bogie. Randall banked sharply to escape the explosion, then banked again so he could watch the missiles strike the slowly drifting disk. What he saw instead was unbelievable. The glowing saucer bounded straight up at incredible speed. There was a series of bright red flashes as the rockets exploded harmlessly where the alien had been only seconds before.

Beed found his tongue first, "Goddamn! How'd he do that? Let's get him with the Gatlings!" In perfect unison the two pilots slackened their speed, made a wide turn, then accelerated toward the disk. Having successfully eluded the missiles, it was again moving very slowly, but as the Eagles approached, it streaked off into the stratosphere.

Randall and Beed cut in their afterburners and were soon at top speed, more shrieking projectiles than planes, tracking the intruder. But it left them hopelessly far behind.

Randall's finger touched the trigger of the cannon, but he told himself not to be silly. He couldn't possibly hit the saucer. His radar computer showed that the bogie was traveling at four thousand miles per hour. Impossible! But incredibly, with still another burst of speed, it was off the screen and gone.

Randall pulled the throttle back and his surging plane slowed, shuddered, stabilized. Below sonic speed again, he circled, followed by Beed. The fire from the airliner was burning on the prairie beneath them, and two strings of ruby-red lights approached the site from different directions.

The radio crackled. It was General Beck. "Foxtrot Leader, this is Foxhole One. Report the result of your attack."

"Negative , sir, negative. The bogie just flew away, first

from our missiles and then from us. We lost him."

There was a pause before Beck spoke again. "Foxtrot Leader, return to base immediately."

"Roger."

Randall looked down once more at the wreckage below. Suddenly he had a deep desire to see his wife and children.

Chapter 6

NILSTROM TURNED away from the radar screen when he heard Straws say, "Operator, I want the Air Carrier District Office of the FAA. And—"

Instantly, Nilstrom pushed down the button on the phone and cut him off. "Listen, mister. Just say that jet crashed. Don't report that it was downed by hostile aircraft. I have authority to slap on security, and I'm doing it right now. Not a word about that other plane."

"Goddamn it, Colonel, you can't classify the fact that a 747 has gone down. This terminal is full of people waiting to meet passengers on that flight."

"No, but if you tell *anyone* the jet was attacked, you'll be violating the National Security Act of . . ."

"My God, half the pilots in the area heard that conversation."

"I want every single one taken into custody until we've had time to talk to them, I don't care whether they're private or commercial. Get them in right away. Move!"

Straws nodded and beckoned to one of the men behind him. Nilstrom took the phone from his hand. "Operator, get me the local office of the FBI—and step on it." He looked up at Straws. "There's another control room in this tower, isn't there? Button it up until they've been cleared by the FBI. And the same for the Denver Center in Longmont.

"Hello. FBI?" Nilstrom identified himself, reported the crash, explained the need for security. Then he placed a call to NORAD.

"Nick! Thank God you're still there . . . Yeah, the FBI is already on it . . . I'd say ball lightning might be the best cover."

Nilstrom fingered the spiraled telephone cord and listened.

"You're right, Nick. I'll call the university in the morning and ask for a leave of absence—no, it's Thanksgiving. I'd completely forgotten my poor children. Well, I'll meet you here at six-thirty. See you then." He dropped the phone and turned to Straws. "How are you coming?" he asked.

"Well, there weren't as many private planes up there as usual. We've contacted all the commercial pilots. Goddamn it, Colonel, what's going on? What is that thing? I flew interceptors for the Air Force until eight months ago, and I can tell you nobody has planes like that. *Nobody*."

Nilstrom said softly, "We'll get him."

Straws looked at him in disbelief. "Hell, Colonel, the Eagle's the best we have. If *they* can't get the son of a bitch, what can?"

Chapter 7

NILSTROM PULLED the collar of his coat tighter. He stood at the edge of the runway on which Beck's plane was due to arrive. His back was to the wind as it howled out of the north, cold and biting. The wind had swept in during the night, and was now bringing clouds. He scowled from the depths of his coat. It was going to be a miserable day.

Then he saw the lights. A small plane was coming in, struggling in the wind. Chris sighed with relief. There was no rational reason to be afraid, he supposed, but he was glad Beck had made it safely. One aircraft had already been destroyed, and the commander of North America's defense system would be a great prize. The fear that the big, friendly general might not make it to Denver alive had nagged at Nilstrom all night, and had grown to unreasonable proportions. Now, with almost childish pleasure, he welcomed the red, green, and white lights.

The plane descended, a small jet used by the Air Force to transport important personnel. If Chris knew his man, Beck himself was flying it. As a four-star general he rated a personal pilot, but at age fifty-three, Nick Beck still loved the feel of an airplane beneath him, and flew whenever he got the chance.

The little jet slid lower, its wings level despite the wind. It was a picture-perfect approach. When the wheels touched, they did so like fingers on a lover's skin. It was Beck, all right.

The plane rolled to a stop. In a moment Beck appeared, first a long leg, then an arm and a shoulder, then another leg, an arm, and finally a head. Getting into and out of anything designed for the average person was hard for the general, who was six-feet-six and clumsy as a puppy. He straightened up and looked around. His arm rose in a wave, and he quickly walked toward Nilstrom.

"Chris! Hell of a day, isn't it?" the general boomed. "Anything new?"

"Nothing," Nilstrom replied. "You know there were no survivors."

Beck nodded.

The two men walked to the waiting limousine. The car was warm, a refuge from the cold and the wind.

"Crash site," Beck ordered the driver. The airliner, or what was left of it, had gone down in the wheatfields twenty miles east of the airport.

"The 747 was at capacity," Nilstrom said. "Three hundred and sixty-two. Skiers and holiday people. It's the worst disaster in the history of air travel."

Beck made no comment. He was tight-lipped, and his fists clenched and unclenched as they drove.

Neither of the car's passengers felt like conversation. Each pictured the scene at the crash site: crews working to separate the victims from twisted aluminum and steel, lighting fires to keep the frigid night away; newsmen taking pictures, shuddering, returning to their warm homes.

With the morning, others would come, the sifters and analyzers, the reconstructors and theorizers. Within hours, ordinarily, the site of such a disaster was crowded with investigators from the FBI, the FAA, the airline, the insurance companies, and anyone else who could convince the authorities he had a stake in the crash. Ordinarily. But this time it was different.

Beck spoke at last. "Let me brief you, Chris. I got permission to sequester the wreckage. FBI specialists from Washington will take charge of the investigation, but I'm responsible for the crash site until they arrive, which should be about noon. Air Police have cordoned off the wreckage."

"Security's going to be one hell of a problem," Nilstrom said. "The press probably got to the scene as soon as the crash crews."

"Affirmative. But from what they can find by just poking around, they'll write stories like 'shattered colossus scattered like confetti across miles of wheatfields.' They can write all that sort of crap they want. It's the ones who know something that bother me. Right now the Air Police are under orders to make sure the airline people don't say anything, but we've got to keep a low profile. For the public record, we're there to prevent looting."

"Yeah, it's got to look as routine—"

Beck interrupted. "There she is."

Up ahead was the six-stories-high tail of a Boeing 747, its graceful lines rising into the gray sky. The severed tail had fallen fifteen thousand feet to land, incredibly, almost upright. The West Central Airlines insignia gleamed red, white, and blue on the polished surface, an anomaly in the drab setting. The huge rudder was there, and so were the horizontal stabilizers. But there the illusion of wholeness collapsed.

Back toward the cold gray towers of Denver lay the rest of the ruined airliner—a million pieces, scattered across the scarred fields.

The car stopped. A man dressed in an Air Force uniform and wielding a rifle peered in the window and recognized Beck. At once he stepped back and, with a precise, exaggerated gesture, waved them through the checkpoint.

Near the tail section a cluster of men stood around a small fire, huddled against the wind. Some wore the insignia and heavy blue coats of the Air Force, others the overcoats of airline employees, state police, and airport emergency crews.

"Stop here, Sergeant."

Beck shoved the car door open and climbed awkwardly out. Chris followed, his muscles stiffening against the cold. Some of the men at the fire looked up, their faces drawn with fatigue, shock, disgust. Like Nilstrom, they had had no sleep, only nightmares.

Chris looked around. Floodlights set up for the crews were now dark. Silent generators hulked under the gaunt framework that held them. Scattered haphazardly around were jacks, carts, tarpaulins.

Beck and Nilstrom moved over to the fire. The others grudgingly made way for them. Numbness was the prevailing feeling: numbness from a night in the subfreezing cold, numbness from shock at what they had found. These men could not yet be done with their work, but they didn't seem to care. With the dawn they had straggled to the fire for warmth, and company, and to get away from the corpses. No one spoke; everyone simply stared into the flames.

Beck held his gloved hands out toward the meager warmth of the fire. The weight of the day rested on the struggling flames—they seemed to have little heat to share.

Two men, shoulders hunched against the cold wind, approached the group. Beck and Nilstrom stepped away from the fire to meet them. One had the West Central Airlines insignia on his coat. The second was an Air Force officer. Hours earlier he must have looked sharp. Now his heavy clothing had come uncinched, his scarf dangled, his trousers were out of the tops of his boots. He wore the twin bars of a captain.

"General Beck, sir?" It wasn't really a question. "Sir, this is Henry Giordino. He's in charge of West Central's field team."

"Thank you, Captain."

The officer turned away, and Beck spoke softly: "It's been a rough night, hasn't it?"

Giordino did not take the offered hand. "General, I've been ordered to cooperate with you. But I think I deserve to know what's going on. This is West Central's plane." His anger was not lost on Beck.

"I understand your feelings, Mr. Giordino. But it's a matter of national security."

"Yeah, I know. Who d'you think's gonna believe that cover story you want West Central to release? The plane exploded with a roar that could be heard all over the state. It was a clear night, midwinter. Nobody who knows shit about meteorology is going to believe ball lightning did this."

"Air Force experts will back you up." Beck knew Giordino was in a rough spot. Over three hundred and sixty people had died in an aircraft operated by his company. God knew West Central wasn't responsible, but the public didn't.

"The Air Force! There are rumors all over the place about the Air Force. Everybody knows there were interceptors in the area when the plane went down, and now this morning there are Air Police everywhere. People are saying this is another gruesome military foul-up, like those sheep you guys killed in Utah a few years ago. They won't believe all the denials, because you lied about the sheep too. And you know what, General? I'm not sure they're that far wrong—"

"Mr. Giordino," Beck cut in with unaccustomed harshness,

"the Air Force was not responsible. I can assure you—"

"Take it easy, Nick," Chris interrupted. "You don't have anything to apologize for."

Beck took a deep breath. "Mr. Giordino, I would like to know exactly what your men have found."

The question brought a change in Giordino. His eyes were suddenly directed at the ground. His voice was soft, tragic. "Things are scattered over fifteen square miles. A lot of bodies were just torn apart; the others were too burned to recognize. And we still have about a hundred missing. When the press was here I kept telling them not to photograph the dead. Some of them got sick." He stopped. The last sentence had been mumbled, "There must've been a lot of heat. See?"

His gloved hand came out of his pocket holding half a dozen spheres of metal, each about a quarter-inch in diameter. They had a dull finish, and seemed to be perfectly round.

"The local people say these fell out of the sky like rain. The metal of the aircraft, vaporized in the explosion, condensed into these."

"Don't remove any of them from the crash site," Beck said quietly. "Any sign of radioactivity?"

"No, and we checked pretty carefully. It wasn't an atom bomb, but it sure was something powerful." He let the metal droplets fall out of his hand.

"Anything else unusual?"

"Well, just the general condition of the wreck. Everything's so incredibly scattered. Only the tail section's intact. There are no other pieces bigger than a few square feet. The explosion was just forward of the wings There's nothing left of the cockpit, which sort of takes care of the flight recorders. We did find the engines—over there

He pointed to the west. A narrow tongue of flame licked upward. It was pale and anemic, but it still burned, eleven hours after the crash.

"Falling from that height, an engine can dig a sizable crater. It's mostly jumbled junk, but the engineers think the engines were on full throttle when the plane exploded.

"There was one other thing. Usually you can smell the explosive. Dynamite and TNT have a distinctive odor that lingers for hours. But we were out here within minutes of the crash and couldn't detect a thing. Also, explosives can coat parts near the blast, but everything we've found so far is as clean as a whistle."

"Okay, Mr. Giordino, thanks."

The tired man moved toward the fire.

"What do you think, Nick?"

Beck shook his head. "There's no question, really. The airspace of the United States has been penetrated, and I couldn't do a damned thing about it."

"You can't catch a hawk with a bear trap. You tried."

Again the ungainly general shook his head. "Remember basic training? What were the three answers you could use?"

Nilstrom grinned. "'Yes sir,' 'no sir,' and 'no excuse, sir.' But, hell, we both know what has to be done now—if you can get the president's permission."

"Affirmative! And if CORADS can't get it, there's no hope. Let's go see the president."

"You sure you want me to go along, Nick? People still think I'm some kind of a kook."

"Are you kidding? After what just happened, they'll call you a prophet. You've been vindicated."

Chapter 8

THE AIRMAN at the door of the projection room stiffened to attention when he saw General Beck's four stars. Beck was accompanied by his aide, Sergeant Arnold Kaminski, and his secretary, Diane Mowbray. He entered ahead of them, and two men rose to greet them. One was Dr. Nilstrom, who nodded absently; obviously his mind was on something else. The other, in army green, was General Edward T. Gray, chairman of the Joint Chiefs of Staff.

"Is everything satisfactory, Nick?" Gray asked. He was a thin man of medium height who limped from old wounds.

Beck looked around the mahogany-paneled room at the chalkboard, beaded movie screen, projectors, and tape recorders. He nodded and said in his oddly loud way, "Looks good, Ed. Waddya say, Arnie?"

A frown of disapproval flickered across Gray's face. Beck's familiarity with enlisted men was generally criticized, and Gray, though a supporter of Beck's, was no exception.

Kaminski checked the audiovisual machinery. "Everything's okay, sir."

"This is Mrs. Mowbray, Ed, my secretary for four years now, best in the Air Force."

General Gray smiled and took the hand she offered.

In quick succession, Admiral Martin Steinhauser, General Herbert Waters, and Marine Lieutenant General Michael O. Jackson entered the room.

Beck's blue eyes sparkled and he whooped with delight when he saw Jackson. "Mike! You old groundhog!"

"Nick Beck! If I'd known you were going to be here, I'd have stayed away and sent an aide!"

Just then the commander of NORAD spotted General Neil Howard, the suave and glamorous chief of staff of the Air Force. "Oh-oh, here comes my boss, fellows. Gotta be good now!"

Howard grimaced at the buffoonery, frostily shook hands with Beck, and immediately took a chair, straightening his trouser crease as he did so.

The chairman of the joint chiefs began. He spoke quietly, but the others fell silent instantly. "I asked Secretary of Defense Scott to brief the president and the others before the meeting this morning, but Nick, you can count on a lot of interruptions from the president. He almost never reads the memoranda and reports, then he thinks we don't tell him anything and he gets peevish." Gray paused, and when he resumed, the edge of bitterness was gone.

"I might add that Scott thinks we're crazy and— Ah, here they come now."

Everybody stood as the secretary of defense entered. John R. Scott was a large fat man who wheezed as he walked. But his eyes were level and steady as he nodded greetings to each of the military leaders.

Behind him came the secretaries of the three services, Vincent Callazarro of the Army, Dale Sanders of the Air Force, and William Summerscales of the Navy. The four secretaries had two things in common, their unflagging loyalty to President Carl Reed, and their basic suspicion of the military. Reed had been one of the most stubborn opponents of the Vietnam war and when elected president years later, immediately made it clear he would tolerate, but never trust or like the military. His appointments reflected that bias. Moments after the introductions had been made, the president entered.

Carl Reed stood as erect as any of the officers present, and his bearing was as confident. He was a handsome man, tanned and healthy-looking. His clothes were flawless, from his expensive tie to his carefully tailored suit and highly polished shoes.

"Good morning, gentlemen. I think you all know Clifton Williams of the CIA?"

Williams, who had entered just behind the president, smiled and nodded to the rest of the group. He was surprisingly old. His hair was almost white and his formerly athletic figure had thickened. He was dressed in a sport coat and held an old briar pipe.

"All right, then, let's proceed."

Gray said, "Mister President, we know the demands on your time. But in view of recent developments we feel it is imperative for you to have a full briefing. General Beck?"

Beck ambled to the front of the room and began recounting the history of UFO sightings, reminding them where it all began. During the Second World War there had been a rash of UFO reports. Military pilots called the UFOs "foo fighters." At the time such sightings were pretty much written off as stress illusions. However, after the war they increased, and in 1947, the Air Force began an investigation that dragged on for years, went through three commissions, and was mostly dedicated to debunking.

A series of sightings at Ann Arbor reawakened public interest, and in 1969 Dr. J. Allen Hynek, an astronomer and long-time consultant for the Air Force, stated that the latest reports comprised "genuinely new empirical data," and he recommended a careful study. But the Air Force had accepted the Condon report, which concluded that there was no reason to believe UFOs were anything other than natural phenomena.

A few years later, numerous sightings were again reported. Descriptions became more consistent, and frequently there were multiple observers, often backed up by radar or photographs. The reports were so impressive that the Air Force set up another investigating commission, headed by a major general, Nicholas Beck. He asked Nilstrom to be the scientific consultant.

Beck paused, then said, "We carried on as complete an investigation as funds would allow, and were astonished to find that we were totally at a loss to explain what was happening.

"However, our orders were to determine if there was any

threat to the security of the United States. Finding none, our commission was dissolved." He grimaced at the memory. "But Chris and I were never satisfied. We asked the Defense Department to conduct contingency studies on the possibility that the UFOs came from outside the solar system and represented civilizations with hostile intent. That suggestion was rejected— and I suspect that we were considered a little crazy." He laughed loudly at his own remark. Dr. Nilstrom grinned, but nobody else responded, and Beck continued, "I was transferred to—"

"Just a minute," barked the president. "I never heard of any proposal for a contingency study."

Beck looked questioningly at Gray who said quietly, "Mr. President, our records show that a copy of the proposal and its rejection were forwarded to you through your military advisor at that time, General Ferré. We have additional copies for you today."

"Well, why didn't Ferré call it to my attention?"

Silence greeted the question; and the president leaned back grimly in his comfortable chair. He nodded and Beck continued.

"Well, Chris got busy and did a contingency study of his own—which he'll tell you about." Beck paused and his bright eyes became serious. "In recent months, evidence of the existence of UFOs has multiplied; and they have frequently appeared over military installations. In fact there has been a series of alarming incidents that have led us to ask for this meeting. Before I recount them, perhaps I should review the structure of the aerospace defense . . ."

Scott groaned loudly.

The president looked sharply at him, but hesitated before speaking: "Some of us lack the secretary's knowledge of military affairs." Reed's dynamism seemed to have evaporated and he was waiting indecisively for a word from Scott.

The secretary waved his hand arrogantly. "Oh, well, go ahead, General."

Beck began again, "The defense of the United States is based on the principle of deterrence—that is, on our ability to punish an aggressor in a retaliatory strike rather than to destroy an attacking force. NORAD is mostly concerned with detecting an attack and passing the word to our strategic forces."

The president nodded.

"For example, NORAD has only a relatively small number

of interceptors, far too few to stop a determined attack."

The president glanced nervously at Scott, who gave no response.

"In line with this philosophy, the United States is surrounded by a wall of radar stations covering all approaches to the continent, and doubly covering the primary attack routes. For example, our BMEWS—Ballistic Missile Early Warning System—scans the entire Eurasian land mass. The Space Detection and Tracking System, SPADATS, monitors all satellites in orbit around earth."

The general went on to describe the orbiting satellites and the dozens of interlocking systems that kept watch over the entire globe.

"On twenty-six August, this year, our Baker-Nunn cameras on Sound Island photographed three objects apparently entering earth orbit from deep space. This is the camera, you may recall, that photographed the six-inch Vanguard satellite twenty-five hundred miles out in space.

"Now, gentlemen, the pictures you're about to see were not taken by a kid in Kalamazoo with his trusty Brownie. They were taken by a crew of highly trained technicians using a camera weighing three tons and standing ten feet high."

He picked up the glass of water before him on the dais and took a big gulp as he nodded to Kaminski to turn on the projector.

"These first photographs were taken at a distance of four hundred and fifty miles and the lighting was bad. They show little spots of light. However . . ." Again he nodded, and the sergeant ran through a sequence of slides. ". . . these later pictures were taken from as close as a hundred and eighty miles and are quite revealing."

The last photograph showed three oval disks flying in formation. Each was thicker toward the center and had a domelike structure on its upper surface. The enlargement clearly showed rocket vents on the rim of each saucer.

The president exploded, "Why, damn it, those things are spacecraft! Why haven't I been notified before? Gray? Scott?"

Kaminski snapped on the lights.

Gray was white with anger. Memoranda and prints of these very photographs had been sent to the president, but Reed was so anti-military that he rarely looked at anything the Pentagon sent him. He depended on Scott to filter all military communications and tell him anything really important.

For once Scott looked embarrassed and said nothing.

"Gray?"

Before the general could answer, Nick Beck looked up from some papers through which he had been shuffling.

"Sir, the report in question was delivered to your office on one September. I have a copy here..."

With huge strides, Beck took an envelope to the president, and returned to the rostrum. He stole a look at Dr. Nilstrom, who was struggling to keep from laughing.

Beck resumed, "Now, sir, we estimate that these ships are ninety feet long and approximately sixty feet wide. They have a maximum thickness of fifteen feet near the center dome, which is itself another five feet high and about twelve feet in diameter. SPADATS radar clocked them at twelve thousand miles per hour but decelerating rapidly as they neared the atmosphere.

"Since that time, we've had eleven radar sightings of unknown objects in orbit over North America, including one on seven September that crossed the United States from northwest to southeast at an altitude of one hundred fifty miles."

"I have a question." Scott was still smarting, and his voice was sarcastic. "I read your reports, but I never took them seriously. I know radar is forever picking up junk that turns out to be an electrical storm or a duck flying in front of the dish. Aren't these 'saucers' something like that?"

"Negative! Our radar is computer-analyzed and makes allowances for such artifacts. The instrument is also capable of such resolution that we were able to make accurate calculations of the object's size and even its appearance. Beyond all reasonable doubt it was one of the saucers we photographed over the Pacific."

"General?"

"Yes, Mr. President?"

"It seems clear that these things are spacecraft. But they are probably probes sent out by the Russians that you spotted returning to earth."

"Negative, sir."

"Why not?"

"Because of our surveillance system. We conduct radar scanning of Russia and have a system of satellites with infrared sensors that detect the engine heat of a missile or other rocket and inform us instantly. We know every rocket launched by the Soviet Union."

The president turned to Clifton Williams, looking for a refutation.

Williams took the pipe out of his mouth and shook his head. "No, Mr. President, our espionage network would have detected the development, much less the use of any such spacecraft."

"Okay, where are we?" Beck asked.

"Eleven radar sightings," Nilstrom reminded him.

"Oh, yes." Beck nodded his big head. "Well, a series of frightening events followed. On twenty September, the aircraft carrier *Independence*, in the Mediterranean, observed an object flying at high speed toward Marseilles. French authorities were alerted. The bogie descended from ninety thousand feet to about twenty and came to a halt, literally hovering over the naval base. It was a saucer.

"The French fired Cactus missiles, which missed, and scrambled two Mirage G-8 interceptors. This is one of the fastest aircraft in the world, capable of Mach two-five. But the saucer just sat there till the fighters came close, and then it scooted up and away. It circled, came back at those planes with tremendous speed, overtook them, and spouted a ball of fire that enveloped both planes. Neither pilot survived."

Beck paused and took another drink of water.

"So they're not ducks," Nilstrom commented acidly.

Scott cast the astronomer a furious look.

Beck gestured to Kaminski, who flicked off the lights and showed a series of slides—satellite photos of saucers taken over Brazil, China, Germany, and England.

"On three October, our optical satellite, Cyclops, took this next picture over the Soviet Union—surely one of the most remarkable in the history of aerospace photography. Please note that two spacecraft are flying in formation, with three Foxbats rising to intercept. With after burners, those planes are capable of speeds beyond Mach 3, but they failed to bring down the saucers."

"Nick, what weapon did the Soviets interceptors use?" General Howard asked.

"The Ash-3 missile, capable of Mach 6, with a range of sixty miles."

Howard whistled.

Beck continued, "We have an amusing tape of the conversation between the pilots of the Foxbats and their command headquarters. If any of you understand Russian, I'll have Sergeant Kaminski play it. . . . No? Well, the pilots referred to the spacecraft as 'American.' I was flattered, but also alarmed that they'd think we'd carry on such reconnaissance operations in violation of our treaty."

When there were no comments, Beck sighed and said, "The French and Russians both had their chance to get a saucer and failed. It was our turn."

Chapter 9

"ON NINE November came the first act of hostility against the U.S. One of the saucers appeared over Norfolk, sweeping in from the sea, so close it could be seen with the naked eye.

"I watched on the screen in Cheyenne Mountain, and could hardly believe what I saw. That son of a bitch was over the greatest naval base in the world, hovering at six thousand feet, obviously observing, perhaps taking photographs.

"The Navy fired three advanced Terrier missiles, and the damned thing took off. The—"

Admiral Steinhauser interrupted angrily, "I want to remind everyone that the Terrier is *fast*. And that saucer just stuck its tail in the air and left those missiles behind as if they were chained to a post."

"Affirmative," Beck said. "They finally had to be destroyed. Now, by an odd coincidence, we were having maneuvers down in South Carolina and had, for that day only, denuded Norfolk of Eagles. Whether the bogie knew that, I don't know. At any rate, I ordered a flight of old F-106s—Darts—to attempt an intercept.

"I was proud of those boys. They scrambled in seconds, and when the saucer came roaring back after shaking the missiles, they attacked. The saucer turned tail again, out over the Atlantic. My boys went right after him and actually gained on him. They fired Falcons, but the saucer apparently jammed their guidance systems and the missiles flew on out to sea.

"Then one of the Darts suffered a malfunction of its afterburner and fell behind the others. Still, it was able to stay fairly close, which was lucky for us, because the pilot had turned on his cameras. He got some pretty darned sobering footage. Sergeant?"

The film was excellent, and the saucer could be seen clearly. When the rockets streaked toward the round, flat object, it seemed they would blow it out of the sky. But, just as Beck had said, they all veered away from the target.

The saucer was flying just fast enough to lead the Darts on. Suddenly the spacecraft left the screen with a turn too tight for the F-106s. The sky spun dizzily as the fighters screamed around in a wide arc, trying to follow. Then the picture shuddered as the camera plane lost its afterburner and dropped back. Almost immediately the alien appeared beside the two leaders, its dome glinting in the sunlight. And it was no longer playing the part of the bird with a broken wing; it was now the hunter, following relentlessly.

There was a collective gasp from the group as the two interceptors burst into flames. Each of them was staring, hoping the canopies would open and the pilots would escape. Then there was stunned silence as the hapless planes exploded.

"Gentlemen, at this point the third plane was ordered home, and he limped in. The alien made no attempt to follow, and quickly vanished over the sea."

The lights came on. Secretary Summerscales pulled out his handkerchief and wiped his sweat-streaming face.

General Jackson, awed, said, "I've never seen a plane turn like that."

Sanders shook his head. "What kind of power plant does it have?"

Everyone looked to the Commander of NORAD for the answer.

Beck shook himself out of his thoughts. "There's only one possibility for the power, and Doctor Nilstrom will tell you about that. But first, let's get on with the rest of the story. We saw nothing of the bastards for a few days. But on fourteen November, there was another demonstration of hostility. As you know, Venezuela gave us permission to carry on simulated amphibian landings on a remote part of their coast. That mock invasion involved thousands of troops. The entire operation was directed from an AWACS plane."

"Oh, yeah," remarked Scott. "I heard you had some incredible foul-up down there."

Beck ignored Scott's remark. "The AWACS plane, as you know, is a Boeing 707 crammed full of electronic gear to monitor and direct battlefield functions.

"It was cruising off the coast when, suddenly, one of the saucers appeared on radar, diving at high speed—from about two hundred miles south. The fleet immediately scrambled a flight of Tomcats. Then something happened that we hadn't encountered before. The radar tracking the bogie got clutter and lost the target. Of course, that means the spacecraft had jammed the radar. Before the computer could sort out the mess, the saucer was over the fleet. The Tomcats were never even in the action. By the time the fleet had visual sighting, the saucer had passed over and headed straight for the AWACS. It tried evasive action, but the saucer let fly another ball of fire and the plane exploded.

"Fifteen men killed and fifty million dollars worth of sophisticated equipment lost.

"The saucer flew back over the fleet. Over thirty missiles were launched by planes and warships. They all missed. I have the photos. Sergeant?"

When the lights came back on, everyone was even more somber than before.

"After this, and with continued sightings inside the United States, I ordered several flights of Eagles to key bases in the interior, away from their usual stations on the periphery.

"Now, I'd like to stop here while Mrs. Mowbray gives each of you copies of the pictures you've seen, and some I am about to show."

Diane took the packets from Kaminski and passed them among the men.

She then returned to her seat and General Beck continued, "The character and intent of the aliens was fully revealed just two days ago on twenty-six November. You have all read about the crash of the 747 east of Denver. Gentlemen, a saucer buzzed that airliner, toyed with it, and shot it down. Naturally, we didn't release that information to the public. "Dr. Nilstrom will tell you more about the tragedy."

Tersely, Nilstrom described what he had witnessed. Kaminski played the bone-chilling tapes of the pilot's conversation with the tower, and showed pictures of the wreckage.

The president was shaken. "Why shoot down a helpless plane? Did he think it was a military aircraft?"

Nilstrom answered, "Mr. President, I haven't the slightest doubt he knew it was a passenger plane. He cruised beside it for several minutes."

"Well, then—my God, why did he do it?"

"There's another question we must answer first, sir."

"What's that?"

"Who are these people? Where do they come from?"

Chapter 10

CLIFTON WILLIAMS asked, "Where do *you* think they come from, Doctor?" He was scraping the bowl of his pipe with his pocket knife.

Nilstrom hesitated, knowing the reaction he'd encounter. But then he said levelly, "From outer space."

"Oh, come now, Dr. Nilstrom!" Scott was scornful. "In spite of what you say, I still think the Russians have pulled the wool over our eyes and secretly developed a high-performance aircraft."

"Negative!" General Beck called out. "*They* tried to shoot down the saucers, too."

The president ended the argument. "Let's hear Dr. Nilstrom out."

"Sir, it may be best to summarize what we know about the saucers themselves before talking about their origin." Chris picked up a sheet of notes, put on his glasses.

"First, it's obvious that they're in a completely different category from anything known to exist on earth. They're capable of at least four thousand miles per hour in the atmosphere, apparently without thermal problems. At that speed, any of our aircraft would simply burn up. They can even fly directly out of the atmosphere into space, where their speed is probably almost unlimited. They're capable of unbelievable maneuvers and seem to have unlimited range—which means unlimited fuel supply; they carry a weapon unlike any known to exist in the arsenals of the world powers; their radar-jamming equipment is much more effective than ours. So far as we know, they have no 'home,' since every country over which we've known them to fly has tried to shoot them down."

Nilstrom paused, took off his glasses, and leaned forward.

"We know that intelligent life does not exist on any of the other planets in our own solar system. But let's suppose that, somewhere out there, a planet orbiting another star *is* capable of supporting life. Suppose it's older than ours, with a civilization technologically more advanced. Would its inhabitants have some of the same characteristics as ours? I don't mean physical qualities, in the sense of two hands and two feet and so forth. I mean the urge to explore and conquer, the willingness to do battle, to kill.

"Philosophers have been trying to tell us for a long time that what distinguishes man from other animals is not his physical makeup, but his intelligence, his freedom to choose what he will do with his life. And the fact that he is intelligent means he can foresee his own death, and is therefore prey to a fear other animals don't have. The knowledge that he will die not only causes him fear, but also humiliation.

Thus man tries to accumulate possessions or achieve power to make himself feel important and immortal. He's adventurous, but, more than that, he's acquisitive and often ruthless in pursuit of what he wants—which makes him dangerous. Well, if any other civilization does exist out there, it has intelligent beings subject to those same forces. They probably have had, perhaps still do have, their wars. And they too could be faced with the problem of overpopulation. Our little planet, so lovely and so hospitable to life, would be very inviting."

Nilstrom looked weary as he paused to take a drink of water. "Even before the recent incidents, Nick and I had become uneasy about the activities of the UFOs. Though they weren't engaged in anything belligerent at first, it looked as if they were thoroughly investigating every aspect of the earth. Saucers were seen in almost every conceivable place: in cities, in the wilderness, over water supplies, swamps, power lines. One was even seen nosing into a tree. And there were bizarre reports by reliable people of being taken on board a saucer for physical and psychological examinations.

"I believe that they're exploring our planet, taking water and air samples, checking the wildlife, the kind of plants earth will support. I think they're checking our cities, transportation, power, communications systems—in short, collecting data much the way the Europeans did when they explored Asia, Africa, and the New World.

"Of course, there's been a lot of romantic nonsense about visitors from space. Most of the speculation concludes that they're superior beings, dismayed at our predilection for war and anxious to lead us to peace. I see no evidence confirming that view. On the contrary, the saucers are now blatantly inviting their own destruction. That has to be the prelude to something. And if they are hostile, if they're intent on conquest, we have a major problem on our hands, for they're unquestionably more advanced technologically."

There was a protracted silence before the president asked, "Dr. Nilstrom, why have they suddenly become belligerent?"

"Mr. President, I believe it's because they've completed their general exploratory mission and are now gathering last-minute military data. I think they're probing our defenses, intentionally provoking a response in order to test our weapons systems. They'd save this for the last, because it's the most dangerous."

"Last-minute data? Probing defenses? Why?" asked Clifton Williams, chewing on the end of his pipe.

"To find out how effectively we can defend ourselves against a takeover of our planet."

"But Dr. Nilstrom, surely those little saucers can't conquer the whole earth?"

"Oh, no. They're only scouts, sending information back to their headquarters."

Secretary Summerscales lit a cigarette and puffed on it furiously, squinting against the smoke. The crow's-feet around his eyes made him look older than he was, but he was still a handsome man. He blew out the smoke and asked, "Doctor, just where do you think that headquarters is?"

"A planet orbiting some other star in our galaxy. However, there's another possibility I hesitate to suggest, but which we have to consider."

Scott had been staring at the floor as he listened. Now he looked up and said with contempt, "What's that? If we're going to play around with ideas like a *War of the Worlds*, we might as well hear it."

Nilstrom looked carefully at the secretary before answering, but he remained cool. "I think there's a strong possibility that the civilization which built the saucers has already launched a fleet, that it's en route, that the scouts are reporting not to their home planet, but to the fleet commander."

Sanders gasped, "My God! What makes you think that?"

"Well, there's good evidence that they've been exploring here for at least three or four decades. I believe the scouts were sent out while the fleet was still under construction. Think how

long it would take to build and outfit such a fleet. In order to
carry out their invasion plans, they would have to bring a
million men billions of miles through space—several light-
years! Imagine feeding that many, keeping them fit.

"The fleet would have to include tankers for fuel, supply
ships with food and clothing and ammunition, battleships and
cruisers, and carriers for smaller attack craft, and God knows
what else. It would be a fantastic feat, undoubtedly undertaken
only by a Spartan-type dictatorship. Probably the fleet would
be constructed in orbit around their home planet while they
waited for word from the scouts. As soon as they received
reports that earth was habitable, they would launch the fleet.
That could mean it's been coming for twenty to forty years.
And to get here from the closest star would take not less than
sixteen years, and perhaps as much as a century."

"A century!" exclaimed the secretary of defense. "Oh, come
now! They'd all be dead!"

"Would they? We don't know how long they live. Maybe
they'd use some sort of suspended animation for the trip. Or
the vessels we see now may be manned by the children or even
grandchildren of the original pilots. At any rate, my guess is
that *right now* there's an invasion fleet within a few billion
miles that intends to destroy us and seize the earth."

Scott began to chuckle. Finally he said, "Dr. Nilstrom, we
all know your love of science fiction. And now you come here
trying to convince us that we are literally on the verge of being
invaded from outer space!" He laughed some more and wiped
his eyes with a handkerchief. "I find that pretty hard to believe!"

Nilstrom's eyes were needles and his voice a scalpel when
he said, "*Why*, Mr. Scott?"

Nobody spoke or moved. Everyone felt the impact of the
simple question. The idea seemed incredible only because it
had never happened before. But it was the only logical explanation of the facts.

Finally the president spoke. "Well, Dr. Nilstrom . . . who
are . . . have you any idea what they look like?"

"No, none at all."

"You mean they could actually be little green men with
antennae?"

"Yes, sir."

"Or sexless creatures that reproduce by growing babies out
of the top of their heads?"

"We have no idea. We'd like to find out."

"But how can we defend ourselves against this—invasion..."

Scott looked up quickly, and the president glanced at him nervously before continuing, "... if there is one at hand? If we can't even destroy one of their little scouts, how can we hope to stop the entire battle fleet?"

Nilstrom said, "I think Nick can best answer that."

Everyone turned to Beck.

"We've got to get more information. So far, other than the general appearance and capabilities of these craft, the only thing we know is their number. Computer study of all verified sightings convinces us there are only three. But we need to know more. So we've got to shoot one down. Since our missiles can't do it, I request permission from you, Mr. President, to use a Graser. The saucers have flown over the Graser sites, and we're sure they'll do it again. When they do, we want to blow the bastards out of the sky."

Suddenly Scott reddened. "Well, *now* I understand, Mr. President! The soldier boys want to play with their new toy, and they've concocted this Buck Rogers story to—"

The president was standing, and had waved his hand for silence. Carl Reed, the "weak" president, the man accused of hating his own military establishment, said, "Permission granted! And I want to compliment the armed forces for the way they have dealt with this threat. I want no discussion of this matter outside this group."

Everyone was numb. It was well known that Secretary Scott had "made" Reed president. It was said that Reed never made a decision without his agreement. Yet he hadn't even permitted the secretary to finish his statement.

"General Beck, does your Canadian deputy commander know the details?"

"Oh, yes, sir."

"Good! I assume you hope to recover pieces of the craft if you are able to shoot one down, and it's possible it'll fall on Canadian soil, which means we must have their cooperation. And General Beck, good luck! Keep me personally informed of every development. Gentlemen, shall we go back to work?"

Scott was livid. His voice shook as he said, "Carl, god-damnit, you don't mean to tell me you're going to—"

Reed's own voice showed neither anger nor fear as he replied calmly, "Mr. Secretary, the first duty of the President of the United States is to protect its citizens from attack. I intend to perform that duty to the best of my ability. This meeting is ended."

Chapter 11

SUSAN HAD already fallen asleep on her father's lap, and Mike was having trouble holding his head up, when Chris stopped reading from *Winnie the Pooh* and declared that it was time for bed. Outside, the temperature had dropped to zero, and two feet of glittering snow lay on the ground. The big evergreen in the front yard was magnificent in its coat of white. The neighbors already had their Christmas decorations up, and the multicolored lights reflected brilliantly on the snow. Inside the Nilstrom's red brick Georgian home, it was warm and peaceful. Chris had built a fire, and the applewood logs crackled and popped.

Nilstrom loved these moments. In some ways he was not a good father, for he was restless and distracted much of the time. But he loved his children and they knew it. Tonight they were in pajamas and robes, and smelled fresh and clean from their baths. Now, as he stood up with Susan in his arms, he buried his nose in her blond hair. She smiled in her sleep, and when he turned to speak to his son, he whispered so as not to awaken her.

"Mike, can you make it upstairs by yourself?"

The sleepy child nodded, yawned, and began to stumble after his father. Nilstrom laughed and, shifting Susan, reached down and scooped Mike up in his other arm. The little boy put his head on Chris's shoulder, and the astronomer carried him to bed. Then, after a kiss for Mike, he took Susie to her room, removed the stuffed animals from the bed, pulled back the covers, and gently tucked her in. She groped blindly for her teddy bear and Chris laid it in her arms as he kissed her.

Downstairs he removed the fireplace screen, poked the logs, and added one more as the flames leapt again. He remembered the times he and Kay had spent before this fireplace. Every

Sunday evening they had a tradition of hot chocolate or cold milk with sandwiches and popcorn before the fire. The kids usually played or watched television in the adjoining study and they had the moments to themselves.

But he remembered, too, one night after they had put the children to bed, when she had said, "Chris, you won't believe this—I never thought it could happen to me—but when I went for my checkup last week, the doctor found a lump in my breast. He arranged for a biopsy and ... well, it's cancerous. He doesn't think it's gotten into the lymph nodes yet, but I do have to have an operation—a radical mastectomy—and ..."

She didn't have a chance to finish, for Chris, aghast, rushed to her and crushed her in his arms.

And it was here, a year later, before this fireplace, that she had told him new X-rays showed the original cancer had metastasized to her lungs. She lived only six months after that. He still couldn't think about it without getting tears in his eyes. He smiled wryly at himself and replaced the fireplace screen.

Then he went to the kitchen for a cup of coffee. His mother always left the pot for him, though she thoroughly disapproved of coffee after dinner, insisting that it wasn't good for a person's heart: "Wouldn't it be awful for the children, already without a mother, to lose you to a heart attack?"

Back in the living room, he settled down in his favorite chair. He picked up the CORADS folder just as his mother entered the room. She frowned slightly as she saw his cup, but said nothing. She was sixty-nine, her gray hair was stylishly done, and her figure defied time. She kept a fourteen-hour day, rushing from her housework to church meetings to book clubs.

"Will you be leaving for Colorado Springs soon?" she asked. "You'll be back for Christmas, won't you?"

"I hope so."

She sighed, knowing he couldn't say more. "Well, your father's asleep in front of the television and you're obviously settling down for a long evening, so I think I'll go on up and have a bath and work on my book review. I'll see you in the morning."

"Goodnight, Mother. And thanks for taking such good care of Mike and Susie. I ..." Their eyes met, and everything he wanted to say was communicated.

Nilstrom opened the folder and began to read the fact sheet.

He was already familiar with the Coherent Radiation Defense System. Operational, or nearly so, were eight stations

across the nothern United States, each with a double battery
of five Grasers apiece. GRASER—Gamma Ray Amplification
by Stimulated Emission of Radiation. Nilstrom smiled; the
military was notorious for acronyms. But he quickly sobered.
There was nothing amusing about a weapon that destroyed its
target with a high-energy beam of coherent radiation. Deadly
gamma rays deriving their tremendous power from a nuclear
reactor—the "death ray" so dear to science fiction had become
a reality. Designed as an antimissile device, the Graser represented a major breakthrough in military technology.

> . . . The beam emitted by the gun is initially eighteen
> centimeters in diameter and is capable of destroying a
> missile or aircraft at ranges of up to five hundred miles.
> Beyond this distance, the spreading beam loses power
> rapidly, but will destroy instrumentation up to six
> hundred miles away. The intensity of the radiation is still
> great enough to kill the crew of a bomber up to eight
> hundred miles . . .

Chris was impressed. He reached for his coffee, mentally
picturing the devastation he hoped the Graser would wreak
upon the UFO. Funny, but had he read this same report a
month ago, he'd have thought only in terms of conventional
aircraft. Now his whole perspective had changed.

He scanned the section about the Graser's limitations. There
were three major ones: first, each firing creates such heat that
the gun must be cooled for three minutes before being fired
again; second, due to its weight, the Graser tracks slowly and
is therefore virtually useless against low-flying aircraft; third,
there were environmental hazards, which were listed and described. Nilstrom's eye caught, "In addition, the radar used
for tracking has allegedly caused sterility in some species of
migrating geese."

Chris shook his head and chuckled, then read on. An incoming missile is reported by the conventional warning system
of BMEWS and DEW, then, when in range, is tracked by
CORADS' own radar until a Laser Guidance Unit pinpoints
the target. The Graser itself is slaved to the laser, and as soon
as the target breaks the laser beam, the gun is automatically
fired. This assures the accuracy of the weapon.

Nilstrom finished reading and leaned back in his chair. He
gazed into the caverns of glowing embers in the fireplace. The

heat and energy even there—imagine it multiplied to a degree beyond comprehension! What a weapon! His mind drifted back to the first time he had heard of the development of the Graser.

It was during his investigation of the UFO sightings. He and Beck were in the officers' club at the Air Force Academy in Colorado Springs. Nick suddenly stood up and gestured to another officer who had just entered the dining room in the company of a young civilian. The two joined them for dinner and Nick introduced his friend, Major General Hart Dobyns, chief of the Research and Development Section of the air force. He in turn introduced Chuck Kellogg. Nilstrom had heard of the young man, a Ph.D. in nuclear physics from Berkeley.

Kellogg was in his late twenties and looked younger. He even had pimples. His shock of unruly hair was poised on his forehead like a wave about to break. He was as gangly as a fifteen-year-old, and his clothes looked as if they'd come from a local Goodwill store and then been slept in. Only Kellogg's darting eyes expressed his intelligence and vitality.

The young scientist clearly didn't like meeting people he did not know or care to know.

"Chuck's our 'Peck's bad boy,'" Hart said. "You'll find him quite intolerable. But you'll also find that he's almost as smart as he thinks he is."

Kellogg looked insolently from one to the other as they talked about him. "And just what do you do in the fucking Air Force, General?" he interrupted. "Are you a bus driver for those pregnant birds that spend taxpayers' money flying congressmen around, or one of the ass-kissers who keep senators happy?"

Beck threw back his big head and roared. "Hey, he really is smart. Just met me, and already has my number."

"Go ahead and tell him, Nick," Dobyns suggested. "He has most of the faults of humanity wrapped up inside him, but one he lacks is a loose mouth. He's cleared for top secret."

"Okay. At the moment, kid, I'm studying UFO sightings. The Air Force was never quite content with the Condon report. Dr. Nilstrom here is my scientific advisor."

Kellogg didn't even glance at Chris; he was fascinated with Beck. Chris thought he saw respect—tentative, but still respect—in Kellogg's expression.

"I didn't think the Air Force had enough sense to see what an ass it made of itself with that report. So you're studying

UFOs again? What do you think?" His voice was surprisingly throaty and he spoke with an exaggerated Groton-Harvard put-on.

"Hard to say, so far, kid. My personal opinion is that alien aircraft are studying our planet—its air, topography, flora, fauna, and us."

Kellogg abruptly turned to Dobyns. "My God, another one. Two intelligent Air Force men at one table, and both of them major generals. As Moses said, 'I will turn aside and see this strange sight.'" Then, jerking his head toward Beck, he said, "He won't last, you know. Just as you won't. An open mind in the military? You'll both be shot. Or retired early."

"Oh, I don't know," Beck said benignly. "Things are no worse in the military than in the scientific world."

"That's for damn sure. Especially since that dipshit Farkas got to be the president's scientific advisor."

"Hold on a minute, Chuck." Dobyns glanced at Nilstrom.

"Don't let me stop you," Chris replied, amused. "Farkas *is* a dipshit."

"My God! Now an open-minded scientist!"

"By 'open-minded,' I assume you mean we agree with you?" Chris asked, smiling.

"Of course." Kellogg grinned, suddenly in good humor. "What's *your* opinion of the UFOs?"

"Fundamentally the same as Nick's."

"Oh?" asked Dobyns. "Then where do they come from?"

"From a planet orbiting another star," Kellogg answered for Chris. "But any idiot can see that. What I want to know is why they're checking us out."

"To determine Earth's suitability for their own needs," said Nilstrom. There was no point in beating around the bush with this young man.

"So you think they're going to stop frightening children and farmers and move in on us?"

"Could be."

"If they do, Nick, can we stop them?" Dobyns asked quietly.

"No."

Dobyns looked thoughtfully at Kellogg. "Well, Chuck, I guess it's up to you."

Beck's eyebrows rose. "Oh? What's the young fellow up to?"

"Nick, this kid is helping us build the ultimate antiaircraft and antimissile weapon."

Chris said, "Really? I thought both the United States and Russia dropped work on Grasers because of the problem with—"

"How the devil did you...I mean...by God!" Kellogg turned to Nilstrom with his mouth hanging open.

Both Dobyns and Beck laughed at his surprise. Then Dobyns said, "During his doctoral work in gamma rays, Chuck got an idea his professor recognized instantly as being the answer in principle to our problem. We're now in reach of producing a workable Graser. We're here to meet with some of the brass to discuss it."

Nilstrom hadn't seen Kellogg since that evening. He knew President Reed had almost dropped the Graser project on the grounds that it was expensive and came close to violating the old SALT agreements. But the determined intervention of G. Whalen Broughton of Mississippi, powerful chairman of the Armed Services Committee, had saved it.

The telephone rang. Chris jumped and looked at the antique clock on the mantle. It was twelve-ten. The phone rang again.

Chapter 12

WHEN HIS radar first picked up the rapidly approaching aircraft, Maxim Bezobrazov, commander of the destroyer *Provedennyi*, wasn't alarmed. The Americans were always anxious to let the Soviet navy know that they considered the Mediterranean their own private sea. His radar officer, Felix Pisarev, reported that the aircraft was losing altitude and was flying at four thousand miles per hour—but any sane naval officer knows such speed is impossible. He would have a chat with young Pisarev later.

Bezobrazov lifted his glasses. And he saw it, saw the sun glint on it, as it bore down on them at almost sea level. He gasped in surprise. That was no American plane. It was round and flat, with a dome on top. And it was bigger than any fighter plane. He squinted through the glasses, struggling to keep it in the field, but before he could focus again, it was upon them. At the last split-second, it hopped upward and missed the destroyer by only a few feet. It made no noise, but in its wake came the shattering, earsplitting sonic boom.

Bezobrazov reached for the microphone with one hand and the alarm button with the other. He hardly needed the latter, for sailors were already pouring on deck to see what had caused the thunderclaps. But now they ran to their stations, pulling on helmets and life jackets.

"Now hear this, now hear this! We are under attack by hostile aircraft. Prepare to fire antiaircraft missiles. Gunnery officer, fire, when ready!"

The saucer was virtually stationary a few hundred feet in the air, half a mile away. Bezobrazov studied it through the binoculars. He imagined he could see someone or something moving inside the dome, but the sea was sparkling so in the brilliant sun that the Russian couldn't be sure.

The first Goa missile blasted away with a deafening roar, and drove flat over the water toward the disk. But the saucer sprang high in the air, and the missile, unable to correct for the sudden movement, went right under it, struck a high wave, and exploded.

Immediately Commander Bezobrazov radioed the fleet commander, Admiral Shuvalov, on a cruiser one hundred and twenty miles away. He had no trouble communicating the problem, for, as they were talking, the saucer buzzed the *Provedennyi* again, and a sonic boom struck.

"Courage, Commander! We are sending fighters! But if he comes so low, why don't use your cannons?"

There was no time to answer. The saucer circled and came again, then again. Bezobrazov gave orders to his panicked sailors to fire every rocket they had, and to use cannon at close range. Four three-inch guns began pounding, sending up huge geysers behind the saucer as it hopped and banked first to one side and then the other.

The commotion was deafening, and the whole ship reeked of the acrid smell of gunpowder.

Then the Russians gaped in terror as the thing took a position directly overhead where the cannons could not be aimed. In a desperate attempt to escape, the *Provedennyi* took violent evasive action and the crewmen reeled about the deck and were soaked by spray blowing over the bow. But the saucer continued to shadow the twisting, plunging ship.

American planes were closer to the *Provedennyi* than the Russians' were. The carrier *Constellation* was cruising only fifty miles away, and launched its fighters the moment the intelligence officer translated the message. Three Tomcats approached from the west, at five thousand feet at the same time the Soviet Mig-25s came toward the destroyer from the east.

The American pilots had just spotted the ship's tortuous wake when eight pillars of fire shot from the underside of the saucer and enveloped the destroyer. The decks burst into flame, the sailors' clothes flashed, their hair crackled with fire, and they were shrunken, smoking charcoal. Belowdecks, it took seconds longer. Men shrieked as the temperature shot from normal to hundreds of degrees. Steel glowed red hot, and water in the toilet bowls burst into steam.

The saucer streaked away, straight up, as the destroyer's magazines and then her fuel oil blew up. Pieces of the ship flew hundreds of feet into the air.

The Tomcats kept their distance and watched as the MIG-25s screamed away in pursuit of the saucer already vanishing into the stratosphere. Then they flew directly over the spot where the *Provedennyi* had disappeared. They saw nothing, not even a life preserver. There was only swirling water and steam.

Chapter 13

NILSTROM HAD been at NORAD's headquarters inside Cheyenne Mountain numerous times, but still it thrilled him. As the Air Force limousine turned off Colorado Highway 115 and began the three-and-a-half-mile climb to the north entrance of the tunnel, he felt his heart quicken. It had been a disappointment to leave his children after so short a stay, but Nick's call about the *Provedennyi* had left him no choice. Chris had hurriedly packed his bag, kissed Mike and Susan, and wakened his parents to tell them his plans. He caught the first plane and traveled all night.

It was early the next morning when he entered the tunnel and rode the third of a mile to the huge blast doors. The tunnel was cut through the solid granite of the mountain. Here and there were steel mesh screens to prevent small rocks from cascading down on motorists. In other places, rock bolts held the walls in place.

The complex had been built in the early sixties, under the assumption that in the event of nuclear attack, the command post of U.S. air defense would be the first target, and if it were destroyed there would be no organized defense.

The mountain contained the hub of communications and center of command for the entire NORAD system. All world-wide air and space attack warning indicators terminated there. Information from the BMEWS and DEW systems, the Space Detection and Tracking System, satellites, the Over-the-Horizon system, radar planes, coastal radar—all poured their messages into this sophisticated center. Here they were fed into computers that automatically updated electronic situation maps and produced an up-to-the-minute picture of the air and of space. In the event of an attack, computers would predict and display time and impact points of intercontinental ballistic missiles and, by backtracking the arc, reveal their launch points—if the space satellites hadn't already given that data. Information from various sensors throughout the world flowed through computers and onto display consoles without ever being processed by human hands. And it was done so speedily that the battle staff could watch the track of an object at almost the same moment it was being made.

The driver dropped Nilstrom off at the guard station in front of the blast doors, where he stopped to present his credentials. At the door, television cameras fixed on him and a young AP saluted.

Beck welcomed Chris to his office overlooking the War Room. He looked more tired than Chris had ever seen him. He was haggard and hadn't shaved. Convinced that the saucers would make more probes of the American defense system, he had come directly from Washington to the NORAD command post, and had been there ever since. A cot was installed in his office. He even had his meals brought in. He greeted Nilstrom grimly, and gave him the details of the attack on the Russian destroyer. Then he related the latest bad news.

"This thing's getting hairier every day. There's just no question about what those bastards are up to. Are you familiar with Ichako?"

Nilstrom remembered what he'd read about the island. When their industries were threatened by the Arabs' withdrawal of their oil supply, the Japanese decided to take drastic steps to make sure their industrial system always had power. The only answer was nuclear power, but understandably, Japanese citizens were terrified of anything nuclear.

So the ingenious planners took over Ichako, one of the small islands in their chain, and relocated its people. There they built a number of nuclear power plants and created a massive web of power lines to the other islands. They cut their consumption of oil to a fraction of what it had been, and now had the most efficient power system in the world.

"That's their atomic island, isn't it?"

"Right. I just got word from our Far Eastern Command that a saucer attacked it. Completely destroyed the plant that generates electricity for Osaka, a damned important industrial complex. And I don't need to tell you that their missiles didn't even come close to getting the bastard."

The two men talked on into the afternoon. Outside Beck's office, rows of men sat at computer consoles watching data flicker across their small screens. At the front of the room, two twelve-by-sixteen-foot screens displayed all important data. Suspicious aircraft were shown until they were proven harmless. At the flick of a switch, the position of any of the more than three thousand satellites and other man-made objects orbiting the earth could be seen.

Suddenly the technician monitoring a satellite that kept its infrared eye trained on northern Russia shouted for his supervisor. Instead of the saucer they hoped to see, the thing they had dreaded for years had appeared on his computer console. It wasn't a picture, only figures. But there was no doubt. Armageddon in electronic green.

"Damn! I'll call the general," said the supervisor. "He'll want a composite on the big screen. Alert BMEWS and DEW for pictures."

He turned and dashed up to Beck's little office where, exhausted, both Beck and Nilstrom were asleep—Beck stretched out on his cot, Nilstrom leaning back in a chair with his feet on the desk. The supervisor didn't let formalities deter him; he shook the general rudely.

"Sir! Something big just went up from Novaya Zemlya."

Beck rose up in disbelief, and Chris shook himself awake.

"Novaya Zemlya? There must be a mistake!" In his stocking feet, Beck stumbled to his desk and looked out across the War Room at the big display boards. Nothing yet.

"Another one!" a technician shouted as he watched the rows of figures on his console. "That makes two!"

Beck shook his head to clear it. He was expecting UFOs,

not Russian missiles! Had the attack on the *Provedennyi* provoked this? Did the Soviets think the United States was responsible for that attack?

"There they are—over the polar cap!"

Two small green dots crawled across the map toward the U.S. from the Russian ICBM base. Slow as they seemed to be, the dots represented objects traveling at tremendous speed.

Beck stared at the display. His hand toyed with the telephone hot line to the White House, then shifted back to the one that connected him directly to the Pentagon. "Only *two*? It doesn't make sense."

Everyone watched for more blips.

"Okay. What do you have on their track?"

"Sir, they're a hundred and twenty miles up and moving at seventeen thousand miles per hour on a direct route to Los Angeles."

Again Beck touched the telephone, but suddenly he slammed his fist down on the desk. "By God! *I* know what's happening! If the Russians were really doing their thing, they'd send hundreds. Those aren't missiles. They're *saucers*. They probably sneaked in near Novaya Zemlya and then took off like big birds, *imitating* missiles! They're either trying to start a war between us and the Russians, or they just want to see what we've got."

"So let's show them." Chris stood beside the big man, watching the dots slide across the screen. The others glanced nervously at Beck. He hadn't alerted the Pentagon or the White House.

"We'll get better resolution in a second, and we'll be able to estimate their size," Beck said. "There! See?" He looked at the paper a technician had handed him, reading the figures as if they were his native language. "That's no FOBS!"

The Soviets had developed the Fractional Orbiting Bombardment System in their SCARP missile. Instead of lobbing a missile over the pole at great altitude so that it fell on a ballistic course, the SCARP put a warhead attached to a small rocket into orbit only a hundred or so miles above the earth and let it glide, then fired small retro-rockets at the precise moment necessary to drop it on the target.

"Son of a bitch! Trying to start a war, are you? Well, you, my little green friends, are going to get the surprise of your life!" Then he did pick up the phone to the Pentagon, and, within seconds, had General Gray on the line. "They're coming right for L.A., sir. They'll pass directly over our Winthrop, Washington Graser site."

While he talked to the Chairman of the Joint Chiefs, Beck watched the two dots cross upper Canada between the 118th and 129th meridians.

"Affirmative! I'll call the president the moment we have our shot."

He hung up and pushed a button on his desk. "Charlie, who's in command at Winthrop?" He never took his eyes off the big screen. "Great! Ginzburg's a good man. Get him on the phone."

Impatiently Beck waited for the call, and grabbed the receiver the second it came. "Colonel Ginzburg? You have the alert and know the situation. Wait till the first bastard is *very* near—say three hundred miles—and then zap him. Your radar ought to pick him up any second now. There! Got him? The other one is about two hundred miles behind and fifty above." Beck looked at the row of swiftly changing figures beside the map. "He's losing altitude—must be down to almost forty miles now. Go get 'em, Colonel!"

The green dots worked their way closer. BMEWS had long since lost them, but the newly improved DEW line tracked them until they crossed the Dolphin Straits and were out of its radar range. Then the Graser's own radar picked up the first saucer and flashed the data to NORAD.

On they came, surely aware that they were being monitored, but apparently unconcerned. High above the frozen Northwest Territory they glided, over Lake Hardisty and Lake la Martre, steadily losing altitude, simulating orbital missiles that had fired their retro-rockets and were ominously, relentlessly descending toward the target.

In Winthrop, the Graser crews were tense. Was this really it? Were they actually going to fire this new weapon, a weapon so secret they weren't even permitted to discuss it with their fellow airmen? The cowling that ordinarily covered the Grasers was now withdrawn, revealing two of the guns. One of the ponderous weapons slowly tracked the first saucer as radar poured data into the computer. It was set to fire when the target reached Mt. Robson.

The sky was brilliantly blue in the late afternoon. There wasn't a cloud. But even by straining their eyes, the men couldn't see anything. Would the target keep coming? Would they really fire?

Colonel Ginzburg felt sweat trickle down the back of his neck as he watched his computer console. Only ninety seconds to go. If Beck was going to withdraw the order to fire and call it a drill, he'd better hurry.

There wasn't a human sound in the NORAD command post. Computers whirred and figures appeared like magic on the display boards, but nobody spoke. In fact, nobody breathed.

The invaders had passed the McKenzie River and were over the province of Alberta, still dropping altitude, the first saucer now only twenty-eight miles high. Silently the dots continued, past the Hoy River, past Fort Vermillion, heading for Mt. Robson.

And silently Chris began to plead, "Keep losing altitude! If you're too high when we hit you, you'll burn up as you tumble into the atmosphere and we won't be able to find the pieces!"

Only ten seconds now before firing, and Colonel Ginzburg was soaked with perspiration. He could do nothing. He could only watch. Computers had aimed the fat, ugly cannon, and computers would fire it. But what a moment! It was history. Or the beginning of the end of history.

Eight seconds.

Six seconds.

Four.

Two. Laser on.

Fire!

From the blunt end of the Graser leapt a line of violet light, light, like a lightning bolt, but absolutely straight. A beam of coherent gamma rays, inches in diameter, but with the power of an atom bomb, would spread to only a foot and a half in the three hundred and fifty miles it had to travel—and it covered that distance and reached the target almost instantaneously, for it moved at the speed of light.

In its wake was a thunder-like crack.

Beck and Nilstrom saw the first dot disappear from the screen. Both could picture the destruction of the saucer. When the gamma rays struck, they burned a hole through the entire craft.

The metal vaporized in the heat of the beam, though that lasted only a fraction of a second, and it was really the vaporized metal that caused the explosion that blew the saucer to bits.

"Now get the other sonofabitch!" Beck snarled.

But it was too late. The moment the first saucer exploded, the second one stopped in mid-air. Then it dove at tremendous speed for the safety of low altitude. In a split-second, it too was gone from the screen.

Softly, viciously, General Beck said, "Chicken, mister?"

Everyone in the command post began to applaud and laugh and talk at once. Instantly Beck was on the phone to the president, reporting that the Graser had shot the saucer down over Jasper National Park in British Columbia.

". . . Affirmative. And I'll alert the Canadians to meet us in Edmonton. The damned thing was so high that the pieces'll be scattered all over the park, but we ought to find something."

Beck put the receiver down. Chris was smiling.

"What's so funny?"

"I was just thinking about Chuck Kellogg. He's the worst brat I ever met, but if he were here right now, I'd kiss the bastard!"

Chapter 14

IT WAS an overcast day again, Chris noted with a pang. The last time he had inspected a crash site, it had been cloudy too. Only then the downed aircraft was a 747 full of people, and this time it was a flying saucer full of . . . what?

He was flying over the flat, rolling hills west of Edmonton, Alberta, heading toward the Canadian Rockies where the saucer had come down. So far the terrain too was like that at the Denver crash site—the ground beneath the plane's wings reminded him of the Colorado wheat fields.

According to the best estimates, the wreckage was scattered along the British Columbia-Alberta border a few hundred miles north of Montana. Chris was not sure what to expect. He had checked the atlas and found that the area was mountainous, the average annual snowfall eighty inches, and the average December temperature ten degrees. It did not sound very hospitable.

The planes carrying the investigators from Edmonton were the tilting-wing C-175s, nicknamed Klipspringers. This transport was designed to carry troops and light cargoes into inaccessible areas. In normal flight it resembled any small cargo plane, but the wings could rotate so that the engines pointed upward, enabling it to land and take off vertically. Then it looked like a toy a petulant child had assembled backwards.

They passed over Jasper, and the gentle, rolling terrain gave way to more and more violent upthrusts as the mountains gathered themselves and humped up toward the little transport. The ride was bumpy as the Klipspringer cut through the mountain-induced updrafts and downdrafts. Chris sat back from the window.

In addition to those in General Beck's party, there were thirty soldiers on the plane, most of them looking uncomfortably bulky in their winter gear. Two Indians, professional trackers, had joined them in Edmonton. Familiar with the area, they could be of tremendous help. They sat together, their faces impassive, their dark eyes flitting around the cabin. The plane was noisy. Nobody tried to talk. Beck sat very still, his boyish face thoughtful. He was an enormous figure, rotund with the heavy parka he wore.

Once the Klipspringers had taken the Americans to the crash site, the four aircraft would shuttle the Canadian troops over the mountains from Jasper where they had been sent by train. Altogether almost a thousand men would scout the area. A lot of troops to expose to the mountains in winter, perhaps, but they were the best, toughened by long training in survival techniques.

Now the mountains seemed closer; the plane was losing altitude. Abruptly the pitch of the engines changed, and Chris felt a tug at his stomach. The little plane bucked furiously and there was a powerful sensation of slowing. He looked forward. The wings were rotating and, as he watched, the engines came into view. The four prop arcs looked like umbrellas along the wings. Chris suppressed a sick feeling. There was something basically wrong about an airplane with a wing like that!

Then came the sensation of dropping. He tried to look down, but the curve of the hull kept him from seeing directly below. On either side, jagged cliffs swept upward. The overwhelming impression was of whiteness, though the snow cover was torn here and there where trees and patches of windswept rock pushed through.

The transport set down with a crunch, and the engines, no longer having to carry the plane's weight, relaxed in unison. The droning settled into a weakening flap-flap-flap, and the propellers windmilled to rest. They had arrived.

There was a flurry of activity. A sergeant snapped orders; the men slung carbines over their shoulders, tightened their clothing, stretched away the cramps.

"What's the temperature outside, Lieutenant?" Chris heard Beck ask the pilot.

"Three degrees, sir . . . Fahrenheit," he added as an afterthought.

Beck merely nodded, but Sergeant Kaminski looked aghast. "Three degrees," he groaned. "and it's the middle of the day. What the hell is it gonna be tonight?"

Another soldier nodded knowingly. His only comment was, "Shee-it."

Kaminski was thoroughly prepared for his assignment. Camera straps crisscrossed his bulky figure like meridians on a globe.

"All right, Lieutenant." Beck pulled his hood up over his head.

The pilot moved to the big panel door, undid the latch, and pulled upward. The cold knifed in, and Chris felt the mucous membranes in his nose shrivel as the air reached him. A huge cloud of snow hung suspended before them, eddies drifting with the wind. From it emerged another transport, kicking up snow as it set down next to them.

Beck jumped out, landing in a heap, and Kaminski followed with an equally awkward attempt. Most of the troops made the two-foot jump without falling. Nilstrom was the last to leave the plane, and the door hastily slammed shut behind him. Covered as he was with layers of official United States Air Force-certified cold-weather garb, Chris wasn't uncomfortable, but the wind that hit his face was insultingly frigid. He moved away from the fuselage. The snow squeaked under his boots. Like the others, he looked around, surveying the scene.

The mountains rose around them in awesome silence, edges razor-sharp in the clear, frosty air. Here and there, trees made a half-hearted effort to climb the slopes, rapidly giving up under the twin burden of sheer cliffs and bitter growing conditions. Snow covered everything else. Chris noticed that they had landed on a perfectly flat expanse. He looked down, kicked the snow away, and his suspicions were instantly confirmed—

solid ice. They had landed on a lake.

"All right, enough sightseeing. Let's get the equipment."
Beck turned back to the plane, reached up, and banged on the
door.

It opened only a few inches. An eye appeared. "My God,
it's cold!" exclaimed a puff of frosted breath.

"So I've noticed," Beck said tersely. "Let's get going."

The door promptly opened the rest of the way and a crewman
jumped out, simultaneously reaching back for a large bundle,
which he pulled out onto the snow. It was followed by another,
and another. The plane was rapidly emptied. Chris chuckled
quietly. Beck got more back-talk than he'd ever seen in the
military, but things were a lot more efficient and organized
than he'd ever seen, either.

The equipment was shouldered by the troops, and Beck
pointed toward the trees. "Let's go."

They reached the edge of the lake in a few minutes.

"I don't see any goddamn flying saucer crash," commented
a soldier.

"And you won't, either," growled another. "How the fucking hell d'ya think that thing'd hold together, falling twenty
miles? It's prob'ly scattered from here to hell's shithouse."

Chris grinned. Military language hadn't changed. "I hope
the good weather holds," he said to no one in particular.

"This is good?" Kaminski's question was sorrowful.

"'Fraid so," offered Beck. "But there's a cold front moving
in. We have a couple of days, at best."

They watched the Klipspringers take off, and then went to
work setting up camp. The transports made the round trip to
Jasper six times, and by fifteen hundred, all the Canadian
troops had been flown in. Chris was billetted with Beck and
several other officers. It was slightly warmer in the tent, so
he removed his gloves and hood. His heavy coat was open,
but he kept it on. Beck was busily making plans with the
others, so Nilstrom pulled out a pen, some paper, and his
calculations. He sat down at a field desk, and within seconds
he might as well have been in his office in Madison, for all
the attention he was paying to his surroundings.

The sun set at an indecently early hour, and they were left
with artificial light. The wind picked up considerably, and the
tent swayed and rippled. The command group clustered around
a small folding table to eat their rations, then most of the men
settled down for the night.

Nilstrom continued to work by the small lantern, occasionally distracted by a loud snore. Finally someone growled, "Turn off that damn light!"

Chris did, crawled into his sleeping bag, and with some difficulty, fell asleep.

Chapter 15

MORNING DAWNED clear, cold, and impossibly late. The camp was a bustle of activity long before the sun showed its face. Chris emerged from the tent feeling lousy. Like most of the men, he hadn't slept well or long enough, and he ached everywhere.

Even before the tardy sun appeared, the search parties started out, leaving a trail of muttering and frozen breath behind.

Beck watched the men go. "Well, Chris, now we wait. Or do you want to go out with one of the parties?"

"I do, but I'm not as young as they are." He looked up at the sky. "What's the latest on the weather?"

"Not good. That front is moving faster than expected. The weather guys suggest we have everybody out by yesterday."

"Do you think we can wait out a storm if we have to?"

"This bunch can. We made damn sure they're all regular mountain goats."

They watched the last party head out. "Come on, you bastards, find something!" Nilstrom said.

Sergeant Ronald Wojekowski led his group up the narrow valley. To his considerable disinterest, he had been told that the mountain rising on the left was Mt. Robson, which reached twelve thousand nine hundred and seventy-two feet. Wojekowski had been born in Leadville, Colorado, two miles above sea level, and, before he was eighteen, had climbed a dozen peaks over fourteen thousand. Anything lower wasn't worth noticing. He had the lungs of a Bolivian Indian, and the thin air of this remote valley didn't bother him at all. His caustic remarks to his men as to their conditioning were not insincere, and in the best military tradition, he felt obliged to chastise them for their foot-dragging weariness.

They had reached a spot higher than any of the other parties, and the sergeant stopped to allow the other to catch their breath and to look back briefly at the frozen lake below.

"Quite a view," puffed one of the privates gamely.

"I've seen better," Wojekowski growled. "What I wanna see is the glacier at the head of this valley. I hate to admit it, but we don't have any in Colorado worth mentioning."

"Shit, Sarge, Colorado doesn't have lots of things. What the hell's so special about it, anyway?"

"Your dear sergeant comes from there, that's what," he snarled. There was a series of hoots. "Shut up, all of you! I've got a reading!" The hoots vanished. He reached for his belt, pulled loose the probe of his Geiger counter, swept it around.

There was a crackling from the counter, and Wojekowski turned excitedly and pulled himself up the steep slope. "Here, it's stronger up here . . ."

He followed the sputtering signal toward the radioactivity it indicated. Above him was a gash in the smooth drift. The counter chattered nervously. His gloved hand thrust into the snow and came out with a piece of badly twisted metal.

Wojekowski grinned triumphantly. "Here, get this down to Old Ironsides," he said, handing his find to one of the privates. "On the double, asshole!"

Chapter 16

WOJEKOWSKI'S DISCOVERY seemed to trigger a rush, and before sunset at least two dozen different fragments had been brought into camp. Chris examined each one. The largest was a piece of metal about six inches square, showing machine marks on one edge, bent where it had been blasted away. It was light, almost as light as aluminum, and it was a silvery gray. Titanium. Lighter than steel and just as strong, as corrosion-resistant as platinum, and able to withstand amazing temperatures. The F-15s that had pursued the spacecraft over Denver were partly constructed of it. Only the relative expense of producing titanium precluded its appearance in everything from cars to dental work.

Chris grinned. The flying saucer wasn't constructed of "cosmonium" or "super lumian," or any other science fiction writer's invention. Titanium. The space-age metal. A perfectly reasonable choice for the hull of a spacecraft.

The pieces were all interesting. In general they were just mangled metal, but some appeared to have been electronic parts. Nilstrom wasn't sure what closer inspection would show, but he believed at least one fragment came from a large integrated circuit.

"Chris! What do you make of this?"

The piece Beck held had just been brought in. It looked like a large metal jar top without any threads. There were three holes drilled in it, in no seeming order. Embedded in the flange were tiny fragments of glass.

"Hmm. Looks like an instrument cover of some sort. But why the holes?"

"Damned if I know."

"Well, it has possibilities, anyway. Is everybody in, Nick?"

"Everybody but the Indians. We haven't heard a word from them."

"Well, I suppose they know what they're doing." Chris looked at the darkening sky. "But I should think they'd want to be back before it gets too much later."

Steven Running Deer knew better than to be so far from camp this late, but he didn't want to return empty-handed. The radio the Americans had given him had crackled all afternoon with news of the success of others, and he should be able to find *something* too, after all his grandfather's teaching. But his grandfather, the insufferable old fool, had never tried to find pieces of a spaceship shot down by a Gamma-ray laser.

The improbability of it all had stopped him for awhile. As a child he had been addicted to Buck Rogers and Flash Gordon. He had dreamed about shooting down invaders from Mars with a ray gun. Now the Americans had actually done it, and he was stuck with finding the pieces. Oh, well, they never had fought fair. When we had the bow and arrow, they had the rifle. Now we have the rifle—he hefted the gun over his shoulder—and they have the ray gun. Well, what of it?

He stopped. Up ahead, through the deepening gloom, he saw a wolf. Steve was lucky, approaching on the downwind side. He ducked behind a tree and peered out carefully. The wolf paid no attention; it was eating. No—it was trying to lick or tear something off a piece of metal. Metal? He yelled and jumped from behind the tree.

In the same motion, he raised the rifle and fired. The wolf slammed over with a shriek. It lay on its side, its legs kicking spasmodically. Steve walked to the carcass. The bullet had hit right behind the leg, tearing through the animal's lungs. A damn good shot, hurried as it was. Buck Rogers would have been proud of him.

He picked up the piece of metal. Yes, there *was* meat on it. It was frozen, of course, but it seemed to have been seared to the metal. It could only be one thing.

Excitement rose within him. Yes, old Buck would have been proud.

Beck heard the shot. He jumped up, tripped over a chair, and stumbled. He regained his balance, and looked out the tent flap toward the sound. Chris was on his feet too, looking toward the woods. So was every man in camp.

"What the hell was that?"

"Gunshot," Kaminski said laconically.

"Thank you, Sergeant," snapped Beck.

There was nothing more. Then the radio crackled.

Beck pounced on the microphone. "Who is it?"

"Steven Running Deer. I found something. A piece of..."

"Who the hell is Steven Running Deer?" barked Beck.

"I'm one of the Indians you signed on in Edmonton."

"Indians? Oh, of course. Sorry, son. What've you got?"

"It's a piece of metal, sir, with what looks like burned meat on it. A wolf ate most of it, but there's still a piece several inches long."

"Good work. But, damn it, Steve, get back to camp. I don't want to lose anybody."

"Yessir. I'm on my way."

Beck's eyes were bright. "Didja hear that, Chris? Could be a tissue sample. It could tell us a lot."

Night had arrived in full force before the Indian returned. Chris examined his find in the yellow light of the lanterns. It was metal, heavier than the others. In fact, it looked suspiciously like stainless steel. The flesh was red, stringy... muscle tissue, perhaps. He could make out little else. He handed it to the officer in charge of everything that had been recovered.

"Keep it frozen. Wrap it and pack it in snow in one of the empty food lockers."

Chapter 17

THE WIND woke Chris. The tent was buffeted by the gale, and he could hear it creak and stretch with the strain. His eyes ground open, fighting the weight of sleep. Pale yellow light filtered through the fabric. It was bitterly cold, and the wind stole any heat as soon as it was generated. The storm had arrived—a day early. Chris crawled out of bed among sounds of dismay from the others.

There was little they could do. A peek outside revealed nothing, for everything was lost in the fury of the blizzard. The wind reached sixty miles an hour in gusts that threatened to sweep them away, and rarely did it drop to thirty miles an hour. The wind-speed indicators fluctuated madly, and the thermometer showed twenty degrees below zero. The shadow of drifted snow moved steadily up the side of the tent. It was a long day, boring and frightening. The officers played cards, pausing to look apprehensively at the tent poles whenever they shuddered and threatened to give way.

Nilstrom worked on his calculations. There was little doubt, he had concluded, that a voyage across the gulf of interstellar space was possible, though the requirements for even the shortest such voyage were staggering.

He spread his notes out on the little field desk and reviewed them. Except for the sun, the nearest star is Proxima Centauri, a type-M red dwarf in the constellation of the Centaur. Since it's a flare star and periodically brightens in a sudden burst of power, there's almost no chance that it could harbor life. But Proxima is the companion of another star system that could.

Alpha Centauri, one of the brightest stars in the southern sky, is actually a double star system, and one of the pair is almost identical to the sun. So the shortest voyage a spaceship would have to make to reach the earth from another star is the distance from Alpha Centauri—four and three-tenths light-years, well over eighteen trillion miles.

Moving at the nationwide speed limit of fifty-five miles an hour, it would take something more than thirty-eight million years to make the trip. The fastest speed yet achieved by man is one hundred thousand miles an hour, attained by the Pioneer XI Jupiter-Saturn probe. Had it held that speed, and had it been pointed in the proper direction, Pioneer XI would have taken almost twenty thousand years to reach Alpha Centauri. If it were possible to travel at the speed of light, the trip would take four years and four months. And this was the star nearest to the solar system. A trip from any other star would take longer. Clearly, he reflected, any such voyage remained in the realm of science fiction as far as human technologies were concerned.

Or was it possible that he was merely trying to force the whole problem into terms he could understand? Perhaps the invaders possessed some miraculous device that allowed them to sidestep the limits of distance. Perhaps they *could* make this fantastic journey faster than light, or even faster than thought. There were excellent theoretical reasons why this was impossible, and there was ample experimental evidence of it as well. But there was also excellent theoretical evidence that quasars didn't exist too—and they did.

So perhaps he was being naive in his speculations.

But the saucers *were* driven by rockets, and they were made of mundane metals like steel and titanium. Nothing he had seen was too far removed from modern technology. The invaders were definitely superior, but not out of sight.

The storm lasted until past noon. An eerie scene greeted them when they finally left the tent. The mountains were the same, the trees and the lake were still there, even the snow didn't seem deeper. But the camp was gone. Everything had been covered by the drifting snow. It was as if the mountains resented the intrusion and had tried to cover it up, as an oyster covers an irritating speck of sand with layers of pearl.

Beck surveyed the scene bleakly. "No use staying now, everything's covered. Let's get the hell out of here!"

Chapter 18

CHRIS WAS in his office at the Chidlaw Building in Colorado Springs when Diane Mowbray called.

"Dr. Nilstrom? General Beck would like to see you."

"I'll be right over." He hung up the phone, stood, and stretched. The office had been assigned to him only a few days before, and it had few creature comforts: an old mahogany desk, a chair that had a weak spring and leaned too far back, and a few pictures of NORAD interceptors on the wall. Chris had brought in a couple dozen of his own books, and they were on the shelves above his chair. Otherwise, the office was bare. He was glad to leave it.

Diane looked up and smiled as he entered.

"Hi, Diane, can I go in?"

The door to Beck's office opened, and the general emerged. "Well, thought I heard you, Chris. C'mon in. I've got the reports on the saucer fragments."

Nilstrom followed him into the office. Kaminski was pinning photographs to a bulletin board.

"These pictures of the *Provedennyi* just came in too, Chris. Thanks, Arnie. That'll be all." The sergeant laid the rest of the photographs on the general's desk and left the room.

Chris studied those on the board. In one, the destroyer was partly obscured by the large saucer above it. Chris bent forward to examine the picture more closely. Without question, the saucer was of the same sort that had been photographed over Norfolk. In the second picture, streams of fire shot from the belly of the saucer. The third showed the destroyer exploding.

"That's quite a sequence, Nick. Terrifying, isn't it?"

"Yeah. To think that one damned saucer can incinerate a whole armored ship!" Beck handed Chris the rest of the pictures. They were less spectacular, but clearly showed the destruction at the power station in Japan.

"What about those lab reports?" Nilstrom sank into a chair.

"Not as much as we'd hoped for. Here, take a look."

The reports were from the Air Force Research Institute in San Antonio. The analysis of the tissue was about what Chris had anticipated. The presence of hemoglobin proved that it was from an oxygen-breathing animal. Spectroscopic studies showed that the elements present were the same as in human tissue, and in the same quantities. Proteins in the cells were identical to man's. Chromosomal structure was similar. Lymph seemed identical. Microscopic examination revealed interesting differences, but nothing of significance.

"At least the invaders are understandable," Chris said. "It's clear why they want earth; it would be as suitable for them as it is for us. They may have seven hands and two heads, but have basically the same needs that we do."

"It looks that way." Beck had moved to the swivel chair, and sat with his size-fourteen feet on the desk, his hands behind his head.

Chris read further. The inorganic material recovered from the saucer was mostly titanium. Several of the fragments were stainless steel. One was an alloy of steel and titanium. There was some aluminum, and a small quantity of copper. The shards of glass sticking to the small disk were a mineral crystal not unlike quartz.

Nilstrom tossed the report back. "Damn! That still doesn't give us a clue about where they come from."

"No, but it all confirms our theory. Maybe now somebody'll believe us."

Chris grunted.

"Have *you* come up with anything?" Beck asked.

"Not much. I've been rereading the old Rand Corporation study, and I think there are several possibilities." Chris shifted to a more comfortable position and put his feet on the coffee table in front of him. "As you know, our solar system is part of the Milky Way."

Beck nodded.

"The Milky Way is an open spiral galaxy about a hundred and twenty-five thousand light-years across, relatively flat—like a pancake—but with arms spiraling from the center and trailing off in several directions. And it has about a hundred billion stars. Spiral galaxies are usually big—in fact, they're the real studs of the universe, bigger than the cloud galaxies.

"Now, galaxies appear in clusters; for example, ours is one in a cluster of fourteen. Of these, Andromeda and our own are the biggest. But there are hundreds of other clusters out there, and every galaxy in them contains millions and millions of stars."

"And each of those stars is circled by a dozen or so planets. It sounds hopeless," interrupted Beck.

"But wait a minute, Nick. Because of the distances, it's utterly impossible for the bastards to be coming from anywhere outside our galaxy. The Magellanic Clouds are fairly close, as galaxies go, and they're two hundred thousand light years away. Spaceships like those saucers couldn't possibly move faster than light—if anything can. They just couldn't have come that far."

"Which narrows it down to our galaxy, down to a few hundred million stars and their planets," Beck said with a lopsided grin.

"But most of the stars in our cozy little galaxy are hundreds, even thousands of light-years away, too. And our solar system is in a sparsely populated part of the Milky Way, in one of the trailing arms, which further narrows down the possibilities.

"Even so, you're right, there are a hell of a lot of stars within a hundred light years of us. However, most of them couldn't possibly have planets capable of supporting life like ours."

"How come?"

"There are a lot of weird stars out there, Nick. Some are too big, like Antares, a super giant. It's so big its circumference is roughly comparable to the orbit of the earth around the sun. The best theory is that it expanded relatively recently, perhaps a million or so years ago. If it had planets, it vaporized them then.

"Some stars are so small they don't give out enough heat to support life, or have enough gravity to hold a planet which, in turn, would be large enough to hold an atmosphere."

"So where does that leave us?" Beck asked. "Those guys gotta be coming from someplace."

"The Rand Corporation estimated that of the nearest stars, only about fifty *could* have habitable planets, and of those, thirty-five are *unlikely* candidates. So they conclude that there are only fifteen stars within a few light-years of earth with a *probability* of having a planet capable of supporting life. I'm confident that the invaders come from among those fifty, and probably from one of the fifteen."

"So how do we find out?"

"Good question. I was hoping we'd find something in the wreckage that would help. What about that instrument dial— or whatever it was?"

Beck opened a drawer in his desk and pulled out the charred metal object. "San Antonio couldn't figure it out. Let's talk about it over lunch. But I don't want to eat here. Usually I like being a big shot and having everyone kiss my ass, but sometimes I can't take it. You know, I've learned something about power. When you have it, everyone wants a favor. But most of the time they won't come out and say so; they just sidle up and give you lots of strokes and lead the conversation around to what they want. Let's go to the Broadmoor. I'll get Diane to call."

As he strode to the closet to get his cap, his face was grim. Chris reflected that he must be exhausted. Beck had amazing resilience and maintained his equanimity through long periods of stress. But when he was tired, things that he usually shrugged off annoyed him. They stopped at Diane's desk.

"Will you call the Broadmoor Tavern for a table? And if you tell anyone other than the president himself where I am, I'll have you assigned to General Locke in Greenland!"

Chapter 19

THEY PARKED in front of the Broadmoor Hotel and walked along the curved driveway to the entrance. The snow still on the ground was rapidly melting in the bright December sun, and the sky was cobalt blue.

The uniformed doorman opened the big door and Beck said, "Thanks, Ben. Beautiful day, isn't it?"

The lobby was the usual throng of people checking in and out, meeting friends, or simply watching the scene in the famous old hotel. Many of the guests wore badges identifying them as members of a teachers' convention.

At the door of the Tavern, the maitre d' brightened. "Ah, General! Your table is ready. Follow me, please."

Once seated in the glass-covered Garden Room, Beck took the metal object out of his attaché case and laid it on the table. "Look at this goddamned thing! The metal is an aluminum alloy, the glass is quartz. But what *is* it? Everyone agrees it covered a dial of some sort, like an altimeter or compass. Looks primitive, doesn't it?"

"Yeah, it does. Must've been improvised. Let's assume it was made by the pilot. But why?" He frowned, and his face hardened in thought.

"I've considered every instrument in a plane or spacecraft, and I can't figure out—"

"Just a minute, Nick, let me think."

As Nilstrom fingered the disk, a waiter appeared. Beck

ordered, looked at his engrossed companion, and ordered for
him too. Within seconds, a basket of fresh French bread and
a dish of butter patties were in front of them.

Chris said, "Look, Nick, if there'd been any kind of dial
under this, the pilot wouldn't have been able to read it through
these little openings." He held the enigmatic disk up against
the sky showing through the glass ceiling. The tiny holes
formed an irregular triangle. Sunlight passing through them
cast three pinpoints of light on his face.

"Looks like stars," Beck commented, buttering a piece of
bread. "But why would he want to sit there and stare at three
points of light?"

Nilstrom looked at him oddly, then back at the disk. A
smile suddenly creased his face. "That's it, Nick! This didn't
cover a *dial*. It covered a *display screen*. Look! These guys
were new to our solar system. Could this have been a navi-
gational aid, fitted over a display screen to block out everything
except what they wanted to see?"

"Yeah, but—"

"*I've got it!* Look! This saucer's been around for years, if
our theory's right, gathering data and radioing it home. But
where's home? A long way away. He'd have to use a high-
energy radio and direct the beam precisely so it wouldn't get
lost in the immensity of space. He probably had to go into
orbit, lock onto some celestial fixed point—maybe a prominent
star—and stay locked on while he transmitted. But what if he
got tired of trying to line up the right stars in his viewer or
display screen? So he took a piece of metal and drilled holes
in it that allowed him to see only the key stars."

"That makes sense, Chris. He'd lock onto one star, then
rotate his ship until the others showed through their holes, and
presto! he's in position!"

"So, by God, the star we're looking for is sitting somewhere
in the triangle formed by those three stars."

"Good thinking! Which one is it?"

Nilstrom frowned. "Alpha Centauri A and B . . . no, there's
nothing in the sky near them that looks like that triangle.
Epsilon Eridani . . . Tau Ceti . . . 70 Ophiuchi A? Hmm. No.
None of those. What were the others? Oh, yes, Delta Pavonis,
no possibility there. HR 7703 A? No, not that, either. HR
8832? Sigma Draconis?"

Beck watched him with amusement. "Chris, don't look
now, but there's a man behind you who thinks you're crazy.

I have to admit that sounds pretty weird. What is all that gibberish?"

"The names of the stars that might qualify. I'll have to check to be sure, but I don't think any of the fifteen are in a part of the sky where there are three such bright stars." He paused. "Out in space, thousands of stars show up, because there's no atmosphere to dull their light. But for navigation, he'd have to choose three brilliant ones, so bright he couldn't miss them. *That's it!*"

"What?" Beck leaned forward eagerly.

"Altair, Deneb, and Vega, a prominent triangle in the northern hemisphere, in the constellation of Cygnus. But wait . . . none of Rand's fifteen are there."

"Well, maybe we can locate the fleet, at least."

"Right, Nick. Still, the fleet and their planet should be almost in a line. There'd be some offset because the stars themselves move, relative to each other. But there *is* a star in that constellation with a low probability for life—61 Cygni!"

"Now you're talking!"

"Well, it's not a very good candidate for the honors. It's actually a binary system, two stars waltzing in each other's gravitational arms. That complicates things for a planet, screws up its orbit, its rotation, its day-night sequence. But 61 Cygni is only about eleven to twelve light-years away, which isn't impossibly distant. That *could* be our bad guy."

The waiter brought their lunch, and the men ate hungrily. Finally Beck put down his fork. "What do we do now?"

"First we ask Green Bank to focus their big radio telescope on the area and see if they can pick up anything. If they do, we'll get LOOTS to take a look. And we'll ask Clem Tillman to see if he can get anything on Pan-European Radar."

"How close would they have to be before we could spot them?"

"Pretty damn close, in terms of interstellar travel."

"Could the fleet already be inside the solar system?"

"I doubt it. The fact that the template was in the saucer, probably in use, makes me think the fleet is still on its way. If they were already in our system, he'd aim his radio in a much different direction."

"This is going to be tough, isn't it?" Beck licked his finger, picked up a large crumb from the tabletop, and decided to eat it.

"Yep. But there's one thing that might help. If the fleet is at the level of sophistication I think it is, the ejecta of their engines must be pure light. If they're decelerating, their exhausts are pointed toward us, and telescopes can spot them billions of miles away."

"Decelerating?"

"Sure. They spend half the trip accelerating, then they turn around and spend the rest of the trip slowing down. Remember, in space, it takes as much time and energy to slow down as it does to speed up."

"Okay, let's get to work." Beck rose to his feet and reached for his hat.

The waiter scurried over with the check, and the general signed it. Nilstrom was still seated, staring at the template.

"Chris?"

"Oh, yeah. Sorry."

At the car, Beck unlocked the door for Chris and asked, "What're you thinking so hard about?"

"Oh, just that with my reputation, it may be hard to get Pan-European and even LOOTS to cooperate. I presume Green Bank will, but—"

"They'll *all* cooperate! I guarantee it. When you're ready, let me know."

Nilstrom looked mockingly at the general. "I thought you hated having all that power, Nick!"

"Well, by God, there're times when it's a help."

Chapter 20

ASTRONOMY RECEIVED its first big stimulus when the telescope was invented, for it permitted scientists to make observations not possible before. Then came spectroscopy and the ability to determine the elements in a star or planet from its light. The construction of the huge reflecting telescopes with cameras, to make sensitive records of light no human eye could detect even through an eyepiece in the telescope, brought spectacular new observations. But optical telescopes, like man, can see only a small part of the radiation that arrives from space.

It was not until the age of electronics and the development of radio telescopes that man could detect some of this unseen

radiation. In 1932, Karl Jansky discovered a source of radio
transmission in the constellation Sagittarius. But when he published his discoveries, few paid any attention. It was the depth
of the depression and a war was approaching.

However, much progress was being made in radar and short-
wave radio techniques, and after the War, other scientists built
telescopes capable of receiving not light, but radio waves. They
quickly discovered that many stars, the sun, and even the
planets give off radio noise.

Perhaps most baffling and exciting was the discovery of
quasars and pulsars. Quasars are sources of radio noise as
powerful as entire galaxies. Pulsars are rapidly spinning neutron
stars that give off radio pulses with such machine-like regularity
that they were at first thought to be signals from an extraterrestrial civilization.

These breakthroughs, possible with no other tool, firmly
established radio astronomy as a respectable science. Soon the
industrial countries were struggling to outdo each other and
build larger and larger radio telescopes. The largest was in a
natural bowl formed by a ring of hills at Arecibo, Puerto Rico.
But only partly steerable, it was restricted in its utility.

The National Radio Astronomy Observatory at Green Bank,
West Virginia was best suited to deal with Nilstrom's request.
The director, Dr. Alex Baumgartner, had agreed to cooperate.
Though he had always been skeptical of Chris's conclusions
about UFOs, he liked Chris and respected him as an astron-
omer. It was almost midnight when he called.

Nilstrom had worked all day on the calculator, and the more
he figured, the more alarmed he became. After a hamburger
at a local restaurant, he was back at his desk in the Chidlaw
Building. He had chewed the erasers off three pencils, and
sworn as each had had the temerity to come apart in his mouth
merely because he had bitten through it. But now he had the
answers. He knew the parameters within which they should
work.

"Chris, what ah you trying to do to me?" Baumgartner was
from Alabama, and his drawl prolonged conversations by thirty
percent. But he was a friendly bear of a man, and Nilstrom
had always liked him. Moreover, he was one of the finest radio
astronomers in the world.

"Did you find something, Alex?" Chris's stomach tightened.

"Ah should say so. Ah suppose ah'll nevah know how you knew where to look, but sure enough, there it was."

"What did you find?"

But there was no hurrying the man.

"We put the big boy on this 'un, the two-hunnert-footer. We locked onto the area you wanted, and we listened and fussed with frequencies and listened some mo'. For a long time we didn't get nothin', 'ceptin' the usual stuff."

"And then?" It was an unsuccessful attempt to get Baumgartner to the point.

"Well, last night, that li'l scribbler began to write the damnedest tune you evah heard. Ah jus' couldn't believe it.

"It kep' on for a while, then stopped and then started again. Ah sat there watchin' that damn thing for six hours—ruined my nightly chess game. Well, ah got to lookin' ovah them scribblin's and ended up spendin' mosta the day. Marianne's madder than hell, 'cause ah nevah went home."

He paused, but Chris made no comment.

"To be brief, Chris, there is someone out there talkin' to someone else. Definitely non-random radio impulses. Ah'm sendin' the particulars by government courier."

Nilstrom suddenly realized that he was covered with perspiration. "Can you tell me where they're coming from?"

"Noooo, ah cain't. But ah don't think the source of the radio signal is 61 Cygni. Mah bet is it's closer than that—and comin' this way."

The perspiration on Chris's brow was suddenly chill. "How fast? How far? When'll they get here?"

"Whoa now, Chris. You always were too quick off the mark. Ah cain't say how far. Or how fast. But they are comin' toward us, and they are slowin' down."

"They would be. They must've passed the halfway point a long time ago."

"Is there somethin' you ain't tellin' me?"

"I think there's a fleet of spaceships out there."

Chris heard the old man suck on his pipe. "Rather thought you had some harebrained idea like that. Trouble is, this time ah don't know as how ah can disagree with you."

"Yeah—but we've got to have more proof. I've been working all day to figure out just how far away they can be seen optically. They'd have to be fairly close, even if their ships are bigger than aircraft carriers—and I suppose that's about their size."

"Ummmm."

"But I've also been thinking about their engines, and I don't think they could make it here from 61 Cygni on the fuel they could carry. They're probably using a Bussard ramjettype engine, scooping up stray hydrogen atoms for fuel. And if they're decelerating, they could be seen for a hell of a long way with a good optical scope."

"LOOTS."

"Yeah."

"But if it ain't a pure light drive, you'd get a better readin' from radar."

"Unless they jammed it."

"Yeah. Well, it's up to you, Chris, but personally I'd use both."

"Thanks, Alex. I'll get back to you." Nilstrom hung up, then dialed Beck at home.

Chapter 21

OPTICAL TELESCOPES had become increasingly more powerful, culminating in the Hale Observatory's famous 200-inch reflecting giant at Mt. Palomar, California. Even so, there were still severe limitations on their use. Not only do city lights create problems by illuminating the atmosphere and blocking out light from the stars, but the atmosphere itself reduces the effectiveness of optical telescopes by inhibiting the resolving power of the lens. The effect is somewhat like looking up from the bottom of a swimming pool.

The ideal telescope should be outside the atmosphere. Early in the space program, the Americans tried to build a space observatory. Skylab I had a small telescope and made some important observations.

In the early eighties, the Americans took a bold approach to a large orbiting optical telescope. They constructed the Stacey Balloon, a telescope consisting of a huge two hundred-foot balloon, half-transparent and half a silvered surface. Then, to correct for the spherical rather than the usual paraboloid reflecting surface, they installed a Schmidt lens. They orbited the balloon, and secured it to Skylab II. But there were still problems—for example, distortion of the image, despite corrections.

So the Americans tackled the project again. And it was Chris Nilstrom who enabled them to have the brilliant success they were enjoying.

The chief stumbling-block in the construction of a true space observatory is the reflector. The two-hundred-inch mirror used at Mt. Palomar had to be cast out of Pyrex and cooled for six years. It took the California Institute of Technology years more to grind it. And it weighed many tons.

Installing such a mirror in an orbiting telescope was not possible, nor was it necessary. The enormous weight of the reflectors used on earth is primarily the result of the reinforcement necessary to keep them from sagging out of shape from the force of gravity. In space there is no gravity. A mirror an inch thick would suffice. But how could such a mirror be transported? If cast on earth, it would sag, even break, before it could be ferried to the orbiting observatory.

Nilstrom had suggested the comparatively simple process of casting a two-hundred-inch mirror an inch thick—in space. His idea was to suspend the half-molten mirror by the edge from a rocket-powered vehicle, then accelerate the rocket until the mirror sagged into the required paraboloid shape. Scientists unfamiliar with space laughed.

But the famous German engineer, Heinz Dillenberger, contacted the American presidential commission in charge of the project and offered to try Nilstrom's method. While the scientific world watched skeptically, Dillenberger went to work. All tools and equipment had to be ferried to the huge Skylab III, but the mirror was successfully cast.

The result was LOOTS, the Large Orbiting Optical Telescope System, the biggest object ever placed in permanent orbit. The entire telescope, laboratory, and living quarters complex was in a four-hundred-mile circular orbit. The satellite quickly became a worldwide object of wonder as it gleamed high in the sky long after the sun had gone down on earth.

Approximately a hundred and fifty feet in length and fifty in width, LOOTS mounted a single Cassegrain-focus reflecting telescope with a mirror width of 248 inches, making it larger than the giant Russian land-based telescope. It had a focal length of 107 feet, giving it a resolution capability of .018 seconds of arc. The light-gathering capability of the telescope was approximately half a million times that of the human eye.

Mounted in a space station and clear of the confusing effects of atmospheric turbulence, temperature change, and gravity, LOOTS was the most powerful such device ever built. It brought new precision and resolution to photographs of the other planets of the solar system and their satellites, and new dimensions to the study of distant stars and galaxies, nebulae, and star fields. The infrared and ultraviolet study of astronomical objects was virtually revolutionized.

Nearly all power came from two seventy-foot solar panels that looked like windmill arms. The energy they gathered was stored in batteries. A small atomic fuel source supplied emergency power.

Weightless in orbit, the telescope needed none of the usual massive supports and complicated steering apparatus. It was steered by six gyroscopes located in the cabin behind the mirror, augmented by eight hydrogen peroxide jets. Thimble jets on the tips of the solar panels were used for fine adjustments.

LOOTS was the envy of astronomers everywhere. Built by the United States, it was operated by the University of California. Astronomers from other countries were often invited to join the crew for a tour of duty, but the rigors of the training required for living in space discouraged most. However, LOOTS scientists agreed to undertake their various studies, and soon had a huge backlog of requests.

The tremendous success of LOOTS had a curious effect on Nilstrom's career. It nearly ruined it. Being right rarely endears one to his peers. The scientists who were proven wrong became themselves the objects of derision, and they naturally blamed Nilstrom. Many were the same ones who had viciously attacked him for giving credence to UFO reports, and who had intrigued to deny him the position at Wisconsin University. Only the acknowledged merit of his work on pulsars, and the support of a generation of younger men, saved Nilstrom from the disaster reserved for those who challenge the tenets and oppose the entrenched and honored princes of orthodoxy.

Nor did his success endear him to the public. There were cynical remarks about the appropriateness of the acronym LOOTS, and Chris became a symbol of scientific extravagance.

The relationship between Nilstrom and the director of the observatory, Bill Robinson, was also affected by the success of LOOTS. Contemporaries, indeed classmates at Harvard, the two shared a mutual respect, but maintained a wary rivalry. Both had meteoric careers and both had national reputations.

Early in life, Robinson had discovered the two secrets to success in any established organization: instead of challenging the prejudices of those in charge, he applied himself to the defense of those prejudices; he understood that a man is more swiftly forgiven for being wrong in support of convention than he is for being right in challenging it. Robinson also used a stratagem which Nilstrom and so many other seekers after truth neglected. If it became absolutely necessary to question a fiercely defended untruth, he did it with such tact as to make the defenders think the new idea was really theirs—an extension of, not a replacement for, their cherished theory.

The only astonomer to have been on numerous space flights, Robinson was the logical choice for the post of director of LOOTS, but the indirect dependence of his own fame on Nilstrom's idea rankled on him, and deepened his sense of competition.

Chris could almost picture Robinson's face wrinkling in disbelief as he told him about Baumgartner's findings and asked him to make observations from LOOTS. But he knew Robinson was aware that if he put Chris off, it would only be minutes before he'd be called by someone higher up. That could damage his reputation and jeopardize his career. And Big Bill Robinson was of his career "a little more careful than of everything."

Chapter 22

Sir Clement Tillman was another matter. He was sixty-three years old and had been in radio astronomy from the beginning. He had personally designed the world's largest radar unit and had persuaded France, England, and Germany to share in its construction. To do so, he had trudged from one European capitol to another. When the plan was almost abandoned during the depression of the seventies, he learned to play politics on an international scale, and got it reinstated in the budgets of the three countries.

Sir Clement did not give the impression that he possessed enough charisma or perserverence to win so huge a battle. A small man, he was pink-faced, with almost transparent skin. His hair was white, and so thin and curly that it stood out like fuzz all over his pink pate. He was impeccably courteous and gracious, but utterly fearless. More than once he had put his own career on the line. Nobody could bully him, nobody could persuade him to do something he didn't think was wise or prudent or necessary.

The demands on his magnificent instrument were enormous. But Sir Clement kept up with every current of thought, not only in astronomy, but in electronics, physics, and politics as well, and firmly resisted every proposal that wasn't high-priority.

Nilstrom reached him at his home outside Toulouse near the observatory.

"Sir Clement, I'm calling on behalf of NORAD and the U.S. Government."

"Yes, rather thought I'd be hearing from you." His voice was cheerful and pitched in a high register. He made a masterful use of it, and was able to fluctuate from a low growl through at least two octaves to a high pitch that was downright musical.

"Sir?"

"Oh, well now, quite obvious, don't you think? First there are more saucer sightings, this time over defense installations. Then the attack on the French planes—oh, yes, know all about it! Hard to keep secrets from an old snoop like me." He was practically singing, he was enjoying himself so much. "All radar installations in Europe have been alerted to report anything unusual—which means they're *expecting* something unusual, right? A group of us who run these things, keeping track of space objects and so on, got together and compared notes. Several of the chaps had picked up those blasted saucers. Then we heard about the American interceptors, the aerial surveillance craft in—where was it? South America? And the airliner. Oh, yes, for mere Europeans, we keep up pretty well. Where do you want us to direct our probe?"

Chris swallowed and managed to say, "Sixty-one Cygni—but, Sir Clement, how'd you—"

"Those saucers, obviously scouts, you know. Dr. Nilstrom, contrary to popular opinion, I agreed with your report on UFOs, though I thought it a bit timid. Well, if the saucers are testing our defenses at last, they must be reporting to somebody. That means an invasion fleet. I began probes last week—thought I'd get a jump on you chaps. Couldn't try Alpha Centauri, of course, so— But what makes you think it could be 61 Cygni? Not a very nice place!"

Nilstrom was limp with surprise, but he found his voice and outlined the events of the past few days. The old man chuckled. It wasn't only that he'd been so correct; he liked the challenge. Suddenly Nilstrom knew how England had once conquered one-fourth of the world.

"Sixty-one Cygni it'll be, then. I'll ring you the moment I find anything. Cheerio!"

Chapter 23

BILL ROBINSON was dressed in his usual coveralls, and their whiteness contrasted with his sunburned face. He was a large, athletic man who had given up football for tennis and sailing as he approached middle age, and he'd just returned from four weeks in Hawaii in time for his tour of duty here in space.

The son of one of California's greatest industrialists, his wealth had enabled him to live an exciting life. Oddly, he had drifted into science, then astronomy and space—a combination assuring him fame and romance. In his young adulthood, he had married a girl chosen by his mother. But it didn't last and he had since shunned marriage. But not women. He was a lover as well as an astronaut, astronomer, athlete, and heir to a large fortune.

He'd be in the space station now for two months, together with five other men. Despite his penchant for romance, he liked the time away from earth, and not only because it gave him a chance to win more accolades by finding new stars or comets, or new information about old ones. He also liked being away from the hectic schedule he kept. His life had settled into a nice rhythm. About the time he couldn't stand the isolation and austere regime of LOOTS, it was time to return to earth. Then, about the time his romantic entanglements became too complicated, it was time to return to space. He liked it.

And he saw nothing ahead but more fame and more pleasure.

But when the first photograph was finally developed, he saw something else, something that sent chills through him. In his easy, successful life he had never really known fear. Once, in orbit around the moon, a serious malfunction had appeared in the engine of his vehicle, and he had been faced with the possibility of death. But even that was exciting.

He was unprepared for the cold dread he felt now, the undefined terror that enveloped him when he saw the picture. He had smiled when Nilstrom called. Good old Chris and his crazy ideas! He had damned near ruined his career once before with his talk of flying saucers. Now he'd really done it! But if the authorities in Washington who made appropriations to LOOTS wanted pictures, pictures they'd get.

In the large photograph, still wet from developing, a layman would have seen nothing, or, to be more precise, he'd have seen so much he'd have seen nothing of significance—hundreds of dots of light superimposed on an utterly black background, some so bright they took up a lot of space, some so weak they hardly registered at all.

But Bill Robinson was not a layman. There, in an area of the sky where there should be nothing, he saw a small, diffuse, weak light, hardly as big as the head of a pin. It was not a star, not a comet, not a planet. He knew very well what it was, and what it meant.

Into his chilled mind came the forgotten science-fiction fantasies of his childhood, where tentacled creatures stood on the bridge of a mammoth spaceship, coolly destroying helpless cities with death rays.

From over his shoulder, Charlie Duetsch whistled. "Where the hell'd that mother come from?"

Robinson said sharply, "Charlie, I want a spectrogram of this thing, and *now*. I want to know what the hell it is. And goddman it, turn up the heat, it's cold in here."

Deutsch looked at his boss. In the two years they'd worked together he'd never seen him agitated, never heard him speak this way. He checked the thermostat. "Bill, the temperature's the same as always. You sick?"

"Oh hell, forget it. I probably caught cold coming back here so soon after Hawaii." It was all he could do to keep his teeth from chattering.

It had been four days since Sir Clement had sent out the powerful impulses from the huge dish which was, at the same time, the world's largest radio telescope and most powerful radar. The instrument was almost as big as the Astrodome in Houston, Texas, and the towers that held it were themselves skyscrapers, more than three hundred feet in height. Although the telescope had been in action only a year, it was already legend. It had detected the mountains of Venus with ease, and got good readings from Pluto, that cold little ball so far out that only the most powerful optical telescopes could even see it. Now the antenna was straining to hear the return of a signal bounced off something more than thirty billion miles in space.

Sir Clement didn't know what he'd get. Multiple pulses, transmitted over a twenty-hour period, would provide several echoes—if there was anything there. Pan-European Radar would be in a position to receive them at any time when 61 Cygni was visible from southern France. Long transmissions were standard technique for distant probes, but this was by far the most distant they had ever tried. Four days and still no return.

The spirited astronomer was standing at the recorders, watching the tape stream through the machine, when the first echo came—when the needles, all four of them, began to scribble at once. With a practiced eye he watched them, reading the scribbling as easily as a stockbroker reads the figures on a ticker tape. He knew the meaning of those little ink lines, knew the immensity of the disaster they implied. Within minutes, he was on the phone to Nilstrom.

Chapter 24

CHRIS HAD had little sleep for five nights. He sat in Beck's office with a sheaf of papers in his hand—papers with equations and figures by the hundreds. But there were words too. Ominous, terrifying words.

"Nick, thanks to that little template—and a lot of luck—we've found the bastards. We have confirmation from three different sources: Green Bank and LOOTS, and—the real clincher—Pan-European Radar got an echo. We *know* there shouldn't be anything out there, but there is. Sir Clement said the echo is from a cluster of objects, not a single target. He has a distance reading of thirty-five billion miles—a little farther than we thought. The Doppler shift in the returned signal indicates tremendous velocity, but also shows they're slowing down. He estimates arrival time at fourteen months."

"Fourteen months!" Beck tugged at his ear. That's not

enough time for your plan. Just not enough time."

Nilstrom took off his glasses and rubbed his tired eyes. "Maybe, but we have to try. Is the meeting with the president set for tomorrow?"

Beck nodded.

There was a knock at the door and Diane entered.

"General, Dr. Charles Kellogg is here for his appointment."

Chapter 25

THE VIEWING room in the Pentagon was crowded, and, despite the weather outside, it was warm, even stuffy. Leaders of Congress had met all morning with the Joint Chiefs of Staff to view films and documents. Now the president and much of the cabinet had joined them, filling the windowless room almost to overflowing. When the destruction of the saucer was announced, the others applauded. Senator Charles Hamilton groaned.

Hamilton had spent his entire political career fighting for peace. When he was a freshman senator, the war in Vietnam was raging, and he spoke out with anguish and shame against the role of his own country. During the Middle East conflicts, he again took up the cudgel for peace. He even ran for president twice, not because he really wanted to be president—indeed, the thought terrified him—but because he abhorred war. He trooped across the United States, indefatigably preaching his gospel of peace.

Now he could see billions of dollars being diverted from antipoverty and environmental protection programs into an effort to stop this "invasion."

Hamilton looked around the viewing room. There was pudgy little Wilbur Sternald, secretary of state. Beside him sat the vice-president, Ward Flexnor, a huge cigar caught between his fat fingers, his black skin glistening with perspiration.

Behind him was young Peter Kerr, who, in the monetary crisis of the seventies, had made a fortune speculating in gold. Now he was the minority leader of the senate, and had more influence than Hamilton. Next to him was thin, skeptical, tough Bertha Fowler, speaker of the house. She had said nothing all day. Hamilton hoped that, as a committed liberal, she might see the implications of what was being presented.

He was sure what the response of J. Whalen Broughton would be. The old warhorse from Mississippi was an extreme conservative. He was Chairman of the Senate Armed Forces Committee and one of the Pentagon's staunchest defenders. Next to Broughton sat Gilbert Doyle, his taciturn counterpart in the house.

Senator Hamilton came out of his reverie. General Beck had finished the presentation, and Dr. Nilstrom was summarizing.

"... To conclude, ladies and gentlemen: their weapon is a plasma gun—which we do not know how to build, but whose principle we understand. They have a far more destructive weapon in their exhausts, which were used to destroy the Russian warship. At this time we possess no weapons system capable of meeting the invasion."

With no expression in his dark eyes, Dr. Nilstrom picked up his notes and returned to his seat. Nobody moved.

Finally the president spoke. "Any questions, gentlemen?"

Vice-President Flexnor shifted his huge bulk in his chair and blew out a cloud of cigar smoke. In a low, sonorous voice he said, "Mr. President, I have listened carefully to the excellent presentation of these two impressive gentlemen. I have looked at the films and the pictures, and I have listened with horror and sorrow, sir, to the tapes of those pilots talking to—"

From the side of the room there was a muttered, "Oh shit!" from Kellogg.

Flexnor glared at the insolent youth, then went on, "Mr. President, it's true that I'm only a humble public servant and not a scientist. But, sir, I can *think*! And I find the conclusion drawn by these estimable gentlemen to be precarious, and tenuous as well, sir." The words rumbled from deep in his chest. "Look at that photograph of the stars! A dot so tiny it strains my eyes even to see it is represented to us as a fleet of battleships. Sir, in my considered judgment, we must have more opinions from leaders of the scientific community. Then—"

"Sure, asshole, why not wait until the bloody bastards are burning our cities? Why hurry? Appoint a presidential commission with you as head—" The shock of hair on Kellogg's head was bobbing, and Hamilton wondered if it would fall into his eyes.

Sternly, the president interrupted again. "Dr. Kellogg, if you cannot be respectful, we'll ask you to leave. We cannot have—"

Kellogg snarled, "Leave? I will, by God! I can't stand to listen to a lot of fucking assholes fart in each others' faces. You're all too stupid to know facts when you see them." He jerked open the door and stormed out.

J. Whalen Broughton was the first to speak. "Mistuh Pres'dint," he said quietly. "Dr. Kellogg's mannahs are atrocious. But look at the facts! It's cleah that a fleet *is* approachin' earth with the intention of destroyin' us."

Bertha Fowler had a voice like a masonry drill, and she used it to the fullest now. "I hate to agree with Senator Broughton on anything, but he's right. We're in deep trouble. Does Defense have any ideas?"

The president turned to Scott. "Mr. Secretary?"

Hamilton smiled at the discomfiture of the secretary of defense. He had never liked Scott, not only because he was head of a department Hamilton hated, but also because he was an arrogant political opportunist.

"Uh, no, Mr. President, I, uh—defer to the Joint Chiefs."

Hamilton could have sworn that Reed smiled thinly.

"Yes, Mistuh Pres'dint, let us indeed heah from the Joint Chiefs. Maligned as they've been, they may yet save us as they have before." From beneath his half-red, half-white eyebrows, old Senator Broughton was glowering at the president who had so de-emphasized the senator's beloved military.

Reed's jaw tightened. "General Gray, maligned as you have been, do you have some idea as to what we can do?"

There was a titter. Gray smiled, left his chair, and limped to the podium. "Yes, gentlemen, we *do* have a plan.

"It is largely the work of Dr. Nilstrom, but has been unanimously agreed upon by the Joint Chiefs. It will require tremendous effort, but we believe it's our only chance. I'll let Dr. Nilstrom tell you about it."

The senator turned back to Nilstrom, who was now standing at the podium.

Chapter 26

CHRIS STROKED his beard and waited for the stirrings to cease.

"Mr. President, ladies and gentlemen . . ."

Then, while the most powerful leaders of the nation hung on his every word, Nilstrom outlined his plan.

Nobody moved. Nobody spoke.

Nilstrom waited.

Finally he added, "Now you can see why we wanted Dr. Kellogg to be here. I'm sorry he was so offensive, but he *has* been working around the clock."

Silence again. Everyone stared at him and tried to assess the practicability of what he had just described, and the dimensions of the menace.

The president broke the silence. "What is Dr. Kellogg's opinion?"

"That we have a chance to pull it off if all the problems I referred to can—"

Bertha Fowler interrupted, talking more to herself than to the group. "It won't work. I don't know about the technology stuff, but, my God, get the Russians and the Japanese and the English and the Germans and those goddamned French to work together? It won't work."

Phillip Walsh, minority leader of the house, had pursed his pale lips. "How much will it cost? I mean, our part? If we should try it?"

Nilstrom deferred to General Gray.

"Well, Congressman, it'll cost a lot. There hasn't been time for a cost analysis, but I would estimate billions."

"Then we can't afford it! It would be fiscal madness. Our budget is already strained to the limit with all the social assistance programs this administration has initiated."

"I agree. My friend Mr. Walsh has stated my position precisely. We can't afford any science fiction nonsense. Flying saucers!" Peter Kerr turned sideways in his chair, crossed his legs.

Bertha Fowler glared at the two men as they spoke. Now she said to Gray, "You see? It won't work because even this group can't agree on anything! We can't make a decision fast enough to stop a glacier, much less a space fleet."

General Gray had suffered through so many meetings with politicians that he was unruffled. In a soft voice, he addressed his words to Kerr. "Senator, you seem suspicious. Which data do you question? The Baker-Nunn pictures? The destruction of the French Mirages? What more do you want? More radar confirmation? Another picture?"

"Hell, no, General Gray, he just wants to hoard his gold until he's sure there's no way out. Then he'll spend a couple of dollars—when it's too late." Bertha was on her feet, her black eyes snapping.

The president stood and interrupted the exchange. His face was drawn and his eyes looked tired. "Please, ladies and gentlemen! This is no time for recriminations. Let's make an orderly decision. Is there anyone who doubts the data or disagrees with the conclusions of the Joint Chiefs?"

He waited, standing beside General Gray. No one moved. "I invite the cabinet members to speak also."

There was silence.

"Then I take it that we *do* agree. Now, does anyone else have a suggestion as to how we should proceed?"

Again there was silence.

"Then we have no alternative except to follow the recommendations of the Joint Chiefs."

There was prolonged silence.

Bertha offered one more comment. "Well, I'm for doing something, and soon, but this plan won't work. Why, it's bigger than the old Manhattan Project, and to make it work, we'd all have to cooperate." She glared at Broughton. "And we'd have to trust the Communists. Congress'll never agree to *that*."

The president looked at Flexnor. The big man wiped his heavily perspiring brow and shook his head. He said softly, "She's right."

Reed was grim as he turned to Sternald and lifted his eyebrows in query. The little man shifted uncomfortably. "No, it won't work. The Russians won't cooperate—or the French or the English, either."

One by one, Sanders, Callazarro, Scott, and Summerscales shook their heads. Only Williams thought the plan had a chance.

Hamilton had said nothing. At last he stood up. His voice was deep and resonant, yet tinged with that anguish of soul that made so many love him—and so many others despise him.

"Mistuh President, I've sat here in great pain at this tuhn of events. It has been proposed that we go all out and destroy these invaders. I disagree. In the first place, it seems cleah that we cannot succeed.

"Suh, I think that is providential, for if we had the capacity to kill all those people—or whatever they are—we would surely do it. So I have an alternative proposal. Let's meet them with love! Mistuh President, I propose that we send up a rocket as a special 'peace ship,' and that we send that fleet a *welcome*. I see no reason to believe that they come with warlike intent.

"Suh, I think they're testing us because of what they've learned about our tortured race, our murderin', plunderin', pillagin' race! I think they're testin' to see if they *can* destroy us, if that need arises. And it's obvious they *can*! So let's meet our brothers from the skies with open arms, and learn from them the ways of peace."

The president paused for a moment before speaking. "Charlie, if we were to send up your peace rocket, they'd destroy it. If they should, by some miracle, stop it, open it, and understand the message, I think they'd laugh. We're not going to be like the Aztecs who welcomed the Spanish Conquistadors. And we're not going to be involved in another Munich. Sorry, Charlie, but I'm responsible for the citizens of this country." He turned away from the pain-filled eyes of his friend.

"Wilbur, I want personal letters prepared for each head of state involved: Russia, England, France, Germany, Japan, India, and China. We must also include Señor Sanchez of the United Nations. I want to sign the letters personally, and I want them delivered by courier.

"Admiral Steinhauser, it has been suggested that we meet somewhere in the Pacific. Because it's crucial that the media not know about the meeting, it will be held at Wake Island. Please make all preparations. We'll meet from the twenty-seventh to the twenty-ninth of December, not in January as Dr. Nilstrom proposed in his plan. Public leaders frequently take off in late December, and it'll be easier for us to be away without arousing suspicion.

"Dr. Nilstrom, you may, as you have asked, call a meeting of certain scientists the day before the world leaders meet. There are things you'll need, actions you'll want to take that I can't foresee. The power and authority of my office are at your disposal. If you encounter any obstacle, call me personally. You may use General Beck's communications system.

"Clifton, Ed—" the president had never before addressed Gray by his first name—"this means we'll have to breach security on the Graser project and on God knows what else." He hesitated, then added, "It looks as if this is the end of nationalism—as we've known it, anyway. Let's hope it'll be the beginning of international cooperation. Strange, isn't it, that it often takes a disaster, or a threatened one, to force necessary changes."

He smiled sadly. Suddenly he looked tired. It wasn't so much the length and tension of the meeting, or even the gravity of the situation. It was that he felt the full weight of the presidency. He looked around once more. He found respect, and it gave him strength.

"This matter must be kept *totally* confidential. Some of you will be expected at Wake Island. We will notify you. Please make your personal preparations, and keep them absolutely secret. This meeting is now— Oh, one last matter. General Beck, you'll want Dr. Kellogg at Wake Island." His face twitched in a half-smile. "Invite him, but see if you can put a bit in his mouth. This meeting is adjourned."

Within a few minutes, nearly everyone had drifted out of the room. Nilstrom and Beck, wordlessly gathering their documents, were suddenly aware that someone was weeping. Senator Charles Hamilton was leaning against the door, tears streaming down his face. The two men stood watching a United States senator weep for his country and for the world—and perhaps for the universe.

"God knows, he's not the only one who's frustrated," said Nilstrom quietly. "All my life I've wondered if there were other intelligent beings in the universe. I'd give my eyeteeth to be able to knock on the hatch of one of those spacecraft and find out what's inside. Instead, I'm trying to figure out a way to destroy them."

The two friends stepped past Hamilton and out into the long hallway. For a while they walked in silence.

"Chris," said the giant general, "Hamilton's a sincere, compassionate man. I think he's wrong, but he's—well, he's a great man."

"No, Nick, I disagree," Nilstrom said in a harsh voice. "He's sensitive all right, but he's not compassionate. And to be great, he'd have to have real compassion—a combination of sensitivity to suffering and the strength to do something about it. Hamilton cries about life and lives in the clouds. He doesn't have the courage to come down to earth and do something *real*."

Beck said, "Chris, you're a hard man."

Together they got on the elevator and Chris pushed the DOWN button.

Part Two

Part Two

Chapter 1

KAMINSKI HAD shown these slides and motion pictures many times. He knew every scene, every scratch on the film. But now, as he flicked the slides on Nilstrom's command, he felt a rising fear. Somehow, what he saw struck more deeply into his consciousness today. Probably it was because of his audience.

The room was dark, the heads of the viewers merely blobs of deeper darkness, arrayed in rows before him. Kaminski could make out Sir Clement Tillman in the front row because of the way his thin white hair stood out in a sort of halo. He knew that Alex Baumgartner was sitting beside the Englishman. Dr. Nilstrom stood by the screen, and periodically his arm intruded into the rectangle of light to point at something.

All of the viewers were scientists. Kaminski knew that somewhere in the group were three Nobel Prize winners. One was the Japanese astronomer, Hiroshi Shigemitsu. He couldn't remember the names of the other two.

As he listened to Dr. Nilstrom, it gave him a thrill that he, a mere sergeant in the Air Force, knew things heretofore unknown to Nobel Prize winners—things that had so shaken the great people that they had hardly spoken at all. He must remember every detail of these meetings. He was watching the making of history.

Kaminski tried to recall the names of some of the others. The dumpy French woman was Marie Monnet. That tall, glum looking Englishman, an authority on—was it plasma physics? How could Arnie forget him? With his long face, he looked exactly like a horse. His name was Cecil Barnstable! And there was Dimitri Solovyev, the Russian, sitting off by himself at the end of a row.

The sergeant wiped his brow. The hot lamps of the two projectors and the almost unbearable heat of Wake Island combined to send the sweat running down his forehead and face.

"That's about it, ladies and gentlemen." Nilstrom had finished the first part of his presentation.

Kaminski turned on the lights, flicked off the projector, and sat back in his chair.

"Chris, why haven't we been told of thees before?" It was the Indian, Narihari Raychandbhai, specialist in radiation physics.

"Nari, my government had to be certain it wasn't aircraft from another nation. Also, we gathered most of this material only in the last few days."

Another hand went up.

"Otto?"

Otto Weber, a German astrophysicist, stood up.

"Chris, you said you recovered some debris—even some flesh. Would you tell us about that?"

Nilstrom nodded. "Due to the extreme altitude of the vessel at the time of its destruction, and the inclement weather at the crash site, very little was recovered. But we did find twenty-two pounds of material, no piece larger than six inches square, the smallest only two inches across."

Kaminski had trouble following what Nilstrom said next. Scientists were crazy! One moment they talked like people, and the next like technical manuals. He gathered that the stuff they'd found in Canada was about what would be expected from a spacecraft.

"The remaining four ounces—organic material—are the most interesting."

The first slide was a photo of the tissue specimen. Several more followed, showing the specimen from different angles. Then came a series of microscopic pictures of sections of the tissue. As Nilstrom spoke, Kaminski threw in the towel. He'd taken biology in high school, but he was immediately lost.

"The microstructure shows elongated membranes and the cells bound together in clumps, suggesting voluntary muscle tissue. We can recognize the normal functional parts." Nilstrom pointed out each one. "Nucleus—folds reminiscent of endoplasmic reticulum—mitochondria. Nothing outstanding about the cells. They're mammalian, and can't be differentiated from human tissue. On a finer level—" Kaminski switched slides— "the nucleus possesses forty-four paired chromosomes, as in human samples, although there are apparently some minute differences. It'll be months before anything more definitive can be deduced from the structure of the chromosomes. Protein and amino-acid analysis determines beyond all reasonable doubt that the animal was a carbon-based oxygen-breather that needed water, air, and warmth at approximately the same levels that we do. Trace-mineral studies reveal some minor differences. Biologists conclude that the creature from which this tissue came could live comfortably on this planet. It's possible that it might require supplemental minerals, but then, so do we. For example, we add iodine to salt to prevent goiter. Are there any questions?" Chris paused for a moment.

"All right, then, we'll move on. What I want to show you now is even more disturbing."

Kaminski began the series with keen interest. These were slides he hadn't seen before.

"First is a picture of recordings taken from the two-hundred-foot radio telescope at Green Bank on the thirteenth by Dr. Baumgartner."

There was a startled murmur, and the sergeant grinned. They acted as if they'd just seen a photograph of a flying elephant. But the figures on the screen were gibberish as far as he was concerned, a graph with spiky peaks and valleys.

"As you can see," Nilstrom said, "this is clearly an information-bearing waveform. There can be little doubt that the signal is artificially generated."

Again there were murmurs. On Nilstrom's instruction, Kaminski ran through the slides slowly, allowing time for the scientists to examine each one closely.

"The signals probably represent a totally alien language transcribed into an equally alien code. Cryptanalysts aren't optimistic about decoding these messages. Sir Clement will explain the next set of slides."

Nilstrom took a seat in the front row, and the cheerful little Englishman bobbed up, rubbing his hands together.

"These are the results of our radar probe." Sir Clement pointed to the chart, and his head was caught in the light from the projector. "The upper half of the screen shows the waveform transmitted December fourteenth. The lower half shows the waveform received ninety-eight hours later, obviously an echo of the transmitted signal.

"Now, ninety-eight hours translates to thirty-five billion miles. The signal encountered a reflecting object where nothing, except perhaps a comet, could be. The characteristics of the reflected signal make it clear that the target consists of hundreds of metallic objects.

"You'll notice that the benchmarks here—" he indicated with his finger— "and here, are Doppler-shifted toward us. The degree of the shift indicates a velocity of two hundred sixty-three kilometers per second, or an English velocity of five hundred eighty-eight thousand miles per hour."

The Englishman paused, letting the silence mount. Then, in a voice a full octave lower, he said, "Extrapolated to zero velocity, this means an arrival in the vicinity of the sun in approximately fourteen months."

A distinct tremor ran through the audience as Tillman quietly took his seat.

"I've saved the real stinker, the clincher, for last," Chris resumed. "Sergeant?"

Kaminski jumped when he realized Nilstrom was speaking to him, and quickly reached for the advance switch. A photograph of the night sky, spangled with stars, came on the screen.

"This was taken December thirteenth from LOOTS. It is, of course, the region of the sky surrounding 61 Cygni. The astronomers among you—"

But Nilstrom got no further; a stream of Japanese interrupted him. It was Hiroshi Shigemitsu, who added self-consciously, "Forgive me, but—there is something there!"

"Exactly, Hiri. There *is* something there." Nilstrom pointed to a fuzzy patch. "An anomalous light source where there was none previously. Next slide, please."

Alert this time, Kaminski hit the advance switch.

"This is a photograph of the same area taken two years ago. As you can see—" he pointed to the blank spot— "there was nothing there then. Will you go back to the other slide, please, Sergeant. This—" Nilstrom pointed to a star near the fuzzy patch of light— "is 61 Cygni. Its proper motion, extrapolated backward, places it directly behind the new light source some thirty years ago. The velocity and rate of deceleration of the objects detected on Pan-European Radar, extrapolated backward, indicates a departure time from 61 Cygni—of thirty years ago."

Someone in the dark room whistled.

"Now, for those of you who are not astronomers, it may be helpful for me to explain the next step. We have a technique called 'photoelectric image enhancement.' The arrival of photons is electronically recorded and computer-analyzed. In this case, an involved pattern of interference fringes was detected, which enabled us to reconstruct the source of light. Sergeant?"

The next slide was simple. On a black field was a square grid of white dots, ten rows of ten each. Every dot bore a double image, like that sometimes seen on an improperly adjusted TV set. The impression was of a second grid of dots behind the first, then more.

Nilstrom made no comment, but waited for them to study it, then said, "We also made a spectrographic analysis."

Kaminski could make nothing of this slide, but the audience gasped almost in unison.

"This spectrum is like nothing I've ever seen. Light is being emitted in the yellow to near-ultraviolet range, with the energy-to-frequency function following an almost perfect bell curve. I don't need to remind you that no natural object, and for that matter, no artificial one that I know of, emits light in that manner. From the amount of light, we calculate that they are using more power than the entire energy output of this planet."

Everyone sat in stunned silence. Nilstrom signaled for the lights, and ran his hand through his dark hair. "I think you'll agree with me that we're about to receive a visit. And judging by the actions of the advance units, it's pretty clear that it won't be a friendly visit." For the first time, his voice sounded tired. "Let's adjourn briefly now, and meet again at three o'clock. Dr. Kellogg and I will present our plan to you then."

The afternoon meeting lasted until the dinner hour. When it was finally over, there was not a single dissenting opinion among the twenty-three scientists. It was a triumph for Nilstrom and Beck and Kellogg.

Where the three got the energy to keep going, Kaminski didn't know. He had only run the projectors, and he was exhausted. Now, although the meeting had adjourned, Beck and Nilstrom were still there, getting ready for the presentation tomorrow.

Chapter 2

ANNA KORNILYEVNA Larin heard the bell and turned back, away from the superb beach. The sky was blindingly blue, the ocean sparkled, and the combers rolled endlessly in to break on the white coral beaches. How far the waves had come, she could only guess. Last night, flying from Hawaii on the last leg of her more than six-thousand-mile flight from New York, it seemed the ocean would never end. Wake Island was the model of the phrase, "the middle of nowhere."

Anna quickened her step when she saw the others converging on the mess hall. Almost everyone had been out for a walk following the shattering revelations of the morning meeting.

Anna was one of the few women here, and none of the men, for all the gravity of the situation, had failed to note her presence. She was thirty-eight and stunningly attractive. Short and thin, she had a beautiful figure. Her hair was almost platinum blond and her complexion was clear and soft.

Once inside the building, Anna sought the Soviet delegation.

She moved between the round tables at which most of the delegates were already seated and spotted her fellow Russians in the corner. The Soviet contingent included Marshal Byacheslav, chief of staff of the army; old Admiral Varsonofiev, commander of the vast Society navy; the still older chief of the KGB, General Semyechkin; young foreign minister Valuyev; the tall physicist, Dr. Solovyev; and the old chairman himself, Fyodor Grigorevich Grigorenko.

Anna bent over and put her arm around him and said affectionately, "Comrade Papa Bear, have you taken your pills? Irina Lvovna will never forgive me if I let you forget." Only five feet seven, stocky in build and eighty years old, his watery eyes flashed beneath shaggy white eyebrows.

She kissed him on his wrinkled cheek, and the old man chuckled happily. "Anna Kornilyevna! I thought you'd forsaken this old man!" His words seemed to flow over gravel.

"Forgive me, Papa Bear, but I went for a walk."

Solovyev held a chair for her, next to the chairman. She smiled her thanks.

Valuyev, said in his high-pitched voice, "Anna Kornilyevna, Comrade Solovyev was just saying that he believes the

Americans are telling the truth about the saucers and the fleet."

There was something about the brilliant, forty-eight-year-old foreign minister that invariably disturbed Anna. She had never had any substantial disagreement with him, and she knew that he honestly respected her. But he was soft-looking, and she suspected he lacked courage.

Anna could not know that Valuyev was a homosexual who realized he had no future in the foreign service if that ever became known. So he had married a stupid, fat woman who seemed likely to make few demands on him. Unfortunately, Xenya Martynovna had turned out to be an ardent lover who became sulky when denied sex. He was never really happy.

Now, pushing his heavy glasses up on his nose, Valuyev leaned across the table, his puffy face tense. "Do you agree with Solovyev, comrade?"

Anna wanted to say what she felt: that any intelligent person could see that Solovyev was right. But she played the game expected of Soviet diplomats: eternal suspicion. Gravely she asked, "Comrade Solovyev, could they be making such predictions because they want something of us? We must be careful."

Solovyev smiled. His crooked teeth, filled with silver, protruded slightly. He was an odd-looking man, as stooped and thin as a wire coat hanger. His clothes were invariably old and unpressed. He always wore gray, his hair was turning to gray, and even his face was gray. He seldom spoke in a group, and rarely appeared at cocktail parties in Moscow. But Anna knew that Solovyev was warm and easygoing with his friends, and could be surprisingly boisterous.

"Comrade Larin, I know nothing of diplomacy. But I can tell you that there *is* a fleet approaching from 61 Cygni."

Anna watched for Grigorenko's reaction to Solovyev's statement. His bushy eyebrows shielded his eyes from her scrutiny, but she could see his face—the set jaw, the deep lines.

In recent months she had worried about him. The old chairman was becoming suspicious of some of the very people he had placed in positions of importance. Young members of the party, with the ruthlessness of the young, talked openly about the way he fell asleep during long meetings, and suggested that he was senile. Anna could smell their ambition, saw them jockeying for positions that would give them an advantage when the change came.

Now, with the threat of the invading fleet, it was crucial that Grigorenko not falter, for only his strength could lead Russia into the alliance that was needed.

Ivan Valuyev shook his head. His bloated face registered dismay. "It's astonishing! First the Americans tell us virtually everything about their radar and satellite network, then . . ."

Anna had never seen the foreign minister so bewildered.

Mikhail Nikolyavich Semyechkin, too, was having a hard time. Nearly seventy-five, he had been head of the KGB for twelve years. The big man had once been a weightlifter, to which his thick shoulders and huge, calloused hands bore witness. His hair and thick mustache looked like patches of snow.

Outsiders and insiders alike wondered why the premier had appointed this old bluff of a former field general. The truth was that Grigorenko wanted a loyal and stupid man in the powerful post. The old general was a flawless choice.

But today Semyechkin was uncomfortable. His KGB was obviously ignorant of the things the Americans had revealed. He cleared his throat, glanced nervously at the chairman, and growled, "Well, of course, Comrade Valuyev, we already knew about their radar and their satellites."

The foreign minister was one of the few persons in the Soviet leadership who understood and approved of Semyechkin's role. He didn't want to jeopardize the old man's position. "Oh, of course, comrade, your department keeps excellent track of such things, but I was impressed with the Americans' candor. When they admitted that their Eagle couldn't shoot down the saucer, I—I was indeed impressed."

"I don't know about you, comrades," Anna said, "but it surprised me to see the kind of pictures their satellites take of the Soviet Union. And the *Provedennyi*! I didn't know about that." Admiral Varsonofiev looked pained. Anna turned to Semyechkin. "Did you also know about the Graser guns?"

Semyechkin reddened, and the white mustache stood out even more against his crimson cheeks.

Byacheslav said bitterly, "Comrade Larin, we knew nothing about the Grasers."

The general's gray hair was cut short, and because his face broadened toward the jaw, he looked like an inverted cone with a flat-top haircut. His face readily flushed, and his blue eyes bulged when he was angry. Though he was Grigorenko's friend, he was nevertheless openly critical of the way the armed forces had been neglected.

"Years ago, the U.S. experimented with the idea of the Graser and then dropped it. There have been rumors that they were working on it again, but—" he looked scathingly at Semyechkin— "the KGB's top agent assured us there was no substance to the rumor."

Foreign Minister Valuyev said urgently, "Isn't this Graser a breach of our treaty?"

The chairman put down his cup. His voice was low, his words deliberate. "The agreements called for limitation on antimissile *missiles*. They have broken no treaty."

"What difference does it make *now*?" Solovyev asked quietly.

"What difference!" Byacheslav exploded. "Comrade, they can fire missiles at us and we can stop a few. But they can destroy all of ours. It will take us years to catch up. And already they're making more sophisticated, miniaturized Grasers that can be transported on ships."

Valuyev fidgeted uncomfortably, watching the old chairman. "But why are they telling us their secrets now?"

Byacheslav growled, "Bah! They're only trying to trap us."

Solovyev said stubbornly, "It's no trap, comrade. Far from being angry at the United States, we should be grateful that they discovered the fleet and shot down one of the scouts."

Valuyev leaned so far forward that his soft face hung just above the salad. "Why have they bothered to call us together?"

Anna drew back from the foreign minister. "It's obvious," she said, "that they have a plan and and want our participation. But also, it's because of the implications."

"What do you mean, Comrade Larin?" Valuyev's owlish eyes were grotesque behind thick lenses.

But it wasn't Anna who answered. It was the old chairman, his voice decisive, deliberate. "If the world is under attack, the world must unite. There will be no more Soviet Union, no more United States—only one people, one government."

"Aha! Comrade Chairman! As always, you've seen through to the truth." Semyechkin sat back in his chair, content that he knew the answer to the mystery."

The old chairman continued imperturbably, "And I think it's clear what the Americans want of us." He glanced at Solovyev.

Anna stared at Papa Bear in astonishment. More than eighty years old, and he'd perceived the plan! She breathed more easily.

The old man was like a father to her, and she was dearer to him than his own daughter. It saddened him that his only child had inherited none of her mother's tenderness and sensitivity. Irina was stolid and intolerably bossy, while Anna was very like his wife, whom he had lost so many years before.

But Anna's success was attributable to more than the chairman's affection for her. Grigorenko had recognized that much of the Soviet Union's problem was the image other countries had of Russia. So he'd slowly phased out the suspicious old diplomats and replaced them with young people—the "bear's cubs," as they were called by cynical old Communists. They were attractive and gregarious, and they dressed modishly and carried to the world a wholly new image of youth and vitality.

Anna Larin was Grigorenko's prize exhibit. She was a startling combination: a feminine, affectionate woman and a tough, even ruthless advocate for her country. After taking her Ph.D in Political Institutions of the West at Moscow University, she distinguished herself in consular offices and was elevated to more prestigious positions. She had served in ambassadorial offices in Paris and London. In each capital, she won the hearts of the people with her warmth and candor and gaiety.

When she was only thirty-two, Anna was sent to the United States as the first assistant to the ailing Boris Ivanovich Volodin. When he died three years later, she became his replacement. Two years after that, she was appointed ambassador to the United Nations.

She was the sensation of the diplomatic community in Washington and then in New York. Once a photographer snapped her picture as she watched films of starving people in India. She was weeping. Nothing in its modern history had done so much to change the image of Russia in the eyes of the world as that one picture. Grigorenko immediately made her chairman of a special worldwide food-distribution task force.

Now, as a member of the Soviet delegation here on Wake Island, Anna was sure she knew what the Americans were about to propose. And she was relieved to see that Grigorenko also understood, for the Soviet Union would have to cooperate or the world was doomed.

She wondered if the others would agree, even in the face of such a threat. She looked around the room, mentally counting the votes. René Molinière, the President of France, and Gerhard Kroner, the German Chancellor, would probably cooperate; the Japanese certainly would.

England? She studies Wakefield Hobbes. Tall, elegantly dressed, haughty, grotesquely egotistical, and a conservative, he was the youngest prime minister in the history of his country. Fiercely chauvinistic and absolutely ruthless, he'd led his failing nation out of near bankruptcy to new heights of prosperity and influence in the world. To achieve this, he'd been harshly businesslike with other nations. Like Professor Higgins, he treated everybody alike: terribly. He regularly insulted the Queen, the entire nobility, members of parliament, and most of the population. A bachelor, he openly installed one mistress after another in Number Ten Downing Street.

Anna had reason to know Hobbes, for he had tried in every imaginable way to seduce her. Anna despised him, even as she admitted his brilliance. She doubted that he'd cooperate.

And what about China? India?

Chapter 3

ON THE whole, Chris was satisfied with the way the morning had gone. Both President Reed and Nick Beck had been persuasive. The general's candor, the frank revelation of "super secrets," and the fact that Sir Clement Tillman had confirmed the American findings gave credence to their conclusions. Nilstrom knew that his own presentation, plus the unanimous agreement of the scientists, had been overwhelming. He had not played his trump card, and he still wondered if he should have. Solovyev had given him permission, but Chris feared that it might cause the scientist trouble.

The afternoon meeting was about to begin, and Nilstrom sat at the front of the room, watching the delegates. The Russians caused him the most concern. Without their participation, there would be no project. And he couldn't make an educated guess as to their response. At the morning meeting, Foreign Minister Valuyev had asked thoughtful questions, and the beautiful ambassador to the United Nations was also impressive. Chris had seen Anna Larin on television, and she was as stunning as he had expected, but smaller and more feminine. He studied her now, as she visited with Chairman Grigorenko.

And he felt a strange, powerful, disturbing sensation.

He had known it once before, five years after he and Kay were married. At a cocktail party he'd seen a woman, not particularly pretty, who drew his attention like a magnet. Their eyes locked and some mysterious electricity poured through the connection. It was as if they were fiercely vibrating to some primitive music others couldn't hear. The feeling startled him, and Kay obviously sensed the moment and was alarmed. So Chris drifted away, never spoke to the woman, never knew her name or saw her again. But he had never forgotten the force of that experience, even though he loved Kay deeply and was completely faithful to her. Now he felt it again. And the one time his eyes met Anna's made him think she felt it too.

He was jerked back to attention as Reed called the meeting to order and asked him to explain his plan. Chris moved to the podium and looked around the room. Quietly he said, "We are virtually defenseless against the forces threatening us. In order to survive, we must produce a new weapon which will destroy them *before* they reach the earth and mount an attack. Therefore, our proposal is to construct a giant Graser able to destroy the entire fleet while it is still deep in space.

"Because of the size and complexity of the Graser, we can fire only one shot, and that must be precisely aimed. We estimate the optimum range to be half a million miles."

He turned and picked up a piece of chalk at the blackboard. "The beam of the Graser spreads as it reaches out into space. At the same time, it loses power." He drew two lines to illustrate the widening beam. Then he drew three lines across the beam.

"If we fire at half a million miles, here—" Chris pointed to the second dissecting line— "Dr. Kellogg and I calculate that the coherent beam will kill the occupants immediately."

His hand moved to the third line. "If we were to fire at a million miles, the chances are the beam would not kill them instantly. You may wonder why we are not proposing a shorter range. We must be sure the beam will have spread enough to encompass and destroy the entire armada."

He drew a rough circle over the first line. "We could wait until they are only a quarter of a million miles away—comparable to the distance between the earth and the moon. Our shot would be more destructive, but at that point the fleet will occupy a wider area than is covered by the beam. I might add that while half a million miles sounds like a great distance, it's

actually trifling. We are waiting until we see the whites of
their eyes!"

Still holding the chalk, Nilstrom faced the delegates. There
wasn't a sound. Hobbes was trying hard to look bored, but
even he didn't move. "We propose to build only one gun, and
to build it in the northern hemisphere."

He turned back to the blackboard and drew first the sun,
then the earth and the other planets in a plane around the sun.
Next he drew a crude picture of the fleet approaching from
above that plane.

"Now, you can see that if the fleet continues on its present
course it will fly right down the mouth of our cannon. Of
course, if it should drop below the ecliptic the gun would be
worthless." Chris brushed the chalkdust from his hands.

"Dr. Nilstrom, even if the fleet comes in above the ecliptic,
the rotation of the earth is such that it will be in the sights of
your gun for only a few hours each day." It was Helmut Stehlen
speaking, a brilliant engineer, systems expert, and, at forty-
five, president of Germany's Hartmann Motorwerke.

"You're right, Herr Stehlen. But I'll ask Dr. Kellogg to tell
you why we propose only one gun."

Kellogg was dressed in track shorts and a T-shirt, and
Hobbes lifted his eyebrows in elegant disdain. But Sir Bernard
Powell, Britain's sixty-five-year-old foreign secretary, smiled
indulgently and his bright eyes twinkled.

Kellogg ran his hand through the tower of curly hair piled
on his head. "Ladies and gentlemen, when Chris first described
his idea I told him he was crazy. But I don't see any alternative.
We'll be trying something unbelievably difficult. Even little
Grasers are the devil to make. Each one has its own atomic
reactor, each is made of beryllium impregnated with ruthenium,
each is cooled by liquid helium. God! You can't believe the
problems we had with those guns! But comparing them with
the monster that Nilstrom proposes is like comparing a muzzle-
loading squirrel rifle with a modern sixteen-inch cannon. For
example, in the existing Graser the power of an atomic explosion pours through an aperture eight inches in diameter. The
heat is terrific! Now we're talking about power hundreds of
times greater. The whole gun could melt. If I had a bloody
five years, I'd panic. To make ten or five or even two Grasers
of this size would be impossible. The odds are heavily against
our making *one*."

As he listened, Chris found his attitude about the young man changing. Kellogg was juvenile in his defiance of customs; right now he looked downright silly. But at least he was honest and forthright. He made rational decisions instead of maneuvering for political advantage. And he worked as hard as a man could.

"I haven't mentioned the worst problem. To fire this gun will require as much power as it takes to light up New York City. We'll need the equivalent of a two-hundred-megaton bomb pouring out through a twenty-foot barrel."

Chairman Grigorenko nodded knowingly.

"*Maybe* we can get the gun built in time—" Kellogg gestured hopelessly— "but the *power*?" He turned to Nilstrom. "That's your problem!" Without another word, he left the podium.

"Doctor Kellogg is right," Chris said. "The biggest problem is power—and that's saying a lot since *every* problem is big. There's only one solution: thermonuclear reactor. And only the Soviet Union knows how to build those. When the United States discovered how to extract gasoline cheaply from coal, allocations to our thermonuclear project were severely reduced and we fell behind.

"But thanks to the leadership of Chairman Grigorenko and the brilliance of Doctor Solovyev, the Soviet Union has harnessed thermonuclear power.

"We Americans have one piece of the puzzle: the Grasers. The Russians have the other piece: thermonuclear power. With those two and the combined brains and expertise of the rest of the technological powers, we have an outside chance."

Chris saw the skepticism on Marshal Byacheslav's face change to smug satisfaction. Anger exploded in Nilstrom like a magnesium flare, but he smothered it. Regardless of how paranoid or stupid others were, he didn't dare lose his temper—or his confidence. His eyes were drawn to Anna Larin. She smiled and he continued.

"You can see that our only hope is for complete international cooperation. Without it, we'll all die.

"We propose to begin immediately. The gun must be located in the desert where work can continue for the next fourteen months without interference from weather. But the site must also be close to industrial facilities so that there will be a minimal wait for parts."

Chris felt suddenly weary, as much from the energy he expended in controlling his emotions as from the long hours of work. Quickly he told them of the organization the U.S. proposed: two chairmen, one political and one scientific; Helmut Stehlen to organize the actual construction of the gun; Jacques Fouché to handle the complicated finances; Takeo Omari to be responsible for the communications network; Sir Clement Tillman to direct the constant optical and electronic observations of the fleet; Beck to be in charge of destroying any surviving ships; Kellogg to design the gun; Solovyev to develop the reactor. Once, when Hobbes rolled his eyes cynically at the international composition of the organization, Chris had to clamp his teeth together to keep from swearing. But he maintained control and introduced Solovyev. Byacheslav and Varsonofiev glared at the tall physicist as he moved forward.

"Ladies and gentlemen, distinguished leaders, I'm honored to be here—though I'm as frightened and confused as you are." Solovyev was so tall he seemed to reach the ceiling of the little meeting room, and the podium that had caught Chris at chest level barely came to the Russian's belt.

"I must begin by sharing with you one more piece of evidence. Upon learning the fleet's location from Sir Clement and from the most remarkable LOOTS telescope, Doctor Nilstrom called me in Paris, where I was attending a meeting. Not only did I know of his international reputation as an expert on pulsars, but—"

Hobbes leaned toward his foreign secretary and whispered loudly, ". . . as a bloody nut on UFOs!"

Solovyev ignored the interruption. "We had met twice before at scientific conferences. I was therefore honored to receive his call. He told me what you have heard today, and on my own initiative I asked for a probe by our Soviet Radio Telescope." He glanced nervously at the Russian delegation. "Ordinarily, of course, I'd have waited for proper authorization, but there wasn't time. I have the results of that probe. They confirm Sir Clement's findings in every detail."

He paused to let the information sink in, and Byacheslav whispered in the ear of the chairman. Grigorenko made no response. Nilstrom feared for Solovyev, but he was glad to have the Soviet probe reported.

"I've been asked to speak about the feasibility of constructing a reactor many times larger than anything we've yet made. I don't know what obstacles we may meet, but I think in principle it can be done. The problem is, of course, time. I can only say that my knowledge and energy are yours if you decide to proceed. After all, there's no other possibility of survival for any of us."

Instead of returning to his seat with the Russian delegation, Solovyev took an empty chair in the front row. Nobody missed the significance of his action.

President Reed rose, grim as he faced the group. He was dressed in a blue leisure suit with a white sport shirt open at the neck. "Ladies and gentlemen, you have seen the evidence and you have heard our plan." He paused, searching for the best way to secure agreement without bitter argument, and decided on the old salesman's trick of assuming the sale was made and leading the customer into a discussion based on that proposition.

"Now, you'll want an opportunity to question the scientists, but before we get even more confused over their equations—" he was interrupted by a chuckle from his listeners— "there are some details to be settled. Obviously, any news of this menace would cause a panic. But confidentiality will be a problem since we'll have to take many if not all of our legislators into our confidence.

"Certainly we must have physical security at the construction site. I believe this can be achieved best by troops from all participating countries. We can leave the details of that to our generals. I might add that the United States will install as many standard Grasers at the site as are deemed advisable by the military commanders. And in order to contribute to the security of each of your countries, we will share with you the full specifications of these guns so you can construct them for your own defense. We also have a limited number available that we're willing to sell."

Reed looked at the Russian delegation. "Since, Chairman Grigorenko, the Soviet Union possesses the largest optical telescope in the world, which may become the target of attack, you may want those Grasers immediately. If so, they are yours."

Marshal Byacheslav exhaled loudly. KGB chief Semyechkin stared in disbelief. Grigorenko's expression didn't change.

"We have two other major problems. One is the countries that are not involved. Quite frankly, each of you was chosen because of your nation's technological skills or because you represent one of the great powers. We dared not expand this group because of the necessity for secrecy. I've asked Señor Sanchez, Secretary General of the United Nations, to be here because it's vital that he be informed of every development. And we need him to deal with those nations that have not been included. He has agreed to help.

"Also of major importance is the necessity for a 'cover story,' as we Americans say. I have a suggestion. For some time we've all been caught up in an energy crisis. Let's announce that we are launching a joint effort to create unlimited power by developing thermonuclear power plants. Of course, the public now knows that conventional atomic power is dangerous and prone to accidents such as the ones in Detroit and at Three Mile Island. Thermonuclear power is comparatively safe and produces no significant radioactive wastes. I think people will be delighted with our efforts.

"Furthermore, I think they will be so relieved to see the great powers actually cooperating in such a venture that the pressure to know details and the anger over not being included will diminish. Also, bitterness can be dissipated if we announce that the results of our experiments will be made available to everyone."

Chris marveled at Reed's adroitness and charisma. He only hoped the President would be able to maintain his confidence in the debate that was sure to come.

"Now, we need an appropriate name for the project, one that will impart to the world our cooperation. Are there any suggestions?" Reed smiled broadly as he invited their active participation for the first time. His ruse worked.

At once, everyone began to talk—in several languages—about the name for a project they hadn't yet agreed to support. There were many suggestions: legendary names from Greek mythology, Biblical names, names from the lore of Communism and from Chinese and Indian history. The discussion was heated, and national differences flared. Marshal Byacheslav insisted that it be called the Leningrad Project after the heroic stand of the Russian people under the leadership of Chairman Grigorenko. The Chinese acidly demurred, maintaining that the greatest achievement of the twentieth centry was the Long

March. Finally Wakefield Hobbes said, "You bloody fools, we'll be here for weeks arguing about this. I'd planned to spend my Christmas holiday under the mistletoe. Instead..."

"Mistletoe! Call it Mistletoe!" someone shouted.

Hobbes shrugged. "Why not? It'd be a charming way to inform the world of our new-found erotic affection for each other. I'm sure everyone would be delighted to see us all disporting ourselves in the same bed."

Sir Bernard Powell said enthusiastically, "By Jove, Wakey, I think you've got it!" The others applauded.

"Well, then, we're in agreement," said Reed.

"Mr. President," said Kroner, "do you know the myth behind the odd little parasite?"

"No, Herr Chancellor."

"In Scandinavian mythology, Balder was the son of Odin and Frigga, and the central figure of many myths. At the time of his birth, his mother bound all things by oath that they not permit themselves to be used to kill her son. But when she came to the mistletoe, she was exhausted. She decided it was too small to hurt him anyway, and didn't bother to extract from it the same promise. Later, Balder's foes discovered this and used a dart of mistletoe to slay him. His death was the prelude to the final overthrow of the gods."

"Herr Chancellor, that makes the name perfect: We'll fashion a dart out of the one thing to which these godlike invaders seem vulnerable! Now, I think we can safely adjourn, and permit our scientists and engineers and—"

"Just one meenute, Meester President. I have a few questions before we adjourn."

Chapter 4

ADAJANIAN SWAMINATHAN was standing, his large black eyes burning in his cadaverous skull. The tall Indian foreign minister hated everyone who wasn't Indian—and most Indians too. Educated at Oxford, he spoke English fluently but with an accent, and in the high-pitched voice so common to his countrymen. Swaminathan had won enemies for his country all over the world by blaming other nations for the famines. The fact that his technique failed to secure aid was perhaps of less importance to the Indian people than the fact that he articulated their own frustrations and bitterness.

"Meester President, I wish to know which desert you have in mind for your fearful gun. Are you referring to the great Sahara, or to the Near East? Or is it perhaps the American desert which you have chosen?"

The president reddened. "Why, uh, yes, it *is* the American desert—near Phoenix, Arizona. You see, we need to be close to the industries that—"

"Ah, yes, I thought as much. You Americans have a way of assuming your country is best in everything. However, may I point out that there are other deserts which would be better suited? Also, if we must build this instrument of death, its construction could benefit the poor people of the country in which it is located. Of course, it is most understandable that you should want this benefit to fall like gentle rain upon the Americans, instead of on the less materialistic and poorer peoples of the underdeveloped world, but—"

"Oh, for Christs's sake, Addie!" Hobbes interrupted.

"Ah, yes, the esteemed prime minister of Great Britain, the nation which found our mother India in peace and prosperity and left her impoverished. Where do *you* think this gun should be located? On the moors in merry old England?"

Reed raised his hand in protest. "Gentlemen, please! We mustn't waste time with private jests!"

Rene Molinière said, "Mr. President, why not build the gun in the Soviet Union? You yourself said they have the technology needed to construct the reactor."

Kroner applauded.

"The winter's too harsh—"

"Oh, but monsieur—"

"The Gobi would be ideal—"

"Only the socialist nations of the world have the discipline necessary to put up such—"

The voice of Wakefield Hobbes cut through the din. "None of this makes any bloody difference! You can build your damned gun on top of the Andes, for all I care. But there's something more important that you haven't even mentioned."

"What's that, Hobbes?" Reed asked.

"Who's going to *pay* for the bloody thing?"

"Why, we assumed we'd share expenses, basing the amount on our gross national product."

Swaminathan shouted, "Aha! Just as I thought! You Americans want the poor people of the world to pay the bills while you reap the benefits."

Reed smiled thinly. "Mister Swaminathan, you misunderstood me. Because of the recent economic difficulties of India and of the People's Republic, we believe the costs should be borne entirely by the other nations repesented here today. India and China were invited as a courtesy."

"Really, Mr. President, there's no need to be so condescending."

Again everyone spoke at once.

"Why *shouldn't* the Indians and Chinese pay their share? They're forever telling us what first-class nations they are."

"You can take your gun and shove it!"

"Don't expect England to pick up the tab for your damned gun, sir!"

"It's only fair that the United States should bear the full expense. They're the ones who angered the invaders by shooting down a saucer!"

"Oh, this is all nonsense anyway! Invaders! More of Nilstrom's quackery."

Reed rapped on the podium. "Gentlemen! Please! Let me speak!"

The President paused, waiting for quiet. "Gentlemen, our differences are ancient, but the menace we face now is without precedent. The decisions we must make are hard. You've heard the unanimous recommendation of the scientists. The plan calls for sacrifices, and success is uncertain. But it's up to you. The U.S. can't destroy the fleet alone. Whether the people of the world will die, or have a chance to survive, depends on you. And you must decide by tomorrow morning, before you leave Wake Island. Each delegation can meet tonight. The scientists will be available for questions at any time. May we have your decisions as quickly as possible? This meeting is adjourned."

Chris remained seated. He looked at the delegates, standing, stretching, conversing. He saw Swaminathan sneering, Hobbes rolling his eyes, the Russians impassive. The time called for giants, and the room was filled with mediocre men.

The other scientists joined Nilstrom at the front of the room.

They waited and watched as the leaders talked, talked, talked. None came to consult them.

Finally, when the last delegation had left the hall, Solovyev sighed and stood up. "It's obvious no one wants to hear from us. I must join the Soviet delegation. Wish me luck."

Chapter 5

As CHRIS neared the housing compound, it was eleven o'clock and most of the lights were out. His walk took him directly past a house he recognized too late as that of the Indian delegation. Before he could correct his path, he heard the foreign minister's acid, high-pitched, whining voice. Suddenly a weary voice interrupted, "Oh, Addie! Shut up!" Chris grinned.

The building where the U.S. delegation was gathering loomed white against the black night. Its windows were ablaze with light that struck the sand in golden rectangles. Large, one-storied, and made of stuccoed-over concrete blocks, it had once served as the lounge where airline passengers whiled away the hours between flights. In recent years it had become a community center for the few people who remained on Wake.

Chris mounted the steps and crossed the wooden porch to the door. His steps echoed loudly, and he heard the talk inside subside into silence. When he entered, those who looked up saw that he was not a courier and returned to their drinking and chatting.

He walked toward a group of scientists at a low, round, Formica-covered table. The German astrophysicist, Otto Weber, dressed in white slacks and a loud, Hawaiian-style sport shirt, waved a cocktail glass and said, "Oh, Chris! Come join us while we wait!"

Nilstrom smiled at the heavyset man and sank into a soft chair. A waiter appeared at his elbow. "I ought to order coffee if we're going to be here all night. But what the hell, give me a gin and tonic."

With Weber were Hiroshi Shigemitsu, Marie Monnet, Hao En-Ching, Alex Baumgartner, Narihari Raychandbhai, and Robert Moore, head of NASA.

"Any word, Bob?" asked Chris.

"Yeah, India, China, and Japan have enlisted, and Marie says the French are ready, but want to talk to the Germans."

"Anything from the English and the Russians?" Chris addressed his question to the whole group.

Shigemitsu, the energetic director of the Osaka observatory, said, "Not a word. I'll bet that sonofabitch Hobbes is holding things up."

Hao, the astrophysicist from Communist China who spent as much time as possible away from his homeland at scientific meetings, said softly, "Hobbes would have been a superb prime minister—in 1880!"

Their chuckles were suspended at the sound of steps on the porch. Molinière and Kroner entered together and walked directly to President Reed. Chris could tell from their hearty handshakes, that they had voted to cooperate.

Two to go—the most difficult, England and Russia.

Weber saw his concern and said softly, "Ah, Chris, relax. They will both agree. What else can they do?"

Marie Monnet chided, "Otto! You are so rational! Always you think others will be the same. But Hobbes? Or Grigorenko? Who understands them?"

Hao said, "I'm not sure Grigorenko's still the power in Russia. That Byacheslav and the old man, Semyechkin! Typical Russians—stupid and stubborn."

Baumgartner took the pipe out of his mouth. "Ah watched them Russians at lunch and ah got a hunch the strong ones are Solevyev and that li'l Larin woman."

Shigemitsu leaned forward. "We know Solovyev is with us. Maybe he can pull Larin along."

Again, there were footsteps on the porch and everyone looked toward the door. Wakefield Hobbes entered, followed by his delegation.

Raychandbhai whistled softly. "The distinguished prime minister looks as if he has just been bitten by a cobra."

Chris watched Hobbes with foreboding. He looked furious, all right.

Chapter 6

WAKEFIELD HOBBES *was* furious. He had just been through the worst experience of his life.

Up to now, Hobbes had had a meteoric career. An M.P. at twenty-five, he became prime minister in his late thirties. Labor had almost bankrupted England by demanding higher wages and more welfare than the nation could afford. Just as the country realized its mistakes, Hobbes appeared with a brilliant gift of speech and a colorful personality. He offered the solution of harder work, fewer giveaway programs, and more initiative in industry.

Hobbes had an arrogant disdain for older politicians, and he looked around at the members of his delegation with contempt.

"Well, now, I hope none of you was taken in by that balderdash about a fleet. It seems a rather obvious trick to lure us into a new world government which the U.S. wants to run." He paused, expecting acclaim.

The foreign minister whom he had bullied for five years, Sir Bernard Powell, stared back with a slightly amused smile. Sir Clement Tillman looked at him with lips pursed in thought. Barnstable and Sir Francis Leonard, Chief of the Imperial Staff, avoided his eyes.

Hobbes then made the mistake of asking for their opinions.

Sir Clement was the first to speak. "Prime Minister, those of us who work with radio telescopy have been aware for sometime that alien aircraft are operating in the world."

"Oh, come now, Tillman!" Hobbes insisted on addressing each of them by his last name to avoid using a title. It stuck in his craw that every other person in the room had been knighted. He was not going to remind himself that the aged queen so disliked her obnoxious prime minister that she resisted every pressure to honor him.

"You chaps can't be serious. You've picked up some damned seagulls on your bloody machine and think it's a space fleet."

Sir Clement's eyes glittered. "Oh, no, you're wrong, you know, quite wrong. Any intelligent person can see it."

Hobbes lunged to his feet, his face engorged with blood. "How dare you—"

"Oh, sit down, Wakey!" Sir Bernard interrupted. "Let's do be reasonable—hard as that is for you."

Hobbes whirled. "Damn you, Powell! I made you foreign minister in spite of your obvious lack of brains, and I can—"

Sir Francis held up his hand in remonstrance. "Gentlemen! We have a difficult decision to make, and no time for personal feelings."

In the three years that Leonard had been chief of staff, Hobbes had never heard him speak so many words at one time. Before Hobbes could regain his aplomb, Leonard turned to the others.

"All right, what do you chaps think? Should we cooperate with the Americans? Sir Clement? Righto. And you, Sir Cecil? You too, eh? Sir Bernard? Ah, that makes three, and you can add me for four. Makes a majority, doesn't it?"

"God damn it, Leonard, I am the prime minister of Her Majesty's government, and I am not going to let two addlepated scientists, a senile foreign minister, and *you* vote to spend a billion pounds on a crackpot scheme."

Sir Bernard interrupted again, this time very quietly. "Oh, now *really*, Wakey. Of course this will cost us money. But what's the alternative? We've got to get on with it. If you refuse, we'll do it without you. And you know, Wakey, I don't think Commons will be as blind to the facts as you are. It'll be the end of your brilliant career. Now, what do you say? Are you going over there to tell the Americans that we want in, or am I?"

Chapter 7

THE GROUP around the scientists' table had grown. Stehlen, dressed in slacks and a baggy sweatshirt, his youthful face with hardly a whisker to mar it, had pulled up a chair, and Barnstable and Tillman had broken away from the politicians to join them.

Sir Clement rubbed his hands together. "Well, Chris, everybody's signed up except the Russians, eh?" His voice was high-pitched and almost singing with excitement.

"Yes, Sir Clement."

"Now, now, Chris! Don't be so formal. Call me Clem."

"Okay, Clem. But the Russians are indispensable. Without Solovyev, we're lost."

"Any chance we could build our own blasted reactor?"

Nilstrom turned to Barnstable. "What do you think, Sir Cecil? Can we do it without the Russians?"

Barnstable's voice was a deep, mournful bass. "No, Dr. Nilstrom—uh, Chris, if I may—in short, no."

Then we just have to hope they come through."

At one o'clock, President Reed asked to talk to Nilstrom privately.

"Chris, we've been discussing the organization of the project, and we all agree that you must be the scientific coordinator. What do you say?"

Nilstrom scratched his beard and lowered his head. Always ambitious, he had hoped he'd be chosen for the post. Now he thought about Mike and Susan, and how much time he'd be away. But he had to be honest and admit that if he refused, he'd only spend his time wondering how the project was going. "What can I say, Mr. President? I accept. Who's going to be political chairman?"

"It's got to be a Russian, of course, if they join us. Probably Valuyev. Another possibility is the woman, Anna Larin. She's young, but people who know her well say she's brilliant, and certainly she knows the western countries."

Chris felt his body grow warm at the thought of Anna. The president looked at him slyly. "You could work with that little beauty, couldn't you, Chris?"

Nilstrom grinned and cocked an eye at Reed, who winked. Then Reed sighed. "Damn! It's one-fifteen. You know, Chris, it's ironic."

"What's that, sir?"

"Right now the future of the world depends on an eighty-year-old man who is half senile."

It was three-twenty before they heard steps on the porch. Many of those in the lounge were dozing. Chris jumped to his feet.

The door burst open and Semyechkin entered, then turned

to hold the door for Anna Larin.

The moment Nilstrom saw Anna, he knew the Russian meeting had been a disaster. Her face was drawn and her eyes were red from crying. She hesitated, searching the crowd, and the pain in her face sealed his sense of doom. Then she saw Reed, walked quickly to him, and burst into tears. Instinctively the dumbfounded president reached out and took the lovely woman in his arms. Semyechkin watched grimly as Reed patted her on the shoulder and said, "Now, now, we know you did everything you could, Miss Larin."

Anna sobbed inconsolably. "It was my fault! If only I'd— Oh, Mr. President, I have terrible news for you—for the whole world." But she couldn't continue. Her back was turned to Nilstrom, and he could see her thin shoulders shaking.

Everyone in the room felt like weeping with her.

Chapter 8

THE OLD chairman had awakened late from his after-dinner nap and had taken time to bathe and have a cup of tea before settling into the big, soft chair. "Oh yes, we must talk about the American proposal, mustn't we?"

He smiled sweetly and nodded for the meeting to begin. For a moment, everyone moved uneasily. Finally, Solovyev said, "Comrade Chairman, I'm only a scientist and I'd have a hard time reducing the intricacies of politics to equations, but—"

Valuyev quickly picked up the ploy and laughed loudly, winking at Grigorenko and Anna.

Nobody else laughed.

"Umm, well," continued Solovyev, "we have to decide if we should cooperate. Now, personally, I think that—"

Byacheslav could restrain himself no longer. "We know

what you think, Comrade Solovyev. Now it's time for you to be silent and let us who are older and wiser speak."

Valuyev saw Grigorenko's head nod slightly at the words "older and wiser," but he leapt into the conversation. "Come now, Comrade Byacheslav! We must listen to the scientists. What do we know of radio telescopes and thermonuclear—"

"I know enough not to be taken in by Americans!"

Admiral Varsonofiev nodded vigorously. During the Second World War, he had almost been decapitated by a piece of shrapnel, and the effort required to speak audibly exhausted and frustrated him. Now his voice was little more than a hoarse croak. "I agree! Never trust Americans!"

Valuyev was perspiring heavily and his soft face was deathly white, but he rushed on, "Comrades! Have you forgotten that our own radio telescope found the fleet exactly where the Americans said it would be?"

Byacheslav roared, "I have not forgotten that Comrade Solovyev *said* they found it there. Neither have I forgotten that he conducted the probe without even informing his chairman."

The physicist stubbornly shook his head. "You're not looking at the facts."

Byacheslav snorted. "Facts? Ha! Radar is notoriously unreliable. Shall I tell you the times I've been alerted by air defense because radar shows a strike of missiles on their way? And if radar isn't dependable at two thousand miles, why should we trust it at thirty-five billion?"

Solovyev grimaced. "Comrade Marshal, everyone knows that radar within the atmosphere is much less dependable than in deep space. Also, what of the non-random radio noise? It's obviously an intelligent message. You saw the analysis."

"Non-random noise! How many times have scientists solemnly proclaimed they were receiving messages from space? Shall I remind you of the furor over pulsars?"

"That was different, comrade, as any physicist or astronomer can tell you. There's no possibility of mistake this time. You saw the amplified pictures A fleet of more than a thousand ships is on its way."

Admiral Varsonofiev croaked, "Those pictures were made by Americans." His voice deserted him. He swallowed hard and whispered, "What could be easier than to doctor pictures? I tell you, this is a scheme to get our reactor. Ask Papa Bear."

They all turned to the old man. He was sound asleep.

"Comrade Chairman!" Byacheslav barked cruelly.

"Urmph! Let us come to order and . . . uh, where were we?"

"Comrade, this cub, this scientist, has been urging us to trust the Americans."

The old man frowned and, under the white eyebrows, his blue eyes stared at something in his past. The others waited for him to speak.

"Trust Americans?" His voice was gravelly and distant.

"Yes, comrade! The cubs have forgotten the past. But we do not forget, do we?"

The old man blinked in confusion. "Comrade, we suffered so terribly. The tsar's soldiers killed my mother and father, our whole village. But we beat them! Then the Americans came, with the British and the French and even the Japanese. Always people try to invade Russia."

The others were staring at him, but he no longer saw them. Anna leaned forward and said tenderly, "Papa Bear?"

He looked up, and she saw that she could not depend on him. Relentlessly, senility was closing in.

"Anna, *we* know, do we not? Trust? Ha! Never turn your back! Tell nobody your thoughts!"

Everyone was aghast. They were witnessing the crumbling of a legend. Anna had tears in her eyes as she looked frantically around the room, wanting the conversation to stop.

But Byacheslav was ruthless, his face hard and his eyes bright. "Comrade! You yourself brilliantly perceived that the Americans want our reactor!"

Grigorenko seemed to emerge from his confusion. In the ruined brain, a few connections clicked once more.

"Yes! They want our reactor!"

Byacheslav pushed his advantage. "Aha! As always, our beloved chairman sees the truth! They want to destroy us. They already have attacked us with their saucers—"

The little man shook his snowy head in bewilderment. "The Americans attacked us? I didn't think they would do that. What will we do?"

Byacheslav smirked. "Do not worry, Comrade Chairman! We will rebuild our armed forces."

"Yes, yes! We must not let them invade Russia!" The old man paused and tears ran down his wrinkled face. "So many have died—so many! Now the Americans . . ."

Byacheslav leered triumphantly at Solovyev and then at

Valuyev. "It's settled, then!" He looked around smugly. "The answer is no."

Anna waited for Valuyev to speak, but saw that he had lost his nerve. He sat motionless, his puffy mouth open, his huge eyes staring. She looked at Solovyev.

The physicist was as gray as a Russian winter sky. But he took a breath and said firmly, "Comrade Chairman, we are deciding the fate of humanity. You must have a vote."

Byacheslav was beside himself. "A vote! Why? Our chairman has spoken!"

"I insist that you take a vote!" cried Solovyev.

The old chairman lurched to his feet, his blue eyes blazing, his face contorted. "You! You dare to challenge me? I am Papa Bear! *I* have voted. That is enough."

He was breathing hard, and he staggered. In all the years she had known him, Anna had never seen him so wild. He was living inside his own senile consciousness. Something in him had snapped.

He turned to Anna, chuckling deep in his throat. Then he bent and took her face in his hands, and his voice was filled with affection and pride. "Anna Kornilyevna! Darling Anna! Go now, and tell the Americans that Papa Bear has spoken! *There will be no reactor in their Mistletoe.*"

He turned, his eyes fixed on Semyechkin, and smiled again. The sight of his old friend—stupid but unfalteringly loyal— gave Grigorenko new strength.

"And you, dear Mikhail Nikolyavich, go with my Anna. Tell the Americans that Russia will live! And there will be no reactor for them!"

Chapter 9

PRESIDENT CARL REED continued to hold Anna in his arms and to pat her back with his big, suntanned hand. The room was quiet except for her sobbing. Finally she got control of herself and stood back, facing Reed and the others. She glanced once at Semyechkin, standing awkwardly beside her.

"Mr. President, gentlemen, it is my terrible duty to tell you that the chairman of the party, premier of Russia, first secretary of the secretariat, the greatest Russian who ever lived, is *dead*. Fyodor Grigorevich Grigorenko is dead! And it was I who killed him."

"Anna Kornilyevna!" The white-haired chief of the KGB stepped forward and put his huge arm around her slender shoulders. "You must not reproach yourself! It was not *you* who killed our great Papa Bear; it was old age."

He lifted his eyes to the bewildered group. Quickly he related the events of the meeting. "Then, when our chairman instructed Anna to tell you Russia would not cooperate, this girl, who loved her Papa Bear too much to let him make a decision that would make him the destroyer of the world, said, 'No, Papa Bear. You've given us freedom. We will vote!'"

"And Fyodor Grigorevich staggered backwards—and then he died. A stroke—or a heart attack.

"We were all in shock, but this little Russian thornbush immediately demanded a vote. Byacheslav and Varsonofiev voted in the negative. Valuyev and Anna voted affirmatively, and—"

Anna interrupted, "And this good man, feared falsely by so many, this man who loved his Papa Bear as much as I, voted affirmatively! Russia has joined the human race! But you must all remember that although Fyodor Grigorevich was too old and had lost his understanding, it was his spirit that guided us.

"Now Comrade Semyechkin is chairman of the party and premier of Russia, subject to confirmation in Moscow. Comrade Solovyev will go to America with you. I—I will accompany the body of our Papa Bear back to Russia. And because it was my words that killed him, I will retire from public life!" Again her big eyes filled with tears.

Semyechkin said, "Anna, Anna, console yourself! You did *not* kill Papa Bear. At the lunch table he was brilliant, but tonight when I awakened him, he was confused. The stroke had begun. If you had said nothing, he would still have died."

Carl Reed said, "Friends, a great man has died, and another has caught his spirit and will lead his country. There is no time for grieving. Anna Kornilyevna, even before tonight you had won our love and respect. But now you have conquered us. Earlier this evening I said to a friend that the fate of the whole world hinged on one eighty-year-old man. I was wrong. He had finished his work. The fate of the world depended on one young woman. Anna, you cannot quit now. You must come to America immediately. You are to be the political chairwoman of Mistletoe."

Part Three

Chapter 1

SO NILSTROM came to Arizona. He didn't get to see his children. There would be little time for them from now until—until what?

The white cold of Canada and the gold-and-blue heat of Wake Island gave way, within days of each other, to the unrelenting sun of the lower Sonoran Desert. It was winter, so the temperature was tolerable, but there was still the sun. It would not fail them. There were no earthquakes and little rain, and they had the hard sandstone foundation on which to work. They were but hours away from the industries of southern California, and there was a rail line close by. It was almost perfect.

The terrain was rough, as if some great animal had died, leaving its scattered skeleton of jagged rocks and boulders strewn on the sand.

Yet it was beautiful. If one could look past the petrified agony of this world, one saw a beauty shared by no other place. The desert was banded in reds, browns, and pinks splashed carelessly across the landscape. The sky was clear, and at night, frosty stars cast soft shadows across the equally frosty land.

More than one man had fallen in love with the desert. More than a few had died here, as well.

The site was just south of the Grand Canyon, and so isolated as to be virtually in a different world. It was fifty miles from any sizable highway, fifty miles of dusty, rutted roads, now packed hard by the tread of heavy equipment.

Chris had asked the army driver to take him to the site, and he found himself in the middle of a forest of surveyor's stakes, each topped by a fluttering orange streamer. Beyond, he could see the river. And the dam.

When the site on the Bright River had been selected, Nilstrom had expressed reservations about building in what amounted to a riverbed, though there was now only a thin ribbon of water. He knew desert gulches were subject to flash floods. However, he had been assured that the river was fully controlled.

Like most dams, this one was large, a wall of concrete blocking off the canyon. Behind it, for ten miles, a lake had formed, storing energy that the hydroelectric plant converted into electricity. Several miles downstream, the low rock walls of the canyon spread out on the plain on which Mistletoe was to be built.

Bright River had never particularly needed a dam. In a truly practical society, it would never have been built. But the United States was not a truly practical society. The dam was constructed as a pork-barrel project in the fifties, and provided irrigation and power for a widespread area. The project had never been as useful as its backers argued, nor as useless as its critics claimed. But now it would provide much of the power needed to build Mistletoe.

Chris tore himself away and asked the driver to take him back to the tent city. Until the prefabricated apartments and office buildings were finished, they would all be eating, working, and sleeping in tents.

Nilstrom's mind was filled with thoughts of the last few days. Meetings, meetings—one after another. And nothing ahead but more meetings.

General Beck watched as the huge Graser assemblies were wrestled through the nose doors into the cavernous holds of the C-5 cargo planes.

"Those two guns would have filled the last gap in the COR-ADS line. The fact that we're giving them to the Soviets for Novaya Zemlya should make it clear that we're serious."

Diane Mowbray said seriously, "It convinces me. Why, every time you've dictated letters about the Grasers, I've had to shred my shorthand notes. Now we're sending them the whole gun."

Beck smiled down at his secretary. "It's rough to break a

lifetime habit of guarding secrets. But Grasers in Russia could
be a nasty surprise for the two scouts."

Diane's eyes got bigger. "I hope so. I even get frightened
driving home alone, knowing they're up there in the sky."

"We'll get 'em. We've been authorized to use nuclear missiles."

"But I thought guided missiles couldn't get them."

"Diane, a nuclear missile like the Genie doesn't have to be
guided, because it doesn't have to score a direct hit. You just
lob it into the area, and the warhead does the rest."

Beck looked back at the C-5s. The nose doors were closed
and the engines were warming up for the takeoff. The exotic
cargo was hidden beneath the smooth aluminum hull. An idea,
barely noticed, began to percolate in the back of his mind.

"I tell you, it can't work!" Kellogg was shouting. "That's the
problem with the fucking things. The core has to be in one
piece." His face was red and he glared at the others.

Stehlen remained calm. "But Herr Doctor, it's simply not
possible to cast a mass of beryllium that large."

"Shit! Don't tell me about impossible. Nobody had built
Grasers at all till I did it."

"How much of the metal will be required, Kellogg?" Solovyev's question was uttered quietly.

Kellogg was defiant. His feet were planted solidly, his hands
on his hips. "One hundred million pounds," he snapped. He
deliberately gave the answer in English units, thus requiring
the Russian to convert into the vastly more practical metric
system.

Solovyev was unperturbed. He picked up a slide rule the
size of a Zulu shield. "Twenty-five thousand metric tons. And
the melting point of beryllium?"

"One thousand two hundred and eighty-four degrees centigrade." The metric measure was a concession to the speed
with which the Russian had solved the earlier problem.

"I see." Solovyev moved the slide and studied the rule for
a moment. His lips pursed in thought. He moved the slide
again. "Allowing for a slow enough cooling to avoid flaws,
it'll take four point six-six times ten to the eighth seconds to
cool to the point where it can be handled." He smiled at Kellogg.

The American realized he was being challenged. He had

a calculator in his pocket, but he ignored it. He thought for as long as he dared. "One hundred and seventy months."

"One hundred and eighty. Much too long, as I'm sure you'll agree."

"I am afraid, Herr Doctor," interrupted Stehlen, "that the laws of thermodynamics won't bend to your needs."

"But damn it, we can't laminate it! Don't you know what happens when a particle crosses a transition layer like that? What are you going to do when you fire the damn thing and it spurts X-rays all over the place, and melts? Piss on it?"

"Chuck—" Nilstrom was trying to head off what he feared might develop into a major confrontation— "the transition effect only applies to charged particles, doesn't it?"

"Yes, of course, but the intermediate reactions involved in the gamma production are carried out by charged particles, and many of them will have to cross the boundary layer."

"I think, however, that the vast majority of these particles move radially to the central axis," offered Solovyev. "Is that not so?"

"About ninety percent of the motion is radial. The rest—" this time Kellog did consult the calculator— "would be enough to raise the average core temperature to seventeen hundred degrees centigrade. Then we'd have the biggest mess of molten beryllium in the world, and about enough gamma rays to sterilize a butterfly."

Chris was dismayed. It wasn't the problem of the "transition effect" that bothered him; he had expected many such. Men of the caliber of Stehlen, Kellogg, and Solovyev should be able to solve them. But the three had to work together amicably.

Kellogg stalked to the blackboard and began to write. "As I think you can see, the difficulty is exacerbated by the fact that . . ."

Nilstrom was able to follow the notation for about one line, then even he could understand only an occasional equation.

At one point Solovyev stood, wordlessly walked to the board, and corrected Kellogg's work. Chris flinched, but the young American merely growled an obscenity and continued. After a while, Chris realized that the two had worked out a truce, however temporary. He left them three blackboards deep in incomprehensible mathematics.

Chapter 2

FROM BENEATH the frigid waters of the North Atlantic, a scant fifty miles from the edge of the Polar ice cap, the mast of a Russian radar picket submarine broke the surface.

Like many others, it maintained a lonely vigil against the day when American ballistic missiles might come over the North Pole. But it was boring duty. Except for a rare long-distance commercial flight or an American patrol aircraft, there was little to see and even less to do.

But today an echo came, weak at first, then stronger. It could only be one thing: an aircraft, cruising low across this desolate part of the world.

A signal went out from the sub. At the speed of light, it reached the Soviet defense command and was relayed, again and again, to ships and airbases. High over the northern end of the earth, a Foxbat supersonic interceptor banked away from its usual patrol course and turned south. At nearly three thousand miles an hour, it reached the submarine in fifteen minutes, received further directions, and turned again. The plane lost altitude and speed until it was barely sweeping over the gray water. Slowly it overtook its quarry.

Hiding his approach by flying low with his radar turned off, the Russian closed on his target. His gloved hand tightened on the stick. Above him was a silvery disk, floating along at a leisurely hundred kilometers per hour. The pilot made adjustments, flipped switches, and four missiles howled out at Mach 6, relentlessly following the target's rocket exhausts.

For a moment, the saucer seemed unaware of the onrushing threat of death. Then, in a brilliant flash, one missile disintegrated, and another. The third twisted away, its homing device wrecked by the heat of the blasts. The scout had destroyed the first three missiles. Suddenly the saucer disappeared in an incandescent flash that briefly outshone the sun as the atomic warhead of the fourth missile detonated. The shock registered on seismometers as far west as the Reykjavik Geophysical Institute. A satellite high above the atmosphere saw it, and so did NORAD's watchdogs.

But the radar of the submarine showed the fleeing disk. For

the first time since the Second World War, a nuclear weapon had been used with intent to kill. It had failed.

At NORAD, General Beck, who had been awakened from a none-too-sound but badly needed sleep, glared at the big screen. "All right," he snapped, "find out what happened."

The airstrip was finished. Or rather, it would be as soon as the concrete set. The freshly laid asphalt of the highway was still sticky, but trucks would be rumbling in by morning. Work was progressing on the railway link, and already, stockpiles were accumulating at the other end of the line. An avalanche of men, equipment, and material poured onto the Mistletoe site, threatening to inundate them all.

"Very well, I'll see what can be done."

Anna Larin hung up the phone. She swiveled her chair away from the desk so it faced toward the tent flap and out into the blinding Arizona sunlight. She had been in this surprisingly beautiful wasteland that was to spawn Project Mistletoe for only a week, and already a major problem had developed.

The fools in Soviet defense had attacked a scout over the North Pole with a nuclear missile, and had not informed the Americans. This was a breach of the Mistletoe Treaty. The Americans were angry.

Anna had a great deal of mollifying to do. Mistletoe was still too fragile to stand up under its own weight, let alone slay Balder.

"Oh, no! Not on your life!" The sergeant was firm.

Takeo Omari blinked at him and said politely, "Sergeant-san, the orders are from your General Beck."

The burly American looked down at the Japanese. "I don't care what no brass hat says. *Nobody* has access to these circuits. They're the main communications lines with Early Warning."

"I know what they are, Sergeant-san; that is why I must see them. We must install devices that will automatically relay information to the Russians." His voice was silky smooth and conciliatory, but the American wasn't listening.

"You're not going to—"

"Sergeant, the orders are correct. Do as Doctor Omari requests."

The soldier turned and found himself staring up at four stars. "But, sir—"

"That's an order, son." Beck watched as the little Oriental moved behind the panels and tore aside the TOP SECRET seals. He felt a mixture of sadness and apprehension. He remembered when the Japanese had attacked Pearl Harbor, and his father had enlisted the next day. And he remembered reading the words Admiral "Bull" Halsey had spoken as he looked over the smoking ruins of Pearl Harbor: "When we're through with them, the Japanese language will be spoken only in hell."

Nick Beck had long since outgrown such primitive passions, but he couldn't help having a vague feeling that, somehow, by giving the Japanese access to America's most guarded secrets, he was betraying both his country and the memory of that day. He sighed, saw that there would be no further interference, and returned to his office.

Anna's voice was reedy over the long-distance phone. Nevertheless, Acting Premier Mikhail Semyechkin grimaced at her tone, and when he hung up, his ears were still ringing with the faraway voice.

"Mikhail Nikolyavich," he reminded himself, "you're a coward to allow yourself to be bullied by a woman." But he didn't feel any less chastised. The cub had grown up. He felt as if he'd been mauled by a grizzly.

He considered what she'd said. Damn it, to have to tell the Americans everything was a gross breach of national security! He couldn't allow it! He suddenly had an acute awareness of what the Soviet Union had agreed to.

Very well, then. He picked up the phone, but he held the receiver a long time before he dialed.

Chapter 3

NILSTROM, EXHAUSTED from a long day, had finally stumbled into his tent, tossed away his clothes, and fallen into bed. But sleep wouldn't come. In the distance, he heard bulldozers, graders, and trucks working through the night. His cot was too lumpy, and a myriad of thoughts and worries persisted. Every time he closed his eyes, he was back in a meeting. He could see faces as if they were with him in the darkened tent.

He tossed from one side to the other. Words swam around him, words of anger, frustration, dismay, delight. There had been a rash of snide remarks about his appointment from his enemies in the scientific community. Some merely questioned the wisdom of choosing an astronomer to head a project aimed at harnessing thermonuclear energy. Others flatly predicted failure for Mistletoe if he became the leader.

He thought of Mike and Susan, and was surprised at how lonely he was for them. Almost every day he chatted with the two children on the phone and he knew they were well cared for, but he couldn't stop the guilt that welled up within him. His mother's cold disapproval of his having accepted the position with Mistletoe didn't help.

And he thought of Anna. He'd liked the idea of working with her, getting to know her better. But the tidal wave that was Mistletoe had swept them away and hurled them in different directions. When he wasn't traveling or in a meeting, she was. They'd no more than smiled at each other in passing.

Finally Nilstrom gave up trying to sleep, and pushed away the wilted covers. He sat wearily on the edge of the cot, noting the tiredness in his back and legs. He put his head in his hands. He could feel the pulse in his temples, and his vision seemed to sway with every beat of his heart.

He stood and pulled on his shirt and pants, stuffed his feet in his shoes, shoved the tent flap aside, and stepped out.

The tent city spread over the low hummocks and dips in the terrain, covering the ground as far as he could see. The night was bright with the glare of arc lights. Work would not stop because of the inconvenience of darkness. Indeed, come summer, with its burning heat, most of the heavy work would have to be done at night.

He looked up at the night sky, toward 61 Cygni. What kind of beings were they, willing to shoot down airliners, willing to wipe out four billion human beings? Were they the barbarians of space, Huns coming to plunder and enslave? Illogically, he strained to see the mysterious fleet as it implacably, relentlessly approached. He shook his head and looked back at Mistletoe.

The project had developed into more than Chris had bargained for. Scientific coordinator. Could he handle it? He smiled. He'd never thought there was a job that Christian Nilstrom couldn't handle, but this one came damned close.

It was all so confused and complicated and ambiguous. All around, invisible in the desert darkness, lay the defensive perimeter, now little but holes in the ground and piles of equipment. Eventually there would be barbed wire, electrified fences, antiaircraft guns, missile launchers, Graser batteries—the best-defended spot on earth.

All over the world, factories were gearing up to produce the components for Mistletoe. Spurred on by huge bonuses, they hired extra workers, tooled machinery, and girded themselves for shifts around the clock.

There were factories in Los Angeles, Detroit, New York, and Atlanta that manufactured the Graser components; plants in Japan, France, Russia, England, Germany, and China made the mountings, sprockets, castings, casings, bearings, moldings, and myriads of electronic components needed. All would pour into this place.

Here were workers from seven different countries: arrogant Americans, stolid Russians, diligent Chinese, difficult French; English, Germans, Indians. Could they all work together?

Here would be raised a weapon that could scorch the face of the moon or wipe out, if they were correct, an entire invading force. The gun would be a giant cylinder of beryllium, rhodium, and ruthenium surrounded by mammoth cooling coils of liquid helium. Three hundred and thirty feet long, weighing twenty-five thousand tons, it was to be supported by a carriage on giant bearings between two pyramidal towers.

Still on the design boards was a huge geodesic dome five hundred feet high and eight hundred feet in diameter. Surrounding it were to be the tankage complex, machine shops, and depots needed to maintain the Graser until its one big moment.

Beneath the dome, underground, would be the largest power plant ever built, a device to fuse hydrogen into helium at temperatures greater than that at the center of the sun. The core of the reactor would burn at the incredible temperature of twenty million degrees centigrade, a heat that would instantly vaporize any material with which it came in contact. Of course, the core would be contained by magnetic fields so powerful they would warp metal out of shape, or cause eddy currents that would burn out components. The reactor would have to be built flawlessly to work.

So great was the power necessary to fire the Graser that no cable could carry it. Instead, huge copper pillars would conduct the current from the reactor to the gun above.

In addition, this reactor would produce the intense burst of neutrons that would be directed up an airless conduit to the gun itself to trigger a complex series of events, involving the rhodium and ruthenium atoms, that would cascade, in a fraction of a second, into the beam of gamma rays.

This would be their weapon.

In an invisible network all over the world were the watchers, under the direction of Sir Clement Tillman. A hundred radio and optical telescopes squatted in valleys, perched on mountaintops, orbited the earth. They watched and waited, and what they learned was sent immediately to the scientists for analysis and assessment.

Also spread around the world were Nick Beck's hunters, tearing through the air, slipping silently beneath the sea, watching from lonely moors in England, and from desolate Siberian tundras. They all searched for the maddeningly elusive scouts that had to be destroyed.

And there was the conspiracy of silence, the governments of eight nations keeping their terrible secret.

Nilstrom thought of the world's reception of the announcement of Mistletoe. At first there had been stunned disbelief, then consternation among the oil-producing countries, then a gush of excitement as everyone realized that cooperation of the eight great powers meant the end of the threat of nuclear war. And if the project succeeded in developing cheap energy, it was the beginning of a new world-wide prosperity. The enthusiasm of the people was almost pathetic; they saw a new world at the very time that, unbeknownst to them, their very existence was threatened. Other countries hastened to offer their cooperation and assistance to Mistletoe—and were miffed and mystified when their help was declined. If only they knew the awful truth. Chris felt like a phony.

He shook his head, watching the moving lights. Somehow it was going to happen, and it was going to happen too fast for any of them to stop and think about it. They had to plunge ahead with a minimum of reflection and no care for expense, replace finesse with brute force, solve problems by fiscal overkill.

Nilstrom was startled out of his thoughts at the sound of approaching footsteps. With a pleasant shock, he realized it was Anna Larin.

"I'm glad you're still awake, Chris. May we talk?" Her blond hair was hanging loose, and occasionally a strand blew across her face. She wore a skirt of undetectable color, and a sweater was draped over her shoulders.

Chris brought two folding chairs from his tent. "So you couldn't sleep, either?"

She shook her head. "I want to talk. In Russia, they're reorganizing. The people who think freedom is dangerous are on the verge of taking over. Semyechkin is a good man, but he isn't smart. Right now, all that is needed is one little issue, and the door will slam shut again. Many still feel that Mistletoe is a trick. And even those who are with us have distrust very close to the surface. Should anything happen to confirm that suspicion . . ."

"Are you trying to warn me that the Soviet Union could pull out at a moment's notice?"

"*Without* a moment's notice."

Chris reached out and took her hand. "Anna, if things do break down, we'll deal with it. We've got to make Mistletoe work!" It occurred to him how hard it was for her to be there, in an alien land, dealing with the alien subject of science. If his work was hard, hers was much harder.

Abruptly she stood up. "I'm acting like a child. I must go. There's lots to be done in the morning."

"Anna . . ." he began. She looked up at him. Chris had never seen anyone more lovely, and suddenly his lips were on hers. He kissed her hard, and she kissed him back. He pulled her to him, and she put her arms around his neck. The kiss lasted a long time. Finally he let her go.

"Good night, Chris," she said, and she was gone.

Nilstrom returned to his cot, and found that he couldn't keep his eyes open. He sagged back, fully dressed, and instantly fell asleep.

The next morning, Chris woke with crusted eyes and a heavy head. He washed absentmindedly, splashing himself with water, and went outside.

Chris was immediately swept up in the day's work. He left the site early and flew to Los Angeles to consult with a group of engineers. From there he flew to Houston, and that evening, met with scientists at the Space Center. With Bob Moore, he presented the evidence of the approaching space fleet, outlined the plan, and asked them to aim the giant Graser with their computers. There was an exhausting discussion before they agreed that it could be done.

For several days, Nilstrom zigzagged across the nation, leaving a trail of worried but frantically working people behind him. He checked in with Solovyev and Kellogg, who were

temporarily ensconced at Cal Tech. The brash young American
was working feverishly, buried in papers. He didn't even look
up when Nilstrom poked his head in. But Chris noted with
amusement that the blueprint tacked up over his desk included
a laminated beryllium core.

Solovyev didn't appear to be busy. He sat behind a desk
littered with empty paper coffee cups, holding a full cup in his
hands, turning it between his palms as he stared out the window. "Greetings, Chris. Have some coffee."

Nilstrom helped himself from the percolator on the Russian's desk. "How're things going, Dimitri?"

"As well as can be expected. Better, even. I have designed
a new type of fusion reactor; they're assembling the model in
the shop now. It'll weigh barely five hundred kilograms, and
if it works, I'll incorporate the principle into Mistletoe's reactor. The main problem is trying to integrate the Graser con-
cept with the fusion reactor. You see, the firing action is triggered by a stream of neutrons. Doctor Kellogg used the best
existing technology in this country to create a momentary fusion; he called it microfusion. But with our idea, sustained
reactions can be produced."

"Yeah—but, Dimitri, can you get it done in time?"

The Russian smiled wryly, crookedly. "I am trying my best.
But we should be building the housing right now in Arizona."

"And we can't till the other two saucers are destroyed,"
Nilstrom said grimly.

Solovyev nodded. "The real question is whether you can
do *that* in time."

Chapter 4

ANNA FROWNED at her aide. "What now?"

Wordlessly, he handed her a letter. She scanned it quickly.
The Americans had ordered the necessary quantity of beryllium
from a mining firm with an unpronounceable name, located
in Brazil. Like most mining companies in South America, it
had been founded by Americans and then nationalized by the
left-wing government.

The note was brief. The Brazilian government stated that

expenses had increased and, regrettably, it was necessary to quadruple the price of beryllium. They would try to make delivery next year, but it would be impossible before then.

Anna recognized their motives. Here was a chance to make a fortune and force the great powers to dance to Brazilian music.

She stood up. "I must see the president immediately."

Anna flew from the new airstrip to Dulles Airport, outside of Washington, where she was met by a limousine that carried her swiftly to the White House. Anna had become so used to seeing haggard faces that she was startled when she saw the president. He looked fresh and rested. His shirt was clean, his suit bore no wrinkles, and his shoes were newly shined. He smiled when he saw her, and Anna wondered in alarm if she looked as unkempt as the others at Mistletoe. This was another world, and she saw it as a prisoner sees the world outside of his jail cell.

Reed became glum as she briefed him on the situation. Then he said, "They tripled the existing price when we needed beryllium for the original Graser project. Now they want four times that."

"Mr. President, the real problem is that they won't even guarantee delivery. We have to go in and *get* that ore."

"You mean—" The words stuck in his throat.

"Military action, Mr. President. It's the only way. Even if we could convince them to hurry, the negotiations would take too long."

"I don't like gunboat diplomacy."

Anna leaned forward, her face hard. "We haven't any alternative, Mr. President. If we don't hurry, New York, London, Brasilia, all will be heaps of smoking rubble."

"All right, all right! But they'll appeal to the United Nations."

Anna was scornful. "Of course they will. Sanchez will have to stall them. But what are they going to do? All the major powers are in Mistletoe."

Suddenly there was a bemused, cynical smile on Reed's face. "What the hell, it'll be a relief to kick somebody in the butt." He sighed. "Power can be exhilarating, can't it?"

She said nothing.

The president swiveled his chair. "Will the others agree?"

Anna shrugged. "What choice do they have? It's better for

us to invade Brazil than—" she raised her eyes— "for those 'people' to invade earth."

"Our first truly international cooperative project, and already we're at war," Reed said bitterly.

Relentlessly Anna corrected him: "Our first cooperative effort *is* a war."

It was January, the rainy season in Brazil. The grasslands around the open-pit mines were damp and sticky. The warmth and swarming insects added to the air of general discomfort.

The attack came suddenly. One moment, the sky was featureless gray; the next, it was speckled with paratroops dropping around the astonished miners. Resistance was too disorganized to be anything but brief. The troops were hard-nosed Soviet veterans flown from Cuban staging areas, and defense of any sort was quickly gone amid the harsh coughing of Russian assault rifles.

The sizable Brazilian Air Force responded quickly. Their orders were incoherent, but all the pilots needed to hear was the improbable and intolerable statement that Russian troops were on their soil, and the planes were off, in twos and threes, streaking toward the mines.

Lieutenant Enrico Ferrara and his wingman took off before their engines were fully warmed, and the little American-made F-5 Freedom Fighters climbed sluggishly away from the airbase. They headed out over the jungle, not waiting for the others.

It was all over before Ferrara realized anything had happened. His wingman was suddenly gone, a falling mass of flame. Ferrara jerked his little fighter around, switching off the cannon safeties. Their assailant was still there—a huge aircraft now turning toward him. Ferrara leveled off just in time to see a flash of light underneath his plane. His right wing disintegrated. He yanked the canopy release and his ejection seat blew him away from the spinning fighter. Limp with shock, he hung from his chute and looked up at the enemy. The big twin-tailed fighter swung away and headed for the coast, and Ferrara gasped in disbelief. On the jet's side, instead of the red star he had expected to see, was emblazoned the white-on-blue of the United States Navy.

Chris Nilstrom saw the headline as he hurried down the airport concourse. He stopped dead in his tracks, fumbled in his pockets, took the newspaper, dropped coins in the outstretched hand of the newspaper vendor, and hurried to the waiting plane. It was not until he was in the air that he had a chance to read it. Well, at least it explained why Anna had left the project site so suddenly. And now they'd have all the beryllium they needed.

It was significant that he, the scientific coordinator, hadn't heard even the slightest hint of what had been about to happen. No rumors had carried the startling news. It was a strange situation, he mused, when truth outran the swiftest of all social phenomena, rumor. And Anna surprised him. He had had no idea she could be so ruthless. He smiled. Somehow it made her even more exciting.

Pedro Sanchez was a soft-looking man with a continually bland expression. But he was an old hand at press conferences, accustomed to bright lights and probing questions. Nevertheless, this time he blinked at the reporters crowding around him as if this were all a new and bewildering experience.

The United Nations was in tumult, facing what many said was its worst crisis, and was certainly its bitterest disappointment. Of the one hundred and thiry-eight member nations, one hundred and thirty had filed formal protests against the joint Russian and American seizure of the Brazilian mine. The statements ranged from sentiments of outrage to uncontrolled hysteria. All demanded immediate withdrawal of the invading forces, a pull-back of the American fleet guarding the coast near the mines, and generous payment of damages.

The eight other nations, those involved in Mistletoe, jointly issued a terse statement defending the action as necessary because of the urgency of the project and the noncooperation of Brazil. Sanchez read the statement before making his own comments.

Sanchez was a practical man. He had become secretary general of a United Nations shot through with dissension. The United States, miffed at being outvoted by Costa Rica and Lichtenstein, had been ready to withdraw its massive support. The Russians sat sullenly in the background, watching the myriad of small nations happily vote in whatever resolution they wanted. Although the achievement was not widely recognized, Pedro Sanchez had saved the United Nations. He had mollified the big powers and quieted the little ones. He was a man of compromise and agreement, and he disliked force.

He was an expert at wheedling and cajoling, at ass-kissing and back-scratching. He was the best secretary general the United Nations had ever had.

"Ladies and gentlemen, the sovereign nation of Brazil has been suddenly and brutally invaded by the military forces of the United States and the Soviet Union, in blatant violation of every precedent of international law. I cannot condemn this action too strongly."

Sanchez paused. The grief he felt at his own hypocrisy filled his eyes with tears. He knew the world would be saying that the reason the eight powers would not let the other countries into Mistletoe was that their cooperation signalized not a benevolent impulse, but an intention to use their overwhelming power to plunder and dominate. The hopes that had been raised so high by the Mistletoe treaty were crashing into the dust. Instead of a step forward into peace, Mistletoe would be seen as a step backward into old imperialist exploitation. Sanchez hated every word he uttered, but he saw no alternative.

"The United Nations has already entered into negotiations to secure the withdrawal of foreign forces from Brazilian soil."

Sanchez knew he would be criticized for that statement. The one complaint about his tenure in office was that he spent too much time negotiating. He always answered that negotiations worked; demands did not. But now he remembered the mildly obscene saying that came out of the United States during the Vietnam days: "If you're being raped, do you negotiate or demand an immediate withdrawal?"

"I would warn the world that negotiations are likely to be lengthy." He could hear the collective groan of the Third World. They were now learning the cold realities of power.

Senator Charles Hamilton was outraged. "My God, Carl, fifty people dead! I find it hard to believe you really did it. It's just like Vietnam all over again."

"I had to do it, Charlie, you know that."

"That's the sort of thing a Nazi would say. Violence is the mark of incompetence."

"Damn it, Charlie, we're fighting for survival! We stand to lose four billion lives."

Hamilton was on the verge of tears. "Carl, can't you see? My God, can't any man in power see? He who lives by the sword dies by the sword. To fight your space invaders, you're becoming like them! Look at the way the people of the world received the news that the eight powers were cooperating in a peaceful project! They were hysterical with happiness! But you betrayed them!

"I'm bound by my congressional oath not to reveal what I know about Mistletoe, but by God, Carl, I'll tell you right now that you'd better stop this insane war of the worlds, or it'll be the end of the human race."

When Hamilton finally left, the president was sick at heart. Charles Hamilton answered to a higher calling than most men, and Reed doubted he'd be able to keep his vow of secrecy. "Higher calling" and "treason" were very close at times. It might well be that Hamilton would see the success—or failure—of Mistletoe from prison. Yet Charles Hamilton, the conscience of the senate, was his friend.

The engineer batted absently at a fly. Rain pounded incessantly on the tarpaulin over his head, and the muggy Brazilian heat made his clothes stick to his body.

"Anything you need," they had told him. "Just get us the ore, and get it fast." But they hadn't counted on the rain that streamed down three days out of four; the pit was always full of water.

He stood up and went to the edge of the lean-to that served as his office. Momentarily he gazed at the huge encampments that housed the Soviet troops. He scratched a mosquito bite and turned back toward the pit. It was a giant gash in the earth, full of heavy equipment trying to wrest the ore free from the mud. How to keep it operating in this weather?

"Anything you need," they had told him. Well, then, why not put a geodesic dome over the pit, one big enough to cover the vein they were working? He ran some figures through his head. It would have to be damned near eight hundred feet in diameter. He scratched another bite. They had said "anything." Hell, he couldn't be shot for asking.

They were as good as their word. The dome was up in weeks. The mining proceeded. What the miners didn't know was that the dome under which they worked was identical to the one planned for the Mistletoe site in Arizona.

It was to prove an invaluable similarity.

Chapter 5

CHRISTIAN NILSTROM shuffled through the photographs. Each was a picture taken from LOOTS. December seventeenth. February third. February twenty-fourth. March twelfth. In each, the dots of light were brighter, bigger, farther apart, closer to earth.

The fleet was less than a year away, and the two scouts were still untouched. How many times had jets arrived at a sighting, afterburners screaming, to find only empty sky?

Yet they couldn't proceed with the most important part of the construction until the saucers had been destroyed.

It was late, terribly late.

For the first time since the inception of Mistletoe, Nilstrom felt panic.

Chapter 6

COLONEL ROBERT WIMMER was suffering. All his life, he had hated Communism. He was convinced that war with the Russians was inevitable, and that military service would therefore provide him with both a career and a fine opportunity to fight for his convictions. And here he was in the Soviet Union, helping them install an American made Graser!

The colonel considered the gift of the Graser nothing less than treason, and he had an intense battle with himself over whether he should obey his orders or resign. Finally he decided that giving the Russians such a secret weapon probably meant the U.S. had developed a much more devastating one.

The work was almost complete, and soon he could go home to Upper Sandusky. For that, he was glad. He hated the intense cold on the island of Novaya Zemlya, the Russian nuclear missile center. Also, because of Soviet suspicions, U.S. technicians were restricted to a small part of the island. Their quarters were drafty wooden houses carelessly built by indif-ferent Russian workers, just where the forest met the tundra.

Colonel Wimmer's Russian counterpart, Colonel Viktor Ivanovich Sobolev, had no better quarters. But the Russian didn't seem to mind the cold. He was a round man with resigned eyes, a big belly, and thick, soft hands, who fortified himself against the arctic cold by repeated tugs at a flask of vodka. His offers to share the antifreeze treatment with Wimmer were archly refused, and Sobolev was informed that no American officer ever drank on duty. The Russian only sighed.

This morning they were walking together toward the concrete structure where the nuclear reactor was being assembled when they heard the sirens. The noise seemed to come from everywhere, from their own compound and from the hills around them. Instantly, Colonel Sobolev dashed for the safety of the building, pulling at the arm of the taller American. "Hurry, Colonel! That's no drill! We're under attack!"

As they ran, they saw a streak of smoke from an antimissile missile. Then there was another streak, followed by the explosion of the first missile, and then the second.

Wimmer lost his footing on the frozen ground, and fell heavily. The Russian turned to help him. But Wimmer was staring at the sky in disbelief. Before Sobolev could see what the American was looking at, an explosion knocked him flat, and the deafening sonic boom crushed them to the icy ground.

The saucer that had flashed out of the sky disappeared almost as quickly as it had come, leaving the squat building where the Graser was housed a mass of flames and rubble.

Sobolev struggled to his feet and pulled Wimmer up, screaming in his ear, "What was that thing?"

Wimmer was still stunned. "It—something flat— and it threw fire!"

Together they stumbled toward the heavily reinforced concrete building. Everywhere, soldiers were running, Russians and Americans, out of the barracks, into the woods. Wimmer saw three bodies near the ruins of the gun building. The smell of burning flesh turned his stomach.

The two colonels made it to the reactor building and wrenched open the heavy metal door just as the saucer attacked again. The whole structure shook under a giant hammer blow. The lights went out, and pieces of concrete tumbled from the ceiling and walls, but the building did not collapse. Designed to withstand devastating blasts, it had defied the fireball.

Sobolev lowered his head and bolted down the stairs into the subterranean depths. Wimmer turned and ran back toward the forest, running until his lungs ached and his legs cramped. Again he slipped and fell. Overhead the huge saucer hovered, only fifty feet above the ruined base. Terrified, Wimmer watched as it moved to a position directly over the reactor building. Suddenly eight pillars of fire erupted from its underside, and the saucer shot upward at incredible speed. Wimmer saw the fire roll down over the building and out across the ground toward where he lay. He died just before the reactor building exploded with an intensity that stripped branches off trees half a mile away.

Chapter 7

THE DOOR to Chris's brand-new office opened without warning, and Anna entered. Chris was on his feet at once, alarmed at the urgency or concern in her face. But it was more than that. It was terror. He took her hand and led her to one of the four soft chairs grouped around a coffee table in the corner of the room.

"Anna, what is it?"

"A courier just arrived from Moscow. After the destruction of the Graser at Novaya Zemlya, the secretariat met and there is a movement to take us out of Mistletoe. Varsonofiev and Byacheslav still maintain that Mistletoe is a trick to get our reactor."

"Oh God, I thought that we had that settled."

"They say the Americans only went through the motions of giving us a Graser, then destroyed it with their saucer."

"What are they going to do?"

"The secretariat has called a meeting for tomorrow, and has ordered Dimitri Petrovich and me home. I think the Soviet Union will withdraw from the project and keep us both in Moscow."

"Anna, I know they won't hurt Solovyev, because they need him. But what about you?"

Anna reached for a cigarette in the box on the table, and Chris lit it for her. Her hand was trembling. She blew out a cloud of smoke and closed her eyes. Then she inhaled again, and slowly exhaled. When she opened her eyes, she was calm. "It could mean a return to the old days of midnight arrests and the Gulag. My father died there, and for me it could be the end too. But that doesn't matter, if only—"

"Stop it!" Chris stood, pulled her to her feet, and crushed her in his arms as he said fiercely, "It matters to *me*! My God, Anna, we've been here almost three months and haven't had ten minutes alone. I can't let you go."

"Oh, Chris!"

For a moment they stood silently wrapped in each other's arms, and then she lifted her face and they kissed, tenderly at first, and then fiercely. The crisis was blotted out in a rush of passion. His hands moved over her tiny body, slid downward, pressed her close. She gave a little cry and her tongue darted into his mouth, her hands gripped his back, and she moved her hips against him.

The buzzer sounded on Chris's desk. He ignored it. It sounded again, longer this time, a power saw cutting through their moment of happiness. He went to the desk, pushed the button on the intercom, and snarled, "What the hell is it?"

There was a second of silence before his stunned, proper, middle-aged English secretary answered, "General Beck and Dr. Solovyev are here."

Virginia Ackerman was a plump, hard-working, capable secretary from London who despaired of Chris. She had always worked for methodical English officials, and she disapproved of Nilstrom's unorthodox ways. She wanted to run an orderly office and to schedule his time carefully. She pouted when he came and went without taking her into his confidence, and the harder she tried to keep track of him and the more she scolded him for his independence, the more he struggled to evade her motherly guidance.

Chris swore now, then said, "Thank you, Virginia. Send them in."

Anna was straightening her hair as the two men entered.

Solovyev was slack, and grayer than usual. The general was stooped and his uniform was rumpled. He looked closely at his friend. "Sorry, Chris. We didn't realize you had anyone with you. You've heard the news."

"Yeah, Anna was just telling me."

Beck and Solovyev slumped into the cushioned chairs. The lanky scientist sighed. "Chris, Anna, I'm not going. Mistletoe must not depend upon the vagaries of Soviet politics. It has to succeed, and without me it can't."

Anna nodded her blond head. "It's right for you to stay, Dimitri Petrovich. But I have to go. I'm a member of the secretariat. Chairman Semyechkin needs me. He is really alone. I doubt Valuyev will be of much help."

Resolutely she stood up, looking pathetically small beside the three men who rose with her. "The courier said the plane that brought him was waiting for us. I'll get my things."

She stepped to Solovyev and took both of his hands in hers. "Dimitri Petrovich, I'll tell them you can't leave for at least a week. By that time, something will have been decided. Do not return under any circumstances unless I return for you. Do not believe anything anyone else tells you, or anything I myself say to you over the phone. Do you understand?"

Tears fell from the scientist's gray face, and he took her in his arms and hugged her. His only words were a choked whisper: "Anna Kornilyevna!"

She turned to Beck. "General, get those saucers! It could make the difference in Moscow."

He shook her hand, then put his arm around her shoulders. "We'll try, Anna."

Anna faced Chris and then went to his arms in an unabashed lover's embrace, kissed him, and leaned against him for a moment as she gathered her courage. Then she walked firmly to the door while the three men watched helplessly. There she turned and said, "When I get done with those old men, they'll wish they'd never sent for me!"

She opened the door, and turned back one last time. "Chris, you really should shave off that beard. It tickles!" The door closed.

For once, Beck's voice didn't boom as he said respectfully, "Chris, you old son of a gun, you've met your match!"

"My God," Chris said, almost to himself, "The least I can do is to see her to the plane. I—"

But Solovyev reached out a hand and caught him. "No, leave her alone. She must show no fear. She must play the game all the way."

The men sank back into their chairs. Finally the Russian asked, "What's the latest on the fleet's progress?"

"Right on schedule," growled Chris. "The larger ground observatories should pick them up any day now. Houston tells me they're still headed right for the sun. They'll have to make a major course correction, probably in January, to reach us. It's already the end of March, but I can't allow Stehlen to start work on the Graser mount or the reactor till the scouts are destroyed. The attack on Novaya Zemlya demonstrated that."

The buzzer sounded and Chris pushed a button on the intercom. "Yes, Virginia?"

"Sergeant Kaminski is here, sir."

Beck leapt to his feet as the secretary opened the door. "Come in, Arnie, old buddy. Have you got those pictures?"

Kaminski, looking embarrassed, handed Beck a large envelope. He'd never gotten used to being treated as a friend by the four-star general.

"Our satellite got these of Novaya Zemlya," Beck said as he laid the photographs out on the coffee table. "The bastards wouldn't let any of our people investigate." He was talking so loudly the overweight Englishwoman gently put her hands over her ears and closed the door.

Chris whistled at the pictures. "No plasma gun could do that to a concrete building. He must've used his exhausts."

Beck roared, "Goddamnit, we've got to get those saucers!" He slammed his fist on the table, scattering the photographs. Kaminski gathered them up and inserted them in the envelope. "Thanks, Arnie," Beck said sheepishly. "That'll be all." Kaminski nodded and slipped out the door.

" Nick, there's got to be a way to get those damned scouts!" said Chris.

But now the general was thinking. Nilstrom, waited, glancing at Solovyev. When Beck spoke, his bulging eyes were bright. "Look, the way we got the first damned saucer was when it flew right down the cannon's mouth, right?"

"Yeah."

"Okay, then we've got to get them to do it again."

"Fat chance, Nick. Those guys have avoided the Graser line like the plague."

"I know, but we've got to make them think we don't want them around so they'll be sure to come."

"Nothing will lure them over the Graser line."

"Yeah, but look, Chris, aren't those new mini-Grasers ready?"

" I don't know."

"I do, General—uh, I mean, Nick. Doctor Kellogg just got back from the arsenal." Solovyev smiled painfully at his mention of Kellogg.

"Good. Are any actually finished?"

"Yes. All but the power source."

"Okay, then maybe my idea will work! When they loaded one of the standard Grasers into a C-5 for the flight to Russia, I was amazed at how it was dwarfed by that huge hold. And I got an idea."

"Okay, let's hear it."

"We'll load one of the new mini-guns in a C-5 with the muzzle pointed out the door. Then I'll get the saucer to fly right into it."

"Good God, Nick! What about the reactor? Have you any idea how much one of those things weighs?"

"That's where I need you two. The other day I saw a couple of the small thermonuclear reactors you made, Dimitri. Those damned things are *little*! Let me hook one up to a mini-Graser and I'll blow that saucer out of the skies."

Chris looked at Solovyev. "What do you think?"

"Let's get Kellogg in here."

The four talked late into the night, and before the meeting broke up, they had agreed to try Beck's plan. The general immediately placed a call to Semyechkin. The chairman was relieved to hear that the Americans were still trying to get the saucer, but also frightened that his opponents would somehow seize on this as one more chance to bring about his doom. Finally he asked, "Where will you set your trap, General?"

"It's got to be over Novaya Zemlya, Mr. Chairman. The bastards know we tried to install the first Graser there, and they'll be watching for another attempt."

"When will you come?"

"Within the next forty-eight hours, sir. I'll pilot the C-5 myself."

Beck called the president and got his approval. Then, still full of energy, he hurried off to his own office.

Nilstrom, Solovyev, and Kellogg wearily left the headquarters building together. Before they parted, Solovyev said, "Chris, sometimes I don't believe that your general is real. He's like something . . ."

"Something out of a musical comedy?"

The Russian nodded, smiling, and he and Kellogg left for their apartments.

Nilstrom looked up at the sky. There was so much light from

the site that he couldn't make out 61 Cygni. Such a pale and insignificant little star! Yet from it a fleet was coming that would turn every city into smoking ruins like the Graser site on Novaya Zemlya. He wondered if a thousand giant spaceships would simply girdle the globe, fire their rockets, and cause all of earth to burst into flame at once. He had a sickening vision of Mike and Susan lying in the charred ruins of his Madison home.

"Stargazing again? Weather's better this time, isn't it?" Nilstrom almost jumped out of his skin as Beck came up behind him.

"Time for bed, Chris. We've got a lot of work ahead of us. And Chris, I have a razor if you—"

"Nick, you son of a bitch!"

Chapter 8

MAJOR ORMAND WILLOUGHBY looked down at the frozen sea. They had come a long way. Their short stopover at Murmansk had helped a little, but still he was stiff and sore. Not that Orm had done all the flying himself; he had shared it with two other pilots including, of all people, a four-star general, the commander of NORAD! Nothing about this mission made any sense, but his surprises had just begun.

General Beck came into the cockpit of the giant cargo plane, took the microphone, and ordered all crew members into their arctic clothing and oxygen masks. "Okay, Major, I'll take the controls now—for the rendezvous."

"Rendezvous, sir?"

"Affirmative, Orm. Look around you."

Willoughby looked out. He saw nothing at first, but then he looked down and to the left and almost fainted. Coming up from below were over a hundred Soviet interceptors. Then Beck was on the radio, and Willoughby listened with incredulity. He couldn't understand a word. Beck was speaking Russian.

"General Zakharov? Beck here. Any sign of the bogie?"

"No sign yet, General Beck."

The Soviet interceptors moved into formation above and below the cargo plane. Soon a flight of fighter-bombers appeared and took positions directly behind the C-5.

Beck spoke into the microphone, this time in English. "This is General Beck. I'm going to open the cargo doors. The hold will fill with frigid air. Be prepared for a sudden reduction in airspeed."

"Sir! We'll crash!"

"Negative. We had the doors specially adjusted so they can be opened eight inches while in flight."

Beck flipped a toggle switch. The plane, huge enough to ferry light tanks, shuddered as if it were going to come apart. Airspeed dropped precipitously, and Willoughby was sure they would fall from the sky, but they continued to fly. He looked out at the Soviet interceptors and fighter-bombers. All had lowered their flaps to slow their speed to that of the lumbering cargo plane.

The cockpit where they sat was sealed and the temperature drop was not significant, but Willoughby knew frost would be covering everything in the hold. How long they could fly in that impossible state, he didn't know. But ice could mount to the point where it would cause them to crash.

"Beck to Zakharov."

Willoughby flinched, reflecting that the general's voice was so loud he hardly needed a radio to communicate with the Russian.

"Zakharov here."

"Shall we move to phase two?"

"Roger."

Major Willoughby understood nothing of the conversation, but he saw what happened next. The dim glow of the arctic morning was suddenly punctuated by hundreds of lights as every Soviet plane turned on its landing lights. Then there was an earsplitting sound on the radio as all the pilots began to talk at once. The sound vanished when Beck switched to a different frequency.

"For Christ's sake, sir, what are we doing?"

"Well, Major, we want the bogie to think these fighters are protecting us because we're important. So far, he doesn't seem to have noticed that we exist. We're trying to raise a racket so he'll attack."

"A bogie in the middle of the Russian arctic?"

"Affirmative."

"But who would dare attack a hundred fighters? The Chinese?"

"Negative. A flying saucer. And the fighters won't worry him; they're just to catch his attention."

The radio crackled in Russian, and Beck was immediately alert.

"Beck! Zakharov here! Bogie at thirty thousand meters, closing at four thousand knots."

"That's our boy! Good luck, General!"

"You too!"

"I'm about to turn on the laser. General, remind your men that they must not fly through the beam! The second it's broken, the cannon fires automatically."

"Roger."

Beck spoke to his crew. "In a few seconds we'll be under attack . . . my God!"

Suddenly the huge plane was rocked with an explosion. The saucer shot by.

"Beck! He got one of our fighters!"

"Move to phase three, General!"

"Roger. Are you damaged?"

"Negative. Where's the bogie?"

"He disappeared into the clouds above at one o'clock."

Major Willoughby watched in disbelief as the Soviet planes, flying close to stall speed, closed ranks around the C-5. It was as if a blanket covered it above and below.

"Beck!" Zakharov screamed from the radio, but there was no time to react. The saucer suddenly appeared in front of them, coming directly at the armada, directly in front of the lumbering cargo plane. But the formation was too tight. At the last second, the saucer rocketed up and over, so fast it was little more than a flash of light.

"Good God!" shouted Major Willoughby. "The son of a bitch is crazy to fly like that."

"Beck! There he is! Insolent pig!"

Beck and Willoughby looked around frantically. The invader had circled and was now hovering at eleven o'clock, a thousand feet above them.

"Flight forty-two, follow me! We shall teach him to fear Soviet airpower!"

General Zakharov's plane and three other fighters streaked toward the spacecraft. The saucer moved away, pulling the four planes after it.

"Negative, Zakharov! He's setting a trap!"

Even as Beck shouted into the radio, the dim sky was illuminated by a tremendous explosion as the four interceptors
disintegrated at once.

"General Beck, this is General Metkov, second in command. I'm going to make a massed attack on the bogie. He
cannot evade all our missiles."

"Negative, General Metkov, it's a trick! Hold your positions!"

But the Soviet interceptors pulled away, eighty planes in
attack formation.

"Damned fools! They're doing exactly what the saucer
wants. Now we'll never get him in front of us."

The flight of interceptors had vanished when Willoughby
cried, "General Beck! Bogie at twelve o'clock high!"

Beck swore and jerked the big plane into a steep climb,
trying desperately to get the nose aimed at the saucer. He
shoved all throttles forward to keep the behemoth from stalling.
The gigantic engines screamed with the effort of keeping the
plane at the impossible angle.

"Sir! this isn't a fighter! You're going to stall her!"

A second was all Beck had before the saucer would be upon
them. He roared in frustration and jerked the stick further back.
The monster plane stalled and began to fall backward. The
saucer was on top of them, huge and silver against the black
cloud behind it.

And it flew directly into the path of the laser.

Instantly, the Graser fired. A blue beam cracked out of the
cargo plane and struck the alien dead center. The blinding flash
of the exploding saucer washed over the C-5, and pieces splat-
tered against it, piercing the cockpit window. The force of the
explosion and the recoil of the Graser threw the mammoth
plane, already stalled, over on its back, and it fell, twisting
and turning, toward the frozen sea below.

Orm Willoughby was momentarily dazed by the shock, and
stunned by the icy air blasting through the broken window.
But he reached for the control wheel. Beck, his face covered
with blood, was slumped forward, and the young major fought
the weight of Beck's body, pushing the unconscious general
away to free the controls.

The aircraft shuddered as human hands tried to bring its
suicidal plunge under control. The engines shrieked. The white

sea, jagged with its ice covering, loomed ahead, but at last the big plane was no longer spinning. Luckily, the C-5 did not fall as fast as it ordinarily would have. With its doors ajar, air rushed into the cargo compartment, slowing the plane slightly, giving Willoughby the extra split-second he needed. The wings moaned under the unaccustomed strain and threatened to snap off, but the plane leveled out.

Then the aircraft was under control again and airborne, climbing to safety.

Willoughby breathed. He looked around. The plane didn't seem too badly damaged. The cold air rushing through the cockpit was like a lance. But it was bracing, and it brought the unconscious general to his senses.

Beck dabbed at his bloody forehead. "Orm, did we get the sonofabitch?"

Major Ormand Willoughby looked across at his chief. "We sure did, sir, we sure did."

Chapter 9

WHEN ANNA stepped out the door of the Soviet jet transport at the Mistletoe airfield, she was disappointed not to see Chris. But she saw Beck, with a bandage on his forehead, and So-lovyev, and a shorter man. She waved happily and started down the stairs toward them.

The field was in utter turmoil. A dozen clattering bulldozers were still gouging out the earth, and clouds of dust blew across the desert. Trucks brought loads of asphalt to be laid and flattened by huge roadworking machines, and a score of fat cargo planes were being unloaded.

Anna picked her way through the chaos toward Beck and Solovyev, and it wasn't until she stood before them that she recognized Chris. He had shaved off his beard. She was as-tonished to see how much more youthful and handsome he looked, but she threw her arms around the gangling general.

"Oh, Nick! Congratulations!"

Beck grinned over her head at Chris, winked, and kissed her on the cheek.

Smiling, Anna turned to Nilstrom and held him at arm's length. "Chris! You look beautiful!" She gave him a warm embrace.

"Dimitri Petrovich! We have won! Thanks to Nick, Mistletoe is saved, and so is Russia. And I have news for you, Dimitri. Your wife has been assigned here as chief computer technician. Look, she's coming now."

The scientist had bent to kiss Anna, but his face froze and the eyes he lifted to the plane were filled with dismay. Chris noticed the change, and turned to see the woman who was approaching.

Olga Solovyev was attractive. Of medium height, she had broad shoulders, an exceptionally full bust, and a remarkably small waist. Her hair was pulled into a tight bun on the back of her head, which gave her sharp-featured face a tense appearance. Her small mouth was thin-lipped.

Chris said quietly to Anna, "You know, it's against our policy to permit spouses here."

Her answer was almost a whisper. "We won back there. Byacheslav and Varsonofiev have retired, and Valuyev was made first deputy premier. But we had to make concessions. Olga Solovyev is from a powerful Moscow family, and she is a friend of many of the old guard. The Soviet Union was entitled to fill this position, so, to placate the opposition, she was appointed. I didn't dare oppose it."

Dr. Solovyev had walked forward to meet his wife. She offered her cheek, handed him the coat she carried, and said, "Oh, Dimitri! You're not still wearing that jacket! I told you months ago to get rid of it. It's a good thing I've come."

Then she was standing in front of the others, and Chris could feel her dynamism—as well as the tension between her and Solovyev.

"Anna Kornilyevna," she said, smiling, "my husband lacks the social grace to introduce me to these gentlemen, so I'll have to depend upon you."

"Madame Solovyev, may I present General Nicholas Beck of the United States Air Force—"

"Well, really, Anna, I didn't think he was of the *Soviet* Air Force!" She put out her hand to Beck, who bent over it awkwardly. "So you're the famous General Beck who shot down the saucer. Very brave!"

"Thank you, Madame Solovyev."

She laughed. "Please, General, call me Olga. All my friends

do." She turned abruptly to Chris. "And who is this handsome man?" She extended her hand.

"Doctor Christian Nilstrom, Olga. Scientific coordinator of Mistletoe."

"Oh, really? I do hope I'll be working with *you*, Doctor."

Anna answered firmly, "No, Olga, you'll be working under Herr Stehlen." There was a trace of emphasis on the word "under."

Olga had not yet released Chris's hand, and he noted that her handshake was as strong as a man's.

As Soviet soldiers in green tunics with red epaulets brought the luggage from the plane to their limousine, the five climbed in, grateful for the air-conditioning and a respite from the noise.

"Anna, did they find anything of the saucer?" Chris asked.

"You haven't seen the report? I'm embarrassed! I asked that it be sent the moment it was completed."

Solovyev interjected, "If it's like most of the cooperation we've had from the Soviet Union, we'll probably get it after the fleet has arrived." The bitterness in his voice startled them.

Olga laughed. "Darling! You mustn't let your disappointment over my coming make you say such things."

She turned to the others. "Please don't be embarrassed. Dimitri and I gave up on our marriage long ago, except for convenience sake. Mostly *his* convenience. You see, I used my influence and position to push him in his career, and then when he—"

"*Please*, Olga!" Solovyev's face was a mask of anguish, his voice raspy.

"You know it's true!" she snapped. "*I* made you what you are!" Abruptly she turned to Anna, and her voice was again silken. "Darling, if you're having trouble, why don't you let *me* make the request?"

Anna never changed her expression, but there was disdain in her words. "Thank you, Olga. I will if I need to."

She turned to Nilstrom. "Chris, I'm sorry you haven't received the report. I'm sure it will come soon. So far as I know, they found nothing new. But there was enough to convince the military that the saucer was extraterrestrial in origin."

"Well, thank God for that."

The limousine pulled up in front of the headquarters building and Chris, Beck, and Solovyev got out. "I suppose you ladies will want to go to your quarters . . ."

But Anna stepped out of the car, asked the driver to take

her bags to her apartment, and said to Nilstrom, "I want to get right to work."

The four entered the low building together, and Beck and Solovyev went directly to their offices. Nilstrom unlocked the private entrance to his office and stood aside for Anna to enter, then closed the door quietly so that his secretary wouldn't know he had returned.

Anna was again dressed in light blue, which brought out the color of her eyes and made her hair look even more startlingly blond.

"Oh, Anna, I thought I'd never see you again." He took her in his arms and they kissed passionately.

She ran her hands over his smooth face, and laughed happily. "You look so young without your beard, Chris, and so handsome."

They kissed again, and Chris reveled in the feel of her body. "Anna, since we've been here, I've been so caught up in this damned project that—well, now it seems to me that however important Mistletoe is, we ought to find some time for ourselves."

"Oh, yes!"

Again they kissed, and Chris's hands roamed hungrily over her beautiful, eager body.

The buzzer sounded on his desk.

"Damn it, Virginia heard us. If I don't answer, she'll come in."

Anna laughed. "We have work to do anyway. But let's save the evening for ourselves."

"Good. We'll go to Phoenix for a decent dinner."

She slipped quietly out through the private door as Chris answered the buzzer.

"Dr. Nilstrom, Dr. Scripps of the Rand Corporation has been waiting for half an hour to see you, and—"

"Oh, yes, Virginia, show him in."

The secretary brought Dr. Scripps into the office, and waited to talk to Nilstrom. She frowned as she saw him wiping lipstick from his face with his handkerchief.

"Hi, Phil, sorry to keep you waiting. Just got back from the airport. Sit down."

But Virginia stood her ground, pursed her lips, and said, "Dr. Nilstrom, I have a great deal of correspondence which must—"

"Yes, I know, I know." He glanced at his watch. "I won't have time to work on it today."

"I'll be glad to work tonight."

"Oh, no, I don't want you to do that. And besides, I'm busy tonight."

"Oh? I didn't see any appointments on your calendar."

"Oh, no, it's personal."

She sighed. "Then I'll come early tomorrow morning and—"

"No, I may be late. Virginia, you can answer most of that mail yourself. Just save the ones you absolutely can't handle, and I'll get at them tomorrow afternoon."

"Your whole afternoon is scheduled, and after Dr. Scripps leaves today, you have an appointment with Dr. Kellogg. And Mr. Boyle wants to talk to you about labor disputes. Dr. Robinson wants you to call him, and MIT has called about—"

"Okay, okay, I'll see Kellogg. I'll call Bill Robinson tomorrow afternoon, but now I want to talk to Dr. Scripps."

When they were alone, Scripps laughed. "My God, Chris, we're on the verge of a space invasion, and secretaries still think they should run things. Why do you put up with her?"

"Because however motherly she is, Phil, she's efficient, loyal, and hard-working. And I know I'm a difficult guy to work for, so what the hell. I take it you've read the reports I sent you, so you know what we're up against?"

"Yeah. How can Rand help?"

"Well, we feel we're on the right track, but we need some thinking done, and we just don't have time. You've read my contingency study?"

"I thought it was superb, Chris."

"Thanks, but it was cursory. We need someone to study what we know and see what can be found out about these bastards. What do they look like? What are their physical characteristics? What would life be like on their planet? What are their ships like in appearance, in shielding, in armament, in mobility, in power? In short, tell us all you can about what we're up against. You know, Phil, sometimes, at night, I find myself staring up there and imagining that fleet, their thermonuclear engines spouting power as they slow down. I picture the admiral—I call him Balder—" Nilstrom smiled wryly and Scripps nodded his understanding— "on the bridge of his command ship, cracking out orders to those scouts here on earth, ordering them to shoot down helpless airliners and to attack ships at sea. I wonder what his plans are. To launch a thousand thermonuclear missiles at us from a billion miles in space? Or to wait until he's in orbit and sear the earth with his exhausts? What's he after? What kind of a man is he—if I can even call him that. Is he a new Viking king, plundering one planet after another? A Genghis Khan who loves butchery? A Tippoo Tob looking for slaves? Or a Cortez or Pizarro wanting gold and territory? Maybe you can find their weaknesses . . ."

Late that afternoon, Chris left the project site for his first evening of relaxation and pleasure since the 747 had crashed in Denver four and a half months before. He and Anna drove a convertible across the desert to Phoenix. There they had dinner at Macayo's, Mexican food and Spanish wine.

It was eleven o'clock the next morning before they got back to Mistletoe.

Chapter 10

As THE time raced by, it became more and more vitally important that the third saucer be destroyed. Stehlen had performed wonders of organization, and the whole complicated plan was taking shape, but they were weeks behind on an already impossible schedule, and the failure to find and destroy the last scout was further delaying them. The excavation was finished and the geodesic dome completed, but they could go no further with the actual construction of the giant reactor. Chris even hesitated to have the components of the Graser gun cradle delivered to the site. Yet it was critical that they be finished in time to test the gun at lower powers before the massive two-hundred-megaton shot at the fleet itself. The estimated number of possible test shots dwindled with each week.

Sir Clement reported weekly that the fleet was proceeding precisely as they had anticipated.

On June fifteenth, Chris, Anna, Beck, Kellogg, Solovyev, and Stehlen met in Nilstrom's office.

Shehlen had lost much of his baby-faced appearance in the months of unremitting work. "Chris, we've got to assemble the gun! With the support Grasers now operational and the whole U.S. Air Force to protect us, do you really think the saucer can harm us?"

"Helmut, I'm as frustrated as you are, but if that scout discovers what we're up to, he'll warn the fleet and they'll come into the southern hemisphere, and we won't even get a shot."

"But Chris," Anna asked gently, "aren't they already likely to know what we're doing? Military aircraft coming and going, Grasers installed . . ."

"I doubt it. They probably think we're establishing another defense center, but—"

"Not that it makes a fucking bit of difference anyway," interjected Kellogg.

Chris winced. Nobody had worked any harder than Kellogg, and if any single part of the project would be ready, it would be the gun. But his behavior grew worse with each week. "What do you mean, Chuck?"

"This fucking Russian won't have his reactor ready. I keep pushing the bastard, but it's like pushing a wet rope."

Solovyev looked at Kellogg tolerantly. "Chuck, the reactor will be ready. I may move more slowly than you—"

"More slowly? Shit! You never even move off your fucking ass!" He turned to Chris. "*I'm* on schedule, but is he? Ask Helmut!"

Chris sighed, but his eyes slid over to Stehlen.

The young German shrugged. "Only Dimitri knows what goes into making the reactor. I can only assure him that we'll get the work done once his specifications reach us."

Still unperturbed, Solovyev said, "I've got some new ideas about how we can improve the reactor and complete the final stages of construction more quickly. I don't want to move until I've had time to think it out carefully, but don't worry. I may be a lazy Russian bear, but I think we'll make it."

Kellogg sputtered, "Did you hear that? The sonofabitch *thinks* maybe he'll be ready. The whole world lives or dies by what he's doing, and he *thinks* he'll be ready."

"Take it easy Chuck. This doesn't help any."

"Oh, fuck all of you! I'm going to California for the weekend."

When he was gone, Anna shook her head. "He's impossible."

Solovyev smiled. "Anna Kornilyevna, he does a good job."

Nilstrom took off his glasses and rubbed his eyes. "Nick, have you any idea where the third scout is?"

"It's a big world. He could be in the wilds of Canada, in the jungles of South America, or . . . hell, he could be any-place."

"Well, damn it, isn't there any sign of him?"

Beck slumped down further in his chair. "The only possible lead we've had are those mysterious explosions."

"What explosions?"

"A submarine patrolling the trade routes southwest of Ha-waii reported hearing some small ones. There's no explanation for them. We're checking it out."

"Well, we're going to have to go ahead here soon, whether or not you find him. Meanwhile, Anna and I are going to take a couple of days off and go to Wisconsin to see my family."

Solovyev showed his bad teeth in a grin. "Chuck will say you're lazy."

Nilstrom walked them all to the door, but Virginia stopped him as the others passed her desk and left the office. "Doctor Nilstrom, that reporter from Los Angeles rang twice this morn-ing. He says he has it on the very best authority that this is a project to meet a space invasion."

"Oh shit! I suppose he got to some congressman. Probably Senator Hamilton."

"Will you talk with him now?"

"Hell, no! Tell him all queries are handled by the Mistletoe public information office. Is there anything else?"

"Correspondence, of course—we're weeks behind. And Mrs. Solovyev has come in twice to see you. She says it's urgent."

"Can't she see Stehlen?"

"She says it's personal."

He looked at his watch. He had seldom seen Olga since that first day, but whenever he did, she was eager to strike up a conversation. It took all of his guile to avoid her. But she did have power with the Soviet government far exceeding her actual position, so he gave in.

"Okay, I've half an hour before I have to leave. Call her office and tell her to come in."

When Olga arrived, she was dressed in a low-cut summer dress that revealed her large breasts, unencumbered by a bra. "So good of you to see me, Chris—may I call you Chris?"

"Of course, Olga. What can I do for you?"

"I wouldn't normally bother you with this problem, but this project is so urgent..."

"What is it, Olga?"

"The Russians here are a close group, and I've been hearing things that might jeopardize Mistletoe. I've heard that my husband is having an affair with Anna. Of course, it means nothing to me personally, since I no longer have any interest in Dimitri. But if it's true, and everyone says it is, then it could be dangerous. I'm going to inform Moscow and ask that both be removed."

Chris turned to ice. Obviously she was lying, but why? Surely she knew her husband was so utterly crucial to Mistletoe that even if he had a hundred affairs, it would make no difference. And she must know about Anna and himself. He looked at the smiling woman; her eyes glittered. Suddenly she leaned over the coffee table for a cigarette, and her dress fell away, fully revealing her impressive breasts. She looked up expectantly as Chris reached for the lighter. The movement brought them close together. He lit her cigarette and set the lighter down.

And he knew what she was after.

She said, "Of course, I don't care if people have affairs. In fact, I think it's nice. It's just that I don't want those two to embarrass the Soviet Union. But perhaps I've been too alarmed."

"In the first place, Olga, I doubt if it's true. And in the second, adults like us don't really care how others spend their private time, do we? Unless you're still in love with Dimitri?"

She laughed heartily and leaned forward to tap the ash off her cigarette, giving him another view. "I have no interest in what Dimitri does as long as he's discreet. It's really that little slut, Anna, that I'm most angry about. She's gone from one bed to another in Moscow, Paris, London, and Washington, and that's embarrassing to a great nation."

Now her plan was even more clear.

"Olga, Mistletoe is more important than personal issues, don't you agree? I think it's best not to interfere."

She laughed again, richly enjoying herself. "Oh, you handsome, sophisticated man! You've persuaded me. But tell me something. What do you think of me? I have the impression that you avoid me, and that makes me unhappy because I find you quite the most attractive man I've ever met."

"Mistletoe is a demanding mistress." His choice of words was a mistake.

She was delighted. "Oh, Chris! All work and no play—how is it you Americans say?—make Jack a frustrated boy? You need to relax. What do you do for sex? A man as young and vigorous as you cannot do without sex. I know how hard it—"

The buzzer sounded. Chris flipped a switch.

"Dr. Nilstrom, the half-hour is up and I must see you about some things before you leave."

"Of course, Virginia. Will you come in, please?" But he heard the click of her switch and realized she hadn't heard him. She picked the damnedest time to be discreet!

When he turned, Olga was standing close behind him, breathing hard, her face flushed. Before he could say anything, she reached up, took his head in her strong hands, and kissed him passionately on the mouth, pushing herself against him. Then she whispered huskily, "Chris, come to my apartment tonight."

Nilstrom drew back against his desk and said coldly, "No, Olga, I will *not* be your lover."

She reacted as if he had struck her. She stepped backward, her face dark.

The private door opened and Anna said as she entered, "Chris, I'm ready if—" Her smile faded. "I—I'm sorry. I didn't know . . ."

Mrs. Solovyev laughed, too loudly. "Oh, perfectly all right, Anna, darling. I was just leaving, wasn't I, Chris?"

And she quickly brushed past Anna.

Chapter 11

CHRIS PAID the cab driver who had brought them to his house, and turned to Anna. "Well, it's not exactly a mansion, but it's home."

She looked around at the apple trees flowering in the front yard, the roses just beginning to blossom, the neatly mowed lawn, the other houses on the quiet, curving street.

"Oh, Chris! It's beautiful!" She inhaled the fragrance of late spring.

He picked up their bags, walked to the door, opened it, and stepped in, placing their bags in the hallway. He turned to hold the door for Anna, then he called, "Hey! Anyone home?" The house was silent. "Now, where the devil is everyone?" He entered the living room, muttering something about his gad-about mother.

He froze.

Standing beside the fireplace was a small figure in a silver space suit and a globular helmet. Its hand held an odd-looking pistol.

"Come in, Dr. Nilstrom. I've waited a long time for you." The thin voice spoke deliberately and sounded electronic. The figure waved the gun toward the couch and Nilstrom obeyed, hoping that Anna had heard and was hiding in the hallway. The late-afternoon sunlight flooded into the room through the front window and he was half-blinded, unable to make out any features inside the plastic dome that covered the creature's head. The rays seemed to set the dome on fire, scattering light in every direction.

"You too, lady, come in and sit down."

Anna followed mutely. The voice of the intruder was reedy but full of authority. Yet the creature was small, and Chris decided to jump him at the first opportunity.

Again the voice spoke, slowly, dramatically: "Dr. Nilstrom, you've made me very angry, making me wait so long. Now I'm going to have to kill you."

The gun lifted, pointed at his head. Chris had no time to spring. The figure squeezed the trigger—and a stream of water struck Nilstrom in the face. The spaceman laughed hysterically and, throwing down the gun, pulled off the helmet.

It was Mike.

"That'll teach you to stay away so long, Daddy!"

Nilstrom's heart resumed beating and he laughed and reached for his son, hugged him, and playfully spanked his bottom.

"You little devil, you scared me to death! Where'd you get that suit?"

"Grandpa bought it for me. Isn't it neat? It has a radio in it. I talked to you through it."

"Where are Grandpa, Grandma, and Susie?"

"They're at the grocery store."

Chris introduced Mike to Anna. Smiling, she shook his hand.

"Wow, Daddy," said Mike, staring, "she's pretty!"

Nilstrom winked at Anna and laughed. "Yup, she is—a little pale, but pretty."

Mike led them through the house as Chris showed it to Anna. Nilstrom was proud of his home. Everything in it had been chosen carefully, from the copper skillets hanging over the stove to the Manet prints in the living room. He put on a tape of a Brahms violin concerto and continued the tour into the den, where his books lined the mahogany-paneled walls. The room now also contained some of the children's toys, and a few of his father's murder mysteries were piled on the table beside the soft leather chair.

They were upstairs, looking at his and Kay's bedroom, now occupied by his parents, when they heard his mother call. They followed the racing Mike downstairs and found her placing bags of groceries on the kitchen counter. Chris hugged her and was about to make introductions when Susan and her grandfather came in with more groceries. Chris swept the little girl into his arms and kissed her a dozen times, shook hands with his father, and turned to Anna, who had watched the scene silently.

"Mother, Dad, Susie, this is Anna Larin, about whom I wrote."

Mrs. Nilstrom had been scrutinizing the young woman openly. "Well, Chris, you said she was beautiful, but I must admit I expected a big, muscular woman. Does she speak English?"

"Mother!"

Anna said, "Mrs. Nilstrom, Chris has told me about *you*, too. You are as pretty as he said—though I must confesss I rather expected a big, rawboned midwestern woman." She smiled sweetly.

For a moment, the older woman was nonplussed. Then she burst into laughter and went to Anna, took her into her arms, and apologized. Mr. Nilstrom welcomed Anna warmly, and they all went into the living room.

Susan quickly climbed into her father's lap and began to chatter about nursery school; Mike got his report card to show Chris, and shyly showed it to Anna, too. Chris noted that Anna's eyes were moist. Mrs. Nilstrom excused herself and went to the kitchen to fix dinner. Anna followed, and soon Chris heard them talking recipes.

At the table, Mike said the blessing and was annoyed when Susan corrected one word. The dinner was delicious, and when Chris complimented his mother on the rolls, she laughed and informed him that Anna had made them. Only once during the meal did Nilstrom get lost in thought, but Mike put his hands around his mouth to imitate a microphone and called out, "Earth to Dad, Earth to Dad—are you there?" They all laughed at Chris's consternation.

After dinner, Chris bathed Susan, checked to be sure that Mike had brushed his teeth, and put them both to bed. Downstairs he found Anna and his parents deep in conversation.

When the elder Nilstroms went up to bed, Mrs. Nilstrom firmly informed Chris that Anna was to sleep in his room, and he would sleep with Mike. Chris smiled agreement with her arrangements.

As soon as they were alone, Chris built a fire and they settled into each other's arms on the couch, watching the flames leap from the applewood.

Memories came swimming back to Chris, memories of times when he and Kay had been there, memories of the long, harrowing months as she had weakened and died. Anna sensed his melancholy and said nothing, but only rested in his arms.

Finally he said, "Well, darling, this is my home, my children and parents. I hope you like them."

But she was crying and put her face against his shoulder. He patted her and kissed her hair, and soon she was quiet again.

"Oh, Chris, it's all so lovely. Kay is everywhere—in the decor, in the warmth of your home, in the children. You must have been very happy."

Tears were in his own eyes, and for a long time, the rock in his throat wouldn't let him speak. Finally he said quietly. "We were very happy. And I'm very happy *now*, too." They kissed then, and sat for a long time in front of the fire before going off to bed in their separate rooms.

Sunday evening, as Nilstrom was packing, his mother came to Mike's room and closed the door, pursed her lips for a second, then said, "Chris, Anna is just lovely! Now, why don't you two get married? The children need young parents, not old folks like us."

He tried to explain that it wasn't possible and wouldn't be for several months, at least. Then their taxi arrived, and they said their goodbyes.

Chapter 12

THE WEEKS dragged on. The gun was nearing completion in California, and the complicated aiming system was finally being assembled and connected with the space center at Houston. Solovyev had given his specifications for the reactor to Stehlen, who declared excitedly that the new ideas incorporated in the latest design would shorten actual construction time by three months.

Even Kellogg ceased to be so offensive.

Mistletoe had reached the point where little more could be done except at the site.

But one critical problem remained: the third saucer.

Stehlen and Kellogg urged Nilstrom to have the mount and gun delivered despite the saucer, but Chris steadily demurred. "How the hell can we hide a gun barrel as long as a football field, and a cooling jacket with a diameter as wide as half of that field?"

On August ninth, an event occurred that caused a near-panic and silenced all doubts as to Chris's wisdom. The saucer flew low right over the gigantic geodesic dome covering the open-pit beryllium mine in Brazil. Antiaircraft missiles were fired, but missed.

It was comforting that the scout made no effort to destroy the dome, but it was obvious that the craft had carried out a reconnaissance over the critically important mine. Beck immediately reinforced the defensive perimeters of both the mine and the Arizona site with the new mini-Grasers.

But the saucer had disappeared.

The military forces of the participating countries were on the alert all over the world, but saw nothing unusual. The recurring explosions in remote areas of the Pacific remained unexplained, and Beck became more and more convinced that they indicated the presence of the alien. More subs were sent to patrol the area; each had orders not to surface beyond periscope level, and if the scout was sighted, they were to attempt to destroy it with nuclear antiaircraft missiles or torpedoes.

Days went by, and still the saucer did not appear.

Chapter 13

ON AUGUST thirtieth, Stehlen and Kellogg requested an emergency meeting with Nilstrom.

"Chris, we can delay no longer," said Stehlen. "I've carefully checked all the specifications. It'll be physically impossible to construct the gun if we don't begin installation immediately—tomorrow. We're allowing no time for errors as it is. If a single hitch develops, we won't be ready. Even if we start now and have no unforeseen problems, we'll barely make it."

Kellogg had lost so much weight that he was nothing but bad-tempered bones put together with taut piano wire. "I've been telling you, Chris! We've got to bring in the sections of the gun barrel and cooling jacket."

The weary Stehlen was dressed in green slacks and a polo shirt that was alarmingly loose on his shrunken frame. Now he stood and stretched, saying, "Even there, we have more of an edge than with the reactor. Thanks to Dimitri's innovations, construction time will be shortened, but after what we learned today, I know that we must begin at once."

"What's that, Helmut?"

Stehlen gestured to Solovyev. The tall physicist put down his paper cup of cold coffee. In the months he'd worked on Mistletoe, he'd become bent-shouldered and developed deep lines in his face.

"Today, Dr. Sydney Knox arrived from the Polk Corporation with the final specifications on the shielding for the reactor. They estimate that it will require three times longer to complete than we'd hoped. We've reached the point where we must begin."

Nilstrom was grim. "Okay, begin tomorrow. But at least

let's have everything moved at night, and camouflaged as best we can manage during the day."

Stehlen ran his fingers through his blond hair, and glanced nervously at Kellogg and then Solovyev. He cleared his throat. "Chris, that's not possible. We've waited too long. The gun barrel is on its way, in sections, on trucks. It will be assembled on the desert floor."

Chris groaned, "My God, Helmut! A three-hundred-and-thirty-foot cannon lying out there on the desert in plain sight? A child would know what it is."

"Chris, there are worse problems. In order to install the gun carriage, we'll have to open up the dome."

"And the whole project will be visible to any fool who flies over! Well, if there's nothing else we can do, let's get on with it. I'll alert Beck."

The men were on their feet at once, but Kellogg asked, "Dimitri, did you mention Sydney Knox?"

"Yes, a physicist who used to work for your government."

"*That* sonofabitch! He worked for me on the original Graser project. A smart bastard, but he moaned about the immorality of working on 'instruments of destruction.' He finally quit, and the next thing I heard he was living in a commune studying Tibetan Buddhism."

"Yes, we were warned by your FBI, but we desperately needed more physicists. He only knows he's working on a thermonuclear reactor, and he's performed well."

"Okay, but don't trust the sonofabitch. Never let him know the real purpose of Mistletoe."

Chapter 14

OLGA SOLOVYEV'S efforts to cultivate suspicion of Anna had backfired. It was clear to her that Chris found her repulsive and that he spent nearly every night in Anna's apartment; she notified Soviet authorities, and was told to mind her own business.

She was frustrated by the fact that she'd been unable to find an exciting sexual partner at Mistletoe. After Chris's rebuff, she fumed for a while, then tried to find another man. But the word was out that she was poison, and she was forced to spend most of her free time alone.

She hated having to eat dinner in the cafeteria by herself night after night, then return to her lonely apartment. Now she went through the line, enviously watching the groups of happily chatting diners around her. As usual, she took her tray to an empty table.

She had just picked up her napkin when a voice behind her asked, "Do you mind if I join you?"

The man who stood above her was younger than she by five years, and at least six feet tall. His smooth face was handsome, his eyes strikingly blue, and his long blond hair was combed back in waves over his narrow head. He was dressed in expensive blue knit pants and a smock shirt embroidered with a bright design. The blond hair on his chest protruded from the open neck.

"Please do sit down. I am Olga Solovyev of the Soviet Union."

"And I'm Sydney Knox—of the world." His impertinent eyes left her face and looked frankly down her blouse.

She smiled.

Chapter 15

ON THE morning of September seventeenth, Nilstrom switched off the video monitor and turned to Beck. "Well, there it is, Nick. The fleet is right on schedule. But we're behind because of that damned saucer. You've got to get it! Every day, I expect to see the bastard come screaming in here, firing his plasma gun like a six-shooter."

"Chris, we can't find him. We've set traps, tried to lure him back to Brazil or to take a shot at another C-5. But no dice."

"What about those explosions?"

"We've checked with every naval power in the world to be sure there was no secret operation going on. We haven't come up with a thing, but the explosions continue."

"It's just got to be the saucer."

"I agree. We've thrown in every carrier we have, and armed every patrol plane with nuclear missiles. Maybe a massed attack can get him—if he's there."

That same morning, Pedro Martinez and his son Juan rowed their little fishing boat back toward Huatabampo on the coast of the Gulf of California. They had fished all night and were looking forward to a rest. Of course, they must first sell their fish at the market, but then their beds would hold their tired bodies for many hours.

The shore was still a long way off when Juan's keen eyes saw the strange sight, and he frowned in surprise, thinking it must be a waterspout. But then he saw that it was moving fast, blindingly fast, and just over the water. It was headed north, toward Arizona, and toward them.

He barely had time to scream "Papa!" before it was upon them. It was so close to the surface that its passage through the air created a suction which roiled the water below it, making it appear to be riding a white plume.

It must have seen them; there was no other boat for miles. And then, too, it gave a slight hop as it passed over. Surely the occupants of the saucer knew what would happen to the tiny fishing boat.

In the few seconds between the time when he first saw it and the instant of his death, Pedro Martinez thought the thing was going to ram them. It didn't, but it might as well have. Mercifully, death was quick. The wall of superheated air following the saucer hit like a locomotive, shattered the boat into fragments, and tore the flesh from their bodies.

Days later, the fishermen who found their remains as they floated ashore were sure they were the victims of a shark.

Chapter 16

UNDER THE irascible supervision of Chuck Kellogg, crews were fitting the last sections of the beryllium barrel together. The dome was open, and huge cranes were lowering parts of the gun carriage into the pit.

Nilstrom was still in his office. Following his meeting with Beck, he had again refused to see Boyle, asked Anna to request that Congress pass a law forbidding strikes on the project, visited with his children on the phone, and had just been informed that the television camera providing direct contact with Mistletoe headquarters had been installed in the LOOTS observatory, when all hell broke loose.

Sergeant Timothy O'Leary was in his dugout and, as usual, was bitching about the blazing heat. He hadn't wanted to leave his native Belfast anyway, and only the fact that he couldn't get a job had prompted him to join the British Army. Now look where he was! Arizona! With Chinamen, Russkies, Frogs, Krauts, and Nips! And to be here in the sun, day after day, on maximum alert, with the cannon fully loaded? And for that matter, an old antiaircraft cannon, when everyone knew only missiles were of any value against jets.

What the bloody hell were they supposed to be watching for, anyway? The blasted Mexican Air Force? Maybe an Egyptian bomber? Christ!

Then the air-raid alarm went off and the sirens deafened him as he rushed to his post, wondering if the world had gone mad.

The alarm system was, of course, automatic. The moment the low-level radar first picked up the saucer coming over the Gulf of California and across the border of Mexico, the alarm sounded. Just as quickly, the saucer used its jamming equipment and the radar screen became a jumble of green lines.

Old-style Grasers swiveled ponderously around. The newer mini-Grasers whined and turned more quickly. At the command post deep in the earth, computers tried to sort out the scrambled electronic messages. Batteries of missiles faced south.

But the invader didn't come from that direction. It approached from the dry, jagged mountain range to the north of Mistletoe, hugging the terrain as it had all through its long flight.

O'Leary saw the saucer before radar could sort out the jumbled data and locate it. "Godamighty, what's that?"

Low and fast across the desert it came. The cloud of dust boiling up behind it looked like a writhing snake as the saucer jumped over the site. The speed was so great that nobody saw anything but the flash of it before the sonic boom hit. Few guns fired, and only one missile roared off in futile pursuit.

The Grasers were still humming as they tried to track the twisting thunderbolt.

Then it was gone. But the alarm continued to sound.

O'Leary strained his eyes at the hills, and again he saw it. This time it approached from the east and, in an evasive maneuver, skipped up and down. Beneath it rose a series of dust clouds not unlike a string of exploding firecrackers.

O'Leary ordered his crew to fire. By sheer luck, the shot burst directly in the face of the saucer. For a fraction of a second it hesitated, but then it came faster than ever, twisting more sinuously, presenting less of a target.

"It's coming right over us," O'Leary screamed. "Fire!"

But before a finger could move, the saucer was gone, fleeing over the desert toward the Gulf of California and the safety of its hiding place.

Chapter 17

IT WAS Tuesday the twentieth, and Commander Alan Ainswright was writing to his mother in Manchester, when the seaman knocked deferentially but excitedly on his door. Ainswright always wrote his mother on Tuesday, and it annoyed him to be interrupted. God knew, writing her took full concentration. Their relationship was close, for she had reared him after his father was killed in Korea. At times he sighed under the weight of it, and grumbled that he hadn't even had time to find a wife, since he spent almost every leave with his mother. But he did nothing to change the routine. Out here in the Pacific, he'd have little chance to post a letter, but his mother liked him to write weekly, even if he sent dozens at once.

He put down his ballpoint pen and called to the seaman to enter. The sailor saluted smartly. "Beggin' your pardon, sir, but those bloody explosions? Well, we got another one just now, sir, and not more'n a mile away, sir."

Ainswright hurried to the control room. The seaman at the console spoke as he entered. "Got it, sir! But I don't know what it could be, such a little pop."

Ainswright knew what it was. He had been thoroughly

briefed before his submarine had been ordered to this godfor-saken part of the world. The *Loch Ness* was the latest in a line of nuclear killer submarines, equipped to sit for days or even weeks, silently waiting for the approach of the enemy.

"All right, lads, this is it! Battle stations! Take her up—periscope depth."

The seamen did as they were commanded, but they looked at each other uneasily. Could it be true that they were going to fire a nuclear-tipped torpedo?

Silently the ship rose, listening for more small explosions.

Ainswright watched the console screen, and saw that their quarry wasn't more than a half-mile away. The ship slowed in its ascent, and stopped.

"Up periscope!"

Ainswright had been authorized to fire on the basis of elec-tronic evidence alone, but he felt squeamish about firing the first nuclear torpedo in the history of warfare without even knowing for certain what the target was. It might only be a Japanese fisherman off-course, who was celebrating an obscure Oriental holiday by shooting off firecrackers.

He squinted through the eyepiece. There it was, floating on the surface. There was no doubt. The sea was calm, and only occasionally did the huge saucer disappear from sight as a swell hid it. The thing that amazed Ainswright most was its size. Somehow, even though the briefing had been complete, he had expected it to be small.

"Prepare to fire number one max potent."

The crewmen looked at each other, but obeyed.

"East three-zero!"

The ship silently turned to aim its torpedo tubes. Not that they had to be very accurate, for the torpedo was self-guiding. It could seek a target miles away and follow a twisting, turning, speeding ship or submarine with deadly accuracy.

Of course, a flying saucer bobbing on the surface was an-other matter. Would it hear the approach of the torpedo and escape into the air? Ainswright smiled. The bloody thing had better be able to take off fast, because, at this distance, the torpedo would only be in the water for seconds.

Suddenly he blinked. By George, there was someone on the deck of the saucer. Or was there? With the thing bobbing the way it was, he couldn't make out any details, but he'd have sworn something upright had moved on the surface of the saucer.

The sights lined up.

"*Shoot*!" Commander Ainswright had been in the Royal Navy all his life, and his father before him, and his grandfather before that. But this was the first time the commander had actually fired a shot except in practice.

As the torpedo hissed out of the tube, the figure on the saucer moved quickly, and Ainswright surmised that the craft's sensors had picked up the sound of the missile streaking toward it. But he would never know. The saucer was tossed slightly by a swell, and the torpedo exploded directly beneath it.

A towering geyser of water was hurled into the air and the *Loch Ness* shuddered, bucked, and rolled from the impact. Ainswright struggled to stay on his feet, and gave the command to check for leaks. He straightened his uniform and looked through the periscope again. There was nothing but a huge, drifting column of water vapor.

"All right, lads, take her up."

On the surface they found an azure sky and great heights of clouds to the east, but not a trace of the saucer. For half an hour the submarine cruised back and forth through the area.

Then Ainswright sent a radio message to his commander that the long search was over. For the first time in the history of naval warfare, a submarine had fired a nuclear torpedo in combat and destroyed its target.

Chapter 18

ON OCTOBER first, Nilstrom, Stehlen, Solovyev, Kellogg, and Anna Larin sat in the conference room, listening to the dauntless voice of Sir Clement on the video monitor. He reported that both the Soviet observatory at Zelenchukskaya and the Hale observatory on Mt. Palomar were getting "splendid" pictures. "Hope you chaps are keeping busy out there in the desert," he said. His face was momentarily tense.

Nilstrom groaned. "We're working our asses off, Clem, and are still weeks behind. But at least now that the scouts are gone, we can proceed without interruption."

"Righto. I say, Chris, did you ever find out what those little explosions were?"

"Yeah. You know how soldiers throw grenades into the water to stun fish, then grab them for food as they float to the surface? We think that's what they were doing."

"By Jove! I must say that suggests all kinds of interesting pictures—little green men in marlin chairs on the deck of a bobbing saucer—or tramping the trout streams of Canada." Tillman's vivid imagination drew smiles even from the grim-visaged scientists. "Ah, well, I'll let you chaps get back to work. Cheerio!" The screen went blank.

Chris stretched and rubbed his stubbled chin. "God, I stink! I haven't had a bath or a change of clothes in three days!"

Solovyev stirred from his chair. "Chris, you need a break. Take time out and get some rest."

"Like you do all the time, huh?" Kellogg's swollen red lids lifted from his tired eyes, and he glanced disgustedly at Solovyev. "If you worked half as hard as Chris, we might make it on schedule."

Solovyev looked sideways at the young man on his left. "I've told you before that the reactor will be ready. I've had to make some changes, but each one has saved us time in the long run."

"And each one has fucked me up and made me—"

"You are quite the most disagreeable man I have ever known, Kellogg!"

"Cut it out, you two!" Nilstrom said quietly. "You're both doing a great job and we'll make it."

Anna said, "Chris, I have a problem. Leaks about Mistletoe have sprung all over the world. For example, one of the British soldiers stationed here was granted emergency leave. While he was home, he told about the scout's attack. The *London Enquirer* printed the story and has called me five times asking for a comment. I lied like Stalin, but I don't think they believed me."

Nilstrom shook his head in disgust. "Is anybody as blabbermouthed as the English?"

"Yes, the Americans. I've had an endless succession of calls from U.S. papers asking about reports they've had of the attack. Apparently some congressman has told them Mistletoe's real purpose. May I invite some of the media to tour the site and see the reactor?"

"No. Not with that goddamned barrel lying out there like a big sausage."

"All right, Chris, but I can't keep the lid on much longer. Something's got to be done."

"Anna, the most we can do is confuse or delay their stories long enough to get the shot off." He leaned back wearily in his chair. "Any more business? Okay, the reason I called this meeting was to hear the new Rand report. Phil Scripps should be here by now." He pushed a button and spoke to Virginia.

The dapper Scripps entered immediately and tossed the report on the table, acknowledged introductions, and began. He stated that the Rand study agreed with Chris's estimate that the fleet had been en route for thirty years, and that their method of propulsion was a ramjet engine powered by a thermonuclear reactor.

"The ships are surrounded by a powerful magnetic field that sucks in loose hydrogen ions, which it uses for fuel," he said. "So in the acceleration half of their trip, the faster they went, the more fuel they picked up and the more they were able to accelerate. But now they're *de*celerating. From the brightness of the engines, we can estimate how much power they're using to slow down, and from the rate of deceleration, we can tell how much they weigh. The best estimate right now is that they average a mass of one hundred thousand tons and a length of one thousand to fifteen hundred feet. The ships are probably cigar-shaped, with a narrow tunnel down the middle. Hydrogen is pulled in one end, and light ejected out the other. The spectrum of that exhaust indicates a very high efficiency."

"Which makes it a devastating weapon," interjected Nilstrom.

"Exactly. You saw what the exhaust of the little scouts could do. Well, that's nothing compared to the big ships. We think they could stand off a thousand miles, and enough of the exhaust would reach earth to do incredible damage. They have a weapon there that dwarfs the biggest hydrogen bomb."

"So you don't think they'll fire a broadside of thermonuclear missiles at us?" asked Chris.

"No, we believe they'd rather wait and use their exhausts. Missiles would leave too much residual radiation."

"Okay, go on." Nilstrom lit a cigarette, grimaced at the bad taste in his mouth, but continued to smoke.

"An interesting possibility is that the fleet may be low on fuel. They've been decelerating for about fourteen years, and probably now must rely on fuel carried with them from the beginning. And that brings us to our most important conclusion." He hesitated and looked around at the tired group.

Nilstrom blew out a cloud of smoke and sighed. "I can see you've got some bad news. Better give it to us straight."

Scripps folded his hands together and leaned forward. "Those three saucers you identified and shot down?"

"Yeah?"

"There's no way they could've gotten here from 61 Cygni."

"What?"

"No way. They just couldn't have the fuel capacity. We considered the possibility that they were originally parts of a more complicated ship—for example, that when they started out, they had a huge scoop and even a giant fuel tank, which were jettisoned when they got here. But the more we studied, the more convinced we became that that wouldn't work."

"Then where *did* the bastards come from?"

"Oh, they came from 61 Cygni all right, but not on their own. Someone brought them."

Nobody breathed. Kellogg finally whispered, "Oh God!"

Nilstrom's face was white under the stubble. "Any other reasons for that conclusion—except fuel?"

"The physiological makeup of these guys. We believe their lifespan is no longer than man's. Now, suppose they did come from 61 Cygni in these saucers. They'd have to be mature, thoroughly trained pilots before starting out. Add at least thirty years for the time en route. Then remember your own speculation that they've been here exploring our planet for thirty-five to forty-five years. Hell, at best they'd be senile, more likely they'd be dead.

"So, if they came alone, they had to bring their own supplies and replacement personnel—and the saucers don't appear to be designed for that."

"That's all pretty damned speculative."

Scripps smiled. "That's what you asked us to be. But it's speculation based on facts. And I'll bet my bottom dollar that if you look around up there, you'll find a big mother that brought these guys. Furthermore, I'll bet it has a whole colony of these bastards living on it—women, children, old folks, everybody.

"Our guess is that she's not really a hot-shot warship, but a ferry. Also, she's probably got optical and electronic gear trained on us constantly. She must have sophisticated laboratories capable of assimilating the data the saucers collected."

Nilstrom felt sick. "Then we're sunk. She can tell the fleet what's going on here, even if the saucer didn't. Now for sure, they'll come in from the southern hemisphere. We won't even get a shot at them."

Scripps handed Chris the report from which he had been quoting, and stood to go. He looked rested and almost cheerful, compared to the others. "Well, if they *are* going to come in that way, I can tell you one thing."

Nilstrom's eyebrows rose. "What's that?"

"They'll have to fire their course correction about two days sooner. So if they do that, you'll know they are coming in from the south."

Nilstrom rose wearily and said dryly, "You guys really know how to cheer a guy up. Can't you do another study and decide there isn't any fleet?"

"Sorry, Chris."

"Got any ideas where the mother ship is now?"

"Sure, it's all in the report. She's probably sitting in one of the moon's Lagrangian Points."

"What are—Lagrangian Points?" Anna asked, puzzled.

Nilstrom looked up and explained quietly, "They're points along the moon's orbit where the gravity of the moon and the gravity of the earth cancel each other. A spaceship can coast there indefinitely with no expenditure of energy."

Anna shook her head in despair. "But why hasn't radar picked up this 'big mother'?"

"Well, virtually all antiaircraft or even satellite-tracking radar is short-range. Also, she probably has electronic gear capable of confusing a radar probe."

When Scripps had gone, Chris looked at his silent, immobilized colleagues and said, "We'd better start praying that Senator Hamilton is right and these guys are peaceful."

Kellogg snorted. Solovyev and Stehlen said nothing.

Chris was lost in thought for a few minutes, then he sighed, "I'll ask Sir Clement to look for the 'big mother.' But right now, let's go to lunch. I'm so hungry I can't think."

Chapter 19

OLGA SOLOVYEV and Sydney Knox were having lunch together, as they did every time Knox was at the site. Usually he also stayed the night with her.

Not that they were in love. Each only used the other for a release of sexual tension.

Today Knox had tried to use Olga for more than that.

Sydney Knox had marched with the resisters against the Vietnam war and had seriously considered fleeing to Canada to avoid the draft. However, his student deferment and a high draft number had made such drastic action unnecessary.

While working for Kellogg on the original Graser, he became so agitated that he stole documents and forwarded copies to Senator Hamilton for use in his effort to stop the project. He always took the precaution to mail them in such a way that even Hamilton didn't know who had sent them. When he left his job, and the FBI routinely warned him not to divulge information about the Graser, Knox was terrified and temporarily ceased taking an active part in the antiwar movement.

When Knox was asked to work on Mistletoe, he was elated. It was precisely the kind of project in which he believed— multinational and peaceful in intent.

Then came the rumors, ever more insistent, that Mistletoe was not what it purported to be, along with wild speculation as to its actual purpose. Knox could contemplate with equanimity the slaughter of a million Cambodians by the Khmer Rouge and call it "excesses by the People's Army"; he could accept with sad resignation the butchery of the South Vietnamese by the northerners, but the thought that his own country was engaged in an effort to defend itself filled him with rage.

He had tried to induce Olga to tell him whether the rumors were true. Indifferent to his concern, she told him nothing, and since he wasn't permitted to leave the headquarters area, he couldn't find out for himself.

But today, when Nilstrom and his weary group trudged into the cafeteria, Knox recognized Kellogg for the first time, and the pieces fell into place.

"I know that bastard," he said, nodding in Kellogg's direction. "Mistletoe is building Grasers to destroy visitors from space, isn't it?"

She looked away from his ridiculously hot eyes, toward Nilstrom's table. There sat her husband, on the verge of being recognized as one of the greatest men of all time. But who would ever know that it was she who had made him great? The new masters of the Kremlin cared nothing for what she had done, and Nilstrom had contemptuously dismissed her. Anna ignored her, and Kellogg, the snotty little American brat, didn't even recognize her when he met her in the hall.

She looked back at Knox and said deliberately, "No, Mistletoe is not making Grasers. It's making one giant Graser to destroy the fleet before it arrives."

"I knew it! They're not satisfied with devastating the earth with war; now they want to fight the whole universe." He leaned over, took her hand, and squeezed it. "We've got to stop them, you know."

"How?" She watched his youthful face carefully.

"I'll get in touch with Senator Hamilton. He'll do something."

"He knows about it, but is bound to secrecy."

"Then I'll go to the *New York Globe*. I'll need aerial photographs."

He was hurting her hand, and she withdrew it. "Out of the question." Her words were hard and clipped. "No plane can get within kilometers of Mistletoe."

"I can get some of the soldiers or construction workers to talk!"

She shrugged. "Some have already, but who believes them?"

"I need documents. You have to help me."

"They won't let me near anything important." It was one of her bitterest complaints that she wasn't permitted to see classified documents.

The young man swore. "The people must know about this! A space war, and they aren't even consulted."

Chapter 20

WHEN NILSTROM got to Anna's apartment that night, he still hadn't bathed or shaved, but he carried a change of clothes on a hanger slung over his shoulder.

"Oh, darling, you look exhausted! Have you eaten?" Anna was already bathed, dressed in a soft velour robe, listening to Beethoven's "Emperor" concerto on her stereo.

"I'm too tired to eat. Mind if I shower here?"

"Of course not, but you've got to eat. I'll order a sandwich."

After his shower and a shave, Anna fixed him a drink and watched as he nibbled at the sandwich. Finally she asked about what was now known officially as Big Mother. "If we find her, can we destroy her with a missile?"

He smiled as she pronounced "missile" with a long *i* in the English fashion. "No, her sensors would detect its approach. But when we have the trial shot for the gun, we'll use her for target practice."

Later, Anna was brushing her long blond hair at the dressing table. She wore only a diaphanous nightgown, cut low in back and front. Chris stood behind her.

"My God, Anna, but you're beautiful! Do you realize how long it's been since we've slept together? It seems like an eternity."

She smiled at him in the mirror, continuing to brush her hair. Then she paused. Dressed only in pajama bottoms, he looked frighteningly thin and his shoulders sagged with exhaustion. His face was deeply lined, but she saw something there besides fatigue, and she felt a hot emotion within herself, responding to it. She stood to face him, and the gown did little to hide her shapely body.

"Anna!" He crushed her to him, his mouth seeking hers. His fingers ran through her hair. He kissed her throat, her shoulders, then the gown floated to the floor and her own hand found the light switch.

*   *   *

An hour later, Anna sat up in the darkness.

"Chris?"

"Umm?"

"When this is over, if we survive, what are we going to do? About us, I mean?"

Anna was leaning on both hands, staring at him. He opened his eyes and answered firmly, "We're going to get married."

"Will you come to Russia to live while I work there?" Her blue eyes were gleaming mischievously.

"Oh God!"

"Shall I give up my citizenship and marry you? Will they let me?"

"I don't know. *If* we survive, it'll be a whole new world." He closed his eyes.

"I've never been a mother before. Do you think Mike and Susan will accept me?"

When he didn't answer, she remained silent, staring into the darkness. After a while she said, "Chris?"

He opened one eye painfully. She was still contemplating him, her chin on her hands now.

"Yeah?"

"Your first name—Christian?"

"Umm?"

"Are you one?"

He opened both eyes slightly, and studied her. "I guess so. Used to be, anyway. I even took a couple of courses in theology once."

"You're a scientist and a Christian too?"

"Lately I've wondered if I'm either."

"I think that's nice—to be Christian. In Russia, many people are going back to the Church. They are much influenced by Solzhenitsyn, I think. Once, in Paris, I went to a monastery. And the monks were holding a—what do you call it—vesper service? They sang chants and prayers for forgiveness. I like it. You know? I saw their faces, and they looked happy, as if they felt clean. I did too. Are you listening?"

He made no answer.

She slithered down inside the covers and cuddled close to him. The air conditioning made the room cold.

It was midnight when the telephone rang, and she grabbed it quickly so it wouldn't wake Chris. It was Sir Clement.

Nilstrom sat up instantly and took the receiver from Anna. "Yeah, Clem?"

The Englishman was uncharacteristically grave. "Just heard from Hale Observatory. There *is* a spaceship, the shape of a cigar and as long as a rugby field, coasting in the leading Lagrangian Point. Thought you ought to know."

Chris swore. "Man, have we got trouble."

Anna hung up the phone, and Chris leaned forward resting his arms on his knees, thinking.

"Chris, this is bad, isn't it?"

"About as bad as it could be, Anna."

"What are you going to do?"

"Well, there's only one thing we can do: continue working and hope that Admiral Balder is stupid, I guess."

Chapter 21

ON OCTOBER twenty-eight, a week before it was humanly possible, Stehlen had the enormous straddle-crane ready. It inched out onto the desert along the new track and dropped its hundreds of lines to attach to the monstrous gun, now hideously fat in its cooling jacket.

The crane had sixteen pairs of legs, and was two blocks long and twenty-five stories high. All day, winches strained and cables coiled. With agonizing slowness, the cannon was lifted from the desert floor. Not a single cable snapped, not a hook let go, not a motor overheated. By midnight the gun was safely secured, ready for the trip to the dome where it would be lowered into position. Stehlen decided to wait until morning to start that trip, giving his primary operator, a French naval officer, a chance to rest.

At dawn the next day, when the officer took his place at the huge console of controls in the crane itself, the air was still cool and the shadows were long over the sand. He pushed the throttle forward and the mammoth machine moved. It had almost a mile to go, and it traveled only a few feet per hour. At nightfall, another operator took over. The move was going without a hitch.

* * *

By November first, the gun had reached the dome. There the carriage awaited it, as a cradle awaits an infant. The sides of the carriage were curved, two giant U's, spreading wide open almost the length of the barrel. Suspended between them was the cradle on which the gun would rest. Like most cradles, this one too could rock, but end-to-end, to allow the giant gun to fire high into the sky. The whole structure was mounted on a turntable so that the barrel could be aimed in any direction.

Everything was ready. The carriage worked with smooth precision. Every part had been checked dozens of times.

But now came the critical moment. The crane inched into the area under the dome, straddled the carriage and the great pyramidal towers on which it rested, reached the end of the track, and halted.

On November third, while President Reed, the joint Chiefs of Staff, and their guests René Molinière and Chancellor Kroner watched, the lowering began, quarter-inch by quarter-inch.

By evening, the gun had settled exactly into place and workers swarmed over it like ants to fasten bolts and make welds.

That night, the president hosted a party.

While the party was at its merriest, Olga Solovyev stole into the headquarters building, using keys she had secured from a janitor she had seduced. A guard on regular rounds frightened her before she had found any revealing documents or pictures, and she left undetected. But she cursed her own fear and determined to return.

On November tenth began the process of filling the coolant jacket with tons of liquid helium. It would take three weeks—if everything went well.

The same day, the thermonuclear reactor was tested for the first time. It worked perfectly. That night, Anna had a party in honor of Solovyev to celebrate the successful test of the reactor.

And during the party, Solovyev's wife stole for the second time into the headquarters building. She went directly to Nilstroms's office. In his files she found the pictures taken by the Baker-Nunn camera and some stills of the saucer beside the hapless Delta Dart Interceptors just before they were destroyed.

Using a miniature camera given her by Knox, she made copies. For an hour she continued to dig into the file, photographing more pictures and documents.

On November twelfth, Sir Clement Tillman predicted that if the approaching fleet intended to come into the northern hemisphere, the ships would have to fire directional rockets on January twenty-fifth. With that information, the shot was set for January thirtieth.

The same day, a rally was held in London by space enthusiasts demanding to know the truth about Mistletoe. The Dean of Canterbury sternly warned that man, the most destructive and bloody creature in the universe, would be sorry if he projected his murderous intentions into space. He himself would be destroyed by the superior beings.

A famous Dutch author also spoke and predicted that the "gods" who built the pyramids of Egypt and the statues on Easter Island were returning to accept mankind into the universal brotherhood of space. He warned that any effort to resist the "gods" would end in total destruction.

On December first, the jacket of the gun was finally filled with coolant. There were no leaks, and the gun could be maneuvered with surprising ease despite its heavy jacket.

The decision was made to test the gun on December twenty-eighth—with a low-power shot aimed at the Big Mother.

On December nineteenth, Olga Solovyev again gained access to Nilstrom's office and photographed dozens of his personal documents. The next day she requested permission to leave the compound and fly to New York for a rest. It was denied. Sydney Knox had not been to Mistletoe for several weeks.

Throughout the world, agitation increased for more information on Mistletoe. A world conference on "relations with other worlds" was called for January seventh in Paris. The leaders of the countries participating in Mistletoe talked via conference telephone and agreed to stonewall it, since the date of the test firing was so close.

On December twenty-first, Big Mother vanished. The scientists speculated that her disappearance meant she had discovered the significance of Mistletoe and was hiding behind the moon.

Panicky efforts to install small Grasers throughout the world were intensified, as it now appeared certain that the fleet would approach from the south.

On Christmas day, Senator Charles Hamilton announced his resignation from the senate and declared his intention to tell the story of Mistletoe to the public. He was immediately apprehended by the FBI, reminded of his oath of secrecy, and told that to talk would violate the National Security Act. Reluctantly he agreed to remain silent.

But his sensational statement prompted the news media to step up their efforts to learn the truth. Since it was only five weeks until January thirtieth, the day set for the shot, world leaders continued to stall.

On December twenty-eighth, a serious leak developed in the Graser jacket. The test shot was postponed for three weeks, making it terrifyingly close to the final shot.

On January eighteenth, the low-power test firing of the gun was a success. Big Mother remained hidden, so there was no actual target. The flash of the firing lit up the noon sky.

Data derived from the test firing indicated that the use of two hundred megatons of power for the shot at the fleet would be an overload. In despair, the scientists agreed to use only one hundred and eighty megatons, though it meant they must wait until the fleet was only three hundred thousand miles away.

Also, the firing revealed a possible leak from the magnetic bottle that constricted the plasma inside the reactor. Solovyev checked the entire reactor, and concluded that a simple adjustment would correct the error.

To make sure, he asked the Polk Corporation to test his theory in their laboratory.

On January twenty-third, Senator Hamilton announced that he had begun a fast that he would continue until the government told the full story of Mistletoe—or until his death.

That same day, Polk's head physicist called to say that he and Sydney Knox would arrive on January twenty-fifth with the results of their tests.

Sir Clement Tillman reported to Nilstrom that the fleet still hadn't made a course correction. "So if they intend to come in from the south, Chris, they'd better hurry. They've only got twelve more hours."

Chris looked at his watch. It was noon, time to meet Anna for lunch. At least, he thought, if they did get a chance at a shot next week, Mistletoe was ready.

Part Four

Chapter 1

TOWARD EVENING on the twenty-third of January, it rained at
the site of Project Mistletoe. Clouds like gray ships advanced
across the desert, veils of rain spreading beneath them.

Many times before, those at the site had seen clouds well
up on the horizon only to fade away, sometimes bathing the
distance as they went, sometimes giving no moisture at all.
But this time they bore down on the site in huge, ominous
columns. Following a few preliminary lightning strokes amid
deep-throated rumblings, the rain came, first in leaded drops
that cratered the dust, then in a sweeping downpour.

Workers ran for cover, where they turned to watch the
magnificence of a desert thunderstorm. Inside the dome, technicians looked up through the transparent roof, wondering at
the rivers that streamed above them.

The rain fell for half an hour, and then, as quickly as they
had come, the clouds recoiled as if in apology for the sudden
drenching. The work ground on, for now there were only seven
days until the firing date.

In his office, Chris Nilstrom paused to look at the dome.
In the months since it had been erected, it had become a land-
mark for them all, a signpost by which everyone oriented himself. The dome was a thing of fragile beauty. Now, washed
clean by the rain, it picked up the colors of the desert and of
the sun low in the sky, and, like an iridescent soap bubble,
cast them back in shades of blue and red and purple.

Under the multifaceted surface, Chris could see the deadly
Graser gun, a dark mass hunkered down under the airy lightness
of the dome that sheltered it. It was an awesome sight.

He turned back to his desk. The storm had helped to lift his
spirits, but even more importantly, Kellogg had informed him

today that the gun was, for all intents and purposes, ready. A few days were needed for final adjustments, but they were minor.

Hard on the heels of the storm came the night. The sun gave up its brief return to power, touching the departing clouds with gold and cinnabar. The stars came out clear and bright, though unseen under the powerful floodlights of Mistletoe. The pure electric blue of mercury-vapor lamps replaced the shimmering colors of daylight reflected on the dome, and glistened on the power lines stretching up the canyon to the dam.

Chapter 2

NILSTROM HEARD the sirens with momentary disinterest, and then with profound disbelief. Air raid? What in God's name . . . ? He pushed himself away from his desk, stood up, and turned toward the door, away from the window. The move quite possibly saved his life.

Exactly what happened next had to be reconstructed from the memory tapes of the computer that ran the defenses of the camp.

For several seconds, the computer had struggled with a spurious signal that kept cropping up on the defensive radar. Whenever the beam swept a certain sector to the west, a blip flickered onto the screen, only to vanish almost immediately. Since it was so momentary a phenomenon, the computer did not register it as a real target. Nevertheless, the signal was vexing enough for the computer to call on the human operator for help.

The ghost image quickly proved to be caused by a signal one hundred and eighty degrees out of phase with the signal broadcast by the radar antenna. Thus it had the effect of canceling any echo from a target. But the human operator realized there must be a target out over the desert, and that it was trying to jam the radar. He also knew that no known equipment could cause such a "ghost."

He reached for the alarm button. Humans are smarter than computers, but they are slow. Too slow.

Even as the sirens blasted, the radar reported four solid contacts moving at low altitude over the hills. The Doppler shift of the reflected signal indicated a speed of six thousand miles per hour, heading directly at Project Mistletoe. Missiles!

The Graser batteries swung around to face the threat. The computer aimed and fired them while the startled gunners were still scrambling for their stations. The first shots destroyed two of the missiles, but the others were approaching too fast for the clumsy Grasers to fire again.

As Chris Nilstrom jumped up from his desk, the computer moved way down its priority list and fired a nuclear-tipped antimissile missile.

It was a dangerous choice, but the only one that might work. A cone-shaped Sprint Missile tore out of its bunker, flashed into the sky and, after a moment of hypersonic flight, exploded, consuming a third missile and sending the fourth out of control. The searing ball of nuclear fire killed thousands of toads, scorpions, and lizards on the desert beneath it. The explosion was far enough away to spare the project site from the blast, but not from the blinding light.

At supersonic speed, the fourth missile plunged into the desert floor only a few hundred yards from the housing compound. It penetrated fifteen feet, before the warhead detonated.

The desert burst into flame as the bomb gathered flesh, concrete, and sand and hurled them, white hot, into the sky. In a matter of seconds, more than three hundred human beings flared into incandescence and were gone.

The shock wave surged over the desert like a mailed fist. Chris Nilstrom, halfway to the door of his office, was thrown to the ground when it shattered the windows inward and shook the building into a flurry of papers, furniture, and crockery. He got to his feet unsteadily, his ears ringing and his vision still swimming from the two flashes.

He looked out the glassless window. The dome had ragged edges where whole panels had been torn away from the shining surface, but it stood. Relieved, Chris saw the gun beneath it, apparently undamaged. He turned to the east. It was an eerie sight. The sky was glowing with a supernatural light. The horizon was hidden by flames as a whole section of the residential area of the project burned. Broken gas mains flared.

"My God, Kellogg and Solovyev were over there!"

The desert brightened again as a Graser fired. Chris knew

he should stay inside the building, but he had to see what was happening. He ran out.

Antiaircraft shells burst all over the sky, and tracers arched upward around him. Against the luminescent sky, framed by the shell bursts, a giant, black, cigar-shaped object moved toward the project with frightening speed. For a moment of madness, Chris thought it was a dirigible. But no dirigible ever flew the way this aircraft did. He gasped as it hurtled directly overhead, not more than a few hundred feet off the desert floor.

"Big Mother! It's Big Mother!" Chris suddenly realized he was shouting, but his voice was lost in the deafening din.

The ship was at least three hundred feet long. As it passed over him a Graser fired, and the front of the great vessel disappeared in a flare of white light. It staggered under the terrible blow, but remained airborne. Then it swept around in a turn, seemingly intimidated by the firepower of the project, and roared out over the canyon, rapidly vanishing in the night.

Christian Nilstrom was fortunate to have witnessed and survived the first true space-age battle. And he had seen the mother ship, the carrier for the three scouts.

But the battle wasn't over. Chris threw himself to the ground as the sky was filled with the light of a third nuclear explosion, farther away this time, up the canyon.

Chapter 3

THE OMINOUS blotch of white grew on the big screen. Nick Beck, who seemed to have the misfortune of scheduling his sleep every time a crisis occurred, stormed into the room.

"Status report!" he snapped, glaring at the screen.

The warrant officer at the master console turned to him. The giant NORAD commander was in pajamas so short that a good ten inches of his long legs thrust out the bottoms.

"Atomic explosion, sir, near the Mistletoe site. What we have on the screen is the infrared view. The white areas are heat."

"I see two bombs."

"Yessir, detonated within a few seconds of each other. Both were a few miles from the site."

"Then they're all right? Have you contacted them?"

"Radio is messed up by the blasts, sir. We're still trying to reach them by ground lines. No luck so far."

"What the hell did it?"

"We don't have anything on radar, sir. And the infrared is all screwed up by the blasts."

Indeed, the huge hot areas created by the bursts had disfigured the screen. Around them were pinpricks of the exhausts of jet aircraft converging on the site. They were Eagles and F-106s launched from bases all over the Southwest. Even as Beck watched, a third smear of white blossomed on the board.

"Sir, geographic readings indicate another ground tremor, epicenter in the vicinity of Mistletoe."

Beck stared at the white. A near miss? It was miles north. But it had to be a nuclear explosion, a small one. He felt a twist. If it *were* a miss, then they must be putting up a defense. Yet there was no word from them. What was happening?

"All right, one of these exhausts is brighter than the others, and moving away. That must be the bad guy. Get the fighters after him."

The orders were transmitted, and as each fighter cut in its afterburner, a satellite far overhead sensed it, and the images on the screen brightened.

"Let's have the composite," Beck ordered.

Instead of the infrared picture, the big screen changed to show a map of the southwestern United States. The position of each aircraft, deduced by computer from all the resources available to NORAD, was marked by a yellow triangle. The larger, faster heat trace was now a big, blood-red triangle. It was flying southeast toward the Gulf of Mexico. The yellows were converging on it.

"Okay, even if he's too low for radar, the satellite has him. Get the bastard!" Beck whispered. But the intruder was clearly outdistancing the interceptors.

Beck wondered what it was, then judged the size of the intruder from the brightness of its heat trace. He sucked in his breath with surprise. "My God, it must be as big as a football field!" he muttered. Then he knew. "Big Mother! How fast is that damn thing moving?"

The sergeant consulted a dial. "Hard to tell, sir, he won't be on radar until he crosses the coast and we get rid of the ground interference, but he's running away from the Eagles, and they're doing twenty-four hundred knots."

"Shit! At that altitude they don't get too much efficiency. And they'll run out of fuel soon. Have the tankers head south. The jets won't have to come back so far."

"Yessir."

"Where the hell is that bastard going, anyway? Why doesn't she just head for space? Do you suppose she's damaged?" Beck glared at the intruder on the screen. It was now over Mexico. The gap between it and the jets had widened, yet they too were in Mexican air space. Illegal, but necessary.

"Only that group from Lackland can catch her now. What's its call sign?"

"Alpine, sir."

"Alpine leader, this is Redwood. Come in, please." Beck could speak directly to any NORAD aircraft anywhere in the world.

"Redwood, this is Alpine leader. Reading you loud and clear." The pilot sounded awed. Redwood was the day's cipher for the Commander of NORAD. Few pilots ever got a chance to take orders directly from Nicholas Beck.

"Alpine leader, change heading to two-oh-five. Target is on heading one-seven-three, speed twenty-five hundred knots. This is Echo One Intercept."

Beck fancied he could hear a gulp as the pilot acknowledged a real combat intercept. "Alpine leader, roger. Course one-seven-three, speed twenty-five. Am proceeding on intercept vector two-oh-five."

On the big screen, four yellow triangles representing the Alpine flight turned south. They now had an advantageous angle on the intruder and would overtake it, despite its superior speed, somewhere over the Gulf of Mexico. It was the last chance that aircraft from the continental United States would get to destroy the Big Mother.

The four Eagles flew over the eastern coastland of Mexico at supersonic speed. They were low, so low that the ground whirled away under them as they covered forty miles every minute. They were wingtip to wingtip, afterburners howling, their sonic boom shattering windowpanes below. Then, in an instant, the land was gone, and they were over water. Another second, and they had the target on fire-control radar.

"You're within range, Alpine leader. You should be tracking the bogie now. Please confirm." Beck's voice was excited.

"Redwood, this is Alpine leader, affirmative!"

Beck watched the four yellow triangles converge on the

larger red triangle of the mother ship. He held the edge of his desk, heard his heart pound, and didn't realize he had forgotten to breathe.

On the screen, two of the yellow triangles spat tiny points of light that moved swiftly toward the bogie, but then slowed and fell away.

"Alpine leader, you're out of range. She's outrunning your missiles. Close and fire again!"

The interceptors edged closer, but the terrible speed of the spaceship kept the gap too wide. Again, missiles were fired. Again, they fell short.

"Goddamnit!" Beck snarled. "That thing is too damned fast! Where the hell is she going?" Beck traced the Mother's course. "The beryllium mines! Sergeant, have you got the Navy?"

"Yessir!"

The nuclear aircraft carrier *Dwight D. Eisenhower* was attached to the fleet that had provided air cover for the takeover of the mines months ago, and was still off the Brazilian coast. Now she was launching her fighters to confront the Big Mother.

"Tell them we've got to get her! They're cleared to use nuclear missiles."

Beck saw the navy fighters deploy. The bogie closed with frightening speed, but they formed a ragged line through which she would have to pass to reach the mines.

Chapter 4

THE RADAR trace was clear. Commander Rodger Livingstone watched it as he held his big Tomcat on course. The range indicator sank toward zero. He was well within missile range, but his orders were to get visual contact. And there was another Tomcat on the other side of the bogie. It wouldn't do to shoot each other down. He strained his eyes to see through the darkness.

The F-14 Tomcat was the navy's primary air-superiority fighter. Though larger and slower than the Air Force's Eagle, it was still an extremely sophisticated flying missile platform, and had proven itself one of the most effective fighters in the world.

Commander Livingstone and his weaponeer were surrounded by ten million dollars of electronic equipment. Four deadly Phoenix missiles rested in recessed bays beneath them. They were high-speed, long-range, high-explosive guided missiles, controlled from the launching aircraft. They had a supreme disdain for any electronic countermeasure system.

On its wings the Tomcat carried shorter-range Genie missiles. Ordinarily the Navy didn't stock nuclear missiles, but Beck had issued them for Mistletoe.

Suddenly Commander Livingstone saw it. Ahead, just above the water that glittered by under the nose of his Tomcat, was a brilliant tongue of flame, so hot it was bright violet. It slipped along the sea, low, breathtakingly fast, and far away. He could see nothing of the bogie's shape, just the nuclear fire that drove it. There was a slight oscillation in its movement.

"Fire!" snapped Livingstone, and behind him, the weaponeer did as ordered. Instinctively, they both closed their eyes against the glare as the Phoenix missiles roared out. A brief adjustment, and they fired two more. The Tomcat continued to close.

Livingstone watched the four missiles streak away, guided by radar by his weaponeer. Right on target!

Then there was a flash of white-hot, almost blue light.

"Damn! The bogie exploded them. Did it get them all?"

The answer came in a cooler, yellowish flash. The bogie's exhaust shuddered. A hit! Then another flash and another shudder. The Tomcat on the other side had scored too.

Livingstone could see the bogie clearly now. He gasped at its size—as big as a destroyer! But it was severely damaged and losing speed. There were two gaping holes in it, and half of its nose was shot away. But it kept going. Somehow the huge craft had taken the two forty-pound warheads and was still flying.

"Tough mother!" Livingstone muttered. But now he was gaining on her. On his radio, he warned the other Tomcat that he was in position to fire his Genies.

"Roger, she's all yours!" The plane veered away.

"Fire!"

Two Genie missiles were on their way. Immediately Livingstone hauled back on the stick, and the nose came up. He took the plane over onto its back, shoving the throttle to the firewall. The Tomcat screamed away desperately, trying to escape from its own weapons, for it had loosed two nuclear missiles.

The Genie was an unguided missile and, once fired, blindly followed a course set by the launching aircraft's computer and detonated at a preset moment. It was too stupid to be confused by whatever electronic countermeasures the target might take.

The blast threw the Tomcat downward. Livingstone still had the fighter on its back, fleeing the fireball, and it almost dragged its canopy on the sparkling sea before he got it under control again. Then he rolled the big plane over, swept around, and craned his neck to look back.

The explosion was ravenous in its desire to consume the darkness, and the night was swollen with orange and red. Livingstone squinted against the glare. He heard screaming in his earphones, but he was so fascinated by what he saw that he didn't answer.

The fireball grew larger, dimmed, then pulled itself upward in a giant, rolling mass of smoke and steam. Finally it began to flatten out, and then slowly assumed the tell-tale shape of the mushroom. Awed, Livingstone flew for a long time before he heard the question being yelled into his ears.

Chapter 5

THE THIRD explosion was miles upriver, but the ground had heaved under Chris. As he regained his feet, he heard a roar rumbling down the canyon. Then he noticed that the lights were out. Big Mother had destroyed the generating plant. No! She'd blown up the dam!

With dread, he listened for the titanic rush of water, knowing Mistletoe was finished.

Part Five

Chapter 1

IT WAS dawn, but the sun was hidden under a murky, rolling sky. Soaked and muddy, dizzy with fatigue, Chris opened the door to his apartment. He found Anna Larin curled up on the couch. Like himself, she had worked most of the night organizing disaster crews, but he had lost touch with her hours before. She came out of an exhausted sleep as he entered.

"Anna, it's over. We've lost."

"Is there no hope?" She had had a shower and was wearing a short nightgown and a bathrobe. He looked dazedly around for a place to sit, but hesitated and said in despair, "It's the water; it brought tons of silt down from the canyon. Even if we could salvage the gun and the reactor, it'd take months to clean them up and . . . oh, hell, Anna, I've got to take a shower before I can even sit down."

He stumbled into the bathroom, dropped his soggy, muddy clothes on the tile floor, and took a short shower. After wearily toweling off, he put on a robe, collapsed on the bed, and closed his eyes.

Anna sat down on the bed beside him, let him rest a few minutes, and then asked gently, "Were many killed?"

He was silent for so long that she wondered if he was asleep, but finally he said, without opening his eyes, "It's impossible to know for sure yet. The atomic missile destroyed a section of the housing area. Most of the buildings were for soldiers and employees, but . . ."

She waited, feeling the depth of his grief.

Finally he said, "Building 'E' was blown to bits. That's where Kellogg and Solovyev and all the top physicists and nuclear engineers lived."

"Oh, Chris!" Anna stroked his forehead with her cool hand.

"I walked through the whole area. Many of the bodies were washed downstream, but on the high ground there were charred corpses everywhere—maybe a hundred."

She leaned across the bed, got a pillow, and put it under his head.

He hardly stirred, but only muttered, "God knows how many more will die from radiation. The fleet will be here in a week, and there's nothing to stop it now." His voice was so low that she could hardly hear him.

She lay down with her head on his shoulder, reached under his robe, and put her arm around his bare chest. "Isn't there *anything* we can do?"

"We have thermonuclear missiles, but . . ." His voice trailed off into silence.

"There must be something *you* can do."

There was no answer, and again she wondered if he was asleep. When he did speak, his voice was close to cracking. "I've given it all I have. But I lost. Balder beat me."

Anna waited, but he said nothing more, only lay motionless beside her. She withdrew her arm and turned on her side, propping herself up on one elbow. "But what about Mike and Susan? Everybody's children? Will they all die next week?"

His face tightened.

"Is there nothing you can do? Chris?"

He groaned, lifted one knee, and opened his eyes slightly. "Anna, Dimitri's dead, Kellogg's dead. The reactor is covered with tons of mud, the gun is half buried, the physicists who worked with Dimitri are dead. We're licked!"

"But can't you try?"

Silence.

"Chris?"

"Helmut has crews working to clean out the muck, and soldiers are collecting the dead. What more can we do?"

"Are you just going to give up?" She waited for an answer, but got none, and went on, "Chris, do you remember Wake Island? I thought it was all hopeless because I could see Papa Bear failing. But do you know what made me *try*?"

"I thought I did." His words were almost inaudible.

"Yes, Chris. I met you, and you were so strong I thought maybe we could do it. You know, Chris, it wasn't President Reed who persuaded the leaders. It was *you*." She waited for a response, but he never moved a muscle.

Frantically she sought words to goad him out of his despair.

"Chris—we can't give up! Those people—or whatever they are—must not get our world."

The telephone rang. Nilstrom rolled over and picked up the receiver. As he listened, his face sagged further in despair. Anna saw the change and reached under his robe, running her hands over his naked body, down his legs. Angrily he wrenched away, then hung up the phone. He was savage as he turned to her. "I *told* you we're licked. Houston says the fleet just made a course correction. They're going south. We wouldn't get a shot even if—"

"But this is later than we thought it would be."

"Anna, our estimate was only approximate."

"So you're giving up?"

"Oh Christ!" He lay back and closed his eyes.

Anna looked at him in disgust. Then she jumped angrily out of bed and went to the window. She threw open the drapes and looked out. The sun had burned off the clouds, and it was a beautiful morning. In the distance, she could see men in radiation suits moving through the blackened area. Earth-moving machines worked near the dome. She looked back at Nilstrom.

"Oh, Chris! It's a new day! And as long as we're alive, we have a chance."

He didn't open his eyes.

She took off her robe. Against the light of the window, her gown was transparent.

"Chris! We've got to get to work, get the gun repaired."

He reared up and looked at her in exasperation. For a second there was a flicker of interest in his eyes. But then he fell back.

"Without Dimitri and Kellogg, we *can't* get the gun working again. Besides, with all that mud, there isn't time. Mistletoe is finished, Anna, worthless!"

Desperate to rouse him from his defeatism, she pulled the nightgown over her head and stood nude against the window. Then she walked over to the bed and lay down close to him. Her arms went around him as she loosened the robe and pulled it away from his body.

"Chris! Make love to me!"

He rose up on his elbows. "My God, the world's coming to an end, and she wants to make love!"

"You refuse?" She sat up, furious. One hand was between his legs. Her yellow hair fell loosely across her naked shoulders, and her eyes were afire.

"What kind of man are you, Christian Nilstrom, willing to surrender to those—those *things*? Willing to let your own children die, rather than try to stop them? Now you even refuse to make love!"

"Well, for Christ's sake! After the night we've had around here, I don't—YOOOOQWWWWW!!!!" He jerked up convulsively, his legs waving wildly.

She had grabbed his testicles.

"If you won't be a man and fight, then give these to me and I'll be the man!"

Bent over in pain, he was halfway across the room by the time she had finished her outburst. "You little bitch! You damned near killed me!"

"You might as well be dead if you're afraid to fight and unable to make love!" she shouted angrily.

"I'm not afraid to fight! But I need some rest and—"

"You're not even a man! You can't even make love!"

"You damned wildcat. I *can* make love!"

"You can't! You're not even a man!"

But he was.

Chapter 2

AT ELEVEN o'clock that morning, Chris, Anna, and Stehlen stood on the hill outside the headquarters building, surveying the damage. Far away to their right, they could just see the airport with its cluster of hangars. Cargo planes huddled unhurt around the primitive little terminal building.

To the north was the dome, less than a mile away. It glittered in the bright winter sun like a many-faceted diamond, even with the holes torn in it. The battered support buildings were almost buried in debris and light tan mud, which trucks and bulldozers struggled to get through.

The wall of water had swept down the valley to the graser site. If it hadn't been for the support buildings, the water would have struck the dome full force.

Stehlen pointed out the route the flood had taken, how it had swirled past most of the housing area, around the headquarters building below where they stood, through the tennis courts and basketball area, and out onto the desert, where it vanished into the sands.

"Helmut, what about the gun?"

The young German shook his head, and his blond hair jumped from the vigor of the movement. His baby face was taut and lined. "Impossible to say yet, Chris. Too much mud. I've been inside the dome—had to wade through pools of water and up to my knees in debris. God, what a mess! The gun itself is pretty clean, but the carriage, the turntable, the motors, aagh!"

"The reactor?"

"Much worse! The mud and sand ran down into the pit. The reactor's completely buried."

"Radiation?"

"None. The water helped us on that. And their missiles were small and efficient. They didn't leave much fallout or residual radiation."

"How long for repairs?"

"Ordinarily, Chris, I'd say months. But here . . ."

"God! It all seems so hopeless, Helmut, and I—"

Anna whirled menacingly and Nilstrom said quickly, "But we'll get it repaired in time, won't we, Helmut?"

"In time, Chris? You mean by next week? No way. And from what Houston says, it doesn't look as if we'd get a shot anyway." For the first time in the fourteen months of unremitting work, the young German sounded defeated. His sloping shoulders were bent in discouragement. He turned toward the housing area, off to their left. "There's the real disaster, Chris. The loss of most of our scientists." He paused and his voice broke. "I don't dare let myself think of them as individuals." He swallowed hard. "But the loss of their talents makes Mistletoe impossible."

Anna looked at the blackened area where the wooden prefab houses and apartment buildings had once stood. For the first time since the attack, Chris saw softness in her face and realized how much she too was grieving. "How many were lost, Helmut?"

He brightened a little. "Well, not quite as many as we'd thought. Chuck and Dimitri and all the very top men have vanished. But some of the other scientists and engineers had gone into town for a party, to celebrate the gun's being ready."

Chris smiled bitterly. "It must have sobered them pretty quickly when they came back from their bash and found this mess."

"*Ja!*" He shook his head. "It's so tragic! Nearly everyone was partying last night. We thought we were ready for the fleet!" He turned back to Chris. "Well, I suppose we're lucky it was only a small nuclear missile. I'm surprised Big Mother didn't fire a thermonuclear device."

"She probably wasn't designed or equipped as a warship. Well, let's get to work. I want a list of the machinery, the men, anything else you'll need. We'll do what we can to put this thing in shape."

"*Ja.* Good God, Chris! What's *that*?" His almost-white eyebrows shot upward.

Down the road from the gate came a caravan of police vans bearing the insignia of the Phoenix police department. Stehlen, Anna, and Chris walked down the hill to the circular drive in front of the headquarters building to meet them.

A police captain stepped out of the first van. He was in his middle fifties and his corpulent body seemed determined to escape his tight uniform. He looked through his yellow-tinted sunglasses at the devastation.

"Captain? I'm Dr. Nilstrom, the scientific coordinator of Mistletoe. Can I help you?"

The officer put out a thick hand to Chris, acknowledged introductions to Anna and Stehlen, and turned back to eye the crater and the ruins. "Heard on the radio you people had an accident. That's quite an accident!"

"Yes, and made worse when the dam burst," answered Stehlen.

The captain looked carefully at him. "German, ain't you?"

"*Ja.*"

"Thought so." He turned back to look at the debris. "Funny thing about that dam. Concrete. Shouldn't have busted that way. Wasn't even much of a storm."

"Umm."

"Some project you people got goin' out here. We're only a little over a hunnert miles from here and don't know a durn thing about it . . ." He peered at Chris, waiting for an answer.

"Yeah . . . the cooperating powers wanted tight security."

The captain grunted. "It's tight, all right." He looked around at the devastation again. "Even those people in Beulah's Corner won't talk about nuthin'. We stopped there on the way here.

Ever' one seemed scared as all get-out. But no one said a word."

Chris and Anna exchanged relieved looks. She asked, 'Captain, what can we do for you?'

He ignored her, said, "Coupla weeks ago we saw a big flash from outa here . . . then all those rumors in the papers . . ." He cocked a quizzical eye at Chris. "Then last night, this 'accident,' the dam bustin' . . ." He waited for someone to say something. No one did. He sighed. "Well, I ain't here to talk about dams. I got some of your people. Seems they decided to have theirselves a little party in our city."

The captain waved, and an officer got out of each van, walked to the rear, opened the doors, and stood back while his passengers got out slowly and stiffly. They looked tired and their clothes were dirty and rumpled. Chris's mouth dropped open. The men were the top physicists and engineers from the project, men he had thought dead. Most of the distinguished scientists studiously avoided his eyes, but a few grinned sheepishly.

"It ain't that we mind a party, Dr. Nilstrom, but these fellers got carried away. They were drinkin' vodka and doin' dances and yellin' and throwin' glasses and pourin' liquor all over each other. The nightclub manager called us, but when we tried to break it up, they turned it into a brawl." He took off his hat and wiped his bald head with a red handkerchief.

The last of the men had climbed out and, squinting in the bright sunlight, walked over to where they could see the ruins of their living quarters. There were forty-two scientists in the group.

"Now, Dr. Nilstrom, I ain't a killjoy or nothin' like that. Hell, I like a little party myself now and then, but I ain't never seen such goin's-on. I understand that Washington granted them all diplomatic immunity, but the nightclub owner ought to be paid. *And* I think you ought to pay the medical bills for my officers who got hurt."

Nilstrom wasn't listening. His sharp brown eyes flicked from one face to another, wondering if they represented enough knowledge and expertise to carry on without Solovyev and Kellog.

"Well, uh, Captain, I certainly do understand your problem, and I want to apologize. These men have been under a lot of pressure and—we'll certainly reimburse you. Let's go inside and see the comptroller and—"

"Now, wait a minute, Dr. Nilstrom. I appreciate that, but I got more to say. It's one thing to let *them* fellers go, but we've got two more. And they were the ringleaders. When we got to the club, these two crazy fellers were doin' some kind of dance down on one leg and yellin' 'Hey!' and throwin' things all over the place. When we tried to arrest them, they just went crazy." The captain waved to the driver of his van.

"Charlie, let them other two out." He turned back to Nilstrom. "We had the damnedest time subduin' these fellers. They darned near killed a couple of my men. One of 'em, the American, calls hisself the 'Cucamonga Catamount.' The other, a Russian, calls hisself the 'Moscow Mauler.' And I am here to tell you, them names are right! We had to cuff and iron 'em to control 'em."

The officer had opened the door, and now he reached up to help the two manacled men. As Nilstrom's heart pounded wildly, Kellogg and Solovyev jumped down onto the pavement. Kellogg's clothes were in tatters, and his face was blotched with bruises and dried blood. His bushy, frizzy hair was a sticky mass. Solovyev's clothes were covered with a combination of liquor and dirt, and the sleeve of his shirt was torn off. His eye was black and his lips were puffy.

"Now, Dr. Nilstrom, I can forgive them *other* fellers if they've got immunity and we get reimbursed. But these two! They've got to be punished. It was them who organized—"

But before he could finish, Stehlen and Chris had rushed to the two scarecrows, who stood blinking in the sunlight. "Dimitri! Chuck! You beautiful bums!" All were talking at once.

Stehlen was almost crying as he pounded the pair on the back. Chris shook their manacled hands and then turned and said, "Get these irons off these men, Captain."

The officer stood with his arms akimbo as his driver unlocked the cuffs and shackles. "Dr. Nilstrom, I must say I'm disappointed to see you treatin' them two as heroes. Why this—" he gestured to Kellogg—"this 'Cucamonga Catamount' damned near bit the finger off one of my sergeants. And this 'Moscow Mauler' kicked Officer Ortiz in the—" he glanced at Anna as Chris choked. "Beggin' your pardon, miss, but he kicked Ortiz right where it hurts a man the most."

Anna looked innocently at the captain. "You are right, Captain! They have acted outrageously." She glared at Solovyev, who smiled sickly through his puffed lips. "Moscow Mauler!"

She turned to Kellogg. 'Cucamonga Catamount!" Her eyes
were withering. Kellogg studied his toes.

"Captain, they will be severely punished! We will put them
on a work detail and keep them busy twenty-four hours a day
until they learn the error of their ways."

The captain nodded approvingly. "Miss Larin, for a Russian, you're a very understandin' lady. Now——" he hitched up
his trousers—"if you'll show me to that comptroller, we'll do
our business and be on our way."

Early that evening, Sir Clement Tillman called excitedly to say
that although he was not quite sure where the fleet was going,
it was *not* heading into the southern hemisphere. In fact, it
wasn't even heading for earth. Within a few hours he would
have enough data to plot its new destination.

Chris called a strategy meeting for the next day, and requested that Tillman—and Robinson, who was about to return
to LOOTS—be present. He also invited Phil Scripps, General
Gray, and Omari.

Chapter 3

"JUPITER?" Nilstrom was incredulous.

"Yes, gentlemen, Jupiter. Their course correction was not
made to bring them in below the ecliptic. They're heading for
Jupiter." Sir Clement's pink forehead glowed slightly from
perspiration, and his voice was high-pitched with excitement.

"Why the devil are they going there?" Nilstrom was actually
addressing the question to himself, but Bill Robinson answered.

"Jupiter's rich in all the elements they need. Maybe we just
made an error in thinking they were coming here."

General Gray turned his cold eyes to Robinson. His face
was, as usual, pinched. "Then, Doctor, why all the probes of
our defenses, the attacks on military installations?"

Nilstrom had asked Gray to represent the military because
Beck was elsewhere, superintending the construction of Grasers.

"Probably to make sure we can't stop them from using
Jupiter."

"Oh, no, Bill. I'm quite sure you're wrong," said Tillman. "Quite sure. Those little fellows can't stay on Jupiter. Why, the atmosphere is filled with methane and ammonia."

"Well, what the hell, Sir Clement, maybe they breathe ammonia the way we do oxygen." Robinson's nose had taken a fearful sunburning, and a beautiful woman he had tried to seduce had laughed at him. He was especially irritable.

"Oh, no, Bill, not possible. Have you forgotten the studies of the tissue found in Canada? It's quite obvious that they need an atmosphere much like ours."

"Well, hell, they could set up an enclosed, floating city with a totally controlled environment. Jupiter would give them the materials they must be short on—if they're anything like us—and they wouldn't have to fight us to get them."

"But what about the heat, Bill?" asked Phil Scripps.

"They could just stay in orbit around Jupiter, and live in their ships."

Scripps shook his head. "I can't buy that. Too much radiation. They're coming here, all right, but why the detour?"

"Good question! Jupiter, for all the jolly legends about it, is not a very nice place." Sir Clement shook his head. "It's the largest planet in the solar system by a great deal, bigger than all the others combined, you know. Quite a heavyweight, and the gravity is crushing."

"Yeah," Chris agreed, thinking hard. "And it doesn't even have a surface. The atmosphere just gets thicker and thicker, until it becomes mush, then solid. But, Clem, did you read my paper in *Annals of Astronomy*, where I conjectured that there might be layers of atmosphere warm enough to support life and thin enough to allow it to move around? It would have to be a fishlike sort of life, but it might—"

"Yes, Chris, I did read that. Didn't you see my refutation in the next issue? It seems the turbulence would be so severe—"

"Oh, yeah, I remember. But that was before we knew about those storms. Lucky guess."

"Nonsense, it was deductive reasoning."

"Luck. But—"

"Ah, gentlemen, could we . . ."

Tillman smiled. "Sorry, General Gray. As I argued then, gentlemen, Jupiter is subject to huge storms, so powerful that they would tear up any kind of structure, and too powerful to permit complex life. In addition, the entire planet is girdled by colored belts, which are almost certainly produced by super-powerful jet streams. And the famous red spot is probably a mammoth cyclone, bigger than the entire earth. So I don't believe there's any kind of life there."

Scripps nodded. "Also, Jupiter is surrounded by radiation, not unlike the Van Allen belts around earth, but much more powerful. The planet rotates so fast that its day is only ten hours long, and the spin gives it a distinct bulge around the equator and flattens its poles. It has thirteen known satellites, which sort of puts old earth to shame. Must be a fascinating sight. I'd like to visit the place someday, but I wouldn't want to stay very long."

"All of which brings us back to the question of why they're going there," interjected Chris.

"Dr. Nilstrom, I can only speak from a military point of view," said General Gray, "but if I were leading that fleet, I'd want some time to exercise my troops, feed them, give them a pep talk, make last-minute plans on the basis of new information. They've come a long way, and to engage in battle immediately would be foolhardy. I'd take time to issue ammunition, maybe practice with weapons. And I'd refuel my vehicles, to be sure—"

Nilstrom snapped his fingers and glanced at Scripps. "Phil, the general's got it! They're refueling! For thermonuclear engines, they have to use some kind of hydrogen compound, and Jupiter's clouds of methane and ammonia would be ideal."

Scripps and Sir Clement nodded, but Robinson was still skeptical. "You mean they've come seventy trillion miles, and now they need to stop at a gas station before the last lousy half-billion? Oh, come on, now, Chris!"

"Bill, we know they've been burning more fuel than they've been able to scoop up for years. They must be getting low."

Solovyev stirred out of his thoughts, and asked through puffy lips, "How will they go about this refueling?"

Scripps shrugged. "Probably just fly down through the clouds and scoop it into the tanks, maybe using a condenser to get more in."

Nilstrom disagreed. "I don't think so, Phil. Remember the radiation belts. Unless our friends are very heavily shielded, the radiation could kill them all. My guess is that they'll send robot tankers down."

Scripps nodded. "You're probably right. And that could provide us with an index as to how heavily shielded against radiation they are. If they appear quickly, it means they must have enough protection to fly down and scoop up the gases. If they take a while, it will mean they had to use tankers. We may get a clue as to how vulnerable they'll be to the Graser."

Sir Clement's blue eyes were bright with excitement. "But Jupiter serves another purpose for them too!" He looked at Chris. "Right now it's on the opposite side of the sun from us. So they can carry on their refueling unobserved, then fly straight at earth for almost five hundred million miles without our seeing them. When they come around the sun and back into view, they'll only be ninety-three million miles away. They can literally pounce on us from that distance."

Scripps frowned. "Won't it be difficult to get a good reading on them if they're coming right out of the sun?"

"What do you think, Bill?" Nilstrom deferred to Robinson.

"Well, no radar can pick them up that close to the sun, and no earthbound telescope can see them until they're very close. Because of the atmosphere, they'd lose the fleet in the corona. Only LOOTS can totally block out the sun and look for it."

"And we'll need to know the second you spot them."

Robinson touched his nose tenderly. "Well, I'll have one of the best astronomers in the world with me." He glanced at Anna. "Doctor Georgi Aristovich Klyuchevsky from the Zelenchukskaya Observatory is going up." Anna smiled back at him.

Sir Clement was busily figuring on a pad of paper. "Ah, there's another thing, Chris. If the fleet comes very close to the sun—say, inside the orbit of Mercury—we'll know for sure that they're heavily shielded against radiation."

"But does any of this matter?" General Gray was depressed. 'The real question is whether the gun will be ready to fire when the fleet does reappear! Exactly how much time do we have now?"

"I think I can answer that," said Sir Clement. "They're close to Jupiter; they'll arrive there in three days. We can follow their progress most of the way. However, we'll lose contact before they reach Jupiter, and we won't see them again until they come around the sun. It'll take them two weeks to get to the sun from Jupiter, since they'll have to build up speed again, so, assuming they use tankers, refuel within twenty-four hours, but don't pause for other reasons, I'd say that we have a minimum of almost four weeks. The earliest they could reappear around the sun is February twelfth, and arrive on February Twentieth."

Chris turned to Solovyev and Kellogg, and his eyebrows lifted. "Can you guys do it?"

Kellogg spoke first. "Yesterday, when I first saw the fucking gun, I thought we'd had it. But this incredible Kraut, Helmut, has—well, he's a miracle worker! He's brought in dredge pumps, pumped *more* water under the dome, and washed the silt out. It's unbelievable! There are some parts that have to be replaced, but not half as many as I'd thought. Give me five weeks, by God, and I'll have it ready."

"Dimitri?"

"The reactor still has a lot of mud in it, so I'm not sure I can make it in less than six weeks, but with luck . . ."

"We don't have five weeks, and certainly not six," Nilstrom pointed out.

Solovyev shook his battered head. "This project has been impossible from the beginning. Now it's more so. Still, I have an idea to discuss with Helmut that *might* work. If it does, it may shorten our time by several days."

Kellogg grinned admiringly at Solovyev. "Dimitri, you fucking genius! You always come up with some idea to save the show!"

Nilstrom asked himself incredulously if this could be the real Chuck Kellogg talking.

"But Dimitri, I don't see any way to speed up the repairs of the gun. I just don't." Kellogg was again despondent.

"May I suggest, Dr. Kellogg, that you try to stay out of the public eye from now until the shot?" said Anna, changing the subject. Despite her fatigue, she was devastatingly beautiful in a white suit that almost matched her platinum hair and contrasted with her skin, bronzed now from the Arizona sun. She looked ridiculously young and took no pains to make herself look more mature. "It's becoming increasingly difficult to maintain our cover story, and your connection with the development of the Graser is not entirely a secret."

She looked at each of them in turn, her face serious. "Speculation is getting closer and closer to the truth. Every day our office is deluged with calls from all over the world. There have been leaks from many sources. For example, Mrs. Ainswright demanded that Parliament award her son the Victoria Cross for having shot down a flying saucer from a submarine. Of course, the government denied the whole story and most people considered her something of a nut. Now, after this 'accident' . . ."
She gestured helplessly.

"At our suggestion, President Reed has announced that the Pentagon will study the nuclear 'accident' here," she continued. "Informed congressmen have assured the newsmen that if the Pentagon investigation is not a thorough one, they'll ask for action from Congress. But of course, they know that by that time—" she made a face—"the issue will be moot."

"Okay," Nilstrom said, "we've got work to do. Let's get to it."

Virginia was at the door as they opened it, with a worried look on her face. "Dr. Nilstrom, there's a...uh...someone who insists on coming in before you adjourn..."

Olga Solovyev appeared behind the heavy secretary. Her dark eyes were burning, but she smiled as she said, "Yes, Dr. Nilstrom, I insist on addressing this group. Please be seated."

Chapter 4

OLGA'S EYES searched their faces arrogantly. Her husband looked as if he could strangle her, but she walked directly to him and patted him on the arm. "Don't be frightened, darling. I'm only going to do what should have been done long ago." She went to the head of the table around which they had been sitting, whirled, and made a sweeping gesture toward the chairs. "Please! Be seated. I will only take a few minutes."

"Dr. Nilstrom, I don't believe I know this young woman," General Gray said icily.

Solovyev responded, "Sir, permit me to introduce—my wife, Olga Solovyev."

One by one, they returned to their places. Since Olga had taken his chair, Chris sat down beside Anna at the other end of the table. Olga wasted no time.

"Gentlemen—and Anna Kornilyevna—I have intruded upon this meeting because of a matter of such urgency that it could jeopardize the success of Mistletoe. I'm well aware that despite the importance of my own work here, I am not a member of this inner ruling body. I can only conclude that there is a reason for my exclusion." She smiled confidently and looked defiantly at Anna and Chris. She was dressed in a red wool skirt and a white silk blouse with squared shoulders and large lapels

open at the neck. Now she leaned forward and folded her hands
on the table.

"What I am about to say is so painful that I can only do it
because I know how desperate the situation is. For, despite the
remarkable cooperation of all eight of the participating countries, despite the brilliance of the scientists, the project has
almost been ruined. Now we have only a few days left to repair
the gun. If there are any unexpected obstacles—" she looked
at Chris significantly—"we will have a catastrophe. In order
to be successful, we must have *two* changes in leadership: a
new political chairman to replace Anna Kornilyevna Larin, and
a new scientific coordinator to replace Christian Nilstrom."

Her eyes flitted from one face to another as she tried to read
their reactions. Olga sought out ambition, greed, and jealousy
as a fly seeks dung.

"Let me recall some of the unfortunate things that have
happened. There was the reconnaissance flight over the mine
in Brazil, then another one here. The saucers were not destroyed until very late. There was the attack by the mother
ship—a disgraceful thing! An imaginative scientist would have
known of the existence of the mother ship long ago.

"It is quite clear that these mistakes are the results of the
inadequate leadership of our scientific coordinator, Dr. Nilstrom." She smiled deferentially. 'It grieves me to say this
because, personally, I like Dr. Nilstrom. However—" and she
spoke very distinctly—"intellectually, he isn't up to the level
of some of his subordinates."

Her eyes darted along the table from one scientist to another,
to see whether that seed had dropped on fertile soil.

"If, instead of Dr. Nilstrom, we'd had, say, Sir Clement
at the head of this project, I'm sure we would have avoided
much that has troubled us." She gave the Britisher her most
dazzling smile. He never changed his expression.

"Or if the chief of the project had been the American genius,
Dr. Charles Kellogg—" she tried to look sexually enticing as
she turned to the sullen young man—"I'm sure the scouts would
have been destroyed long ago, and the gun finished months
earlier." Kellogg smiled brightly, and she grew bolder.

"Or Dr. Stehlen, who has performed so brilliantly, could
have led us to success."

Stehlen kept his eyes on the pad of paper before him. On
it he drew one circle inside another.

"And Dr. Takeo Omari, who performed such prodigies with

communications, could have done the same." She saw him start at the mention of his name, but his face remained impassive.

"Ah, and what if the brilliant director of the LOOTS observatory had been in charge?" She smiled simperingly. "He has worked for years in a highly difficult situation with few of the comforts of life. Yet he treats his co-workers with such respect that they do not fight among themselves."

She knew she had scored. Robinson smiled, making a slight gesture of diffidence. And the way he had been admiring her figure convinced her she could safely take another step. "And certainly all the *ladies* would work with him gladly," she chortled coyly. Robinson smiled broadly. Nobody else reacted.

"There's my own husband, whom I haven't mentioned because I don't want to seem biased. But for all his deficiencies, with a little help in personal relations, even he could have done a better job than Dr. Nilstrom."

Chris watched every response of his colleagues. His staggering sense of fatigue, which had been partially banished by sheer adrenalin, now returned. Bitterly he remembered the times he had defended Kellogg, and when the young man smiled at Olga, Chris almost threw an ashtray at him. He saw Robinson warm to Olga's vulgar flattery, and he thought of how he had had to plead with Robinson even to get him to look in the direction of 61 Cygni. Damn it! Had everyone forgotten it was *he* who had studied the template and guessed the origin of the fleet, that the whole idea of Mistletoe had been *his*? Why didn't somebody say something?

Olga was smiling.

"Doctor Nilstrom's mistakes in judgment have jeopardized the safety of the project. He must be dismissed."

She paused, then her face became lugubriously sad. "But I have said that there are *two* leaders who must go—Nilstrom and Larin. I say this reluctantly, for Anna is an *old* friend. A fellow Russian! But it's obvious that she must be removed. Consider the Brazilian invasion—a ghastly imperialistic act which earned the hatred of the persecuted and emerging nations of the world. A leader of skill and sensitivity would have obtained their happy cooperation.

"But now I come to the worst part of this sad affair." Olga lowered her head in sorrow. Chris watched her performance with disbelief.

"You all know that one of the rules adopted early in the life of Mistletoe was that no families would be permitted to live at the site. This has been a hardship on most everyone, though such a rule was a necessity. I myself saw the wisdom of it when I arrived, and I decided that my husband and I would not take advantage of our position. So Dimitri has his apartment and I have mine." Her eyes dropped demurely.

For a moment she was silent, then her voice cracked like a whip and her eyes burned. "But it was *not* that way with *all* of us! Oh, no! Not for Anna Kornilyevna Larin, the whoring disgrace of the Soviet diplomatic service, who wouldn't have lasted a day in a government run by anyone except a sentimental man like Chairman Grigorenko! Nor has it been that way for Dr. Nilstrom! While others were dedicated enough to give up their personal lives, he—I hesitate to say this—he and Anna Larin have been lovers, spending hours together that could have been devoted to their work! Oh, yes! It is not *only* their lack of ability which has prevented Mistletoe from succeeding; it's also that they cannot tear themselves from their bed long enough to direct its future!" Her strong voice, resonant with moral outrage, finally quivered into silence, and she leaned forward, picked up the pitcher of ice water, poured herself a glass, drank from it, and set it down again. All eyes were lowered, staring at the table; only Robinson looked at her.

"Please forgive me, I seldom lose control like that. But when I see the rest of you sacrificing, working so brilliantly, and I think of how you have been betrayed, I— Well, this is what I have to say: these two must be replaced by more capable people who will not let the project fail while they debauch themselves! Not that I see anything wrong with sex! I'm no prude! But we should be willing to sacrifice our own desires for the salvation of the world! Therefore, I propose that you inform the participating countries that the brilliant successes of Mistletoe so far have been *in spite of*—" she waved her hand sadly at Anna and Chris—"not *because of* these two; and that the near disasters are due to their mistakes. You should then ask that they be replaced, Dr. Nilstrom by one of *you*, and Larin by—whom? Well, I think it should be a *man*— someone strong, yet with finesse. Perhaps Señor Sanchez, or someone from the emerging countries. An ideal choice would be Mr. Adajanian Swaminathan of India.

"But—" she gestured self-deprecatingly—"you are far more qualified to judge than I. I only came to say publicly what is being said secretly by countless others." She sat down, daintily extracted a handkerchief from her sleeve, and wiped her eyes.

Chris waited for someone to say something.

Olga looked up shyly, smiling bravely to reassure them just how difficult and distasteful it had been for her to come.

Nilstrom could hardly believe the silence. Surely one of those present would speak up for Anna and for him. Were they so anxious to seize power and honor for themselves?

The silence became unbearable.

Out of the corner of his eye, Chris saw Anna move slowly, and he turned his head to look at her more closely. There was no fear in her face, or even anger, but amusement. His eyes fell to the hand she rested on the table in front of him. Her fingers were making a prehensile, cuplike movement.

He jumped at the significance of her motion, and said, 'Gentlemen—and Anna—Mrs. Solovyev has made some accusations and some suggestions. I would like to respond. And if she wishes, Anna may also.'

"First of all, Mrs. Solovyev is partly correct. I should have thought of Big Mother. Otherwise, I have no apologies. As to my personal life—" he waved a hand at Olga in disgust— "it's none of her goddamned business."

A few stirred, Olga showed a trace of a smirk, then Bill Robinson spoke. "I didn't know about any of this." He was being cautious. Though he could smell the possibility of an opportunity for his career, he also knew it was dangerous to commit himself before he was sure of how the others felt. "But I certainly think it took courage for Mrs. Solovyev to come in here and—"

Kellogg interrupted, "You're right, you know, Bill! It did take guts, and I for one am grateful."

Olga was so excited she wriggled in her seat and turned her triumphant smile on Kellogg. She possessed three smiles. One was her "I'm enjoying this" smile. It was her best, but she rarely gave it. The second was her conspiratorial smile, which she used when trying to entice a man into her bed or to flatter a person into accepting her point of view. She had already let them have that, full force. It was too tight and thin-lipped, but she had learned to soften it and project at least a fascimile of innocence by opening her eyes wide. But now she flashed her triumphant smile—lips pursed, but gleefully twisted at the ends—a grotesque combination of a smirk and a suppressed giggle.

Kellogg smiled back. "Yessir, it really did take courage to come in here."

Chris felt his ears heating up. Just as he was about to explode, Kellogg said, "You know, Dimitri, when we had our little party the other night, you told me a lot about Olga—how determined and persistent she can be, all that sort of thing. But you never told me she had such courage!"

For once Solovyev's face wasn't gray, it was red.

"Really, friends, now don't you agree?" Kellogg searched the faces around the table. Most avoided his eyes. "I mean, to walk into a room filled with people who have always thought that Chris Nilstrom is the most brilliant and strongest man they know, and that Anna Larin is the most beautiful and toughest little lady in the whole world, and tell us that they're really idiots—that took guts!"

Olga's smile faded and her eyes became wary.

"I think it must be like undressing in Macy's window during the Christmas shopping season, don't you?"

The corners of Sir Clement's mouth twitched. Olga froze.

"I mean, to come in here like this and make such an utter asshole of herself, to display herself as a jealous, stupid whore . . ."

"You swine!" Olga was standing, shrieking, her large breasts heaving.

"As I was saying, it took guts! All of us know perfectly well that Dimitri doesn't sleep with her because he can't stand her. And we know she tried every way she could to put the make on Chris, but that he told her to go screw herself."

Olga was shaking from head to foot. Her teeth were chattering from rage.

"And of course, we all know that the only reason she even has a job here is that some fat-assed Russians wanted a spy they could count on. She knows about as much about computers as a barmaid."

Olga's face jerked so convulsively that she couldn't speak. But her husband held up his hand to restrain Kellogg.

"Please, Chuck! Olga is simply—" he looked at the ruin that had once been his wife, and bitterness and pity were mixed in his voice—"simply the old Russia!" Then he turned to Anna Larin with affection. "And Anna Kornilyevna is the *new* Russia." There were tears in his eyes, but he forced himself to go on. "Olga thought she could play upon our jealousy of Chris."

He smiled sadly, and looked at Nilstrom. "Oh, yes, Chris! We *are* jealous of you! Handsome, brilliant, successful, and you have won the love of the beautiful Anna Kornilyevna. If I didn't respect you so much, I'd probably hate you!

"Someday, if we survive, you and Anna will marry and have happiness. And *I*?" His eyes swiveled to Olga, still standing at the end of the table, gripping its edge with her brightly polished nails. Everyone looked at her in contempt.

But she was tough, if nothing else, and she gathered herself and quickly left the room without looking back.

Sir Clement pushed his chair back and went over and put his hand comfortingly on Solovyev's shoulder. His voice was husky with emotion. "Friend! I'm so sorry. When she first began, I didn't know what to say. I thought she must be speaking for you."

Solovyev looked apologetically at Anna and Chris, still sitting motionless at the end of the table. 'What can I say?"

Stehlen said quietly, "It's so sad to see a human being fall apart like that."

Omari shook his head. "I could hardly believe it."

Solovyev was still staring at Chris and Anna. 'What a dreadful experience this was for you!"

"Dreadful?" asked Kellogg, bewildered. He looked at Chris. "You didn't really think any of us were taken in by that—" He looked back at Solovyev. "They know perfectly well the way we feel about them, Dimitri. Let's not get sentimental!"

General Gray so rarely altered his expression that what happened to his face now was less a smile than a hairline fracture. He said dryly, "For a moment, I thought that woman was going to shake Chris, and I said to myself, 'Maybe he isn't the man we need.' But when he told her off, I said, 'By God, that's still Chris Nilstrom!' "

Chris turned to Anna. She winked at him, and her hand relaxed. He said, "I don't know about the rest of you, but I need a drink!"

Chapter 5

FOR THREE hours, Olga lay on her bed, staring at the ceiling. The pain of her humiliation was so acute that she even contemplated suicide, but decided 'they' would only laugh. That she could have fallen so far from the prestige she had once possessed in Moscow was incredible. It was all Dimitri's fault. And he owed her so much!

As the daughter of a woman who had utterly dominated both her husband and child, Olga had developed a contempt for all men. Yet she was obsessed by them. She had been attracted to Solovyev when he was still a young physicist teaching at the university. Sensing his greatness, Olga wanted to be part of his success, and she wooed, seduced, and married him before he could quite catch his breath. At first the marriage went well, but her dominating, scheming tendencies soon caused Solovyev to withdraw into his work. His brilliant successes only infuriated her. Few paid any attention to his neurotic wife, and over the years, her smothering affection turned to hatred.

Now, as she lay on the bed, her heartbeat slowly returning to normal, Olga knew there was only one way to get even with those who had humiliated her. She would destroy Mistletoe. She lifted her arm, no longer trembling, and looked at her watch. It was four o'clock. Olga knew that, at that moment, Sydney Knox and another representative of the Polk Corporation were meeting with her husband. She wondered if Knox would change his mind about the fleet when he saw the devastation wrought by the mother ship. She hoped not.

She got up and went into the bathroom to the shower, where she unscrewed the shower head and extracted from the pipe a long, thin package wrapped in plastic. Back in the bedroom, she tore it open. Out tumbled tiny magazines of film. She hesitated a moment, for she didn't really have any sympathy with Knox and his ideals. She'd actually rather work on a project to destroy a fleet of spaceships than conspire with Knox, who prattled on about peace. But she had tried to help Mis-

tletoe—and she had been rejected! The thought of her humiliation removed any hesitation.

She knew that if she was successful, Mistletoe would be
effectively paralyzed or even destroyed, and there would be
no way to stop the fleet. Well, it would serve them right! They
had forced her to get the documents for Knox, forced her to
destroy Mistletoe.

She had just finished putting the films into a false-bottomed
attaché case when Knox called.

Chapter 6

IT WAS six days later, February first, before Knox could finish
the laborious task of developing all the magazines of film in
his Boston apartment. A few of the photographs of documents
were not clear, but most were of superb quality. Olga had done
her work well.

Knox took all that day to study the material. Occasionally
he swore to himself at the militaristic bloodlust of those who
had prepared them. They just assumed that men from another
star system would be as cruel and avaricious as themselves.
Now they had so provoked the spacemen that there had actually
been attacks!

At five o'clock, he called Randall Evans at the *New York
Globe*. Evans didn't quite know what to think of the slightly
effeminate young physicist with the blond hair and the intense
eyes, but as he listened, he knew he was on the threshold of
the greatest scoop in the history of his paper, greater than the
Pentagon Papers or Watergate. He agreed to meet Knox at
Kennedy Airport.

Knox immediately packed an overnight bag, put on his
sheepskin coat, and headed for the airport.

It took him five hours to tell the whole story and to show
the papers he had so tediously prepared. Evans had called his
editor-in-chief, Arthur Tangerman, and the publisher, Roger
Ulrich. When Knox had finished, Ulrich, who had said nothing
throughout the presentation, asked bluntly, "How much do you
want?"

Knox turned on him angrily. "How much? I want a new world, devoid of war! I want to be able to tell my children that—"

Ulrich took the cigar from his mouth and crushed it out. The room was overheated and he was sweating. "Bullshit! How much do you want?"

"Not a damned cent!" Knox was red-faced and quivering in rage.

Ulrich sighed. "Okay, okay, I'll put it this way: *what* do you want?"

"I want a new world. I—"

"Oh Christ," Ulrich ran his fingers through his gray hair. "Will you cut out that shit and tell me what you want?"

"I want you to print this stuff, goddamnit!"

Ulrich closed his eyes in disgust, and thought for a few seconds. Then he opened his eyes and looked across the table at Tangerman. "Arthur?"

Tangerman was a tall young man who had risen meteorically in the *Globe* hierarchy. Though he was dressed elegantly, his shirt too was open at the neck. His all night chain-smoking had been interrupted only by his coffee drinking.

"We'll have to verify it."

Knox leaned over the table, his face tight. "Okay, but hurry."

Tangerman drummed his fingers. "Roger, if you thought things were hot after Ellsberg, you haven't seen anything yet. We'll have the courts, the FBI, the CIA, the Army, Congress— Jesus! We'll all be sued for millions if this stuff is bogus, and be arrested for breaking fifty laws if it's authentic."

Ulrich nodded, picking a fleck of tobacco off his thick lip. "It'll either be the biggest scoop in the history of journalism, or the biggest boo-boo." He turned back to Knox. "You know, don't you, Knox, that it'll only take the FBI about two days to find out where we got this stuff? Then, both you and your girlfriend are in the soup. Are you willing to go to jail? To have your career ruined?"

Knox was flushed and sweating, but he thought of how he'd backed out of revealing the truth about the original Graser project, and his voice was firm. "Yes, I am! We've got to stop this stupid war!"

Ulrich rubbed his stubbled chin and eyed the young fanatic. "Yeah, but maybe that fleet *is* on its way here to wipe us all out."

"Well, if they are, we should reach out and show them we're not all warmongers! We ought to meet them with the hand of—"

Ulrich closed his eyes and said softly, "Jesus!"

Knox paused, then said loudly, "The people must be told!"

Tangerman nodded and said quietly to Ulrich, "Regardless of who's right, the people should have the information."

Ulrich licked his lips and grimaced at the way his mouth felt. He took a sip of cold coffee and frowned at that, too. "Well, frankly, I'm not so sure. We could cause a panic."

"Roger," Evans said quietly, "this'll be the greatest scoop ever."

Ulrich studied his coffee cup while the others waited. Finally he looked up and nodded solemnly. "Okay, we print it. But first we check."

Knox was nervously chewing on the inside of his lip. "*When* will you print it?"

Ulrich looked at the calendar on the band of his wrist watch. "February sixth, if it checks out. The biggest edition we've ever published."

"Okay," said Knox. He leaned toward Ulrich and his eyes burned fiercely The publisher leaned away from him. "Will you print a personal note from me in the same issue?" Knox asked. "A call to peace-lovers all over the world to gather at the ruins of the Bright River Dam for a Peace-Rock Festival in protest against Mistletoe."

Ulrich shrugged, then nodded. "Yeh, sure . . . why not?"

Knox stood up.

Tangerman asked from across the room, "Won't the whole area around the dam be radioactive? The Big Mother hit it with an atomic missile."

"These advanced people used 'clean' missiles. They left no radiation. Olga says men are already working at the dam site on the power plant."

Chapter 7

THE GLOBE's researchers spent days going over Sydney Knox's documents. They found no signs of a hoax. Reporters probing official sources ran into a wall of silence wherever they went, and concluded that the documents must be authentic.

On the third of February, the *Globe's* world-famous Washington correspondent, Martin Cooke, had lunch with his old friend Wilbur Sternald. He asked a number of pointed questions. Sternald not only refused to give any information, but frankly warned Cooke not to indulge in speculation about Mistletoe.

Immediately Cooke phoned Ulrich and told him that Sternald's total refusal even to discuss the issue was unprecedented in all the years he had known him. Cooke was convinced the documents were genuine.

Meanwhile, Sternald had called the director of the FBI to warn him that the *Globe* had some inside information. He feared a crack in security inside Mistletoe itself.

On the morning of the fourth of February, an FBI agent called the *Globe*. He was referred to Ulrich, who blandly suggested they meet the afternoon of the sixth.

On the same day, Arthur Tangerman went to Washington to see Charles Hamilton. The senator, weakened from his fast, sadly refused to discuss anything he knew, but his friend said, "Charlie, I know you can't talk, but you can tell me if you think what we have is false."

He handed Hamilton the story scheduled to appear on the sixth. It filled forty-five pages and included pictures by the score. The senator scanned it quickly and smiled broadly. "Arthur, do you remember what I said when I began this fast? That I'd fast till the truth came out about this Mistletoe? Well, I'm goin' to have a big juicy steak tonight! And I'll tell you somethin' else, Arthur! When I've had some time to regain my strength, I'm headin' for Arizona."

Tangerman called the office from the airport before returning to New York. The newspaper had made its final check.

All that night and the next day and night, the *Globe's* presses rolled. Employees were sworn to silence. One who threatened to alert the authorities was physically detained while the printing went on.

At midnight on February fifth, Sydney Knox left his apartment with a suitcase in his hand and headed for the airport. Then he vanished.

Chapter 8

THE MOMENT the messenger delivered her copy of the *New York Globe* on February sixth, Anna knew she was looking at disaster. Hurriedly she glanced through it, her hands wet with cold perspiration and her heart sick, then she headed for Chris's office. Before Nilstrom could say a word, she spread the paper out on his desk. Everything was there: the Baker-Nunn pictures, the story of the Russian destroyer, the destruction of the scouts and Big Mother, even pictures of the specks of light that were the fleet.

"My God!" exclaimed Chris. "Where the hell did they get this?"

"Look." She pointed to a picture of Knox over the article which included his call for a peace-rock festival. "It says *he* got the documents for them. And I know where."

"Olga! Damn it! Kellogg warned us about Knox."

"I'll have her arrested immediately," Anna said. "But she's a minor problem. The real question is, how will the public react?" She walked away from the deck and began to pace the floor. Her hair was piled high on her head and it made her seem taller, but it also gave her a severe look that emphasized the concern she felt. "Can you suggest a cover story?" she asked.

Chris got up from his desk, walked to the window, and looked out. "Would it really help?"

"It may make a difference. We only need a couple of weeks." She came and stood beside him at the window.

He looked at her, at her exquisite figure, her beautiful face and flawless complexion, and marveled at how she excited him, even in the midst of a terrible crisis. He put his arm around her waist and drew her close.

"Okay, then let's say Knox got hold of an old contingency study I did for the Pentagon."

"What about the pictures?"

"I'll say we prepared the study as a problem for the defense forces, and that the pictures were fabricated as part of the exercise. That might work. You know, a few years ago, a professor told his students an asteroid was going to crash into the United States, and asked them to figure out a way to stop it. If someone had gotten hold of his statement and their solution, he might have had a problem. Say this is the same sort of thing."

"That might help," she said.

Nilstrom sighed and looked back at the paper. "So Knox is calling for a peace-rock festival, eh?"

"Yes, what is that?" He loved her when she looked so puzzled, and when her speech took on the sharp edges of her own language. He smiled and said, "It's kind of hard to describe. A lot of people get together to listen to music and to protest something."

"How many people?" She looked alarmed again.

He shrugged. "You can never tell. There were half a million at Woodstock."

"Chris, anything like that could be a disaster! It would be . . . how does your saying go? A powder box?"

"Powder keg."

"This festival must not be permitted!" Her blue eyes blazed.

"What do you suggest?"

"Nobody must be allowed into this part of the desert."

Chris was exasperated. "Anna, we can't prevent people from congregating."

"We have to. In Russia—"

"Damn it, Anna, this isn't Russia. It's their constitutional right. Even if we close the roads, they can get across the desert in four-wheel-drive vehicles. We might slow them down, but it'd just publicize the thing more. No, it may be one of the disadvantages of living in a free country, but we can't stop them from coming."

Chapter 9

AT TWO o'clock on the afternoon of the eighth, a Chinese sentry assigned to the northeastern sector of Project Mistletoe walked his rounds between the first and second fences, pausing occasionally to scan the horizon with his binoculars. The little soldier walked with the casual swagger of a man thoroughly bored. When he reached the perimeter phone, fastened to a fencepost, he muttered negatives to a Chinese interpreter.

He resumed his walk, then stopped and lifted the binoculars to his eyes. The distance leapt closer. The man grunted in satisfaction. The glasses were Japanese, and of better quality than any he had used before. It was unfortunate they were unavailable in China.

Then he gaped. No, it was not a mirage! That blot on the desert had to be people. And the highway leading to the blot was jammed with traffic. *Why* they were there, he didn't know, but it was bound to be important. He turned back to the phone.

Anna was so furious she pounded the desk as she looked at the video monitor.

"Mr. President, I asked for that road to be closed!"

"I know, Miss Larin, and it's being closed—right now."

"But there are already thousands of people there. I saw them myself, just a few miles outside the perimeter fence."

The president was worried, and the video screen did not hide the lines that had crept into his face.

"Now, Miss Larin—"

"Don't 'Miss Larin' me! That road was supposed to be closed hours ago! And it still hasn't been done."

"All right!" Reed snapped back. "I know it. I don't have any jurisdiction over that highway because it isn't on federal property. I had to go through the governor, and he's not too happy about the whole thing anyway. What do you expect those people to do? Storm the fences? Against all those troops? I've got my hands full as it is. That damned *New York Globe*! We have a worldwide panic on our hands. We had to close the switchboard at the White House, and half of the eastern sea-

board is swarming around the gates. I had to call in extra
guards to control the crowds. You and Beck are just going to
have to handle it yourselves, Miss Larin."

Anna sighed. "Yes, sir. But if they *should* try to storm the
site, I can't answer for the consequences."

"I don't think they will. It's supposed to be a *peace* festival
anyway. They'll probably just listen to music and speeches,
and then picket. As long as nothing happens to really set them
off, I'm sure you'll be okay."

Anna's voice was soft and conciliatory. "I hope so. Thank
you, Mr. President."

Chapter 10

BY EVENING on the ninth, when Sydney Knox finally arrived,
the crowd at the festival had grown to ten thousand, and
hundreds more were still arriving. He got there after nightfall,
bouncing over a dirt trail with a Jeep-load of long-haired teenagers. He had suggested that the festival be held on the banks
of the Bright River because it was close to Mistletoe and they
would have water. In the dark, he could see little except a
huddle of people and tents that faded away into the night. There
were few campfires. He threw down his sleeping bag between
two cacti, crawled in, and fell asleep.

He awoke to the sound of running water and looked up at
the figure of a young man in an army-surplus jacket, urinating
near his head.

"Hey!" Knox rolled over, feeling the imprint of every rock
he'd slept on. "What the hell do you think you're doing?"

The young man zipped himself up. Stringy hair streamed
down his back and a beard down his front. He grinned. "Just
fertilizing the cactus, man."

"Well, goddamit, you were fertilizing my sleeping bag too."

"Be cool, man. This is nature. Animals don't use toilets.
When they gotta go, they just go." He sauntered away.

Knox looked around at the "nature" the young man had
referred to. For a hundred yards in every direction, and down
the riverbank as far as he could see, the ground was covered

with people in various postures, most still asleep. The air was still bracing from the night, but the sun was up and promised a warm day. The odor of unwashed bodies hung over the camp.

Knox picked up his sleeping bag, stuffed it under one arm, slung his knapsack over the other shoulder, and set out to find a place less damp with "nature." After several minutes of stepping over prone forms, he found a relatively smooth, flat place, and dumped his belongings.

He found himself next to two bearded men camped by a Jeep. He cocked an ear toward their conversation.

"Man, that dude, he's the best, I mean, the greatest since Daniel Ellsberg! I mean, man! Did he blow the whistle on those pigs! I mean, wow!"

"Man, like you got the right handle, but you don't have enough of it. He ain't the greatest since Daniel Ellsberg. I mean, like, he is the greatest *ever*."

"Yeah, I guess you're right, man. He *is* the greatest. I remember when I was in college, those physics dudes were really up-front people. Just think about all those pigs, man, looking all over the place for him. I mean, wow, I'm glad they don't want me that bad."

Knox smiled proudly.

One young man then terminated the conversation. "You got another joint, man?"

Knox frowned.

He decided to take a look at the dam, even though he knew there was little to show it had ever existed. The riverbed in which they now camped bore no sign of the torrent that had swept through two weeks ago. The river flowed idly by, not seeming to care that it had been released from its bonds.

Knox climbed the trail that twisted along the east wall of the canyon. It wasn't a hard walk. Bright River Canyon didn't really deserve the name. It was more like a valley with low, jagged walls on either side.

There wasn't much left of the dam. The ends still clung to the canyon walls, but most of the center was now a giant U-shaped gap that extended almost all the way across and very nearly reached the bottom. Water flowed through the gap and into the river. There was no sign of the power plant or the spillway, just the remains of a concrete wall, crumbling and blackened by the tremendous heat of the alien missile.

Behind the dam was a pond, only a small remnant of the sizable lake it had once been. The valley still showed the outline of that lake. Above a clear line was the sparse desert vegetation. Below it nothing grew, and the sandy yellow of the soil gave way to mud.

Knox gazed at the scene for a long time. Finally he breathed, "Magnificent!"

"Eh?" The man standing next to him was dressed in a conservative blue suit, so the physicist was not sure he could trust him. He decided to enlighten the man.

"Do you realize what they did here? The destruction of this dam saved the lives of hundreds, probably thousands of their fellows out in space. They hurled themselves through a ring of man's greatest weapons to get at this dam. They must have known they couldn't survive. Yet they died so that others would live! It shows how great they really are!"

"Yes," the man replied sadly. "All Saturnians are like that. They consider their lives secondary to the good of the race. And they did it for us too. Now we will benefit from their wisdom."

"Saturnians?"

"They told me that some day they'd come to save us from the ravages of greed. I didn't think it'd be this soon, but the pictures in the *Globe*...."

"You idiot, they're not coming from Saturn, they're coming from 61 Cygni, a class-K binary star in the constellation of Cygnus."

The man shook his head determinedly. "They come from Saturn. It's just another CIA lie that they come from Cygnus."

"Listen, buddy. Saturn is a big, cold ball of hydrogen. Nobody could live there."

"Have you been there?"

"Of course not!"

The man smiled. "Saturn is a beautiful planet, full of lawns and gardens, with cities whose towers reach toward the ringed sky..."

Knox turned on his heel and left. His anger grew as he stormed down the path. Head down, he almost bumped into a man coming up the trail.

"Senator Hamilton!"

The legislator was dressed in blue jeans and a sweatshirt. He started to push on past. "Yes. Glad to meet you. Excuse me..."

"Senator, I'm Sydney Knox."

Hamilton blinked in surprise. "Of course! I'm glad to see

that you've managed to stay free. A great many pow'ful people are very angry at you."

"Well, I'm traveling sort of incognito. I haven't even made my presence here known—and I won't, either, until there are enough people to prevent my being arrested. I'm glad you decided to join us, Senator."

"Well, Mr.—or is it Dr.—Knox, for once, by God, just for once, we must meet strangers with love instead of bullets."

The senator's last words triggered a rush of affection in Knox. "Senator, you're so right! We've got to stop this thing."

Hamilton looked at the men still working in the debris of the base of the ruined dam, and his eyes twinkled. "The Cygnians may have stopped it themselves."

Knox looked down the valley. In the distance, the huge dome glittered impossibly, a bubble cast up on the plain. Beyond it, the circular pond that was in fact a bomb crater shimmered under the sun. He gestured toward the dome.

"My contact told me they expect to have it ready soon."

Suddenly there was a shout, and the two watched as the workmen pulled a body from the rubble and wrapped it in a tarpaulin.

"Ugh," commented Sydney Knox. "It's too bad so many had to die."

"But what else could the Cygnians do?" asked Senator Charles Hamilton. "They have a right to defend themselves."

Chapter 11

FOUR HUNDRED and fifty miles above the rapidly developing peace festival, LOOTS swung by in its serene orbit. The eye of its giant telescope was pointed unflinchingly at the sun. For days now, it had not turned away.

Waiting and watching are always boring, and this wait and this watch were no exception for Dr. Georgi Aristovich Klyuchevsky. Being here was exciting, but waiting was not.

The screen before him held the image thrown by the telescope. The sun itself was blotted out by a huge black disk that permitted him to see, undazzled, past its rim. He watched with the trained patience of the professional astronomer, but he watched with only half of his mind. The other half was wishing the United States employed female astronauts. Indeed, only the presence of some one billion dollars of astronomical equipment consoled him.

With a heavy shock of blond hair that tumbled over his ears and neck, and a boyish face that belied his thirty-five years, Klyuchevsky had always made a hit with the girls. At eighteen, he had been admitted to Moscow University, where he excelled at astronomy and discovered his second big interest in life. It was said, with justification, that he knew the location of every star in the heavens and the bed of every pretty girl in Moscow.

Upon graduation, he had the honor of being assigned to the new observatory at Zelenchukskaya, which possessed what was then the largest telescope ever made. In spite of his profligate personal life, he had rapidly advanced to a position of prominence.

Now, here in LOOTS, he saw things in his imagination that not even this telescope could see. Hidden by the glare of the solar furnace was Jupiter. Klyuchevsky understood clearly why the others had concluded that it was a refueling stop. But he also knew that violent planet would not detain the Cygnians long.

Once refueled, they would fire their rockets to begin a long fall toward the sun. Earth was hidden from them, just as they were hidden from earth. The Cygnians would fall faster and faster until they almost brushed the torrid surface of the solar system's mighty lord, and then swing outward on a trajectory that would carry them past the sun and on to earth.

The sun. Everything that Jupiter is, the sun is more. Jupiter has been described as a star that never got going. The sun made it to full stardom. Where the temperature at the core of Jupiter reaches fifty thousand degrees Fahrenheit, the core of the sun burns at an incredible thirteen million degrees. At that temperature atoms collide so hard they fuse, releasing even more energy into the blazing core. The center of the sun is so hot that it shines with hard gamma rays. But those rays are bounced around by the packed atoms time and time again, until, perhaps a million years later, they crawl to the surface, tamed to ordinary light. A million years to reach the surface, yet a moment in the life of the sun, now four billion years old and in the prime of life.

The surface of the sun is called the photosphere. Through a heavily filtered telescope, it looks like a sea of seething rice grains. Above the surface is the sun's atmosphere, the chromosphere, a region where solar flares erupt into red arches and prominences that fountain thousands of miles into space. And all of it shines with a white heat, a light so intense it exerts a measurable pressure.

Still farther away is the corona, the shimmering outer atmosphere, almost a vacuum, hotter than an exploding hydrogen bomb. The outer edge of the corona streams away as the solar wind, wafting the tails of comets, flickering into a moment of incandescence seen on earth as the Aurora Borealis.

Somewhere near this god, moving under cover of its unrelenting glare, was the Cygnian fleet, ready to pounce on earth as a bomber dives out of the sun.

That was what Klyuchevsky was waiting for.

In another compartment of LOOTS, Bill Robinson was shaving. There was really no point in it, since his only company was male, and Robinson felt no need to impress the newest member of his crew. But you never knew what might come up. There might be a television relay.

Shaving in weightlessness was no easy task. One used a sticky cream that clung to the face and kept whiskers from floating free where they could wreak havoc with delicate equipment. It was necessary to have a towel handy to gather in any blobs that floated away. And one had to be anchored in order to have both hands free and not drift around the room.

Robinson was something of an expert, having logged more time in space than anybody else. He was nearly finished when Klyuchevsky stuck his head down through the hatch. "Bill! Come quickly!"

"Oh yeah?" he replied, irritated at the cultured accent of the Russian. "You got something?"

"There's a light moving away from the northwest limb."

"Just one?"

"So far."

Robinson hurriedly wiped the remaining lather off his face. Then he gave a push with his feet, floated up through the portal without touching the edges, and emerged right by the control seat of the telescope. With one easy motion of his hand, he levered himself in next to the Russian astronomer. It never hurt to give the less experienced Klyuchevsky a lesson in free-fall maneuvering.

"Now where . . . ?"

But the Russian was staring in astonishment. Robinson fol-

lowed Klyuchevsky's eyes to the screen. Then he too gaped.
Over a hundred flecks of light, each mirroring the brightness
of the sun, were clustered at the edge of the light-mask. As
they watched, another row appeared. Robinson tried to count
them, but more appeared constantly. Finally he gave up. He
knew from previous observations that there would be over a
thousand.

"February twelfth—the bastards are right on schedule," he
breathed.

The Soviet astronomer was chalk white, and the lines of his
handsome face were stretched into gauntness. "I didn't really
believe they would come," he said softly.

Chapter 12

As EMERGENCY calls always seemed to, this one jangled Nilstrom out of bed.

"Chris, Clem here. Bill Robinson is on the line with me."
He paused. "We have some rather frightful news."

"Christ! You've seen the fleet?"

"Righto. Bill, maybe you'd better tell him."

Robinson's voice came through an electronic blurring that
told of his remoteness. "We've got them, Chris. One thousand
mirrored ellipsoids came around the sun at four-thirty this
morning, your time."

"Damn it! What's their course?"

"They've moved north of the ecliptic, and are coasting along
on a course that'll bring them into the vicinity of the earth right
on schedule, eight days from now."

Chris didn't believe his ears. "Did you say *north*?"

"Yep," Robinson replied. "Indicated speed is almost one-
half million miles per hour, decelerating from the sun's
gravity."

"My God, they're flying right down the mouth of the cannon!" Chris fumbled in the drawer for his calculator. "Do you
have an ETA?"

"Well," said Tillman with an inexplicably cheerful voice,
"they'll have to make a mid-course correction to reach us. The
best time for that would be 5:15 A.M. your time, February

eighteenth. The burn should last for hours, probably a full day, and slow them down to fifty thousand miles per hour. They should start final orbital injection retroburn at 9:00 P.M. on the twentieth."

Nilstrom was busily figuring. "Then we have to fire about 4:00 P.M. on the twentieth." His heart was pounding so rapidly it was hard to concentrate.

"That's what I figure. Can you make it?"

Chris gave a worried grunt. "We'll *have* to make it. But it'll bust more than a few asses!"

"By the way," said Robinson, "closest approach to the sun was nineteen million miles."

"Damn! They must have some radiation shielding."

"Rather powerful air conditioners too, I imagine," said Sir Clement. "However, we estimate they spent twenty-eight hours at Jupiter, which almost certainly means they used robot tankers for refueling. And that means they haven't a *lot* of shielding."

"Yeah, but whatever they have reduces our chances of getting them."

Nilstrom put down the phone with a trembling in his stomach. Eight days left! After fourteen months of frantic activity, it would all be over in a week. One way or the other. He lay back in bed and thought how long it had been since he'd seen Mike and Susan. He counted backwards, found the days turning to weeks, and the weeks to months. But he'd talked to them as recently as last week and told them he'd be home soon. Either he would be, or they'd all be dead.

Chapter 13

VIRGINIA BUZZED Chris on the intercom and told him that General Beck was in the office. Nilstrom realized he'd be glad to see him, but when the general entered, Chris stared in astonishment. He was stooped, and his usual good cheer was missing. There was a noticeable tremor in his face.

"Nick! How are things going?"

"It's probably futile, Chris, but I've been all over the world installing Grasers."

Nilstrom saw that it was more than fatigue that was wrong

with Beck. "What's eating you, Nick?" he asked gently.

The tall man looked at Nilstrom with haunted eyes, then smiled bitterly. "Frankly, Chris, losing all those people...I...I don't know. I feel like I failed them."

"Bullshit!"

"Eh?"

"Nick, goddamnit, you're mortal. Nobody could have defended this place better. Look at what happened. You fought a split-second battle against a technologically superior opponent, scared off the Big Mother, chased her halfway around the world, and shot her down. If it hadn't been for the dam, the damage to Mistletoe wouldn't have been bad."

Beck nodded gloomily. "Well, anyway, Chris, I came to see you about security. We think there are three hundred thousand people camping along the river below the dam. We estimate there'll be half a million by next week. And some big names have shown up. Roberta Venezia arrived yesterday. Stockton Williams has announced he'll attend. Charles Hamilton is already there, and we're pretty sure Sydney Knox is. It's going to be big."

Nilstrom frowned. "Can you handle them, Nick? That's a lot of people."

"I've beefed up the ground defenses. The fences are heavily patrolled twenty-four hours a day. I have troops ready to move on a few minutes notice, and we're flying in riot-control devices. Water cannon, foam machines, tear gas, that sort of thing."

"We only have to hold out for eight days, Nick, and it'll be over, either way." Nilstrom told the general about Sir Clement's call.

"The retro-burn for that course correction could cause trouble here, Chris."

"Yeah, they'll be able to see it, all right. It'll look like a bright star. You think it might touch them off?"

"It could start a religious uprising," Beck said wryly. "That idiot Hendricks has shown up. FBI infiltrators report that he's been delivering sermons."

"Hendricks?"

"Yeah, the guy who's been saying for years that the flying saucer people bred us from apes, and are, in fact, our gods. Now he's been claiming they're coming to make us part of the Greater Universe, and that we should greet them like the returning gods of Olympus."

Nilstrom made a face. "I suppose every nut on earth is there."

"Yeah, but it's the ones who are serious, really dedicated, that bother me the most. Roberta Venezia can hit people right in the soul with her singing. Hamilton is a convincing speaker; Stockton Williams is a respected ecologist. There are veterans of the Vietnam War, many of them in wheelchairs. People are flooding in from all over the world. Immigration is trying to keep them out, but most of them find a way. Then, too, lots of people are coming across the border illegally because the Mexicans are ticked off that they weren't included in the project and won't cooperate with security." The general seemed to be relaxing. He put his feet on the coffee table and said, "But what the hell, Chris, tell me about the fleet."

"They really put on a show this morning. They seem to have an albedo near unity."

"Albedo?" Beck wrinkled his forehead.

"That's the amount of light reflected. They're like a fine-quality mirror, which is strange. I got a good look at Big Mother when she was here, and she was as black as a coalbin on a dark night."

"Maybe they can change, like chameleons."

"Great idea, if it'd work. I guess that's one more unresolved question. And speaking of unresolved questions, Chris, how come the fleet's coming in north of the ecliptic? I was sure they'd swing south."

"So was I, Nick. But I've been thinking about it and I think I've got the answer. Big Mother thought she'd destroyed Mistletoe and must have told the fleet that. After all, we were flooded. But she never got to the mine."

Beck looked puzzled. "Which isn't dangerous."

"I know that, you know that, but Big Mother didn't. She probably thought the mine was another Mistletoe."

"Of course! The domes are identical! So the fleet is coming in to the north to avoid what they think is an undamaged Graser in Brazil."

"Yeah. Will you be here for the shot?"

"Sure. I'll be here almost constantly from now on, in case those 'peace lovers' get violent."

Chapter 14

THE VAST crowd was deathly quiet that evening. Bobbie Venezia's voice was strong and lovely, and it floated across the enthralled throngs to the tent where the rally leaders, Sydney Knox, Charles Hamilton, and Stockton Williams had gathered. They were meeting that day, the seventeenth of February, to discuss how to stop Project Mistletoe.

"Gentlemen, our tactics haven't been workin'." Hamilton was firm. "We must try somethin' much more drastic."

"Like what?" Knox asked testily. "We have thousands of people picketing twenty-four hours a day. Pretty impressive, if you ask me."

"And pretty ineffective," Hamilton said. He ran his hands through his long hair. His frustration and grief over the folly of mankind had given his face an almost ethereal appearance. He sighed and said, "We're hampered by not knowin' when they're goin' to fire their damned gun."

"Olga told me they should have the gun ready . . . let me see . . . well, in the next few days. You know, I wonder what's happened to her."

"Yeah," growled Williams. "God knows what they've done with her." A professor of biology and ecology at the University of Oregon, he was a handsome man, tall, with blond hair just turning white. He wore a leather jacket, stylishly cut, over gray trousers and expensive hiking boots.

"Gentlemen," Hamilton interrupted, "may we get back on the subject? We believe the firin' will be this week. We have no reports on the fleet's progress."

"Yes we do," interrupted Williams. "A young man came to me today. He's been working at the Space Center in Houston and he says the fleet is only a few days away, and should make a mid-course correction early tomorrow morning. The retro-burn could be visible from here just before sunrise."

"With the naked eye?" asked Hamiliton incredulously. "How far away will they be?"

"Eighty million miles," said Knox. "But remember, Senator, there are a thousand of them, with powerful engines. We should be able to see the light from the exhausts."

Hamilton was uneasy. "Well, then, let's alert ever'body to look for it. We can have a predawn gatherin', and then, after the sun comes up, we can send a delegation to talk to the leaders of Mistletoe."

"Well, I can't go. I'm wanted all over the country. If I show up, they'll throw me in jail."

Hamilton said, "I'll call the president, Mister Knox. He's gone crazy, but we were friends once. I'll see if he has enough decency to offer us safe passage in and out of Mistletoe."

"Okay," answered Williams. "Good enough. But I think we should also consider what we're going to do if we don't get anywhere with them. Because I don't think we will!"

Sydney Knox looked grim. "Well, then we'll have to stop them by force! We have a half-million people here. Quite an army."

Chapter 15

ANNA'S FACE was clear and sharp on the monitor screen. "Chris, I've informed the world leaders, and they're all planning to be here for the firing day after tomorrow. President Reed will arrive tomorrow afternoon, and the others on the twentieth. How much time is there now until retro-fire?"

Nilstrom looked at his watch. "If Sir Clement's right, only fifteen minutes. It's five o'clock now."

"I'll be right over."

"Okay, Anna, hurry." Her image vanished. Chris stepped out of the blockhouse into the cold Arizona darkness.

When Anna arrived in a jeep a few minutes later, he had his binoculars trained up the canyon. She nudged him. "What do you see?"

He gave her a kiss. "I was surprised to see so many fires over at the peace festival. Something must be up. Anybody with sense would be in his sleeping bag at this hour."

"Including us?"

Chris put his arm around her and offered her the glasses. She looked through them briefly, then said, "There does seem to be a lot of activity. Do you suppose they know about the retro-firing?"

"Probably. Maybe it'll sober them."

Anna shivered, and pressed closer to Chris. "I hope so, but—" She broke off with a gasp. Chris pointed at the sky in the east, where a brilliant point of light had suddenly flared.

"My God!"

The light was even brighter than Venus. Chris raised the binoculars. After a minute, he handed them to Anna and said, "So that's Balder! And he'll be here in two more days!"

Within an hour, the sky lightened and the flare in the east grew dimmer. Finally the sun peeked over the horizon. The morning sky was its familiar blue, devoid of anything sinister. Chris turned the binoculars back on those at the peace rally. Many were still staring into the sky.

Chapter 16

PHYSICALLY, NILSTROM was a wreck. He had been up for so long he'd forgotten what bed looked like. The only sleep he'd had for two days was a catnap. But, although he could hardly believe it, he knew they were ready. They were actually going to fire the gun in thirty hours, when the invaders arrived at the critical point three hundred thousand miles deep in space.

Thirty more hours, and the long nightmare would be over, for better or for worse. Now, as he listened to the technician who was explaining to him and to Solovyev, Stehlen, Kellogg, and Anna the way the blockhouse would function during the countdown, he marveled at what they had done.

It was impossible, but the gun was repaired. Because they had used expensive and highly corrosion-resistant metals, the damage from the flood was less than they had anticipated. They were going to make it! And Balder was going to get the surprise of his life!

Nilstrom lifted his tired eyes to the wide slit in the block-house and looked out at the hills beyond the dome. Even at this distance, he could see smoke rising from the campfires of the peace-rock festival. The latest count was in excess of half a million people. Having that many so close and so dedicated to preventing the shot was nerve-wracking. He realized he was letting his mind wander, and forced himself to listen to the technician.

"The fifty-eight consoles with TV screens are for monitoring the subsystems in the reactor and in the Graser. Each one has a switch so the operator can stop the countdown and prevent—"

"Uh-uh!" Nilstrom interrupted vehemently. "No technician is going to stop this. The countdown doesn't even pause unless Dr. Solovyev, Dr. Kellogg, Dr. Stehlen, and I agree. If it's some minor thing, we go ahead. All the technicians can do is to notify us of what's happening."

The young man pursed his lips in disapproval of such recklessness, and went on, "Here is the master console, where . . . uh, the men whom Dr. Nilstrom just identified will sit. I understand the president will be here, so we have added a chair for him. And this row behind the master console is for other distinguished persons. The seat in the center is for Miss Larin, and the one next to her is for Chairman Semyechkin. This one is for . . ."

"Okay. Okay! Skip the protocol. Just tell us if this damned system is in working order."

"Oh, yessir. *Yes sir!* Checked, double-checked, and triple-checked. At four o'clock tomorrow afternoon, when you fire the gun, I can assure you that everything will function perfectly in this blockhouse. At least it will, ha ha, if you don't flip that toggle switch!"

Chris was too exhausted to be amused by the technician's attempt at humor. Wearily he asked, "What switch?"

"Well, sir, as you know, the cannon will actually be fired from Houston, but we've got to be able to stop it if anything goes wrong. So that switch at your desk can disconnect Houston from the Graser and stop the firing."

Nilstrom grunted and asked for a test of the TV monitor connected to the telescope on LOOTS. The technician reached over to Nilstrom's desk and pushed a button. Immediately the gigantic screen above the windowed slit lit up with a picture of the moon. The orbiting LOOTS was on the other side of the earth and could not now see the fleet, so their lens was turned on the moon. The familiar ridges and valleys stood out brilliantly.

Chris marveled again at what Takeo Omari had accomplished. The picture sent to them from LOOTS via satellite was clear and bright. They would all be able to watch the fleet for much of the remaining time, even during the shot itself.

"Okay, it looks good," Chris said. "Just how the devil you guys put this thing back together, I don't know, but..." He began to laugh. The three scientists were as grimy and ragged and red-eyed from lack of a bath and sleep as he. "I guess I *do* know how you did it. You worked your asses off! My God, but you guys look awful. You even smell! What the hell have you been doing with yourselves?"

They grinned back, but then Kellogg asked Anna sharply, "What I want to know is if you're going to be able to hold the peaceniks off our backs long enough for us to save their fucking skins?"

"How I hate the newspapers!" she exclaimed. "If anybody deserves to be exiled to Siberia, it's those publishers! The whole world is in turmoil today because of them—parliaments demanding explanations, others demanding that we fire missiles at the fleet—and that festival."

Kellogg ran his fingers through his dirty, tangled hair. "I'm not afraid of the politicians. They'll talk and talk and do nothing. But I'm worried about those peace-pricks up there in the hills."

Anna glanced out through the slit-window. "So am I. Nick's reconnoitering the area right now from a helicopter."

Nilstrom stretched painfully. "Well, I'm going for a shower and a nap before the countdown begins this evening."

Anna touched his sleeve. "Sorry, Chris, but you can't. We've got to meet the delegation from the peace-rock rally."

"The *what*?"

"President Reed phoned that Senator Hamilton and some others want to see us, and Reed thinks it may calm them down if we humor them."

"Hell, I'm no public-relations type."

"No, Chris, *that* you are not!" Stehlen agreed softly.

Nilstrom glared at him as Anna continued, "The president promised Hamilton that none of the delegation would be arrested. I rather imagine Sydney Knox will be with them."

Kellogg's eyes flashed. "Then, by God, *I* want to be in on the conference!"

Anna smiled and said with amusement, "Why not? The meeting won't do any good anyway, and you *do* seem to have a way with words, Chuck."

Chapter 17

IT WAS two o'clock that afternoon when Anna, Chris, and Kellogg met in Anna's office with Senator Charles Hamilton, Sydney Knox, and Roberta Venezia. Nilstrom shook hands stiffly; Kellogg clasped Miss Venezia's hand warmly, distastefully accepted the senator's handshake, and then glared at Knox as if he were a viper that had just crawled through warm cow dung.

"You fucking Judas! Get your sweaty, effeminate hand out of my way before I break all your fingers."

Knox shrugged, but his face, already flushed, became deeper red.

Anna cordially invited them all to be seated around the low coffee table, and Hamilton began in his most sonorous voice, "Now, I'm sure we can speak candidly. After all, I was at the original briefin' regardin' Mistletoe. I made my feelin's known then, and I haven't changed them."

Anna smiled warmly. "What can we do for you, Senator?"

"We've come here on behalf of all the peace-lovin' people of the world to demand that you abandon this mad scheme."

Nilstrom was too tired to be courteous. "You represent *all* the peace-loving people, Senator? May I congratulate you? I didn't know there'd been an election. How did you go about identifying the peace-loving people? Was it just announced in the papers that all peace-lovers should dash down to their local polling places and cast their ballots for—"

Knox snarled, "Why don't we cut out the funny stuff, Nilstrom? You know everyone has a right to know what you're doing here. The people are against you and you're not going to get away with it."

Anna said firmly, "Dr. Knox, perhaps you can tell us why you're here?"

"We're here on behalf of the people."

Nilstrom said in despair and disgust, "Oh Christ!"

Hamilton smiled benevolently, and his eyes had a faraway look in them, as if he were saying what had to be said but he had no hope that his words would be heeded. "Well, now, it's obvious that there are some things we aren't goin' to agree on. But I do think we have a right to ask that the decision to fight the aliens be presented to the people of the world in a referendum. For you to commit all of us to a millenium, maybe more, of warfare with our space neighbors, without askin' the people's permission, is wrong."

Anna said gently, "But Senator, in *your* country, I understand that it's the practice for duly elected leaders, congressmen, and the president to make decisions about war, is it not? And as you well know, they have authorized the participation of the United States in Mistletoe. Furthermore, you ask something we can't grant. You must see the president and your own Congress."

"Miss Larin." Roberta Venezia's hands waved like the fronds of a palm as she spoke. "I must say, I am really impressed, and I mean it, that you, a woman, are one of the leaders of this phenomenal project! I am *impressed*." Her voice was soft and her eyes, as black as her long, silky hair, were pleading. "But is it *right*? I mean, think of all the people in the world, not just those from the eight countries that are involved in this thing. Think of the *whole*, especially the people of the Third World. They haven't anything to say about being involved in this space war."

Anna smiled and said confidently, "Miss Venezia, you may or may not be right, but that was a decision made by the sponsoring powers. We are only the people they asked to take charge of the project. If you want to object, go to the president, Congress, the other world governments."

Hamilton said serenely, "Miss Larin, I don't want to seem disrespectful, but isn't that the same thing the SS leaders said? 'We're just followin' orders!' No, I must respectfully hold each of you responsible for what is happenin' here now."

Kellogg was so slumped in his chair that he looked like a pretzel. But neither his intellect nor his temper had relaxed. "Hamilton, don't threaten us! I hold *you* responsible for having added one more problem to this project—maybe making it impossible—and for causing a worldwide panic. And I would feel guilty if I did not do everything I can do to stop the slaughter of mankind by a lot of psychopathic star-hoppers."

Nilstrom sadly studied the senator. There was something winsome and noble about him. "Senator, did you see the retroburn?"

"I did, Dr. Nilstrom! I did indeed. But then, I never doubted that there was a fleet approachin' earth. Your data was most persuasive, suh!"

"Did you see the pictures of the bodies from the 747? The Delta Darts being destroyed? The Japanese power station? The Russian destroyer?"

"I did, yessuh." The senator seemed detached, disinterested, as if he were so firmly in possession of a higher truth that he listened only out of courtesy, not to learn.

"Well, then, do you think that a handful of you should decide for the rest of the world that no resistance be made to such murderers? Do *you* have the right to decide that *they* will die? Or go into slavery?"

Hamilton smiled imperturbably. "Ah, you have turned the tables on me, Dr. Nilstrom! And as an old debater, I admire your skill. But I feel that even if the invader is hostile, we would do better to yield and then win them with love rather than perish in futile resistance. I think it's our own warlike behavior that has caused them to act as they have."

Kellogg groaned and put his face in his hands.

Bobbie Venezia crossed her thin, brown legs, and leaned so far toward Kellogg that her chin seemed to rest on her knees. Her long hair fell almost to the floor, and her voice was a feathery whisper.

"Doctor Kellogg, I can see that you are *very* brilliant, really! And this is obviously a great, a *really* great thing, this Mistletoe. But it's so—unfriendly. I mean, don't you think we can win them with love? I really believe in the power of love."

For a time Kellogg didn't answer, but when he did, his voice was uncharacteristically wistful. "Miss Venezia, I've listened to you sing your song, 'The Power of Love,' a hundred times. And you almost make me believe it! I wish I *could* believe it—but I don't. I'm absolutely convinced that if we don't stop those bastards, they'll turn their exhausts on the world and burn up every man, woman, and child of us. They've shown that they're psychopaths."

Her eyes widened and she whispered, "Oh! Do you *really* think so?"

Knox stood up. "It's obvious that we're not getting anywhere. I have only one more thing to say—if you don't stop this insane project, we'll stop it for you."

Nilstrom rose too. "Who's 'we'?"

"The peace-loving people of the world. We'll throw our bodies across your gun if necessary. Just when is it, Dr. Nilstrom, that you plan to fire this thing?"

"Knox, if you'll promise to throw *your* body across the Graser, I'll tell you."

"Senator," Anna said, "you understand that we've met with you as a courtesy to President Reed. But we're not authorized to stop this project on your request."

As the six of them walked to the door, Kellogg fell into step with Roberta Venezia. "You know, I've been an admirer of yours for years. I even bought a guitar and tried to play and sing like you do, but I sounded like fingernails on a blackboard."

"Oh, I'll bet you *didn't*! You have such a nice speaking voice! Really! And you're so brilliant you can do anything."

"Say! I have a couple of hours, Bobbie. Why don't you come swimming with me, and then we'll have a quick dinner?"

"Wow! That'd be nice! It's awfully dry out there at the festival. But I don't have a suit."

"Hmm . . . well, I'll tell you what." He looked at Knox, then winked at Anna. "We'll go by Olga Solovyev's apartment and get hers. She won't need it anymore."

Knox whirled on Kellogg. "You sonofabitch! What have you done with her?"

Kellogg smiled innocently. "You know, Knox, it was really a relief for me to find out that you like girls. I always had you pegged for a fairy. But don't worry about your girlfriend."

"What have you done with her?"

"Don't worry, Knox. She stood up to torture very well. She didn't really do much talking until we shoved the red-hot poker—"

Anna burst out laughing and stopped him. "Chuck! Don't be cruel." She turned to Knox and said, "Olga is a Russian, and under the Mistletoe treaty she will be tried under Russian law. She is being detained for transport home."

Chris and Anna watched from the window as the group left the building. They were amused to see Knox and Hamilton shaking their heads in despair as Kellogg and Miss Venezia walked toward his apartment, hand in hand.

Chris glanced at his watch. "Three-thirty! Two hours before we begin the countdown. Let's get an hours's sleep."

But they never got out of the headquarters building. The loudspeaker paged Nilstrom, and he and Anna went wearily to his office. Tillman was on the video relay.

Chapter 18

"Two MINUTES to reacquisition," announced Klyuchevsky.

"Check," acknowledged Robinson. Both men scanned the dials in front of them. One out of every four hours, they lost sight of the fleet as LOOTS passed behind the bulk of the earth. The crew often used this interlude to recalibrate the aiming mechanism of the huge telescope. This time they had sighted on the moon as a check. As usual, things were running smoothly, and the telescope easily swung back to its original heading, ready to pick up the fleet again.

For days, LOOTS had watched the approach of the Cygnians. Robinson, and now Klyuchevsky, had grown almost used to the picture on the screen. Every time the satellite emerged from behind the earth, the picture was the same—the unchanging formation of ships, arrayed like squares on a three-dimensional chessboard. The retro-firing had changed that image briefly, but now it should be back to normal.

The two were silent as the edge of earth crept off the screen and more and more stars appeared.

"There they are," Klyuchevsky asserted. "Bigger than ever. Hey!"

"My God!" breathed Robinson. "What happened?"

"There are a million of them! Where did they all come from?"

"No! They're spread out! The're spread out all over the damned sky!"

"But why? Oh my God!" The Russian's face had suddenly gone white.

Robinson reached for the phone. "Wait till Sir Clement hears this."

The other nodded numbly, still staring at the screen.

The Cygnians had deployed their fleet for battle.

"Clem, you know what this means."

"It means you'll have to shoot the cannon about ten hours earlier than is optimal because if you wait, the beam won't be wide enough to catch all the ships in its embrace, right?"

Nilstrom was rapidly making calculations. "Yes, damn it! We'll have to fire tomorrow morning at about six, when the fleet is eight hundred thousand miles away. And their dose of gamma radiation will be a fraction of what we planned."

Tillman was subdued. "And we know they're shielded to some extent. "There's only one thing to do, Chris."

"Yeah?"

"You've got to increase the power to the two-hundred-megaton range you planned in the first place."

"You know what can happen if we do?"

"Well, I dare say it could melt the cables, fuse the bearings, even warp the barrel. But you only have time for one shot anyway."

"Clem, the cooling jacket of the gun is filled with liquid helium. If it overheats, it'll blow up with the power of an atomic bomb, scattering gamma rays in every direction except at the fleet. I'd rather take our chances on a low-power shot that would at least reach the fleet."

When the image of the Englishman had faded from the screen, Nilstrom turned to Anna grimly. "Okay, get in touch with the eight national leaders and tell them the countdown will be abbreviated and will begin immediately. We'll fire at 6:16 A.M. our time, at a distance of eight hundred thousand miles, and increase the power as much as we dare."

Anna swiftly took notes. Nilstrom got on the phone and relayed the news to Solovyev, the Houston Space Center, Kellogg, and finally Stehlen. "Helmut, since the shot will be so early in the morning, the fleet will be very, very low on the horizon. You'll have to remove the lower section of panels from the dome, but shield that operation from those idiots in the hills. If they know we're going to fire tomorrow, they may really go nuts."

As he hung up the receiver, Anna asked, "Chris, just how bad is this news?"

There was no expression on her face, but her lips were pale, and he hesitated before answering. He decided to give it to her straight. "It reduces our chances from fifty-fifty to . . . damned near infinitesimal."

He took her in his arms and held her tightly. Neither of them said anything for a long time, and then Anna pushed him away.

"Chris, if—if it is this bad, then there's something you must do." Her steady blue eyes were level and determined. "You must call Mike and Susan. If you wait, you may not get another chance."

Wordlessly he picked up the phone, punched out the number, waited a minute, then said, "Mike? This is Dad. How are you, tiger?"

The little boy cried out, then began to sob. He wept uncontrollably for several minutes before he was able to say, "Grandma, it's Dad..." Even as the child handed over the phone, Chris could hear him begin to sob again.

"Christian Nilstrom!" His mother's voice quivered with fury and fear. "Do you *know* what you're doing to your children?" She paused to regain control of herself, but before Chris could respond, she swept on, "You haven't seen them in months, haven't written in weeks, and haven't called in days! There is a terrible accident at Mistletoe, and we learn about it on the ten o'clock news. We only know you're safe because the newscasters quoted you denying that sabotage caused the accident. The papers are full of stories of scientists saying the accident would never have occurred if a physicist instead of you were heading up the project. Some even call you a quack. Then we hear that Mistletoe is really building a gun to destroy a fleet of space invaders. Your children have been miserable, lonely, and frustrated. Now their schoolmates are telling them their father is a fool."

Nilstrom tried to calm her by saying how busy he'd been, but she furiously interrupted him. "Just tell me one thing, and I don't want any excuses about national security! *Is* there a fleet of—people—coming here to kill us or not?"

Chris decided it was too late for secrecy. "Yes, Mother, there is. And it's up to me to stop them. Let me talk to Mike again, will you?"

He heard her gasp, and knew she was handing the phone to Mike. This time the child was calm.

"Hi, Mike. I just called to say that this nightmare is almost over. I'll be home in two days, and this time it won't be for a few hours. It'll be for good."

The boy began to weep again. "Oh, Daddy! We miss you so much! Where have you been? We tried to call you so many times and they can never find you—and you don't call back. Please come home."

There were tears in Nilstrom's eyes and a knot in his stomach as he said, "I told you, Mike, *two days*. Then we'll go on a vacation, school or not, okay?"

The sobbing slowed. "Daddy, people are saying terrible things."

Nilstrom fought to control himself now, and Anna came and wiped away the tears that were blinding him, and kissed his face.

"Mike, don't worry about the dumb things people say. Just remember, I'll be home soon. Now let me talk to Susie."

It took fifteen minutes to calm both children, reassure his mother, and chat with his father. Anna spoke to each one too, confidently and cheerfully. Then the call was over.

Nilstrom felt wrung out. He grinned at Anna. "Sorry about being a baby, but those kids have already put up with so much." He stopped, and Anna put her arms around him and snuggled close. They sat for five minutes in silence.

Chris looked at his watch. "Got to go. Countdown!" His voice was strong. He even sounded refreshed.

He could not know that Anna had asked him to call his children not only for their benefit, but also to give him the catharsis he needed, and to infuse him with fresh determination.

At the door, he turned. "Anna, we're going to get those bastards! We're going to blow Balder out of the skies!" He glanced at the hills, where the smoke from the festival was staining the blue desert sky. "If *they* let us," he added.

Part Six

Chapter 1

THE MP guarding Olga Solovyev at her apartment knew she wasn't considered dangerous, or she'd be in the project jail. So when she asked him to play gin rummy, he willingly obliged. And he thought it uncommonly kind of her to offer him some iced tea.

He was writing down the scores when she returned with the glasses, put hers down, and circled behind him to put his on the table. He was still adding up the score when she picked up the brass vase of dry flowers. He only caught a glimpse of her flashing arm descending.

Olga knew she had four hours before the next guard came on at midnight. Breathless because she had struck again and again, she dragged the MP's body into her bedroom and undressed him. The little man's uniform fit her perfectly. It took a minute to wash the blood off the collar, but then she was outside, looking for his Jeep. She found it and headed for the road to Phoenix, but some unusual activity at the dome caught her attention. She stopped the Jeep and watched. Baffled, she drove closer. Workmen were tearing panels from the geodesic dome, near the base. Then it came to her. It wasn't so much a logical conclusion as an intuitive one.

They were preparing to fire.

At the south gate, sleepy guards waved the jeep through without looking at her identification or even her face.

Once outside, Olga drove west on the highway toward the dirt road that led north to the dam. Twice, patrols made her slow down, but seeing her uniform, let her through. When she reached the dirt road, she drove even more rapidly and arrived at the festival site at eleven o'clock.

Olga had never seen so many people in one place before. Everyone was listening to music from the center stage, where a rock group was performing.

She walked away from the light of the campfires, searching until she found an empty tent, where she stole a dress and changed into it. Then she asked a group of campers where to look for Knox and Hamilton. Twenty minutes later, she found them.

When Olga explained what she'd seen at the dome, Knox exploded. "Those bastards! They must be planning to fire that monster tomorrow morning, if they're tearing out the lower panels on the east side. What'll we do, Senator?"

Hamilton no longer looked quite human. His eyes seemed to be fixed on something far away, and his smile was unreal, as if he had suffered so much in this world that he had withdrawn from it.

"Senator, what'll we do?" Knox repeated.

The older man looked at him and said, "Don't you worry, son, I'll stop 'em."

Knox squinted at Hamilton in the darkness, and he knew he was alone. Hamilton was living in a dream. Violently, Knox turned away and led Olga to the bandstand. Once there, he spoke quietly with the young man who was the emcee. The red-haired youth jumped to the platform and stopped the music. The huge crowd grew so silent that only the crackling of the fires and the wind off the buttes could be heard.

Knox took the microphone. "Hey, all you peace-lovers! We've had our fun out here, making music, making friends, making love. But now we've got to *do* something. You all know I'm the man who gave that information to the *New York Globe*, and now I'm a fugitive from the Gestapo FBI because of it."

Knox had mounted the platform with his elegant leather jacket only draped across his shoulders. Now, as he waved his arms to acknowledge the cheers and applause, the jacket slid off to the platform.

"Well, tonight we have with us the one who got those documents for me. Because she did, she's been tortured and illegally imprisoned. But she escaped and is here to tell us the whole story of Mistletoe. I think when she's finished you'll agree that the time has come for the people to seize power. Listen to her!"

Out in the hills, the patrols that had been posted by General Beck heard the roar that followed Olga's speech.

Then they saw the torches and flashlights and headlights of five hundred thousand people as they began to move toward Mistletoe.

It was after midnight and they had miles to go.

Chapter 2

IT WAS 12:30 A.M. on the morning of the twentieth when the president arrived at the blockhouse. And since the shot would be some ten hours earlier than planned, he was the only one of the Mistletoe leaders who would be there in time to witness the firing.

Carl Reed didn't come alone. With him were Secretary of State Wilbur Sternald, Secretary of Defense John Scott, Clifton Williams of the CIA, and Gilbert Doyle, Chairman of the House Committee on the Armed Services.

Anna jumped up immediately to greet them. Her two-piece light gray suit was smudged and her hair was coming unpinned, but excitement had revived her so that her cheeks were red and her eyes bright. "Ah, President Reed! Please come with me, we have seats for you."

Nilstrom, Kellogg, Solovyev, and Stehlen sat at the console, watching the green display screens in front of them. All of the scientists were unshaven and in shirtsleeves. Periodically, through the microphones that were part of the headsets each wore, they spoke to technicians conducting the countdown.

Reed looked around the huge blockhouse, at the dozens of men at monitors, at the giant TV screen. He was grim with fatigue and anxiety, but his smile returned as he thought of their achievement. "Miss Larin, this is simply unbelievable! I thought we were doomed after the flood."

"We thought so too, Mr. President, but those men . . ." She looked across the room at the scientists and shook her head in wordless admiration. "Just keep your fingers crossed that all goes well in the next six hours."

"Everything's set, isn't it?"

"Yes, but there's the countdown. A broken circuit, a loose rivet, a leak in the coolant jacket, a thousand—no, a million things could go wrong. And now our countdown can only check out the major areas of potential problems. We haven't time for the detailed check used for space shots."

Anna led them to the coffee bar next to the wall and each man accepted a cup. Some also took sandwiches from the table. Even the men at the consoles next to the coffee urn took no notice of their presence; the din of their voices continued unabated.

"Miss Larin, before I sit down, I'd like to speak to General Beck," said the president. "When we flew in a few minutes ago, there were thousands of lights moving this way."

Anna nodded, and while the others took their seats, she led Reed to where Beck sat before an array of display screens. Over her shoulder she said, "Dr. Omari has set up a command post here for General Beck. He has TV monitors and radio communication with his field commanders."

The group clustered around Beck parted slightly as they approached, and the president could see that Admiral Steinhauser, General Gray, and General Howard had arrived before him. They nodded grim greetings.

"Hello, Nick. Everything under control?"

"Affirmative!" In contrast to the impeccably dressed Chiefs of Staff, the tall general was unshaven and dirty, and his blue uniform was torn. His bulging eyes were veined in red, and his hair was uncombed. "Please excuse my appearance, sir. I was out reconnoitering the line of march and supervising the installation of new barbed wire barricades, and unfortunately I stumbled into one myself."

Reed smiled.

"We have two long barricades now, three miles apart, one at the narrows and one near the mouth of the canyon, in addition to the high double fences here at the site. We have armored trucks with water cannons or foam guns, troops with tear gas, and helicopters with noise machines, blinding lights, and emetic gas bombs. I've ordered all commanders to fall back slowly rather than to open fire. I think we can hold them long enough to get the shot off. The terrain between here and there is pretty rough, full of arroyos and rocks. The road from the dam is on high ground on the west side of the valley, but we've cratered that and dynamited the upper part. It's virtually impassable for any vehicle."

"Good work, General. Continue to avoid violence. What set the crowd off? How did they find out the time for the shot?"

Anna answered the president's question. "Olga Solovyev killed her guard and escaped. Again, we Russians are ashamed."

Reed said grimly, "Well, it was an American who fed it to the press. And God, what a mess!"

Beck was still watching the monitors. The pictures were coming from helicopters spotlighting the crowd. Jeeps and trail bikes led the way, winding slowly down the hills through the gullies and arroyos, at times splashing through the shallow river. People carrying torches and flashlights followed. A few vans and sedans had begun the march, but were soon abandoned because of the rough terrain. Beck could see youths in Levi's and sweatshirts, women in pantsuits, men in tweed jackets, clergymen in collars, nuns, Hindu cult members in flowing saffron robes, entertainers in elegant attire—and one girl in the nude. He knew there were businessmen, housewives, professors, nature freaks, children, minor politicians, and several motorcycle gangs in the mob. Most of the crowd were responsible, intelligent people sickened by endless wars. Beck sighed. He was in sympathy with them, even if he couldn't agree with them.

Anna asked softly, "Mr. President, what's the reaction around the world, since the retro-firing was so widely seen?"

"Panic. There's been a rash of suicides, and preachers are calling on us to repent. The ACLU demands that we release all data on Mistletoe immediately, and the Veterans of Foreign Wars demand we arrest the ACLU. It's unbelievable."

Anna brushed away a strand of hair. "At least it'll be over soon, one way or the other."

He nodded. "But what a disaster!"

They followed the aisle between the guests and the busy technicians back to the master console. Beside Nilstrom was a chair for the president. But before he could sit down, Anna laid her hand on Reed's arm and whispered in his ear, "Sir, these men are exhausted and so busy they haven't even paused for coffee. Just observe, please, and don't talk to them."

Reed frowned. "But Miss Larin, surely a little greeting from the President of—"

"No! You asshole!" Reed cringed at the outburst. "We're *not* going to stop this countdown! It's just a defective sensor. Climb down there and look!" It was Kellogg snarling into his microphone.

"I had hoped Dr. Nilstrom could do something about Dr. Kellogg's language," the president said with a smile.

"You idiot! You left a cap on the vent! Get up on that scaffold and get the damned thing off before it explodes and blows your balls over the moon!" This time it was Nilstrom, oblivious to everything around him.

Wordlessly, the president shook his handsome head and sank into his chair.

Chris didn't acknowledge Reed's presence for an hour and a half. Then, at 2:02 A.M., he flicked off his headset and turned to the president. He smiled wryly and said, "Morning, sir. Want to see something? LOOTS is in position to view the fleet again." He snapped a switch on his desk, and the huge screen above the slit-windows lit up with a picture of the heavens. A number of stars could be seen, but in the center, in geometric formation, were hundreds of large, silver, elongated objects.

Reed whistled. "So that's the fleet? My God, what a picture! How far away are they?"

"Just about a million miles, and traveling at fifty thousand miles an hour." Nilstrom never took his eyes off the screen.

"There are so many!" The president was whispering in awe, and Nilstrom could hardly hear him above the voices of technicians. "How big are they?"

Chris turned and faced Reed. "Each is approximately a thousand feet long, or about the size of a tanker. There must be many types, but they all look much the same because of the requirements of space travel. If you look closely, sir, you'll see they're ellipsoid."

"Oh, yes, I can see that." Reed studied the screen a few seconds longer, then said, "You're tearing out part of the dome. Why bother? The Graser beam would go right through, wouldn't it?"

"Oh, sure, but it'll vaporize everything in its path, including that section of the dome. And when something vaporizes, it, in effect, explodes. Also, that vaporized metal and plastic would be radioactive, which would complicate any work in the area later." Nilstrom yawned, took off his glasses, rubbed his eyes, and replaced his glasses again.

"But isn't the firing of the cannon like an explosion?"

"Well, yes and no. You won't see anything but a violent flash, like lightning, but straight as an arrow. It'll be so bright that anyone intending to watch through the slit-window will need to wear goggles. And there'll be one hell of a noise, like a clap of thunder, but much louder. That's from the overheated air—which is what causes thunder."

Reed looked at Chris closely and asked quietly, "Will the beam have enough power to kill everyone in the fleet?"

"Very debatable. We don't really know how much shielding they have—quite a bit, we're afraid. We know the beam won't have enough power to destroy their instrumentation, much less the ships themselves." He shook his head.

"If we could wait until they're only three hundred thousand miles away, as we planned, and if the gun works well, we could kill them instantly. We might even see some of the ships explode. But eight hundred thousand miles? That's three times the distance to the moon!"

Reed nodded solemnly and Nilstrom started to turn back to his console, then hesitated. "Two other things. LOOTS will be in position, so we'll be able to watch the fleet as the beam hits, eight and six-tenths seconds after the Graser fires. It takes four and three-tenths seconds for the beam to reach the fleet, and the same time for the picture to get back to us. We have all the radio telescopes in this area of the world trained on them too, so we'll be able to hear whether they send any messages. Not that we can understand them, but we've been monitoring them all along, and it's amazing how they chatter with each other."

"You said it takes four and three-tenths seconds for the beam to reach the fleet? Will they see it coming and take evasive action?"

Nilstrom laughed. "Excuse me, Mr. President, but you see, gamma rays travel at the speed of light. The Cygnians won't know a thing until the beam passes through them. Of course, their sensors will tell them something has happened even if the beam doesn't cause immediate physical injury."

"Hmm. Okay. I understand. What's the second thing you have to tell me?"

"See this toggle switch?" Nilstrom frowned. "If anything goes wrong here at the last minute, we can flip the switch and disconnect the aiming and firing controls in Houston. Now, unless we have a major mechanical failure, it's unlikely that *I* am going to have any reason not to fire. But if for some reason *you* decide not to go ahead with the shot, there's the switch."

Reed smiled wearily. "Not much chance of that, is there, Chris? Besides, I'm only one of the eight leaders."

"Yes, sir. But you're the only one *here*. You represent them all."

"You're trying to tell me that it's my responsibility, aren't you? You're beginning to sound like Charlie Hamilton." Reed looked out the slit-window at the glow of lights moving from the festival site. "I wonder," he mused sorrowfully, "if Charlie is out there. He must be brokenhearted."

Chapter 3

BUT HAMILTON was not with the thousands who were pouring down the valley toward Mistletoe. Sydney Knox was there, in a Jeep, standing, waving everyone on, calling out on a bullhorn. And with him was Olga Solovyev, sitting in the back seat, lost in her own thoughts, watching the sea of humanity swarm across the ridges and gullies of the rugged desert like a giant amoeba.

It was hard going, and many times the flowing mass had to stop at an impassable gully, backtrack, circle, and find another way. Many had fallen and were injured, and others had dropped out to care for them, but the mass swept on.

At 2:48 A.M., those in the lead reached the first barbed-wire barrier at the narrowest part of the canyon. Beyond it, the terrain leveled out into a wider valley and easier going, but across the low wire fence were blinding lights. Knox knew they represented armored cars and possibly even light tanks.

While the vast throng piled up before the barrier, he reconnoitered, and found that the wire stretched from one canyon wall to the other. He climbed as high as he could, and saw another line of lights about three miles ahead. Guessing that it was another barrier, he called together some of the more aggressive young people.

Soon they were circulating through the ranks of Jeeps, motorcycles, and trail bikes. They returned with sixty-three pairs of wire cutters and pliers. Slowly they began to cut their way through the barrier.

As Knox had suspected, they were not fired upon, but a bullhorn warned them to stop where they were. They continued to cut the wire. A dozen searchlights snapped on, and tear gas grenades were lobbed in. The cutters retreated, gasping and weeping. From the crowd, rifles fired at the blinding search-lights.

The sound of the shots sent a wave of terror through the mob, but when the fire was not returned and the lights went out one by one, the leaders became more aggressive and rushed forward. The gas drove them back again.

It was Olga who suggested that enough of the wire was gone so that they could storm the barrier. Jeeps and four-wheel-drive trucks led the assault, and within minutes they broke through. Masses of people followed, coughing and weeping as they moved through the clouds of gas lying in the lower areas. The troops had retreated.

On level ground now, the crowd moved faster, confident and with high spirits. Still in the lead, Knox and Olga saw the project site draw closer by the moment.

Up to their right on the hillside was an antiaircraft battery connected to Mistletoe by a small access road. Knox sent a task force of motorcyclists up with orders to outflank the next barbed-wire barrier. He watched their lights as they picked their way toward the road. With them they carried the weapons for their assault; They carried dynamite.

Chapter 4

SENATOR CHARLES HAMILTON had spread a blanket on the ground under the wing of the little Cessna that had brought him to the festival. He was lost in meditation. He heard nothing of the singing or the shots. The heavy responsibility he felt for the follies and sufferings of mankind had lifted, and in their place was the joy that comes for a great, selfless decision.

Senator Hamilton had made his peace with God, with the universe, with his fellow man. He was finally happy. Soon he would make the ultimate sacrifice for his convictions, and that gave him peace.

Chapter 5

AT 5:00 A.M., the monstrous gun responded to electronic nudges from the Houston Space Center and began to lower to a nearly horizontal position. The hole in the side of the dome was large enough now, and soon, if all went well, the Graser would be fired—just before sunrise, just as the earth rolled around and the fleet came over the horizon. A twenty-foot-wide coherent beam of vicious gamma rays would stab eight hundred thousand miles out into space to meet the fleet gliding toward its rendezvous with earth.

The barrel of the Graser was three hundred and thirty feet long and, in its cooling jacket, eighty feet in diameter. A covering of frost added another two feet. The technicians who had checked every detail left the dome now. The Graser was ready.

Others continued the countdown on the reactor. But within a few minutes, the reactor too was ready for its one titanic effort.

Inside the blockhouse, Kellogg, Stehlen, Solovyev, and Nilstrom reviewed their decision to use the equivalent of a hundred and ninety megatons of power for the shot. The four admitted that there was still an element of risk; none knew whether their decision was the correct one.

Nilstrom waited apprehensively for Reed to interfere. He knew how Reed hated war, hated the thought of people dying violently. But the president listened carefully and said nothing.

The last stages of the countdown went on.

Chapter 6

ONLY TWO miles from the gun and three from the blockhouse, the leading elements of the crowd reached the second barrier. Soon there were thirty thousand shouting people facing less than a thousand soldiers across the wire.

Hotheads threw rocks at the troops, but they fell far short. Others dashed to the barricade to cut the wire. Loudspeakers blared at them to stop, but they went ahead, cutting their way through the incredible tangle. Behind them, the crowd swelled to nearly a hundred thousand, spreading across the valley, then to two hundred thousand. Searchlights illuminated the scene and helicopters circled overhead, playing their intense spotlights on the huge crowd. The noise became an ugly roar of frustration.

There were spurts of light as cannisters of tear gas were fired. One by one, the cutters abandoned their work and retreated, wheezing, to safety. But Knox urged them on, reminding them that the shot would soon take place. Other young men took up the cutters, only to retreat when the gas got too thick.

Knox swore violently. Where the hell were the motorcycle shock troops? There were three hundred thousand in the crowd now, and those in the back pressed the others forward into the wire. Some were cut and many were sick from the tear gas. Again, wire cutters went to work, but they were pinpointed by searchlights and engulfed with more tear gas. Marksmen in the vast mob tried to shoot out the searchlights.

Suddenly the helicopters swept down and released a cloud of nausea gas over the crowd. There were screams of fear and outrage, and the riflemen turned their fire on the helicopters. Thousands were vomiting, and the monstrous crowd began to retreat.

The helicopters flew back and forth over the throng, and their loudspeakers drowned out even the roar of their own motors and the flap, flap, flap, of their rotors: "YOU ARE ILLEGALLY ON UNITED STATES PROPERTY. PLEASE LEAVE IMMEDIATELY BEFORE MORE DRASTIC ACTION IS TAKEN. THIS IS BY ORDER OF THE PRESIDENT OF THE UNITED STATES."

Their lights played over the crowd constantly. Specially designed for riot control, they were so bright they left afterimages in the eyes.

Knox was throwing up and his eyes burned fearfully, but he would not give up. He noticed that the wind had sprung up and was carrying away the gas, so he shouted to his followers to move forward again. There were fewer this time. Those unaccustomed to great physical exertion, and those surprised at the violent resistance, had retreated up the canyon.

There were still thousands to press the attack, and suddenly they got their break. Inside the barrier, a cluster of lights appeared, racing toward them. It was the motorcyclists, who had walked their bikes around craters and along what was left of the road, and circled the military forces. Now they charged into the maze of wire, hurling sticks of dynamite.

The peace people recoiled from the explosions, but when they saw great holes in the barrier, they dashed forward and poured down the valley.

The soldiers were mostly Indian and Chinese, with a few American liaison officers and one English contingent. Terrified at the marauding motorcyclists firing small arms and racing along the wire toward them, the Chinese returned the fire. One rider fell and his cycle continued to race forward, hit a rock, and hurtled into the air, then fell back and snarled on its side in a futile circle. A housewife from Illinois and two Oregon teenagers were shot as they ran through the barrier, and their screams joined the cacophony.

The American liaison officers soon had the Chinese under control, but the attempt to stop the crowd peacefully had been abandoned long enough to provoke mass passions. In a fury, the mob ran through the ranks of soldiers, throwing rocks, firing rifles and pistols. The commanders ordered their men to retreat, and trucks and Jeeps roared into life and disappeared.

They were replaced with armored riot-control vehicles bearing high-pressure water cannons. Men and women were knocked to their knees or thrown back upon the wire by the powerful streams of water.

But it was too late to stop the movement. Olga jumped out of the Jeep, grabbed a stick of dynamite, lit the fuse, jumped onto an armored car, and stuffed the dynamite down the exhaust. The explosion killed everyone inside, and the other cars wheeled around and headed for the safety of the site enclosure, leaving a cloud of gas behind.

But now the crowd was free of obstacles, and it surged across the flat desert floor toward the electrified fence surrounding Mistletoe. They weren't singing now, but shouting, screaming, roaring in defiance and rage. Knox and Olga were again in the lead Jeep.

A helicopter seeking to impede their progress broadcast prepared sounds so irritating to human ears that they could in time drive people mad. People screeched in pain and covered their ears. Those with rifles fired at the copter, and suddenly it tipped crazily, spun in circles, plummeted to the desert, and exploded in a ball of fire. The crowd swept on.

Chapter 7

SENATOR CHARLES HAMILTON flew above the moving mass. He had smashed the lights of his plane so it could not be easily seen. Now, as he looked down, sadness disturbed his supernatural calm. He circled once, high above the copters but low enough to see the bodies of the injured and slain in the light of the numerous spotlights. Would it never end? Would men slay each other forever? He hauled back on the stick and sent the little plane high, high up into the air over the desert, heading east, away from Mistletoe.

Chapter 8

WHEN BECK commanded his men to pull back behind the electrified fence, he knew he had to do something more to slow the mob's progress. There was still time for them to reach the dome before the shot. He called for more helicopters to lay down clouds of gas, and the civilian workers were issued fire hoses and stationed at the fence, but again, he ordered his men not to fire. He had little need now to watch the TV monitors. He had only to lift his eyes to the slit-window to see hundreds of lights bobbing on the desert, relentlessly moving toward the Graser, now waiting for its signal from Houston. Like the wall of water that had surged down the same valley only three weeks before, the mob seemed unstoppable.

It was five-forty when those in the lead reached the electrified outer fence and stopped. Cannisters of gas drove them back—for the moment.

Chapter 9

CHRIS HAD just refused a technician permission to reenter the
dome to check a sensor that was proclaiming a faulty circuit
on the reactor. Nilstrom knew there wasn't time, and besides,
he was sure the sensor had merely shorted out and was giving
a false warning. At least he hoped that was it.

The president was still seated next to Nilstrom, perspiration
streaming down his face, his hands shaking, as he looked out
at the masses of peace-hungry citizens. He knew that it would
now be an unbelievable catastrophe if the gun blew up, for all
the people on the desert would be killed. Nilstrom watched
him, desperately afraid Reed couldn't stand up under the growing pressure.

Just at that moment, the huge screen above the slit-window
lit up. LOOTS was again in position to observe the fleet. When
the image came on the screen, there was a collective gasp, for
now the fleet was so close that there was a dramatic improve-
ment in the picture. Each ship could be clearly seen. Long,
cigar-shaped, silvery, they glided through the black sky. There
was no exhaust fire to give life to the eerily beautiful scene.

These ships had flown for thirty years across trillions of
miles of empty space, probably carrying a whole population
of men, women, and children. Those now in charge had probably been no more than young cadets when the trip began. The
first commanders had almost certainly died en route.

Chris found himself wondering if there were children playing in nurseries. Or were they in some sort of deep storage,
kept in an undreaming sleep until arrival? What were the
women like? Smiling housewives or stern amazon warriors?

What had it been like to build the fleet, which had almost
certainly been done in great docks orbiting in space? He could
picture riveters in spacesuits crawling over the great hulks. He
could even imagine the excitement, the sense of relief when
at last the fleet was ready, a thousand gigantic ships orbiting
the strange planet with the two weaks suns, and when word
arrived that a new home was ready—for conquest.

How unfeeling they must be, he thought, to contemplate

wiping out four billion beings in order to steal their homeland.
But maybe they saw themselves as something like the Holy
Children of Israel, who invaded the Promised Land after forty
years in the wilderness and exterminated the Canaanite inhabitants. Did the Cygnians consider humans a race of moral and
intellectual inferiors not worthy of the planet on which they
lived? Perhaps the invaders were puritanical, ruthless religious
fanatics, invading a "pagan" land. Was the fleet commissioned
in a great religious ceremony before being launched on its long
journey?

He shook himself. Whoever they were, they wanted the
lovely little green planet God had given man. And by God,
they weren't going to get it if Chris could help it.

"Sir! Mr. President!" A young soldier stood beside the
master console.

Reed swiveled to face him. "Yes?" His voice was an-
guished.

"Sir, we have received a radio message from a light plane
east of here. General Beck said to give it to you. The pilot
claims to be Senator Charles Hamilton, and he insists on speaking to you."

"Oh my God!" Reed started to rise, and Nilstrom noted that
his shirt was sopping wet with perspiration. He pulled the
distraught chief executive back into his seat.

"Here, sir." He flicked a switch. "Speak into this microphone."

Reed picked up the mike. "Hello? Charlie? What the devil
are you doing?"

Chapter 10

SYDNEY KNOX told Olga to stay at the fence, and as the crowd
grew, to keep it moving farther and farther around until they
had outflanked the soldiers or spread them out so much that
their defenses would be ineffective. Then he told her to attack
and blow up the fence. Once inside, they could tear down the
non-electric inner fence.

Knox himself headed up a task force of a hundred motorcycles and Jeeps that were going to circle the site and attack

from the south. He had a box of grenades and two automatic rifles the cyclists had found in the hastily abandoned anti-aircraft emplacement.

He had to hurry. It was five-fifty.

Chapter 11

THE SKY was changing from deep violet to pink, and on the desert below, birds were singing and chirping. Not that Senator Hamilton could hear them. He heard only the sound of the little motor, the rush of wind past his cabin, and the voice of the president in his earphones. The two men argued for several minutes. Reed claimed that if he did *not* go ahead with the shot, earth was doomed. Hamilton claimed that if he *did*, mankind was doomed. The president reminded Hamilton of the mistake of Munich. Hamilton reminded Reed of the futility of saying that "one more war" was necessary before peace could come.

Finally, with a resigned and even happy smile on his face, the senator wheeled the little Cessna around and headed for Mistletoe, flying precisely at the huge gun barrel staring dully out of the hole in the dome.

"Carl? Ah'm sorry to have to do this, but if you fire your damned cannon, then ah'll be the first person to die."

The senator knew that dozens of antiaircraft missiles and even Grasers were pointed at him—waiting only for an order from the president to destroy him. And he knew that order would never be given.

Chapter 12

AT EXACTLY six o'clock, Knox's shock troops attacked Mistletoe from the south. They quickly killed the few guards stationed at the gate and threw grenades at the fence. High-tension wires snapped and fell to the ground writhing like snakes, spitting blue sparks, but Knox and his men poured through the opening and headed for the blockhouse. A small patrol of surprised soldiers met them and there was a brief firefight. But the Jeeps and motorcycles broke through, seized weapons from the dead and wounded, and swept on.

Then they split forces. Half went north and attacked the troops and civilian defenders from behind. Taken by surprise, they broke and ran. Then dynamite was thrown against the outer fence, and it was breached. Hundreds and then thousands pushed through to the inner fence, demolished that, and headed for the dome.

Knox's group had reached the blockhouse. He knew he had to get inside to stop the shot. But the heavy doors were shut. They raced to the side, then to the front, and looked through the two-foot-thick slit-windows at the technicians and politicians inside. In futility they kicked at the glass, fired at it. But it was intended to withstand tremendous explosions, and they could make no headway. They had no more grenades or dynamite.

The mob, with Olga in the lead, ran, walked, and crawled toward the dome. They knew it was open and undefended.

But they would never reach it. A squadron of armored cars appeared before them. A hundred yards from the hysterical crowd, they swiveled their cannons, fired, and continued to fire. The startled people found themselves in monstrous, billowy clouds of foam. Instantly, everyone was sliding across the slippery desert, unable to stand. And the foam covered them, got in their eyes, mouths, noses. The desperate attackers were helplessly caught in a surrealistic world of white. Jeeps and motorcycles tried to storm their way through the foam, but spun and skidded helplessly, bumping each other and slamming into those on foot.

Chapter 13

THE PINK sky was now turning to soft gold. Soon the sun would be over the horizon. But just a few minutes ahead of it would come the fleet, invisible to the unaided eyes. Or to be more precise, the earth, in its stately, rotating trip around the sun, would roll around so that the fleet would be low in the eastern sky beyond Mistletoe.

At six-twelve Sydney Knox, weeping and hysterical with frustration, suddenly knew what he had to do. Mistletoe had been constructed so quickly that many electrical lines which ordinarily would have been buried were strung on towers between the blockhouse and the dome.

"Quick! Shoot those lines down!" he shouted. At the same time, he began to climb one of the towers."

Chapter 14

REED WAS still pleading with Hamilton when the first of the consoles went blank, then another, and through the slit-window, those in the blockhouse saw a string of lights go out at the dome.

Nilstrom jabbed at a button on the console and snarled into his microphone, "Nick! Those bastards are shooting at the electrical lines. If they should hit the one attached to the safety switch, it'll cut the Graser off from Houston Control. You've got to stop them."

"My God, Chris, don't you have a backup system?" Beck roared back.

"No, it's one of the many things that didn't get done in the rush of this goddamned project."

Chapter 15

HAMILTON LOOKED down at the dome in front of him, at the muzzle of the huge Graser, larger in diameter than the wingspan of the Cessna. And he knew the president was not going to stop the shot, even if it meant his best friend would be killed.

He pressed the button of his radio, and at the same time pushed the throttle of the plane forward, sending it into a shallow dive right at the gun.

"Carl? Sorry we couldn't agree after all these years. Now ah'm going to save you from yourself. Goodbye, friend, and forgive me. Ah've got to do it."

He was only a short distance from the dome, traveling at full speed. The air rushing past the cockpit increased in pitch until it was a screaming hurricane. Still he dove. He knew that when he hit the gun, the cooling jacket would rupture and explode, killing all the people on the desert. But he had no choice. He had to stop the shot.

Chapter 16

"FIRING MINUS twenty seconds."

The fat technician was counting even as he stared out the window at Knox, who had nearly reached the top of the tower. The horrified people in the blockhouse saw him reach out and sever a line with his cutters. A whole row of display screens went blank. He reached for another as he balanced precariously on the crossbeam.

Beck saw Hamilton's approach on his radar screen and shouted, "That sonofabitch is playing kamikaze!"

But there was nothing he could do without the permission of the president, and Reed sat immobile, watching the screen in front of him.

Knox crawled farther out, snipping lines, blacking out lights in the dome, display screens in the blockhouse. But the line containing the little safety wire was another level up. Now he inched back to the center pole and climbed to the next level.

"Ten."
"Nine."
"Eight."
"Seven."

The armored car reached the blockhouse. A soldier appeared at the turret, swiveled a .50-caliber machine gun around, and opened fire. The bullets lifted Knox's body off the crossbar and hurled it outward. He made no sound as he fell, but the young people watching from below groaned in unison.

"Six."
"Five."
"Four."
"Three."

The dome before him was now as big as a mountain. The ugly Graser was just in front of the nose of his plane. The senator felt no fear, no anger, only a deep sadness. He braced himself for the crash, but his hand was steady on the wheel.

Nilstrom had torn his eyes from the onrushing plane to glance at the screen above the window. The relentless battle fleet came on, unaware of the drama far below on earth.

He looked at the president, whose face was a wet, gray mask of anguish, then his eyes dropped to the president's hand on the console beside the toggle switch. The hand did not move.

"One."
"Zero."

Hamilton never saw the beam leap from the Graser he hated so much. He saw nothing, heard nothing, felt nothing. He merely ceased to exist.

Chapter 17

A TITANIC flash of blue light erupted from the dome, a flash twenty feet in diameter. Before its brilliance, the people on the desert—those who had tried so hard to prevent it and those who had fought to protect it—all were momentarily blinded. For some, it would be days before their sight fully returned.

But it was the sound that really dazed them. The shock wave was a hammer that sent people reeling and staggering. It wasn't only the superheated air around the beam; it was also the explosion of the Cessna. Hamilton was just a hundred yards from impact when the Graser fired. The plane, and Senator Hamilton as well, instantly turned to vapor. Only the tip of the right wing was not caught in the beam, and it floated down to the desert like a sorrowful dove.

The Graser did not explode. Water cascaded from the barrel as the frost melted from the heat of the firing, but the jacket held. The copper towers connecting the reactor to the gigantic barrel glowed as more power than that which lights New York City poured through them. The concrete wall surrounding the reactor became so hot that crickets crawling on the desert above it died instantly.

For a long time everyone—soldiers, protesters, workmen— stared at each other in mute agony. Then they silently began to help those who were hurt. Out on the desert and up in the hills, others from the festival watched in mournful silence.

The first space war had begun.

Nobody inside the blockhouse spoke after the thunder clap from the Graser. Every eye was glued to the screen, to the silent, silver ships sailing imperturbably toward earth. As Chris counted to himself, he flipped the knob that connected his console to the radio telescope at Prescott. He wanted to hear the Cygnians' reaction when the gamma rays pierced their fleet.

Over the loudspeaker came the now-familiar low level of chatter. It was the Cygnians talking to each other, from one ship to another. It may have been some kind of code, Chris could never quite decide. The sounds were certainly not like human speech. They were more like Morse code dots and dashes.

"... seven, eight, pow!" he said to himself. The loudspeakers fell silent. Chris hoped against hope that the rays had killed the invaders. Seconds passed, and there wasn't a sound—from the Cygnians or from those in the blockhouse.

But then the chatter began again, hugely increased in volume. It seemed as if everybody aboard the fleet were talking at once. Chris swore softly, and the president turned to him. "So we've lost after all—they didn't die."

Chris listened to the radio noise and watched the fleet on the screen, and he felt sick. The silvery ships glided serenely on. "Well, I didn't think the beam would be powerful enough that far out to kill them all instantly. But I *hoped* it would."

The president watched him closely, and there was fear in the chief executive's eyes. "But doesn't all that chatter mean they weren't hurt?"

Nilstrom leaned back in his chair, still studying the fleet. "No, I don't think so. In fact, their immediate silence and then the burst of chatter indicates that *something* happened. It may have been an alarm system warning them of radiation, or they may have felt some immediate reaction in their bodies. I don't know."

Reed quietly persisted, "Do you think it did the job?" His voice was shaky.

Nilstrom never took his eyes off the fleet, although if anyone had asked him what he thought he'd see, he'd have been unable to tell them. "I don't know, sir. I just don't know. It may have been only enough to give them a headache—or maybe enough to kill some but not all."

"When will we know?" He was getting better control of himself.

Nilstrom stood up, took off his headset, and threw it on the console. Around the president were Beck, Steinhauser, Howard, Gray, and the president's guests, all waiting for his answer.

Nilstrom looked at his watch. "Well, if they're going into orbit, they have to make an injection burn at nine tonight. Otherwise, at their speed, they'll keep going right on past earth and out of the solar system. So we'll know for sure by nine tonight, and maybe even before that if, for vengeance, they fire a broadside of missiles at us."

"It's going to be a pretty rough fifteen hours!" said Reed.

Nilstrom nodded mutely. "Well, at least the seven other national delegations will be here soon. We'll sweat it out together."

Once outside, Nilstrom stood with Anna and the other scientists and Beck. Slowly they looked all around them. A funereal silence reigned over Mistletoe. Even the ambulances picking up the wounded kept their sirens silent. Everywhere, people were stumbling dazedly, seemingly oblivious to the presence of the masters of Mistletoe who had left the blockhouse and stepped into the morning sun.

Dimitri Petrovich Solovyev left the group and walked out toward the vast retreating crowd, looking for Olga.

Not twenty feet from where the group stood lay the bloody, broken body of Sydney Knox, his eyes staring sightlessly at the blockhouse.

"Well, the sonofabitch had the courage of his convictions anyway," said Nilstrom. He was startled at his own harshness. He continued to stare at the body, and suddenly he was filled with a torrent of conflicting emotions. He was glad Knox was dead! Not only because his death meant the Graser had fired, but for deeper, darker reasons. He groped inside his own consciousness, and knew at last that he had hated Knox so much because the young fanatic had made him feel uneasy about his own decision to fight the Cygnians. Nilstrom had thrown himself so utterly into the battle that he had not really considered the possibility that the Cygnians were not intent on conquest. Knox had stirred those latent doubts, stirred his own inclination to pacifism, and made him wonder if the battle was indeed the disaster Knox and Hamilton thought it was—if it was a step into endless interstellar warfare. He was honest enough to recognize that at least the death of the strange fanatic stilled the voice of guilt, the impossible questions. Chris felt self-revulsion. What had happened to him? Had the war brutalized him, as wars usually do to those who fight them? He looked around at the dead, the injured, the grieving. How many had died already in this war? He remembered the night in Denver when he'd first heard the cry of the 747 pilot. That same evening he'd called the air aces of the First World War the last of the chivalrous warriors. Had he seen Mistletoe as a battle like the old dogfights, a romantic jousting? If so, where did Knox and Hamilton fit in? Were they good guys or bad? Knox had killed people in his effort to stop the shot. Was that kind of killing justified? Was the killing Nilstrom had done justified? Was killing ever justified? But that was what Hamilton had been saying. He felt confused and sick.

Anna's soft voice called him back to the present. "You know, Nick, your General Sherman was right."

Beck's unshaven face was creased with anguish as he asked gently, "Sherman? You mean . . ."

"War is hell!"

Again they fell silent, watching the zombielike people around them.

Out of the blockhouse came Kellogg with Bobbie Venezia. Nilstrom and the others gaped, then, almost hysterically, they began to laugh, releasing their tensions.

Furiously, Kellogg looked at them. "Well, goddamnit, I wanted Bobbie to see what we were trying to do, so she'd know we weren't a lot of warmongers. I just dressed her up in overalls and everybody thought she was one of the concessionaires making coffee and sandwiches."

Chris finally got control of himself, wiped away his tears,

and asked her, "And did you see something convincing?"

Bobbie was drawn and her eyes were huge, her lips white. "Oh wow! Really, I mean, wow! I never knew what you were up against!"

Oddly, Nilstrom felt comforted.

Stehlen put his arm around Kellogg's shoulders. "Chuck, you're the most predictable person I've ever met. You always do the totally unpredictable!"

Chapter 18

WAKEFIELD HOBBES and Sir Clement were flying over the North Atlantic when they heard the news that the gun had been fired.

Chairman Mikhail Semyechkin had just left New York City when he heard it.

René Molinière and Gerhard Kroner were over Kansas, close enough to see the flash. The Chinese, Japanese, and Indian delegations were just crossing the California coastline. By 2:00 P.M. of the twentieth, all eight heads of state had reached Mistletoe.

Anna Larin greeted them as they arrived, giving each a brief account of the morning's happenings. There wasn't much left to see. The bodies of the dead had been picked up, and the damaged fences were faint lines in the distance. Farther up the valley toward the festival site, one could see only clouds of dust and smoke from the few remaining campfires. Most of the people had already left, and the rest were preparing to do so. Everywhere the sand was crisscrossed with the treads and wheelmarks of the riot-control vehicles and ambulances. One side of the huge dome gaped open, but not much else had changed.

But the shocked faces of the men and women of the project bore witness to what had happened, and a palpable sense of exhaustion, apprehension, awe, and relief hung over the project.

There was also the waiting. The air was heavy with it.

At four in the afternoon, Nilstrom called the leaders to a

conference room in the headquarters building. First he showed the television pictures being broadcast from LOOTS. Each of the silver spacecraft still held its position. Not one had faltered or wandered out of formation. Silently they came, steadily growing larger on the screen. There was no clue to what might be happening inside the craft.

Chris also reported that the amount of radio noise had gradually decreased ever since the Graser had been fired, eventually tapering off to the complete silence they were now monitoring. So far there was no sign of any counterattack.

One after another, the leaders asked the meaning of the ominous silence, and Chris admitted he didn't know. Perhaps they were bracing for battle; perhaps—he was almost afraid to voice the hope—they were dead. Kenzuki Takahashi remembered the radio silence of the American B-29s before their bombing of Japan. Kroner remembered the silence of the Ardennes Forest after the Battle of the Bulge. Chris remembered the silence of the Colorado wheatfields. The calm before the storm? Or the silence of the graveyard?

"Gentlemen, Sir Clement will brief you on the timetable."

The pink-faced Englishman was subdued as he walked to the front of the room. "Lights, please," he said quietly.

The first slide showed a drawing of the earth as seen from space, and of the moon.

"As you know, we've maintained constant radar surveillance of the fleet, and now optical telescopes can make out the individual ships clearly, so we can predict their possible actions with accuracy. Let me show you."

From the pointer in his hand, a small triangle of light appeared on the screen. "The fleet is heading for orbit and will probably try for a one-thousand-mile circular orbit, inclined fifteen degrees to the celestial equator. In order to achieve this, they will have to shed some thirty-five thousand miles per hour of velocity.

"We expect them to begin orbital injection burn at exactly 9:11 P.M., which will put them in orbit by nine-forty-three. If there is no burn, the fleet will reach its closest proximity to the earth about nine-thirty-eight."

Tillman nodded to Kroner, who was waving a hand.

"Sir Clement, let me see if I've got this. If our weapon did not work, then they'll fire their engines at nine, uh, eleven, was it? And enter orbit." The handsome German looked drawn.

"Yes, Herr Chancellor."

"And if it did work, they will not fire their engines and we shall be safe?"

"Righto. The decisive time is nine-eleven this evening." He consulted his watch. "About five hours from now. Yes, Mr. President?"

"Sir Clement, assume for the moment that the Graser did kill all of the crew. What will happen? Will they fall into the earth, or will they just go right on by?"

Nilstrom noted that Reed seemed to have grown from his harrowing night. He was clearly the dominant figure of the eight leaders. Almost by reflex, Chris glanced at Scott. He was gray, and held his face in his hands.

"The latter, Mr. President," Sir Clement answered. "They're not on a collision course with us. If they do not fire the orbital injection burn and slow down, they'll miss us entirely. The nearest ship will pass by about five hundred miles from earth, somewhere north of Hawaii."

"Will we be able to see them?"

"Unfortunately, they'll be on the other side of earth. Oh, I say, Chris, won't LOOTS be over Hawaii about then?"

Nilstrom looked up. "Uh, let me see . . . why, yes, Sir Clement, they will. So if the fleet doesn't enter orbit, it'll pass almost directly over LOOTS. I'll get right on that." He rose and, without a further word, left the room.

Nilstrom went directly to the blockhouse, where communications had been restored, to contact the orbiting lab by satellite relay.

Bill Robinson and Georgi Klyuchevsky got his call at four-thirty-three, Arizona time, and immediately set up a small Schmidt-type telescope that would be best suited for closeup viewing of the fleet. LOOTS would be much too close to use the giant telescope. At five-thirty, they notified Chris that everything was ready.

Shortly after six, the leaders left Tillman's briefing and began to arrive at the blockhouse. Despite the fact that almost three hours remained, there was no other place to be, nothing else to be done. They could only wait.

At seven, a meal was served in the blockhouse, but few ate more than a morsel. Those who did ate with distraction, continually looking up at the timer that was now counting off the hours, minutes, and seconds remaining until the burn. When the dishes had been removed, Chris finally allowed himself to look up too. One hour and thirty-two minutes.

Takahashi, Kroner, and Molinière stepped outside and gazed into the night sky, but there was nothing to see and they soon wandered back in.

There was little talk in the control room. Everybody watched the monitors. In addition to LOOTS, half a dozen other telescopes followed the fleet's progress, and periodically the picture would vanish as the fleet, like the sun, set in one part of the world only to rise in another.

But the clock never stopped.

Fifty-six minutes.

Chapter 19

HIDDEN FROM the fleet by the bulk of the earth's sphere, the silver-and-black form of LOOTS began to turn. Tiny jets at the tips of her winglike solar panels fired. The observatory slowly rolled over, her wings turning like windmill arms. The jets fired again, and she stopped. Then more powerful jets on the main body fired, and she moved again, this time swinging around. Shadows, pure black against the silver of the outer hull, shifted as she turned.

The giant telescope left the bearing it had maintained for so long, and swept away to stare uselessly into space. But now the smaller telescope was on target. The jets spurted intermittently as the crew steadied the spacecraft on her new heading.

Robinson looked through the eyepiece of the scope. All he could see was the earth itself, still blotting out his view of the fleet. He turned a focusing knob, then called Mistletoe.

Nilstrom took the call at his console. "We're getting a beautiful picture, Bill. Keep her at that heading, and you'll get one hell of a view. And keep this line open. I want to see everything that happens up there."

"What do you mean?" Klyuchevsky's image appeared behind Robinson.

The American looked over his shoulder at the Soviet astronomer and answered for Nilstrom, "Georgi, if those crews are still alive, who do you think's going to be the first to get it?"

"Oh." Klyuchevsky understood perfectly.

"All right, Chris, we'll stand by. How much time left?"

Nilstrom looked at his timer. "Twenty-three minutes."

Chapter 20

THE ATMOSPHERE in the blockhouse grew heavier with each passing minute. Silence hung over the men, silence too dense even to permit fidgeting. They waited.

LOOTS curved around the earth and passed over Norway, Spitzbergen, and the North Pole. Radio telescopes in Japan waited, listening. They heard nothing.

Twelve minutes.

In Brazil, a helicopter lifted and flapped away into the night. The only passenger, the superintendent of the beryllium mine, was the last foreigner to leave. Come morning, if morning came, the mine would be back in the hands of its original owners.

In the blockhouse, Nick Beck looked up at the clock. "Five minutes!" he boomed needlessly.

Ten miles up Bright River Canyon, Stockton Williams paused in his packing. His Jeep was almost ready for the trip back to Oregon. He pulled out a pair of binoculars and climbed up on the Jeep's hood. He sat down crosslegged and turned the glasses toward the west. He could see nothing. Around him, others constantly glanced upward as they too prepared to leave. He knew none of them could see the fleet enter orbit, but nevertheless they waited. He looked at his watch.

"Two minutes," Beck announced.

Chris looked down and realized he was gripping the arms of his chair so hard his hands were cramping. His breathing was intermittent; he repeatedly forgot to exhale. He tried to quiet the pounding in his chest, but soon gave up.

*   *   *

"One minute!" This time Beck realized it was unnecessary, looked abashed, and, like the others, stared at the screen.

Chris watched the second hand of the timer make its revolution. It crawled. He looked back at the television screen. The optical telescope on Midway had the best picture now. Each ship of the fleet was easily, ominously visible, though appearing to wobble slightly as the earth's atmosphere shimmered. He wished LOOTS could have been in position.

Ten seconds. He looked at Anna. She was staring at the screen.

Five seconds.

Four.

Three.

Two.

One.

Chris stiffened.

He stared at the picture.

Nothing happened.

Each ship continued on its course.

There was no burst of light. There was no noise for the radio telescopes to hear. He gaped, afraid to believe it. Perhaps Mistletoe's calculations were off by a few seconds.

He watched.

The seconds dragged on.

The images on the screen grew, then started to elongate as they slid past the watching telescope. Chris longed to rush outside and look up at the sky, but he knew there was nothing to see.

He continued to stare at the screen.

The others began to stir and looked around at each other almost furtively.

But nobody spoke.

Chris couldn't take his eyes off the screen.

Now there was no doubt; the ships were passing. Finally he turned and looked up at the president, sitting in the gallery above him. Reed showed no sign of emotion.

No one dared speak, for even in the drama of the moment, nearly every person in the room was acutely aware that the first words uttered would go down in history.

"Sonofabitch!" boomed General Nicholas Beck. "We got the bastards!"

Chapter 21

GEORGI ARISTOVICH Klyuchevsky felt distinctly cheated that they had not been able to see the fleet at the moment when it was supposed to fire its orbital injection burn. Instead, LOOTS was hidden behind the earth, watching by television as the earthbound telescopes saw what happened—or failed to happen.

But now he and Robinson were to be repaid many times over for what they had missed. From LOOTS, they were going to see the fleet closer than any other man ever would. It would be mankind's only chance for a closeup look, for once it had passed, the fleet would be gone forever. It would continue on out of the solar system, never to return.

The leaders of the most powerful nations on earth would be watching on television; only the LOOTS crew would see it for real. All the equipment was ready, the dozens of cameras and other devices that would record the passage of the giant fleet.

Klyuchevsky watched the screen intently, waiting for their orbit to carry them into the fleet's path. Only a few minutes now. He looked at Bill Robinson, beside him in the control seat, and wondered vaguely what he was thinking.

The horizon was steady in the eyepiece. The two astronauts kept their eyes glued to the lenses. Suddenly a row of silvered dots sprang up over the earth's edge. They grew alarmingly in size and number, and then, before either man could suck in his next breath, LOOTS appeared to be in the midst of the Cygnian armada.

One after another, the ships filled the viewing field, then slid past, only to be replaced by more. They were huge! Each dwarfed the big observatory. Klyuchevsky tore his eyes from the telescope, and looked out the port. Sure enough, even with the naked eye he could see them, hundreds of them, streaming past, miles distant, like a gigantic school of silvery minnows.

Again he looked through the telescope, and the powerful device showed the individual ships for what they really were, great galleons of space. He could see no portholes, no hatches, no guns—only curving, shining metal, punctured at each end by the dark maws of the intake and exhaust ports. One was fat, swollen with an unknown cargo, another slim and deadly-looking. Some were huge, the size of the Empire State Building, others smaller. All were roughly the same shape, circular in cross section, tapering to a blunt, rounded tip at either end. One seemed to be covered with bumps, and Klyuchevsky realized it was encrusted with little scout ships, clinging to their huge carrier like barnacles.

There was no sign of life.

He knew what he was seeing: lumbering troopships, mighty battleships, agile destroyers, assault ships, cargo carriers, tankers, all sweeping by in a silent, ghostly procession.

For several minutes the two astronauts watched, entranced, just as they knew those on earth would be watching. Then the fleet was gone, returning to the endless night of space, now carrying a cargo of the dead blindly back into the void.

Man would never know what had happened inside those silver hulls. The radiation had done its job, that much was certain. Apparently it had taken several hours for the crew to die. What a scene of carnage it must have been, with the crew dying in droves, collapsing upon the decks, lying still in chairs, slumped across each other.

Were they all dead? Or had a few survived? Perhaps infants, living in specially shielded nurseries, now waited in vain for parents to return. Perhaps some miscreant locked in a shielded cell was the lone survivor, cursing and tearing at the door. His jailers would be dead, and he be helplessly borne away.

Perhaps, mercifully, all were dead, staring with sightless eyes at instruments that showed the ever-increasing distance from their destination.

The Russian and the American watched the fleet recede. The last any human would see of it would be tiny flecks in the most powerful telescopes, and then it would pass from mankind's sight forever.

Perhaps, one day unimaginably far in the future, some other spacegoing race would find the phantom fleet, still in perfect formation, still manned by its crew of corpses. They would wonder where the fleet had come from and what had happened to it, but could they ever know?

Klyuchevsky turned to Robinson, who was still staring through the eyepiece, thoughtfully stroking his nose.

"It's over," he said.

Chapter 22

As THE blockhouse burst into applause and cries of relief, Anna quietly pulled Chris away, out into the hallway.

"Come on, Chris. A jet's waiting. We're going to Wisconsin. Now."

Part VII

Chapter 1

PRESIDENT CARL REED rolled the superb Havana around in his mouth before lighting it, and he smiled comfortably. This was the high point of his life, and he intended to savor every moment of it. God knew he deserved it. He had suffered through the criticism after the shot—for the secrecy that had surrounded Mistletoe, for letting Hamilton and so many of the peace-rock people die.

But movies of the fleet's approach and silent exit from the solar system were shown all over the world. Reporters were permitted to visit Mistletoe and were told the full story. The site was even opened to visitors and designated an international monument.

Slowly at first, then more quickly, the world returned to normal and any criticisms were buried in a landslide of approval. The eight nations were lauded as saviors of the world. Reed was called the "warrior for peace," and even intellectuals ceased calling him a monster, dictator, and murderer.

When he eulogized Senator Hamilton for his devotion to peace, and proposed that the senator's bust be placed in the rotunda of the Capitol, he was called a true statesman. And when he refused to permit prosecution of the *New York Globe*, even his harshest critics were silenced.

Reed was aware that today every major newspaper in the world carried a breathless description of the splendid presidential banquet and ball held here in the White House last night. And they all speculated as to the specific content of the proposal he was about to make to the seven other Mistletoe leaders.

He blew out a cloud of smoke and watched it circle in the

light. This was, without doubt, a moment historians would someday relate with delight and admiration. Reed smiled as the old Soviet chairman, Semyechkin, entered. With him were the odd little foreign minister, Valuyev, and the tall physicist, Solovyev.

Reed's mood was shadowed for a moment when he saw the scientist. For he knew that Solovyev's wife Olga had been found dead in a dirty little hotel in San Francisco. Apparently she had fled Mistletoe with one of the motorcycle gangs. Three men wearing leather vests had been arrested by the FBI and charged with her murder.

The president's eyes shifted to the figure of Kellogg, and he almost laughed out loud. The impossible man was dressed in a Brooks Brothers suit and radiated good humor. What a difference love could make! The president had seen pictures on TV of the happy couple leaving the church. The marriage of a popular peace-rock singer to the mastermind of the Graser had caught the fancy of the world.

But the wedding all Mistletoe people expected had not occurred. Reed glanced at Nilstrom. Certainly he and Anna Larin seemed to be in love. She wore a new ring, and they were sitting together. But he looked depressed. Reed couldn't understand it, and felt a fleeting moment of resentment. He knew Harvard had offered Nilstrom its presidency. Maybe it was the bitter statement by Smythe of Yale, who had said that if some more competent person had headed up Mistletoe, they would not have come so close to disaster. At least, Reed thought, his preliminary announcement should cheer Nilstrom up.

Slowly the room grew quiet, and the president rose. Everywhere he saw answering smiles. He greeted them warmly, and slyly said he hoped everyone had recovered from the evening before. Contented chuckles answered his words.

"Ladies and gentlemen, before moving to the business of the day, I have some good news. The Nobel Prize Committee has just concluded an unprecedented early meeting. And I have been granted the privilege of announcing the awarding of separate prizes to Dr. Helmut Stehlen, Dr. Dimitri Petrovich Solovyev, Dr. Charles Kellogg, and Dr. Christian Nilstrom."

The room erupted into thunderous applause.

"I also have the honor to announce that a special Peace Prize will be awarded posthumously to a man whose great accomplishments made this project possible: Chairman Fyodor Grigorevich Grigorenko."

Again applause shook the room. Reed didn't report to the gathering the fact that the committee had intended to give *him* the prize until he related the story of Wake Island and persuaded them to make the change.

"I have the further honor of announcing the award of the regular Peace Prize to the person whose diplomatic skills contributed so much to the success of Mistletoe: Anna Kornilyevna Larin!"

This time the applause threatened to lift the roof. The president looked at Miss Larin and Nilstrom. They were holding hands, but Nilstrom only smiled wanly.

"Now, ladies and gentlemen, on to the order of the day. What I wish to propose will come as no surprise, because each of you has been thinking the same thing since the conclusion of Mistletoe.

"What has been accomplished is unique. We must not—we dare not—let it pass without reaping the full harvest of benefits. We have discovered that we *can* cooperate, we *can* trust each other. We do *not* have to waste resources defending ourselves against each other.

"It is admittedly sad that after all these centuries of wondering if there were intelligent beings anywhere else in the universe, we found that there are—only to be forced to do battle with them. Nevertheless, out of that tragedy came the discovery of unity. And *think* what we can accomplish together!" He paused and smiled. For the first time in history, they were all unabashed friends. He continued.

"Therefore, I propose the creation of a special task force to explore the most creative uses of our unity. And I propose for the agenda of this task force the following items:

1. Exploration of ways to devote to peaceful pursuits that part of our budgets formerly designated for defense, with particular emphasis on the renovation of our cities, the education of our people, the cleansing of our environments, research into the prevention and cure of disease, and the eradication of poverty.
2. Development of renewable energy resources and methods of transmitting energy on an international basis so that inexpensive energy will be available wherever and whenever it is needed.
3. An open and full sharing of all scientific knowledge.
4. Open and tariff-free trade among all nations.

5. A pledge to ourselves to engage in no belligerent action without the consent and participation of the other seven Mistletoe Treaty nations.
6. Free travel and open emigration among our several nations, including the right of marriage between citizens of our countries."

Chairman Semyechkin shouted goodnaturedly, "Nyet! Nyet! No marriages! The Soviet Union would lose its most beautiful flower!"

A roar of laughter followed the chairman's words, and Reed joined it, glancing at Anna Larin. She smiled and even blushed.

Then the president asked for discussion of his proposal. There was instant agreement that such a task force be formed, and for over an hour the conversation rolled on, from one agreement to another.

Only Nilstrom remained glum.

At last the president turned to him. "Dr. Nilstrom, for the first time in its long history, mankind stands poised on the threshold of devoting its energies to peaceful purposes. You and your team of scientists have made this possible. Would you like to speak to this assembly?"

Nilstrom rose to warm applause.

"Mr. President, distinguished leaders, I have been so stimulated and encouraged by what I have heard here this afternoon that I'm reluctant to introduce an element of unpleasantness. But I must." He looked over the heads of the group. "Nick, will you tell them?"

Reed was paralyzed with apprehension as the tall, gauche general slowly came forward. On his chest were the many decorations awarded him by grateful countries. They were topped by the Congressional Medal of Honor.

"Mr. President, I come here with a heavy heart. Just this week, after the glow of our success wore off, I was approached by Dr. Nilstrom with some disturbing thoughts.

"He pointed out to me that the crews of the Cygnian fleet survived for a few hours after receiving the fatal shot of gamma rays from our Graser. During those hours we may be sure they sent messages about their fate to their home planet. The inhabitants of 61 Cygni will receive those radio messages in about eleven and a half years. We must expect that they will retaliate. They may outfit and dispatch another force. To follow up the success they confidently expected, they may already have equipped a second fleet to bring more colonists to earth, or to invade some other planet. Of course, all this is speculation. But it fits with what we know about this advanced, ruthless civilization.

"Now, every year, our technology advances. Theirs probably does too. The ships and weapons they possess now must be superior to those of the fleet they launched over thirty years ago, which we destroyed. And soon they'll learn of the Graser, and will build their own. Certainly they'll bend every effort to find defenses against it.

"Dr. Nilstrom has made a cursory contingency study. He estimates that we can expect a retaliatory response from the Cygnians in forty to one hundred years, with more advanced spaceships and weapons.

"To meet that threat, we must begin *now* our own massive program of research and weapons development. It will cost—"

"*Non!*"

"*Nyet!*"

"*Nein!*"

"No, by God!"

The uproar was instant and unanimous.

But finally it was René Molinière who gained the floor and most eloquently expressed the grief and defiance all felt. "*Non! Mon general*, we are *not* going to do that! We *are* going to cooperate, but not in new wars, rather in peace, in vanquishing poverty and ignorance and hunger!"

Beck said nothing as they roared their approval of Molinière's statement. At last, when silence had returned, he said quietly, "I understand perfectly. I too would like to see our money spent and our mental energy devoted to making this planet the garden of peace and prosperity it could become.

"It is my duty, however, to point out to you that if we ignore this threat, it's likely that when the invaders return, they will find a very happy, healthy, prosperous people on earth, helpless to defend themselves. Our children and their children will have had decades of peace before they are incinerated."

The silence was so total that the loudest sound was the ticking of the huge grandfather clock in the corner.

Beck looked at the stricken group, at Nilstrom sitting with

his head lowered. Then he glanced over his shoulder at the president.

Reed's face was bloodless as he said in a strangled whisper, "My God, what have we done? Charlie was right."

In answer to his comment, unheard by many, Beck said, "But if we hadn't made the Mistletoe effort, we'd all be dead now."

Molinière said, "Maybe not, *mon general*! The fleet did not launch a salvo of missiles after the gamma rays went through them. Why not? They lived long enough to do it."

"Quite frankly, we don't know," Beck admitted quietly. "They may not have *had* missiles, or were too sick after the Graser hit them. Or perhaps their admiral felt that our own effort to survive deserved success, that nothing could be achieved by adding our deaths to their own."

"Or," mused Takahashi, "perhaps their intent was not hostile in the first place and we killed them needlessly."

"Sir, remember the airliner, the attack on your power station?" Beck replied. "And even if you're right, after what we've done, the people on 61 Cygni are sure to be vengeful now. They'll attack when they're able."

Again there was bitter silence.

"If we're to avoid the fate you describe for our children and grandchildren," Kroner began tentatively, "what kind of expenditures will be required?"

"Uh, well, Dr. Nilstrom's study is only a preliminary one, but it's not optimistic. You see, we already know they're far ahead of us in technology. Therefore, to catch up, we must make an all-out effort, use every resource. We'll have to leap whole generations of weapons and try not only to match their thermonuclear engines, but to go beyond them. The whole thing will cost hundreds of times what was spent on Mistletoe, and will require the best minds of the world.

"In general, here's what we suggest: even more powerful Grasers strategically placed—first, all over the world, then on the moon, on Mars, possibly in some of Jupiter's moons. And when we've developed our technology enough, we must build mammoth satellites, armed with the most advanced weapons, to orbit millions of miles from earth. Then..."

As he talked, Beck's enthusiasm became more ardent and his voice rose to its usual booming volume. But suddenly he sensed that the silence was too complete, that despair around him was as deep as the pit of hell. He looked up from the notes he had been reading. And he saw the leaders of eight nations staring at him in mute horror.

The only sound was the relentless ticking of the clock.

An unspeakable evil lurks in the shadows...
fighting to extract a terrible revenge. It will stop at nothing...
to inherit ... THE TABERNACLE!